TRUST NO ONE

After ten years in London, working for a City law firm, Clare Donoghue moved back to her home town in Somerset to undertake an MA in creative writing at Bath Spa University. In 2011 the initial chapters of Clare's debut novel, *Never Look Back*, previously entitled *Chasing Shadows*, were longlisted for the CWA Debut Dagger award.

You can say hello to Clare on
Twitter @claredonoghue, or Facebook:
www.facebook.com/claredonoghueauthor.

Also by Clare Donoghue

Never Look Back
No Place to Die

CLARE DONOGHUE

TRUST NO ONE

PAN BOOKS

First published in the UK in 2016 by Pan Books
an imprint of Pan Macmillan
20 New Wharf Road, London N1 9RR
Associated companies throughout the world
www.panmacmillan.com

ISBN 978-1-4472-8429-1

1 3 5 7 9 8 6 4 2

A CIP catalogue record for this book is available from the British Library.

Typeset in Minion by Palimpsest Book Production Ltd, Falkirk, Stirlingshire
Printed and bound by CPI Group (UK) Ltd, Croydon, CR0 4YY

Visit **www.panmacmillan.com** to read more about all our books
and to buy them. You will also find features, author interviews and news
of any author events, and you can sign up for e-newsletters
so that you're always first to hear about our new releases.

For my father. Now and always.

CHAPTER ONE

Wednesday

I've got to do something. He's left me with no choice.

I know what should happen, but that doesn't mean anything. There's not much you can't find out from the Internet these days, but what if it doesn't work? I feel sick if I think about it for too long, but that's normal, natural even. It's not like I haven't given this any thought. I've done nothing but think about ways to make him stop. Are there alternatives? Of course there are; but this is the best way – the best way I can think of. I just need it to stop. I can't take it any more. I really can't.

You probably think I'm just scared, don't you? You might even think I won't have what it takes to do it when the time comes, but you could not be more wrong. I always stand by my word. Always. I don't make decisions without thinking. If I say something, I mean it. I will do it, and no one can stop me. Who would want to anyway? If they knew what I know they would reach the same conclusion. I know it is the right thing to do and I know that I am the only one who can do it, who has the courage to do it. So whatever you think, you'd better think again. I'm no coward.

CHAPTER TWO

30 July – Wednesday

Richard Taylor stepped back from the barbecue, craning his neck in a vain attempt to avoid the plume of smoke that was engulfing him. 'Harvey, bring out the meat and grab my sunglasses on your way out, would you?' he shouted, looking up at the back of the flat.

He had arranged, with the agreement of the other tenants, to have the back of the three-storey townhouse power-washed last month. It looked great, a shining beacon amid a sea of weather-worn grey. It put his neighbours to shame. 'Shit,' he said, spotting the open window. 'And close the bathroom window,' he yelled. 'Bloody house will stink for days,' he muttered to himself. He sucked in air through his teeth, glancing next door as the column of smoke changed direction and drifted over the fence. Most of their windows were open too. That should impress Mrs Chakrabarti, Tommy and the mysterious female tenant in flat three who he had yet to meet. He had toyed with the idea of going over to ask for a cup of sugar or whatever, just to find out who she was, but after almost three years of not knowing, it seemed pointless.

'Where are they?' a voice called back.

'In the fridge,' he shouted.

'Why are your sunglasses in the fridge?'

'The meat, Harvey . . . the meat is in the fridge.' He ran his hand through his hair before shading his eyes. 'My sunglasses should be next to the microwave.' He stepped up onto the small patio. The barbecue needed a few more minutes to calm down. The hairs on his arms felt singed from the heat.

'How much lighter fluid did you put on there, Dad?' his son asked as he pushed open the back door with his foot and walked down the stone steps that hugged the back of the house. Richard's flat was the middle one of three. When he bought it, the back steps had led to a shared garden. However, after some nifty negotiations he had managed to persuade his downstairs neighbour, Desmond, to agree to a separation. Some money had changed hands, of course, but Richard had snagged the lion's share of the space, leaving Des with his side-access squared off to the end of the building. It might be small, but Richard didn't feel too bad. Des had needed the money, and never used the outside space anyway. It was a win-win.

He watched Harvey descending the steps with care, carrying a bowl of salad under one arm and an assortment of cutlery, a bundle of red gingham napkins and numerous packages of meat in his hands. 'Nuking the food, are you?' Harvey said, nodding his head towards the flames.

'I barely used one squirt,' Richard lied, using a tea towel to fan the smoke away whilst kicking the almost-empty can

3

of lighter fluid under the barbecue, out of sight. 'The coals are just dry,' he said with a shrug. 'It'll settle in a second.'

'Mum doesn't use lighter fluid.'

Richard and Harvey both turned. Olive, Richard's twelve-year-old daughter, was standing in the doorway at the top of the steps, Richard's sunglasses resting on the top of her head. She was wearing cut-off jean shorts and a T-shirt that showed off her midriff. He had thought it was a cute look when she was ten, but now he wasn't so keen. 'Mum says it's bad for the environment and makes the food taste rank,' she said, lolloping down the steps. She reminded him of a sloth on the move. Each step was slow, as if the energy required was too much for her young limbs to bear.

'Your mother knows nothing about barbecues,' he said, walking over and putting his arm around her. 'Whereas I, on the other hand,' he added, giving her a playful squeeze, 'am an expert.'

Olive squirmed. 'Urgh, you stink,' she said, pushing him away. She was scowling but he could see she was holding back a smile.

'Charming,' he said, as she turned away. He reached down and pinched the back of her thigh, making her jump.

'Dad,' she groaned, stretching out the word.

It was unfair and perhaps unwise to torture a near-adolescent, but Richard couldn't help himself. She was so easy to wind up these days. Everything he said or did was 'sooo lame' or she was 'sooo over it'. It aggravated the hell out of her mother, but Richard just found it funny.

'When are we gonna eat?' Harvey asked, dropping the napkins and cutlery on the A-frame picnic table that Richard had spent last weekend painting green at Olive's behest. 'I'm hank marvin.'

'Not long,' Richard said, edging closer to the barbecue as the flames and smoke subsided. He blew the remaining smoke out of his way, picked up a long-handled fork and poked at the coals. 'There, you see?' He looked over his shoulder at his son. 'Give it ten minutes and we can get cooking.'

'Ten minutes,' both children chorused.

'Jeez, calm down, you two. I said ten minutes, not ten hours.' He cocked his head to one side, admiring his handiwork. 'You have to wait until the coals are glowing and all the flames have gone . . . otherwise you end up with burnt, undercooked meat and that can only lead to . . .'

'The shits,' Harvey said, at the same time as Olive said, 'Salmonella.'

'Salmonella's from eggs, dummy.' Harvey poked his sister, who was now sitting at the picnic table.

'Err, no it isn't,' Olive said, taking her smartphone out of the pocket of her jean shorts. Harvey followed suit, both of them tapping away furiously in order to prove each other wrong.

Richard chuckled. 'Technically you're both right,' he said. 'There are lots of different bacteria, and salmonella *is* one type, and . . .' He waited until they both looked up from their phones. 'And all of them give you the shits.' Harvey smiled, but Olive wasn't quite ready to let the issue drop.

'Listeria, staphylococcus and . . . salmonella,' she said, enunciating each syllable.

'Swallowed a dictionary, have we?' Harvey countered. 'You need to get out more.'

5

'Least I *can* read,' Olive muttered under her breath.

'Hey,' Richard said, holding up the fork with a raw beef-burger attached. 'That's enough. I don't want to hear another word like that, thank you.' Both children fell silent. Olive appeared to be entering full sulk mode. Harvey seemed to be considering the same, but his eyes soon settled back on his touchscreen phone, and his face cleared.

Harvey was, for the most part, loving and attentive to his younger sister – but his dyslexia was not to be talked about, let alone joked about. Richard had no doubt Olive would pay for her insult when no one was looking. Big brothers will only take so much, he thought with a smile and a shake of his head. He had given more than his fair share of dead legs and chinese burns to his sister, Louise, when they were growing up. She had driven him nuts, always playing the 'I'm the youngest' or 'I'm a girl' card.

He turned away and began tearing open the other packets of meat: sausages, kebabs, chicken and king prawns. There was enough to feed a family of twelve, but at least they would all have what they wanted and there would be no squabbling. Olive's tastes and preferences changed almost daily at the minute, and Harvey's appetite was scary. The boy should be the size of a house, the amount he consumed. He glanced over at them. Harvey was now sitting down next to Olive, his arm slung around her shoulder. He was holding the phone in front of them both, showing her something. Richard's heart squeezed in his chest. He was a good boy, a good brother: better than Richard had ever been.

He was only thirty when Harvey was born. When Nicola told him she was pregnant, Richard had been in a state of shock, and remained that way for about the first three months of the pregnancy. He had never really considered whether he wanted children, let alone whether he was ready for them; but all that had changed the second he held Harvey. How could something so little be a problem, an imposition? A year of sleepless nights had almost dulled his joy, but nothing could make a dent in the euphoria he felt every time Harvey looked up at him and smiled. He turned and resumed prodding his fire.

Olive had been another surprise, but this time Richard had been ready. He picked up a metal skewer and one of the prawns, threading it on before reaching for another. Olive's delivery had been tough on Nicola, much to her chagrin. 'Second babies are meant to be easier, Rich,' she had said over and over again in the birthing pool. She had spent hours in the water, only to be told she had to get out and move up to a different ward in case they needed to do a C-section. Richard couldn't help smiling. He could hear her voice now. 'You can tell that effing doctor that if he makes me get out of this effing water, I'm going to effing well hit him.' Nicola had been determined not to swear during labour. 'I don't want our baby to come into the world hearing me effing and blinding.' Richard had pointed out – not helpfully, it turned out – that his wife had sworn for the entirety of Harvey's birth, and he didn't seem any worse for the experience. 'We don't know that yet,' she had said. 'He's only two, Rich. Any minute now, he might open his mouth and tell us both to eff off.'

Richard picked up the empty prawn packet and shoved it into the Sainsbury's bag he had tied onto the leg of the barbecue. He still missed his wife, even though the divorce had been his idea. She had been his best friend before she was his wife and the mother of his children. She had always been able to make him laugh, and he had always been able to talk to her.

'Dad, Ben just texted,' Harvey said, coming to stand next to him. 'Can he come over for lunch?'

'Sure.' Richard gestured at the food. 'I think we've got enough. Olive?' He turned. 'Do you want to invite anyone over for lunch, Freya or Ella?'

'Freya's not talking to me,' Olive said, looking through the slats of the table at the grass below. 'Ella's on holiday with her mum and dad. They've gone to *America* for their holidays.'

'That's 'cos they're loaded,' Harvey said.

'OK, OK,' Richard said, wary of his daughter's tone. 'What about Kirsty?'

'I'm not bothered,' she said, resting her head on the table.

Richard pushed away his irritation and walked over to the table. 'Are you feeling all right, honey?' he asked. 'You don't seem your cheerful self today.' He wanted to say *this year*, but knew that would be asking for trouble. 'Do you think maybe you're a bit hot?' He ran his hand over the top of her head and forehead. 'Harv, will you go and get your sister a hat and bring out the sun cream, please? The factor 30's in the bathroom cabinet.' Harvey was texting, and walked back up the steps and into the house without looking up or acknowledging Richard's request. 'Come on, honey,' he said, sitting down next to her and putting his arm around her waist. 'Let's get you a drink of water and then, how's about you help me cook the kebabs. You're the only one who knows just when to turn them.' He felt her body stiffen for a moment.

'OK,' she said, her voice thick.

He stood up, pulled her out of her seat and over to the barbecue. 'Now let's get that shade up before you get cooked too,' he said, looking around for the umbrella. The picnic bench was new, but the sunshade wasn't. There was so much rust on the pole it was almost impossible to tell it had once been white.

'Daddy,' Olive said.

'Yes, honey.'

'Did you love Mum when you married her?'

He opened the umbrella in his face, hitting his nose square on. 'Bloody h—' He stopped himself. 'Almost took my eye out with that.' He pushed the umbrella into the ground, swinging it left and right until Olive's head was in the shade. 'What a thing to ask,' he said. 'Of course I loved your mother when I married her. It would be a bit daft to get married if I *didn't* love her, now wouldn't it?' This was the fourth, maybe even the fifth time his daughter had brought up the question of love and marriage since she had broken up for the summer holidays. 'Why do you ask?' It was a genuine question, but he couldn't deny his trepidation. Nicola had mentioned that talk of 'girl stuff' and 'periods' would be on the cards pretty soon, which had left him in a permanent state of high alert.

'Harv said some people get married for the wrong reasons,' she said.

He looked down at her. She wasn't sulking now. She was just talking, running her toes over the grass. He had to remind himself that she was twelve years old, not two. She wasn't his baby any more. 'Well,' he said, considering the best way to answer her question without lying, upsetting her or talking about his ex-wife for the rest of the afternoon. 'I don't know about that . . . but what I do know is that marriage is a very important thing and people who get married should want to be together for the rest of their lives . . .' Olive opened her mouth to speak, but he carried on, '. . . that's why your mum and me got married.' He bit his lip. 'But even though we loved each other very much, we couldn't live together. Remember we used to argue a little bit, maybe even shout sometimes?' Olive nodded. She still didn't appear upset, so he decided to keep going with what felt like a practised speech. 'Well, we realized that we loved each other but that we were better friends when we didn't live together, and then we could be better parents to you and Harvey. We didn't want you two growing up in a house where we were shouting all the time.' He bent down and tilted up her chin. 'That would be rubbish, wouldn't it?'

'So you love Mum as a friend now?' she asked, looking up at him, her eyes large and wet.

He nodded. 'That's right. I'll always love Mum, always. She's just more like a best friend now.' He tried not to change his expression as the lie left his lips. 'We love you and Harv masses and masses, and all we want is for you two to be happy and healthy.' He stroked her hair. 'Does that sound OK to you?'

She pushed his hand away. 'I am happy and healthy.'

'Well, that's OK then.' Richard pulled her into a hug. 'Now, are you going to help me with these kebabs or what?'

'Or what,' she said, laughing as she ducked out of his arms and towards the steps, taking them two at a time. She met

Harvey at the door. He shoved a faded pink sunhat onto her head.

'That better?' he said in a babyish voice. Olive punched his arm, but he manoeuvred her until she was in a headlock before leading her back down the steps, despite her protests. 'Ben's cycling over,' he said. 'He'll be here in half an hour.'

'Sounds good,' Richard said. 'Now if you can stop torturing each other for five minutes, I need a pee. Get this lot started, will you?' He nodded towards the piles of meat. As he passed he gave Harvey a playful shove, and pinched Olive's nose. 'And your sister is in charge of the kebabs.'

The inside of the flat was cool and quiet. He hadn't realized until now quite how much noise there was outside; the whirr of half a dozen lawnmowers, kids playing, laughing and crying and some blokes up the hill obviously watching football in the garden, shouting at the TV when their team failed to score. He walked down the hallway, past the kids' bedrooms and into his own. The en suite had been a godsend. Olive seemed to spend longer and longer in the bathroom every time she came to stay. He shook his head. She would be thirteen soon – a teenager – worse than that, she would be becoming a woman. He grimaced. 'That's going to be hardcore,' he said to his reflection.

He was just about to flush the toilet when he heard a scream. Without thinking he ran down the hallway, through the kitchen and out the back door. Harvey was standing at the barbecue, the long-handled fork in his hand. Olive was clutching her arm, tears already streaming down her face. 'What on earth's happened?' he said, rushing down the steps and over to his crying daughter.

11

'She got too close to the barbecue,' Harvey said, his face pale. He was shaking. 'It was an accident . . . I didn't do it.'

CHAPTER THREE

31 July – Thursday

Jane listened and heard nothing, so turned, burying her face into the back of the sofa, relishing the darkness. She didn't need to look at her watch to know it was seven. Her body clock woke her at the same time every morning, whether she liked it or not. She wasn't due in to the office until nine. She tilted her head back and looked over the arm of the sofa at the gap between the lounge curtains. It was raining.

Her mother didn't think it was necessary for curtains to close unless they were in a bedroom. 'It's a waste of material, darling,' Celia Bennett would say. 'Besides, it looks cumbersome and spoils the overall look.' Jane smiled, surprised to find comfort in her mother's idiosyncrasies, rather than her usual frustration. She watched the rivulets of water coming together and dividing over and over as they made their way down the window pane. At least she didn't need to worry about watering the garden or topping up the pond. It was a miracle the pond had ever even been finished. Her father had been working on it when he had his TIA, or mini-stroke as the doctors kept calling it. He had only just installed the

13

pump and fountain when the full stroke hit. Jane closed her eyes and chewed the inside of her bottom lip. She could feel the tears wanting to come. 'No,' she said, shaking her head and pushing herself up into a sitting position. The cycle of guilt felt never-ending. It was with her as she struggled to get to sleep. It was with her in her dreams, and it was with her as soon as she opened her eyes. 'Come on,' she said throwing off the duvet and standing up, arching her back.

She walked through to the kitchen and flicked on the kettle, easing her neck from side to side. She had been so exhausted last night, even the thought of climbing the stairs to her parents' spare room had felt like too much effort. Besides, she hadn't wanted to risk disturbing her father. She pulled her shoulder blades together, and let them go again. The sofa had been comfortable for the first hour or so, but then she had become sweaty and hot. She poured out some cereal, took the milk out of the fridge and sat down at the kitchen table, grumbling to herself. She looked at the jagged edges of the cereal flakes and winced. Her consultant had pronounced her throat healed, except for a small amount of bruising. Jane swallowed, aware of the action. She had been out of hospital for over two months, back at work for one; but neither her throat nor her dreams seemed ready to forget what had happened. She heard a thump from upstairs. She was out of her chair and taking the stairs two at a time before her spoon even hit the floor.

'Dad,' she called, knocking on her parents' bedroom door. 'Are you OK?' She waited for what felt like hours before knocking again. 'Mum, Dad?' Her heart was hammering in her chest. She opened the door, preparing herself.

'Sorry, honey,' her father said, his words almost lost by his leaden tongue. He pointed to the floor. 'I dropped the iPad.'

Jane let out a breath, stars dancing in front of her eyes. 'It's fine,' she said, walking over, bending down and picking the iPad up before sitting down on the edge of her father's bed. 'You sleep OK?' Her heart was still jumping. It took her breath away. 'Mum in with Peter?'

'Yes, and . . . I assume so,' he said, 'unless she's left me.' He reached out and squeezed Jane's hand. 'How about you? I didn't hear you come up.'

'I ended up on the sofa,' she said, pulling her mouth to one side.

'An error of judgement on your part,' he said, smiling.

'That's for sure.' She leaned down and kissed him on the cheek. 'I was just making a cuppa. Want one?'

'I'll come down.' He moved to get up. 'I'm starving.'

'No, no.' Jane pushed his shoulders back onto his pillow. 'I'll bring you up some toast. Put the telly on and we'll watch *BBC Breakfast* together before I head off to work . . . and before you-know-who wakes up,' she said, jerking her head towards the other side of the house.

'You-know-who, as in your mother?' he asked. 'Or you-know-who, as in your son?'

Jane laughed. 'Either,' she whispered. 'I'll be back in a sec.' She handed him the remote and left the bedroom, pulling the door closed behind her.

She ran her fingers through her hair as she tiptoed down the stairs. She could cope with a heightened state of tension at work – if she wasn't disturbed by murder and mayhem, something really would be amiss. She could even cope with a certain amount of anxiety at home, with Peter and his routine, but now the haven of her parents' home had been turned into a stress-fest too, especially since she and Peter had been 'staying' here.

Her mobile was ringing in the kitchen. She jogged down the last few stairs and along the hallway. It stopped the moment her hand closed around it. 'Typical,' she said. She used her thumb to swipe up the bar locking the screen and looked at the missed call log. It was Lockyer. No surprise there, then. Her finger hovered over the call button for a second, but she put the phone back on the counter and nodded her head, impressed by her restraint. If it was important, he would call back. Lewisham's murder squad and her boss could cope without her – a fact they had proved not too long ago, when she had been off for over a month.

It was the longest she had ever been away from the office since Peter was born. Her consultant had tried to persuade her to take another week, but Jane had been itching to get back to normality. Of course, no sooner had she come out of hospital and started the process of putting it all behind her and she was back in King's College A & E with her father. The Bennetts weren't faring very well at the moment, her mother included.

In the first few weeks after the stroke, Celia Bennett had been a trouper, as was her way. She had turned caring into an art form. She had insisted Jane and Peter move in with them, so that she could keep an eye on everyone at the same time. Jane had resisted, but given her own weakened state, she hadn't had the fight to stand firm. There was no denying

Celia's verve for the job; she was fussing over all three of them day and night. Each week Jane tried and failed to move herself and Peter home, her mother seemed to have the argument prepared and won before Jane had even started. 'The doctor said you need rest, you *need* to be here for your health,' or, 'You're going back to work. Who's going to take Peter to and from school? I can't come and collect him from all the way over at your house. I can't leave your father for that long, but if you're here, it's simple.' Or, the most recent: 'It's the school holidays. Who's going to look after Peter all day while you're at work?'

But when Jane had come down one morning to find her mother dusting the house with her underwear, she realized things had shifted. It was her mother who needed the help, who needed looking after. So Jane had stopped fighting and taken on the role of lead carer in the Bennett household. She buttered her father's toast, poured out two cups of tea and added milk to her cereal, which she was going to let her father eat. She just couldn't face it. She would grab something at the office.

Peter had turned eight in the middle of the Bennett family crisis. He had been understanding – or as understanding as a child with autism and separation anxiety could be, under the circumstances. The separation anxiety was a new challenge, something Jane was struggling to deal with. She had tried suggesting that she could throw a birthday party for him and all his friends when she and Grandpa were feeling better. Peter didn't understand. How could he? All he knew was that his mummy was in the hospital, where they had a cafeteria with cakes and biscuits, and that Grandpa had been to stay at the same hospital. Peter wanted to know why he couldn't stay there, too. He liked the nurses and the doctors, everyone buzzing around with clipboards and pens that they let him use. He didn't want to be at home or at Grandma and Grandpa's house, and he didn't want to be by himself, ever. It was a setback in his behaviour that Jane didn't need or have time for. 'Poor little bugger,' she said to herself. She took a sip of her tea as she looked around for a tray to carry her father's breakfast upstairs on. He would be getting impatient, no doubt. The stroke might have changed John Bennett in a lot of ways, but his appetite had been unaffected. If anything, he was eating more than ever. Her phone started ringing again. She glanced over at the screen. It was the office. She had been wrong: it seemed neither the murder squad nor her boss could live without her after all. She picked up the phone.

'DS Bennett,' she said, searching for a pen and paper.

'Morning, boss. Sorry to call so early.' It was Chris Wall, one of the murder squad's younger detective constables, although having a five-month-old baby at home had given him a grey hair or two that made him look older than his twenty-five years.

'Not a problem. What's up?' She picked up her father's mug of tea and put it in the microwave. If it wasn't nuclear hot, he wouldn't drink it.

'DI Lockyer asked me to call you. He's been called out to an unexplained death over in Crystal Palace, Gipsy Hill. He wants you to meet him there.' The end of Chris's sentence was muffled – Jane guessed, by a bacon sandwich or some other delicacy. She would never understand how coppers, her male colleagues in particular, seemed equipped to eat grease morning, noon and night.

'Is his team or mine taking it on?'

'Err . . . he didn't say,' Chris's mouth was still full.

Jane wasn't surprised. She had been running her own team for her last half a dozen cases at least, but Lockyer, it seemed, wasn't ready to let her fend for herself yet. He was more like an overprotective father than a boss these days. 'What's the address?' She grabbed yesterday's newspaper from the counter, and a pencil that was stuck to the fridge by a big yellow magnet.

'63 Gipsy Hill, Crystal Palace, SE19 1QH. Adult male, forty-four years old, last name Taylor, first name Richard.'

Jane scribbled down the details. 'OK, thanks Chris. Can you call Lockyer and tell him I'll be there in about . . .' She looked at her watch. 'Forty minutes?' There was silence from the other end of the line. Jane wondered if Chris had choked to death on his cholesterol-laced breakfast. 'DC Wall, did you get that? Forty minutes, OK?'

'Sorry, boss,' he stammered. 'I just thought . . . does it take that long . . . I mean . . .'

'I'm going to put some clothes on first, if that's all right with you, Constable?'

'Of course – sorry, boss, sorry. It's just, DI Lockyer said he'd called and you didn't . . . I mean, never mind. I'll tell him you're on your way.'

'Thank you.' Jane hung up, and smiled. She knew why Chris was so rattled. Lockyer had been lead detective of the murder squad in Lewisham for years now – since long before Chris joined – but his attitude of late was something to be wary of. He had always been a vocal boss, and a tad short-tempered if things weren't done his way, but since Jane's return to the office he had been bordering on officious. For a detective who had always followed his instincts more than the rule book, he was a changed man. If anyone challenged him he would go bright red in the face and shout, 'I'm thinking about your safety, the team's safety. I am responsible for you lot, whether you appreciate that or not. It's my job to ensure you get home to your wives, girlfriends, husbands, mothers . . . Following the rules, doing as you're told, keeps you and your colleagues safe. Understand?'

Jane smiled again. Not one officer on the squad had been stupid enough to do anything but nod at that point in the speech. The irony was not lost on her. In all the years she had worked with Lockyer he had been the maverick, whereas she had been the rudder, the one keeping him abreast of the rules. To say the tables had turned was an understatement.

She waited for the microwave to ping, took out her father's tea and headed off up the stairs. She wasn't going to have time to enjoy *BBC Breakfast* or a shower, it seemed. Lockyer wanted her, and he wanted her now.

CHAPTER FOUR

June

Message from Dee_28:

Hey handsome,

Could my day get any worse?

Some guys came into the bar tonight who would not take no for an answer! What am I, a piece of meat? I told them to feck off but then my boss dragged me into his office and threatened to fire me. He said if I couldn't handle some rowdy customers on a Wednesday night then I had no chance on a weekend shift. I reckon a blow job would've shut him up but it's only my third day and I was saving that for 'in case of emergencies', haha!! ☺

How's your day been? Better than mine I'll bet. You're so lucky to have a job you actually like. I did one of those aptitude tests at the job centre and it said I should be a financial advisor or an airline attendant! Errr, I can't do maths and I've never left London, let alone flown anywhere. I'm surprised they didn't tell me I had just the right set of skills to be a fire hydrant ☺

Now for the big question . . . I don't want to scare you off but I was wondering if you fancied meeting up for a drink sometime? This weekend maybe? Nothing major . . . I'm not expecting dinner, flowers, candles or anything like that . . . unless you want to, of course, but just a quick drink somewhere, to see if we get on. I mean, I kinda know I like you already but I get the feeling you probably have a lot of offers with your eyes (and the George Clooney butt shot in your second photo)!

No pressure. Let me know xx

CHAPTER FIVE

Thursday

It's hard to describe how I felt, like standing on the edge of a cliff, ready to take the leap. I swayed back and forth but the compulsion to jump into the abyss was overwhelming.

What have I done? Is this what I wanted to happen?

The words circled my mind like vultures over their prey. I could almost hear their screeching cries. But then another feeling, much stronger than my fear, took over. I was excited. I felt excited and, I guess, righteous. How little everyone around me understood about who he was. They've seen what he wanted them to see: a man, a father, a family man. That's not what I saw. I witnessed the darkness. The darkness he tried to hide behind a winning smile. He wanted you to believe, but it was all a lie. It always was.

What kind of person would I be, if I had turned away from the precipice and let him get away with it? He had to be stopped. He thought he could carry on regardless of anyone else, but he was wrong. So arrogant, but then, who could blame him? No one had ever told him no. He had always taken what he wanted: like a parasite, just eating, eating and eating. But not any more. The feast is over.

CHAPTER SIX

31 July – Thursday

Detective Inspector Mike Lockyer stood at the foot of the bed, arms crossed, one hand resting on his chin. As a scene, it was unremarkable. He wasn't sure he needed to be here.

Richard Taylor was lying on his back on the right-hand side of the bed, his eyes and mouth closed. A blue and green patterned duvet cover was folded back on itself, as if it had been thrown off during the night. Taylor was wearing a pair of black cotton pyjamas, piped in yellow with an emblem embossed on the breast pocket. A Christmas gift, no doubt. Lockyer slept in a T-shirt and boxers or nothing, depending on the weather and his mood, but that didn't mean he didn't have dozens of pyjama sets stuffed in a drawer that Megan had given him over the years. He looked again at Taylor. Only married guys or guys with kids wore, or indeed owned, proper PJs, surely? Lockyer took a deep breath to clear the distraction. Taylor's feet were uncovered, poking out of the bottom of the duvet. His expression wasn't pained or distorted. If anything, he looked relaxed, like he was sleeping.

'Are you sure he's dead?' he asked, turning to look at Dr Dave Simpson, the senior pathologist for the area.

Dave smiled. 'As a doornail, my friend.'

'I've never seen such a . . . peaceful corpse.'

'Not everyone dies screaming, Michael.' Dave shook his head. 'I fear your profession is beginning to taint your view of the world.'

Lockyer laughed, but he couldn't disagree. The last six months had been filled with violent deaths, more so than even he was used to dealing with. 'It's just a change to see a dead guy and not think, "Thank God I missed that show".'

'Do you want me to wait for Jane?' Dave asked, going to the bedroom window. 'You can get back to the office if you like and I can fill her in on the details. My morning's pretty quiet.'

'And why would I want to do that?' Lockyer asked, frowning.

'Well, given Roger Westwood's ascent to Superintendent, I'm assuming the squad is going to need an appropriate DI or DCI to take on his SIO role. That coupled with the fact that you've asked Jane to come down, I'm assuming that you're possibly passing this case on to her team, for her to run. So you can get back to doing whatever Senior Investigating Officers do.'

'The gossip network is working well, I see,' Lockyer said, taking a deep breath. 'Yes, Roger has officially appointed me as SIO for four of the teams. But as it happens, I'll be Jane's SIO as well.'

'Oh, she will be pleased,' Dave said. Lockyer opened his

mouth to retort, but Dave beat him to it. 'Any mention of a move up to DCI rank?'

'No, not yet.' Lockyer stepped back to lean against the wall.

'It'll happen,' Dave said, 'and then you'll really be earning your crust.'

'Or stuck behind a desk on the same pay grade.'

'Ah, finding the positive as always, Mike,' Dave said, his tone brimming with sarcasm. 'You've a real talent for doom and gloom sometimes, you know that?' Lockyer shrugged and refolded his arms. 'So, why don't you get back to the office,' Dave continued, 'and I'll fill Jane in on everything and she can get things started.'

'What's she said?'

'Who?' Dave's face was a picture of innocence.

'Oh, pull the other one, Dave. Don't ever join the bad guys. You're a terrible liar.'

'I don't know what you mean,' Dave said, but Lockyer could see he was tightening his jaw. 'OK, OK. Jane *might* have mentioned – in passing, mind you – that you've been a touch overprotective since she's been back in the office.' He held up a hand to meet Lockyer's protest. 'It's perfectly understandable, Mike. I know that. She knows that. I wasn't trying to interfere, mate, honestly.'

'Sure.' Lockyer rolled his eyes. 'You're getting more and more like a gossiping old woman every day.'

'I was only suggesting you might have better things to do than stand here looking at a dead guy. Hang around if you want to. It's no skin off my nose.' Dave slipped on his glasses, a new addition he was very sensitive about, took a notepad out of his trouser pocket and started making notes, not looking up and not smiling. The guy might be in his fifties, but he could sulk like a teenager.

'All right,' Lockyer said, trying his best not to grind his teeth. It felt as if he was giving in and saying sorry far too often these days. The price of dropping his hard-arse exterior, it seemed, was that once he let one person in, others followed, whether he liked it or not. 'I want to get a better idea of where the case might be heading before I hand it over to her . . . and yes, that is because I don't want to overload her too soon.'

Dave stopped writing and looked over, surprise evident on his face. At least Lockyer wasn't the only one to find the changes in his personality jarring. 'As I said, Mike. It's completely understandable and I'm sure Jane appreciates you looking out for her.' He paused. He had more to say, Lockyer could feel it. 'That said, I think it's worth remembering that she's a grown woman and a senior detective sergeant, a role you encouraged her to go for. Give her a bit of credit. She'll tell you if things get too much. She's never exactly been backward in coming forward, has she?'

'No, she hasn't.' Lockyer felt himself conceding yet more ground. He hated it when Dave thought he knew more than he did; hated it even more when Dave was right. 'I'll back off.' He balled his hands into fists. 'I'll *try* to back off.'

'She'll appreciate it, Mike. I'm sure she will.' Dave moved around to the other side of the bed.

'Mmm, no doubt,' Lockyer said, stopping himself before he could enter a sulk of his own. He forced a smile. 'How long have you been waiting to bring this up with me, then?'

Dave laughed. 'Not that long, don't worry about it. Despite what you might think, I have a somewhat demanding profession, and looking out for you isn't in my job description. I do it on a very part-time basis.'

'Thanks, mate.'

'Pleasure. And congratulations on the bump up to SIO. I'm sure you'll fill Roger's shoes with ease.'

'Thanks.'

Both men fell silent for a moment as Lockyer looked at his watch. 'I'll admit she's capable and all that,' he said, 'but what the hell is taking her so long? What's she doing . . . walking here?'

Jane looked up at the address. As far as she could tell, there were three flats to each townhouse: ground floor, first floor and top floor. From the buzzers, it looked like Richard Taylor's flat was on the first floor.

She turned, aware of anxious stares from passers-by and curtains twitching in neighbouring properties. Gipsy Hill was a nice area, a pretty tree-lined street – not a regular for her, or the murder squad. She looked over at an area of grass on the other side of the street. The sun shone through the trees, creating a dappled light that made even the council flats tucked away opposite look charming. The fish and chip shop on the corner was immaculate, its owner already outside sweeping the street and straightening his signage before he opened for business later in the day. It was nice, Jane thought, to see people taking care of where they lived, rather than waiting for an overstretched council to clean up their mess. She took a deep breath. A killing here, depending on the circumstances, could make national news. The police presence would be freaking out the locals, no doubt. A woman holding the arm of a young girl was heading Jane's way.

'Is everything all right? Has something happened?' the woman asked, the girl next to her squirming. Jane wasn't so good with ages once kids were out of nappies, but given the sullen expression, she would guess the girl was a teenager and her mother a long-suffering forty-something.

'Do you live in the area?' Jane asked, conscious that the woman looked more stricken than the average Joe public.

'Yes, at the top of the hill. My daughter,' she said, indicating the girl at her side, 'Kirsty and I . . . well, we were on our way to the shops and thought we'd see if Olive wanted to come with us. Flat 2. Her father is Richard, Rich Taylor?'

Jane hoped her face didn't register surprise at hearing the name of the deceased. It wasn't uncommon for neighbours and relatives to turn out, sometimes en masse, the moment there was a hint of trouble. It was as if they were wired in to the police frequency. They seemed to just *know* the second a tragedy had befallen their loved ones. It was weird, and sometimes a bit eerie. Why had this woman chosen this morning of all mornings to show up unannounced? 'Can you tell me your name?' she asked.

'Chantelle,' she said. 'Chantelle Bullion.'

'And could you tell me your address, telephone number?' Jane took out her notepad and jotted down the details, her curiosity piqued by the woman's demeanour. There was, as yet, no crime-scene tape. There was only one squad car. There were two unmarked cars, but this woman wasn't to know that, and yet she seemed close to hysterics. Maybe she was just a bit highly strung. Jane looked at the girl, who was dragging her feet along the pavement in exaggerated circles.

'Mum, can we go?' she whined, trying to shake free of her mother's grip.

The woman continued as if her daughter hadn't spoken. 'Has something happened?' she reiterated.

'We're responding to an incident at this address. I can't give you any details at this time,' Jane said, trying to sound reassuring. She couldn't very well say, *your daughter's friend's father is dead and it might be murder, but we're not sure yet, and while we're at it, why are you so jumpy?*

'But can you tell me, is it Richard's flat?' Chantelle asked, her eyes wide.

'I'm afraid I can't say,' Jane said, 'but someone will be in touch if we need to speak with you.' She waited a moment for the woman to compose herself before turning back to the main door of the building. She could feel Chantelle Bullion's eyes boring into the back of her head. If this case was assigned to Jane, which it seemed it would be, she would no doubt be passing the woman's details to a member of her team, and Chantelle would end up being far more involved in her daughter's friend's father's life – or death, as it was – than she ever intended.

CHAPTER SEVEN

31 July – Thursday

Jane tipped her head back, rested it against the wall in the hallway and closed her eyes. You would have to be either deaf or in another country not to hear her boss. His voice carried even when he wasn't shouting, and right now he was in full rant mode. Chris had been right – taking her time getting here had been an error.

She pushed herself off the wall, took a deep breath and went into the room. 'Hey, sorry I'm late,' she said, trying to look casual. 'Stanstead Road was mental.' She made sure not to look at Lockyer as she took out her notepad. 'Before I forget, I just spoke to a friend of the deceased . . . Chantelle Bullion. She was passing just now, downstairs. Her daughter is friends with Olive Taylor, Richard Taylor's daughter.' She heard Lockyer take a breath, but ploughed on before he could speak. 'I've taken down her details. One of the team will need to speak to her in due course, I'd imagine.' She looked up and caught Dave's eye. He was smiling. It was clear from his expression that she wasn't fooling anyone. 'Morning, Dave,' she said. 'How are things?'

'Things,' Dave said, 'are good. You?'

'Can't complain.' Jane was aware of Lockyer moving towards her.

'We've been waiting for over an . . . '

'How's your father doing?' Dave asked, interrupting Lockyer. 'On the mend, I hope?'

Jane was caught off guard by the sincerity of Dave's question. 'He's doing OK,' she said, swallowing. 'A bit better each day.'

'Good,' Dave said. 'That's really great. If he's anything like his daughter, he's made of pretty strong stuff.' He smiled.

Jane had to resist the urge to jump over the bed and hug him, dead guy or no dead guy. He hadn't asked about her father to divert Lockyer's rant, though of course it had helped. He had asked about her father because he cared – because he cared about her.

'Thanks, Dave.' She took a deep breath through her nose and turned to Lockyer. 'Boss, what have we got?' The seconds passed. She looked at Lockyer. His expression was unreadable, but then his eyes cleared.

'Richard Taylor, forty-four years old, lived alone, divorced, shared custody of two minors.' He looked down at the pad he was holding. 'Ex-wife is Nicola Brown, also forty-four – Harvey Taylor-Brown, fourteen, and Olive Taylor-Brown, twelve. Names were hyphenated after the divorce,' he said, rolling his eyes. 'The kids were staying here. The son, Harvey, found Taylor at about 6, 6.30 a.m. He didn't respond to stimuli, no pulse, so the kid called 999.'

'Cause of death?' Jane asked.

'Don't know yet.'

Jane looked down at Richard Taylor. His expression was untroubled. She felt as if they were intruding, that at any moment he was going to wake up and be, understandably, pissed off that two coppers and a pathologist were standing in his bedroom watching him sleep. 'Could it be natural causes?' He was shaking his head. 'Suicide?'

'Suicide?' Lockyer repeated, pursing his lips and raising his eyebrows as if the idea hadn't occurred to him. 'I mean, it could be, I suppose; but look,' he said, leaning over the body and clicking on a pen torch he had taken from his pocket. 'There are some fibres around his left nostril.' Jane looked and nodded. 'And there are a few more on his bottom lip.'

'Suffocation?' Jane said, straightening up and looking at Dave.

'It's possible, yes. There are a few broken blood vessels around his mouth and his right eye is slightly bloodshot, but I really won't know until after the . . .' Before Dave could finish his sentence there was a shout, followed by a thumping of feet and slamming of a door. 'Who the hell is that?' As if in answer to the question, the bedroom door burst open to reveal a teenage boy, puce with fury.

'Get away from him,' he screamed, barrelling past Lockyer and throwing himself at Dave, fists flying, knocking Jane to the ground in the process. 'Leave him alone,' the boy shouted, pushing Dave back onto the bed, onto the body of Richard Taylor. 'Don't touch him . . . I won't let you touch him.'

Jane pushed herself up off the floor just as Lockyer reached the wrestling pair. He leaned forward, put his hands over the boy's shoulders, back under his armpits before locking his elbows and pulling the boy towards him, off Dave and off his feet in the process. He had to have five or six inches on the boy. Jane tried to take a step forward, but found herself rooted to the spot. She wanted to help, to throw herself into the fray, but her body had other ideas. Her muscles twitched in strained protest.

'Bloody hell,' Dave said, rolling off to one side to avoid the feet flying in the direction of his head. 'Have you got him, Mike?'

Jane looked at Lockyer. He had a good hold, but the kid was putting up a fight and then some. He was kicking and screaming, his legs pinwheeling three feet in the air. Two other officers who Jane didn't recognize were standing in the doorway, looking equally floored by the scene.

'Some help would be good,' Lockyer said, backing away from the bed towards the doorway, allowing the two PCs to approach the boy from the side and take a leg each. 'Let's get him back in his bedroom.' The three of them manhandled the boy through the doorway, down the hallway and into a side room, the door slamming behind them, no doubt due to the boy's still kicking feet.

Jane turned to look at Dave, who was sitting on the end of the bed panting, loosening the collar of his shirt. 'Are you all right?' she asked.

'Well,' he said, leaning back and taking in a deep breath, 'no wonder you two are always walking around like wounded soldiers. I'm going back to the mortuary suite where it's quiet and no one ever jumps me.' He managed a smile. 'Who the hell was that? He was so strong. I just couldn't get him off me.'

'I'm guessing,' Jane said, 'that's Harvey. Taylor's son.'

CHAPTER EIGHT

Richard – June

Richard ran his fingers through his hair for the umpteenth time and readjusted his shirt. He felt sick. Was that normal? He couldn't remember. The last time he'd been on a proper date he was a gawky teenager, and the date had turned into a marriage and two kids.

He had thought about nothing but this meeting all day. One of his patients had very nearly ended up with a root canal instead of a filling, he was that distracted. He checked his appearance one more time before walking out of the bathroom, turning off the light. It was just a drink. There was no reason to be nervous. Without thinking, he picked up his phone and checked his messages.

Fingers crossed this is the last first date we ever have to get ready for!! ;-) Nervous? I am ☺ x

He plonked down onto the bed. How had he managed to get himself into this? They had only been messaging for a week. They knew nothing about each other, not really. Was the

35

intensity of their texts and emails a good thing? Lots of his mates had met their wives or girlfriends on dating sites. He counted them off in his head: Paul, Julian, Spencer, Dave, Ian. In fact, Ian had found both his first and second wives online. Not that he was a very good example. He was still using the sites, married or not; searching for wife number three, it seemed.

Richard remembered Spencer regaling them all in the pub with endless stories of a good thing going bad. He was adamant that chatting too much beforehand was a mistake, created too much pressure before you were even out of the starting gate. He also said that excessive chat wound the girls up into such a frenzy that they would turn up to the date in a wedding dress, metaphorically speaking. Had Richard done that? Had he been too forward, too open? He realized he was sweating. He reached for his deodorant on the bedside table and, unbuttoning his shirt, gave his underarms another generous spray.

Date or no date, he wasn't sure the Internet was the right medium for him. In real life people were always telling him how funny and easy-going he was, but he didn't think that side of him came over very well by email. How did you make dentist, divorcee, solvent, father of two translate into exciting prospect, not to be missed? He had tried to be himself, to be honest about his life, about how much time he had to give to any new relationship. He might be self-employed in a thriving practice, but he didn't have the luxury of time off or long holidays. He had a mortgage to pay, not to mention an ex-wife and two kids to support. He had been up-front about everything, but had that been the right thing to do?

He let out a long breath, aware of his heart thudding in his chest. He was going to meet a stranger and yet this stranger *knew pretty much everything about him: his height, his salary, what he looked like, where he lived, his hobbies, his physique, his hair colour, eye colour, skin colour. The only tick box missing was penis size. Of course, that wasn't strictly true. He smiled and covered his face with his hands again as he fell back on the bed. They had talked about sex last night, about specifics, which had turned Richard on and terrified him in equal measure. Then it hit him. He might have sex tonight. He didn't know whether to run out the door, or back into the bathroom to throw up.*

CHAPTER NINE

1 August – Friday

'You should come with us tonight,' Penny said, as she took a left onto Catford Road and joined the South Circular. 'Max has offered to ferry Joanne and Scotty home afterwards so we can all have a few drinks. He'd be happy to drop you back to your folks.'

Jane raised her hand to thank the van driver who had let Penny join the line of traffic. It was a force of habit, even when she wasn't driving. Penny was a DC in Lockyer's team. Well, she had been. Now she was Jane's senior detective constable. The shift from Jane assisting to running her own cases had been subtle, especially as they all worked in the same office and manpower often overlapped, but Jane could feel the difference. She didn't have to ask if she could take Penny with her to see Richard Taylor's ex-wife and children over in Penge. All she had to do was complete an action log, tell Lockyer where she was going, as he was acting SIO for the investigation, and then she was free to run her team as she saw fit. It felt good.

'Thanks, Pen, but I can't tonight,' she lied, staring out of the passenger side window at the rain. It was August, for goodness sake. It was meant to be summer. It was depressing.

'OK, but next week.' Penny turned on her windscreen wipers. 'Just you and me – one drink. I'm happy to come your way if it's easier. Max will drive me.'

'This Max is sounding more perfect by the minute,' Jane teased, changing the subject. 'A social worker; caring for others; picks you up; happy to drive your work buddies all over the place. Is he always this wonderful, or is he trying to butter you up for something?'

Penny laughed as she flicked on her indicator and turned right, following the signs to Sydenham and Crystal Palace. 'Funny you should say that,' she said, as she and Jane both raised their hands in sync to the driver behind. 'I have a feeling he's going to propose.'

'Wow, that's soon,' Jane said, before she could stop herself. 'I mean, that's great. You've been dating, what, six months?'

'Nine,' Penny said in a monotone. 'We've been living together for six.'

'Oh blimey, a long time then. I didn't realize.' Jane tried to drag her feet out of her gaping trap. 'How do you think he'll do it?'

'I don't know.'

Jane rubbed her eyes. 'I'm sorry, Pen. That really is exciting.' She paused for Penny to answer, but when she didn't, decided to grovel a bit more. 'No wonder you need a girls' night out. You need to practice your "yes" and your surprised face.' She touched Penny's arm and felt her tense for a second before relaxing again.

'Exactly,' Penny said, '*that's* why I wanted you there.' She stopped at the traffic lights next to the Pawleyne Arms. 'Another time,' Penny went on. 'Anyway, how do you want to handle this morning? Do you want me and the FLO to keep the kids occupied while you talk to the mum and then switch, or vice versa?'

'Anne Phillips is the family liaison officer who's been assigned. She missed this morning's briefing but I've spoken to her and she said she was happy to prep the family. If you can speak to Ms Brown, I'll observe the kids with Anne and assess whether they're suitable for video interviews.'

'I can't see why they wouldn't be.' They turned right onto Clevedon Road. 'What number is it?'

'Twenty-eight,' Jane said, checking her pockets for her phone, notepad and a pen.

'The boy's fourteen and the girl's what, twelve? I've observed interviews with children much younger than them, for sure.' Penny slowed the squad car to a crawl as she craned her neck looking at house numbers.

'Me too,' Jane said, 'but you can never tell how minors will react to trauma. The boy, Harvey, had a complete melt-down at the father's place yesterday. He almost knocked Dave out. He sent me flying. It took Lockyer and two other officers to get him under control. There,' she said, pointing up ahead. 'On your left, the one with the brick frontage.' It was another tree-lined street, but Jane didn't think it was as nice as Taylor's street. Gipsy Hill had more of a village feel, rather than this south-east London suburbia. The rain didn't help. All the houses looked dull and unappealing.

'Got it,' Penny said, accelerating and then pulling into a space right outside the house. 'Are we going to be OK, just us, then?' she asked. 'I'm no weakling, but if it took three guys to take the kid on, what chance have we got?'

'True; but don't worry. I spoke to him after he'd calmed down and he was fine. It was just the shock of finding his father, and the invasion of his home, I think. Bless him. He'd obviously been holding it together for the sake of his sister, but once the aunt arrived to pick them up he just couldn't any more. I had to stop myself from hugging the poor kid once he started crying. He looked so lost. He won't be any more trouble, I'm sure.'

'Fair enough. You ready?'

'Yes.' Jane opened her door. 'I don't want to take too long with this. The quicker I can assess them, the quicker we can get them over to Caterham Road to the video suites.'

Penny raised her eyebrows. 'Whoever called them suites has some sense of humour. I always feel like I've arrived on the set of that TV programme where the old lady who wasn't really an old lady interviewed celebrities . . . Mrs Merton. There's way too much burgundy furniture going on for my taste.'

Jane laughed. 'I don't think the decor is to anyone's tastes, Pen. Mrs Merton is about right – everything's twenty years out of date and given the Met's current budget, I don't see them updating the sofas anytime soon.' She looked over the roof of the car at Penny, still smiling, until she saw Harvey Taylor-Brown glaring at them from the lounge window of his mother's house. Jane wondered if her 'he won't be any more trouble' assurance might have been a bit presumptuous.

*

'I'm sorry about Harvey,' Nicola Brown said as she ushered Jane and Penny into a lounge to the left of the hallway. At the same time a door slammed so hard upstairs that Jane wouldn't have been surprised if it had come off its hinges. 'He's not taking any of this very well. I mean, his father's passing or . . . any of it, you know?' She sniffed.

'Of course,' Jane said, motioning for Penny and Nicola to go ahead of her. 'We understand. It's a difficult time for you all – your son particularly.' She looked around. The walls were painted a light grey, the skirting boards and window frames a darker shade. The curtains were also grey, broken up by swirls of a warm mustard colour. The carpet was yet another shade of grey. It could have looked depressing given the colour palette, but Jane couldn't help thinking her own lounge could do with a makeover and this style was perfect, almost serene.

'He was diagnosed with ADHD three years ago,' Nicola explained. 'We thought it was just the dyslexia . . . he would get so frustrated, couldn't focus, but his behaviour has definitely . . . changed in the last year or so.' She paused, then went on, her voice guarded, 'I heard about yesterday. He has trouble with impulse control.'

Jane realized she was talking about Harvey's tussle with Dave. She nodded her understanding. 'It's all right.' She took out her notepad, and scribbled a note to remind herself to check the boy's medical records and speak to child services again. There was no reason he couldn't be interviewed, but there would need to be extra support specific to his needs. 'It isn't uncommon for relatives to lash out. You mustn't worry about it, and neither should your son. It's forgotten.' The truth was, Harvey's unexpected entrance had stayed with her. Not because she was frightened of a fourteen-year-old, but because she was shaken by her own inability to act. She looked at Nicola, deciding whether she needed to say more, to further reassure her; but it seemed her words had had the desired effect. Nicola's shoulders dropped. Had she really thought they would have her son up for assault, after what he had been through?

Nicola sighed, and gazed out the window. 'I had to give him a couple of sleeping tablets just to get him to settle.'

'Prescribed?' Jane asked. 'Please take a seat.'

Nicola waved the question away.

Jane let the dismissal pass, and stood for a moment debating how best to position herself in order to observe the children. There was an off-cream sofa that looked way too pristine for actual use, or two black leather and teak easy chairs with accompanying footstools. They were Eames chairs. Jane had been following something similar on eBay the week before and it had ended up going for four hundred quid, about three hundred and fifty quid over what Jane was prepared to pay. She opted for the chair next to the reconditioned fireplace, and sat down. Nicola Brown was doing well for herself.

'Anne's in the kitchen,' Nicola said, 'making a pot of tea. She's been wonderful to the kids and to me.' She covered her mouth with the back of her hand, stifling a sob. 'Rich and I have been divorced for over three years, separated for more, but . . . it's still an awful shock. We've always been close, even after . . . maybe not as close, but I still considered him a friend, a close friend.' Penny stepped forward and guided a now sobbing Nicola to the sofa before sitting down next to her.

'Of course,' Penny said, her voice low and soft.

'I'm sorry. I know you're not here to talk to me.' She raised her head, pushed away her tears with her fingertips and shook her head. 'Sorry. It's just hit me harder than I expected.'

Interesting choice of words, Jane thought. 'It's all right,' she said. 'Is your daughter home?'

Nicola nodded. 'Olive, yes. She's up in her room. Do you want me to get her?'

'In a moment,' Jane said. 'Would you mind if we asked you a few questions first?'

'Yes . . . I mean, no, I wouldn't mind. Please, go ahead.' She took a deep breath, sat back and crossed her legs.

'You're a dentist, is that right?' Jane asked, looking down at her notepad. She had a list of questions she had prepared before that morning's briefing.

'Yes. I'm a partner in the White House Dental Practice. It's just down the road near Penge West.'

'A partner? That's impressive.'

'I was lucky,' Nicola said. 'One of the existing partners wanted to retire. He stayed on as an associate while I made the transition, held my hand, so to speak; and I had help. My sister is a dentist – so is my brother. So was Rich,' she added, her hand going to her mouth again.

'A family profession,' Jane said, nodding.

'Yes, my father was a dentist. My mother was his dental nurse. You know the story,' she said, without enthusiasm. 'He wanted all of us to be professionals, as he saw it. He said it didn't matter whether we were doctors, lawyers or dentists, but we all knew he wanted us to follow in his footsteps.'

'He must be very proud,' Jane said, curious that Nicola's emotions, so raw moments ago, had for the time being disappeared without a trace. Her eyes were dry.

'I suppose. My parents were killed in a road traffic accident two years ago.'

'I'm sorry to hear that.' Jane made a note, not only of the death but of Nicola's demeanour, which had changed beyond recognition.

Nicola shrugged. 'That's OK.' She stood up. 'I'll just hurry the tea up so we can get on with this. I'm sure you have better things to do than sit here chatting about banalities with me. I know I do.' She left the room before Jane or Penny could answer.

'Wow,' Penny mouthed, looking at Jane, pulling her mouth down at the edges.

'Wow is right,' Jane whispered. 'Devastated one minute, dismissive the next. I'd say that was natural, given her ex-husband has just been found dead; but there's nothing natural about her, is there?'

'She's wound pretty tight, for sure,' Penny said in a low voice.

Jane shook her head. 'Why do I feel like my day just got longer?'

Penny smiled. 'I'll go and help, send Anne in to talk to you. Maybe she's got a better read on the family set-up.'

'OK, thanks, Pen.' Jane let her head drop back and rocked herself in the chair. God, it was comfortable. Not four hundred quid's worth of comfortable but not far off either.

'You here to see me?'

She sat up with a start. Harvey Taylor-Brown was standing in the doorway of the lounge. His eyes were red and swollen, his skin mottled and pale.

'Yes, Harvey,' she said, standing. 'Please, come and sit down.' She gestured at the sofa opposite and waited for him to sit before sitting herself. 'How are you doing today?'

He shrugged his shoulders, just like his mother had done. 'What do you think?'

'Like I said yesterday,' Jane said, trying to make her voice sound as soothing as possible whilst choosing her words with care, 'you've had a terrible shock. It's perfectly normal to feel sad, angry, frustrated, numb . . . a whole range of emotions. Anything and everything, that's the norm when things like this happen. You seem calmer today?'

'Do I?' he said, looking at his hands. 'Did I knock you over . . . when I came in yesterday? You were on the ground. Did I do that?'

'No, no,' she said shaking her head. 'Forget about it, honestly. My main concern is you. You and your sister.'

'What about my mum? Does anyone even give a shit about her?' Harvey stabbed his finger towards the kitchen. 'It's all about my dad, isn't it?' His voice was rising. 'Well, he's dead, isn't he? His problems are over. My mum, she's left with two kids and a business to run. How's she going to manage now, with me and my sister and everything else?' He shook his head and folded his arms. It was obvious the rant had originated elsewhere. He was repeating what, Jane would guess, his mother had said either yesterday or this morning. She knew from experience that second-guessing a family member's reaction to a traumatic death was nigh-on impossible, but for Nicola to be worrying about herself so soon felt wrong. 'Who cares, right?' Harvey said. 'Not your problem, is it?'

'It's perfectly natural to be angry.'

'Err, do you even listen?' he said. 'You're like one of those call centres in the middle of bum-fuck-nowhere, reading off some cheat sheet. It's pathetic.' He spat the words out. If he'd been sitting any closer, Jane was sure she would have had his saliva on her face.

'OK. What do you want me to say, Harvey?' She opened her hands in a placating gesture. 'I'm a police officer. You found your father. It's my job to find out what happened. You can understand that, I'm sure? And I do care about you and your family. It's my job.'

'Whatever,' he said.

Jane had to remind herself that Harvey was only fourteen. He might be taller than her – and built like an Olympic swimmer, all shoulders – but he was still a kid. 'I just want to help,' she said.

They sat in silence for a minute or so until Harvey said, 'I'm sorry.'

She let the apology hang in the air for a few seconds before responding. 'You've got nothing to be sorry for.' Her heart squeezed in her chest as she watched two tears roll down Harvey's face. The desire to go over and comfort him was almost overwhelming. It was like watching her own son – at war with his own emotions, powerless to defend himself – and her, powerless to help.

'Did you manage to get any sleep last night?' she asked. 'Your mum said she gave you something to help you relax.'

'It was just some herbal shit,' Harvey said, wiping his nose on his sleeve. 'Everyone knows that stuff doesn't work. No point telling my mum that, though. She's got more pills than a pharmacy.'

'How about your sister? How's she doing?'

'You'd have to ask her.' His voice lowered. 'She's not been out of her room this morning, and if you're waiting for my mum to make her, you're wasting your time. Olive's sensitive,' he added, in a tone conveying both resentment and genuine concern.

'I'm sure that won't be necessary,' Jane reassured him, crossing her fingers it wouldn't be. If Harvey's sister wouldn't come out of her room, it was going to make assessing her for video interview impossible. Then again, at least Jane knew one thing: despite his mood swings, Harvey would be fine for video interview. He might not like it much, though.

'You're the police lady from my dad's house.' Jane and Harvey both turned to see Olive Taylor-Brown poking her head around the door to the lounge.

'That's right,' Jane said.

'Will you catch who killed my daddy?'

CHAPTER TEN

1 August – Friday

Lockyer rocked his head from side to side, his neck cracking. He hated interviews involving kids, and he wasn't even going to be in the room. Jane had tried to get both sessions pushed back until tomorrow, to allow Harvey and Olive to grieve and adjust, but as a new SIO Lockyer couldn't allow it: time was against them. Whether the death was listed as suspicious or not after the post-mortem, these kids needed to be questioned now – before they could forget, before time distorted their young memories from fact into fiction. Besides, given what Olive had said to Jane this morning, there seemed little doubt in Richard Taylor's daughter's mind that this was not a case of 'death by natural causes'.

He shifted in his seat, his six-foot-three frame cramped and awkward. The tech room was just next door to the video interview suite, and calling it a 'room' was a bit of a stretch; it was more like a broom cupboard. What with the equipment, the tech officer, Lockyer and Lockyer's legs, there wasn't room to swing a cat or any other small mammal. To add to his discomfort, he would be observing and making notes on the interview of Olive Taylor-Brown, twelve years old. She looked small, sitting alone on a gold velour sofa in the interview suite. She was wearing a green hoodie, a white T-shirt and skinny blue jeans. She looked younger than twelve.

He rubbed his face and tried to focus his attention on something else in the room, but the orangey-puke coloured curtains, the mishmash of furniture and the brown patterned carpet were an assault on the eyes. His attention shifted back to Olive, the tendons in his neck tightening. Ever since his daughter, Megan, was born, Lockyer had found it difficult to separate his protective father's instinct from the job.

'A couple more minutes and we're good to go,' the tech officer said. 'If you want to stop the interview or add a question, just give me a nudge and we can pause the session.'

'Thanks,' Lockyer said, trying to sit back. This room was not designed for anyone who had issues with personal space. 'Which monitor's which?'

'The two on the left will show the interviewee, full shot and close-up of her face, and the monitor on the right is a wide shot to capture the entire room.'

'Great, thanks.' Lockyer looked at the screens. The social worker was crouched in front of Olive, explaining what was going to happen. The sound quality was impressive. On the sofa opposite was a specially trained child protection officer. She was the only one qualified to interview children. Lockyer didn't recognize her, but from what he could see she had a kind, open face. It took specialist skills to get kids to talk about a traumatic event, to get every detail without causing unnecessary distress or influencing their answers.

Lockyer would make a rubbish CPO, and he knew it.

Megan was nineteen going on fifty, and he still hadn't perfected talking to her. She was more than happy to boss him about and poke her nose into his private life, but she was cagey when it came to talking about herself. Given her reluctance to divulge personal information, and his inability to engage in sensitive dialogue of any kind, they were pretty much stuffed. He pulled on his ear, massaging the lobe as if trying to squeeze the tension away. Things were so much better than they had been, but he sensed the slope was slippery, and he needed to put in some serious effort if he was to keep their relationship going uphill. Thank God for his ex-wife. He didn't think that very often, but without Clara there was no knowing where Megan might have ended up, emotionally speaking. Clara had always done the heavy lifting when it came to girly stuff when Megan was little, and even now she carried the bulk of their daughter's emotional baggage.

And of course now there was Brian, Clara's new fiancé. According to Megan, Brian was wonderful and talked to her like a grown-up. Lockyer was sure she only said stuff like that to wind him up, and wind him up it did. He didn't care if Clara got remarried. Well, he didn't care as long as he didn't have to attend the wedding, or hear about Brian more than once every five or ten years.

'Ready?' the tech officer asked.

'Sure.' Lockyer rested his notepad on his knee, his pen poised, pleased to be distracted from his bad-father guilt trip. 'What's the CPO called?'

'That's Cathy, PC Catherine Jones. The social worker is Marie Knight. DS Bennett briefed the three of us earlier.'

'Naturally,' he said, jotting the names at the top of his pad. He had no doubt Jane's briefing would have been thorough, to the point of giving the CPO a list of questions. She wasn't the kind of person to leave things unclear. He admired that about her, and of course it would make his job as SIO that much easier. He wouldn't have to chase her for progress reports or the action list – unlike Roger, who had spent pretty much his entire career chasing Lockyer.

The social worker had taken her seat next to the CPO. Lockyer looked down at his pad to refresh his memory. Marie and Cathy. Olive sat alone. Lockyer knew this was how it was meant to be: no family members, no close contact. It was designed to ensure the child wasn't influenced in any way, or fearful to tell the truth or go into detail in front of a relative.

'Olive,' Marie said, 'this is Constable Jones, but you can call her Cathy.'

'Hello, Olive,' Cathy said.

'Cathy is going to ask you some questions,' Marie said. 'All you have to do is answer her as best you can, and if you get stuck, don't worry. You're not in any trouble. OK?' Lockyer turned to look at the monitor that was focused in on Olive's face. She nodded, but her eyes didn't leave her hands, which were resting in her lap. 'If you have any questions or are worried about anything, you can talk to me, or to Cathy. We're here to look out for you. OK?' Again, Lockyer glanced at the close-up of Olive's face. She nodded again.

'Right, Olive,' Cathy said in a firm but level voice. 'Can you look at me? Would that be OK?' Lockyer could feel himself beginning to sweat. He was glad he wasn't in that room. He watched as Olive lifted her chin and locked eyes with the CPO. 'Thank you. Can you tell me how old you are?'

'Twelve,' she replied in a voice that was both clear and delicate. Her eyes were like saucers, her pupils taking in every ounce of light. Lockyer shook his head. She looked like the bloody cat from *Shrek*, one of Megan's favourite films. There was a scene where it widened its eyes and purred so the ogre wouldn't eat it, or something, Lockyer couldn't remember the storyline. This was torture. He couldn't help but compare Olive's voice with his own daughter's at that age. He had to remind himself that twelve-year-olds these days were smoking, drinking, doing drugs, getting into fights, bullying other kids on the Internet, having sex – having children. Adulthood didn't begin at sixteen like it used to; not that it ever really had. But he could see that Olive, like his own little girl, wasn't like that. He doubted she had ever been left alone, neglected or witnessed her parents having a drunken fight that spilled over onto her. Like Megan, she had been protected by her parents, and then without warning she had been thrust into an alien world of police officers, cameras, social workers and adults wanting things from her that she couldn't understand – that she shouldn't have to understand at her age.

'And do you understand why you are here?' Cathy asked.

'Yes.'

'Can you tell me?'

'My dad's dead. Someone killed him. You need to find out who did it.' Her statement took Lockyer by surprise. He knew she had said something similar to Jane a few hours ago, but she sounded so calm, so sure.

'What do you think happened?' Cathy asked. Lockyer wasn't looking at the CPO any more. All his attention was focused on the two monitors that showed Olive on the sofa and the close-up of her face.

'I don't know. Someone killed him.'

'OK,' Cathy said. 'You're doing really well.'

'Do you feel OK, Olive?' Marie, the social worker, asked. 'Do you want a glass of water or anything?'

'No, thank you,' Olive said, looking back down at her hands.

'Olive,' Cathy said. The girl looked up at the sound of the CPO's voice. Lockyer found it amazing that Cathy had managed to become an authoritative figure in under five minutes. 'You say *someone* killed your father. Do you know that someone?' Lockyer watched as Olive's eyes began to twitch. She looked left and right as if searching for the answer.

'No.'

'Did you see someone?'

'No.'

'Did you see someone in your father's room?'

'No.'

'Can you tell me why you think someone killed your dad?'

Olive's head jerked backwards and she screwed up her face as if the question struck her as stupid. 'Because Harvey said so. Dad didn't just *die*. Harvey said so.' Olive sniffed, but no tears fell. She was a brave little thing. Muscles in Lockyer's jaw were jumping from the tension, but Olive was managing to take the interview in her stride. The resilience of children, especially children under stress, never failed to amaze him.

'So your brother told you that someone had killed your

father?' Cathy confirmed, her voice somewhat louder. Lockyer wondered whether the tech and the social worker had noticed the change.

'Yes,' Olive said.

'Did Harvey see someone? Did Harvey know who it was?'

Olive screwed up her face. 'He . . . no, no, I don't know.' She was shaking her head, and her face had paled. 'I don't know *exactly* what he said,' she rushed on, the words coming out like machine-gun fire. 'He came into my room . . . told me something was wrong with Dad, that he wasn't breathing. He said we had to call the police. He said Dad was dead . . . that someone had killed him in his bed. He said we had to call the police.'

Cathy held up her hand. 'It's all right, Olive,' she said, shifting on the sofa. The atmosphere in the tech room had changed, so Lockyer could only imagine what it felt like to be in there. 'Take a deep breath, OK?' Olive's left hand was shaking. She took several halting breaths. 'Do you want to take a break for a minute?'

Olive was already shaking her head. 'No, I'm fine. I'm fine,' she said, although she didn't sound fine at all. Lockyer had to resist the urge to run in there, scoop the kid up and make a run for it.

'OK,' Cathy said. 'You and your brother were staying with your dad, is that right?'

Olive nodded. 'Yes,' she said, 'since the weekend.'

'Can you remember what the three of you did that day?' The CPO's voice had changed again. Her tone was lighter, more conversational, relaxed.

Olive pulled at the sleeve of her hoodie. She was silent

for almost a minute before she spoke. Lockyer realized he was holding his breath. He was not cut out for working with kids. He was about ready to jump out of his skin. 'Dad went for a run in the morning.'

'Did your dad run a lot?'

'Every day, before work, before breakfast,' Olive said with a sigh.

'And then what happened?' Cathy had her head cocked to one side, as if she was listening to the retelling of a normal family day.

'Not much. Harvey was playing on his Xbox, like he always does. We watched telly . . . went to the shops. Dad promised Harvey we would have a barbecue if it was sunny . . . it was sunny.'

'Do you remember what shop you went to? About what time?'

'We went to Sainsbury's,' Olive said. She seemed to pause before continuing. 'I don't know what time. I don't like barbecues . . . Dad and Harvey love them . . . Dad always burns everything, makes me ill.' Lockyer could hear the bitterness in her voice. He had heard the same tone from his own daughter more than once. It was the resentment of a child whose life, through no fault of their own, has been split between two houses, between two parents. Clara was always banging on about consistency when Megan was growing up. *'We need to be consistent for her to feel safe. This is all so unsettling for her.'* He wondered now how Olive had fared with her parents' separation. It seemed to him that, in that one sentence, she had revealed that she wasn't just a little girl mourning her father – she was still mourning the divorce. Again, he had an urge to run in and rescue her.

'Did you have the barbecue in your back garden?'

'Yes,' Olive said.

'Just the three of you?'

She shook her head. 'Ben cycled over.' Cathy looked as if she was about to speak, but Olive continued before she had a chance. 'He's one of Harv's friends. He came over. They ate everything. I went in . . . it was too hot.' Lockyer sat forward, studying the girl's face. She had the sullen attitude of a teenager, coupled with the fragility of a child. She seemed stuck between the two. Adolescence, he thought. Never an easy time.

'Do you know Ben's surname?'

'Nicholls,' she said.

'And did Ben stay over . . . spend the night?'

Olive shook her head. 'He went home after lunch. Him and Harv had a fight.'

'About what?' Cathy asked.

'Nothing,' Olive said. 'Xbox . . . Harv was losing. He doesn't like losing. It's his ADHD.'

'OK,' Cathy said in a sing-song voice, as if breezing over Olive's reference to her brother's condition. 'And what else – what about the rest of the afternoon, the evening? What did you do?'

Olive shrugged. 'Not much. Dad and Harv watched a film. I phoned Mum to say goodnight.'

'What time would that have been?' Cathy asked.

'Eight . . . eight thirty,' Olive said with a shrug.

'Did you talk to your mother for long?'

'Not really,' she said, shaking her head. There was a pause and Olive shrugged again. 'Then I went to bed.'

There was a noticeable pause before Cathy asked her next question. 'Can you remember if you woke up in the night?' Olive frowned, but then nodded her head several times. 'Did something wake you up?'

There was a beat before she answered. 'Yes.'

'What was it?' Cathy sat forward. 'What do you think woke you?'

Olive was picking at a thread on her jeans. 'I heard a noise.'

'What kind of noise? Could you describe it?'

'A bang, like a door closing,' she said, looking at the CPO with wide eyes. She looked desperate for some kind of approval, something to tell her she was saying the right things.

As if the CPO had heard his thoughts, she said, 'Good, that's really good. Was it a loud bang, like a door slamming? Or just a normal bang, like the noise it makes when you shut a door without slamming it?'

'Normal,' Olive said. 'I thought it was Harvey.'

'You thought it was your brother?' Cathy's head had tilted to the other side now. Lockyer wondered if she was aware of her body language. Mind you, it wasn't as if a twelve-year-old was going to be an expert in the field.

'I thought he must be going to the loo,' Olive said. Lockyer saw a trace of a smile on her face. It seemed everyone was susceptible to toilet humour, no matter the age or circumstances; or perhaps she was just embarrassed to be talking about her brother's bodily functions with strangers.

'So, you heard a noise – a bang – and you thought it was Harvey getting up to go to the toilet. Is that right?'

'Yes.'

'What time do you think it was?' Cathy asked, her head tilting back to the first side again.

'Um, I don't know.' Olive's brow crinkled into a frown. 'I can't remember.'

'Well,' Cathy said, 'was it still dark outside?'

Olive was nodding. 'Yes. Yes, it was still dark.'

'Does Harvey or your dad sometimes get up to go to the toilet in the night?'

'Sometimes Harvey does,' Olive said. She resumed picking at the thread on her jeans. 'Dad's got his own bathroom. He won't let me use it.'

'OK, so do you remember if Harvey turned on the light in the hall or maybe in the bathroom? Do you remember that?'

'He didn't turn on the light,' Olive said.

'Would you be able to see if he did?'

'Yes, but he didn't. He usually does.'

'Why do you think he didn't turn the light on?' Cathy asked.

Olive frowned again. 'I don't know. Ask Harvey.' Lockyer could see she was getting agitated, losing concentration. It didn't last for long with kids. Another ten, maybe fifteen minutes at a push, and this interview would be over.

'Thank you, Olive. You're doing great. Now, if you can, see if you can tell me everything you remember from when you heard the bang until your Aunty . . . Kate, arrived to pick you up yesterday morning.'

'Everything?' Olive asked, her mouth open and her eyes wide.

'Everything you can remember, yes,' Cathy said. 'Take your time, there's no hurry.'

'Would you like a drink of water now?' the social worker asked.

Olive nodded. Lockyer watched the monitor that showed the whole room. Marie turned to the CPO, who nodded. She got up and went over to a table at the side of the room. She seemed to be making a big show of setting out three glasses, picking up the water bottle, opening it and then starting to pour drinks for the three of them.

'Go on, Olive, you can start while Marie gets you the water,' Cathy said. Lockyer now understood the 'show'. It was meant to distract Olive, give her something to look at so that she could access her memories, even the distressing ones, without too much anxiety.

As expected, Olive continued to watch Marie but started to talk. Her voice was a monotone, as if she'd been hypnotized. 'I heard a bang, like I said. It woke me up, but it was still dark. The light in the hall didn't come on. Usually I can see it.' She started to chew on her lower lip. 'I went back to sleep.' She was in the zone now, it seemed. 'In the morning I woke up. It was early in the morning, six, six-thirty maybe. I could tell it was going to be sunny. Dad said if it rained we would go into London for the day, go on the London Eye, but if it was sunny we'd have a barbecue,' she said, her eyes narrowing. 'I put on some socks because it was cold . . .' She seemed to think for a second. 'The ones I wear to go skiing. My normal socks are at Mum's house because I don't keep all my clothes at Dad's, only what I'm going to wear. I wanted to go to the loo . . . toilet, so I got up and went.'

'Was anyone else up?' Cathy asked. Lockyer was impressed by Olive's recall. On the whole children had better memories than adults, but when it came to trauma, things changed and shifted much quicker in a child's mind, in his experience.

'Harvey was up. His bedroom door was open,' Olive said. 'I wanted to watch telly in the lounge . . .' Olive was still watching Marie as she handed her a glass of water. She took it, said thank you, and took a sip. She said thank you again, cupped the glass in both hands in her lap and crossed her legs at the ankle. She took a deep breath. 'But it was too early, so I went back to my bedroom.'

'When you were up, did you hear anything? Or maybe smell anything?'

Olive frowned, her eyes shifting from left to right. 'Smell?' she asked.

'Yes, think back. What could you smell? Close your eyes if you like,' Cathy suggested. 'It sometimes helps.'

Olive closed her eyes and sniffed. She began to shake her head, but then stopped. 'Daddy's aftershave, I could smell that.'

'Good, that's good, Olive. And what did you hear?'

Olive opened and then closed her eyes again. 'I could hear Harvey talking to Dad.'

'What were they talking about?'

'I don't know. I couldn't hear what they were saying. I couldn't hear Dad, only Harvey.'

'And then what happened?' Cathy took the glass that

Marie was handing her, and thanked her. Marie took her seat, and sat back.

Olive opened her eyes. They were wet with tears. Lockyer had to look away for a second. When he looked back, the expression on Olive's face made him want to run screaming from the room and get a job in a library.

'Then . . . then Harvey was banging on my door. He banged really hard. I shouted at him. He scared me but he kept on banging,' she said, sniffing. 'He kept banging and shouting, *Dad's dead, Dad's dead. He's not breathing. You've got to come out, someone's killed him, someone's killed Dad . . .*' Tears flowed freely down her cheeks. Lockyer wanted to look away again, but he needed to see this, to hear this. This was his job.

'Then what happened?' Cathy kept her voice level, giving no sign that the kid's emotions were affecting her. She must be made of stone, Lockyer thought. His sympathy for tears was limited, but the scene before him was heartrending.

'I . . . I opened the door. Harvey grabbed my arm. He grabbed it really hard,' she said, looking down at her left wrist and rubbing it, as if the memory made it hurt all over again. 'He dragged me down the hallway. I didn't want to go. I was frightened. He was hurting my arm.' She looked up at Marie. She wasn't looking for authority now; now she needed care and sympathy, and that was Marie's role.

'It's OK,' Marie said. 'You're doing ever so well. Tell us what happened next, Olive.'

'He . . . he pulled me into Dad's bedroom. He . . . Dad was lying on his bed. He was sleeping. He was wearing the pyjamas I got him for Christmas. I paid for them with my own pocket money.' Neither Cathy nor Marie intervened.

Both sat back, waiting for Olive to finish, waiting for her to say what they all knew she was going to say. 'Harvey was shouting, *He's dead, he's dead. Look at him, he's dead. What do we do?*'

'And what did you do?'

Olive was shaking her head. She had stopped crying, but her face was still pale. 'We didn't know what to do. Harvey said we should call Mum but I said we should call the police. He said we could go and get one of the neighbours . . . that we should try to do mouth to mouth.'

'Did you?' Cathy asked. Lockyer was wondering if the fibres Dave had found on Richard Taylor's nose and mouth might have been from his children trying to save his life.

'No. I don't know how, and Harvey didn't want to.'

'So did you phone the police?'

'No,' Olive repeated, shaking her head. 'Harvey did. He left me with Dad while he went to get the phone. He left me with him. He was so cold.'

'You touched your father?'

'I only held his hand.' Olive dropped her water, covering her face with her hands. 'I just wanted to hold his hand.'

CHAPTER ELEVEN

1 August – Friday

Jane listened, making notes in shorthand as Harvey talked. The CPO, Carl Jenson, was good. She had met him before the interview to brief him. It didn't seem like he needed the guidance. He was asking all the right questions, steering Harvey without antagonizing or upsetting him, maintaining a clear authority over the interview and at the same time creating an easy rapport with the teenager. The whole process had felt more like an informal chat than an interview – which, Jane guessed, would have been the CPO's intention.

'Did your folks talk much about the divorce, about what went wrong?' Carl asked.

Harvey shrugged. 'Mum talked about it . . . well, more than Dad did, anyway.'

'What did she say?'

He shrugged again. 'Dad had an affair with someone from work.'

'And your mum found out about it?'

'Yeah,' Harvey said, pushing his index finger into the corner of his right eye. 'She said Dad admitted it, came home one night and told her everything, said it wouldn't happen again . . . cried, said he was sorry.'

Jane shifted in her seat, unable to concentrate, trying to ignore the tiny shard of panic that was needling her. She had discovered, not too long ago, that she was somewhat claustrophobic. The tech room was tiny. The tech officer felt way too close for comfort. She could feel herself starting to sweat, and she could swear the walls were closing in on her.

'Do you know what depression is, Harvey?' Carl's question broke into Jane's thoughts and prompted her to refocus.

'Yes,' Harvey said, pulling at the skin on the back of his hand.

'What do you think a depressed person would be like – act like?' Carl asked. 'How would they seem, do you think?' Jane knew he was working his way around the suicide theory, as she had asked him to, but she didn't think he needed to be this obtuse. Harvey was fourteen. If the kids she encountered were anything to go by, he might well know far more about depression than most adults. She wondered if he would have been counselled after his ADHD diagnosis. She assumed he would, but either way, if Harvey realized the implication of Carl's question he wasn't showing it.

'They would be sad,' he said. 'Not want to be around people, cry maybe.'

'Was your dad ever sad, Harvey?'

'What – about the divorce?' Harvey's lips curled up at the edges. 'That was ages ago. No. Dad was fine. He was . . . happy, really happy.'

'Good. That's good. Did your father ever talk to you about the marriage breakup, or any problems they might be having?'

'No,' Harvey said. 'He didn't think me or my sister needed to know about any of that. He didn't like that Mum told us what happened, that she talked about it all. But that was after.'

'After what?'

'The divorce,' he said, like it was an obvious statement. 'They stayed together and did the whole separation bit without me and Olive knowing. I was only eleven when it all kicked off. Olive was eight. Dad moved out just before Olive's birthday.'

'That must have been hard,' Carl said, nodding as if agreeing with himself. Jane rolled her eyes. He was good, but he also had a bit of a know-it-all edge about him.

'It was shit,' Harvey said. 'Olive was really upset, thought it was her fault or something. She was so little – she didn't know any better.' The tenderness in his voice was touching. Jane would bet not many older brothers were so caring towards their younger sisters.

Harvey sniffed. 'Mum was crying all the time too, or shouting. She was buying her practice. Uncle Tommy and Aunt Kate were helping her, so they were over at the house a lot. Mum shouted a lot.'

'She was obviously very angry with your father,' Carl said, resuming his nodding.

'Yeah, I guess so,' Harvey said, throwing his hands in the air, 'but like she said herself . . . she was the one who kicked him out. He admitted it . . . said he was sorry, so why kick him out? Mum told Olive Dad didn't even want the divorce. It was all Mum's idea. And then she goes on crying and screaming about being left alone. Doesn't make any sense, does it? Dad didn't cry or shout . . . or anything. He just moved out. Olive started wetting the bed after that . . . an eight-year-old wetting the bed. That's not right. Not right.' Jane could see that he was holding back tears. She wondered if the 'one of the guys' rapport Carl had created might, in fact, be inhibiting Harvey.

'Do you think your mum might still be angry with your father?' Carl asked. Jane and the tech officer sitting next to her both took a sharp intake of breath at the obvious change in direction.

'That's a bit leading, don't you think?' the tech officer asked, looking at Jane.

'I'd say so,' she said, getting up out of her chair. 'I'm going to stop the interview before—' She didn't get to finish her sentence.

'I doubt it somehow,' Harvey said, his voice low. 'He's dead – or did you miss that part in the handover? Can't be angry at a dead guy, can she?' he spat. 'Or have you decided that if my dad wasn't depressed enough to top himself, then my mother must have killed him instead? Is that what you're saying? Is that what you're fucking saying?' He was standing now, moving towards the CPO. Jane was tempted to let Harvey land a punch, given Carl's behaviour, but her more sensible side prevailed as she ran out of the tech room and into the video suite.

'Whoa, whoa,' she said, positioning herself in between Harvey and the shocked-looking CPO. 'Carl, can you step outside? Now, please.' She didn't bother to look at him but heard him get up off the sofa, and the door close. 'Harvey, take a breath, come on,' she said.

'Did you hear that?' he shouted. 'Did you? He as good as came out and said my mum killed my dad.'

'Please, Harvey, calm down. That's not what Officer—'

'I am *not* stupid.'

Jane looked up at him. She felt small all of a sudden, and very much on her own. 'No, Harvey,' she said, making eye contact with him. 'No one thinks you're stupid. Officer Jenson did not mean that your mother was in any way implicated in your father's death. He could have phrased the question better, and I'm sure, given the chance, he would be happy to do so.'

'I'm not talking to that prick again. You can't make me.'

Jane had to remind herself that the man towering over her was in fact a fourteen-year-old boy. 'OK, fine,' she said. 'Please – just sit down.' She held her breath. If he didn't comply, she was going to have to ask the tech officer to get help. That was liable to make a bad situation worse. She just needed to get him calm, get him to talk. It was clear he wanted to. The pain he was holding in seemed to be coming off him in waves. 'Please, Harvey, sit down,' Jane repeated.

His shoulders dropped, he stepped back and without speaking he turned, walked away and sat down. He looked out of place on the burgundy, Nineties-throwback sofa – as if he had stepped back in time, rather than just across the room. 'Thank you,' she said.

'My mum's been through enough,' Harvey said, puffing out his chest.

'It's OK,' she said, thinking, as she often did, how hard it must be to be a guy. Girls were allowed, no, encouraged to be touchy-feely, to express their emotions; but for boys it was different. There was a club, and if you wanted to be in it, you had to be tough. You couldn't show weakness, and above all, you couldn't cry. It was archaic and wrong, but despite all the changes and calls for equality of the sexes, the 'club' still existed – and the boy sitting in front of her proved it as he bit his lip, refusing to give in, refusing to cry because he had found his father dead only twenty-four hours before.

'Are you sure this is a good idea?' Lockyer asked.

Jane stopped on the stairs and turned to face him. She had given Harvey a ten-minute break after the interview with Carl. In her opinion that was enough time for the boy to calm down and she, for one, didn't want to lose any time rearranging the interview for another day. The more time passed, the more these kids were liable to forget – or embellish. Lockyer's expression told her he disagreed. She smiled. 'It's meant to be me dragging my heels, and you harassing me to get things done quickly.'

'That is true . . . but since when have you and I had a conventional working relationship?'

'Not for a while, sir,' she said, holding onto the banister. 'Whatever happens, someone has to interview him. Cathy agrees I'm suitable, given I've already got a connection with him and she'll be present. The mother's fine with it, and I don't want to lose a day waiting for another CPO to be assigned. Cathy is more than happy to supervise, and the social worker . . . '

'Marie,' he prompted.

'That's right, Marie will be in the tech room observing, so everything is covered. Besides, Dave is doing the post-mortem late afternoon. I want this finished so I can get back for that. If Dave says it's natural causes . . . '

'He said that was unlikely,' Lockyer said.

'I know, but I'm trying to keep an open mind,' Jane said, 'despite what the kids have to say.'

'And you still think suicide is a possibility?'

'I honestly don't know, but either way, I want to know what I'm doing next. Am I passing the case over to the coroner, shutting down my investigation altogether or, if Dave finds foul play, kicking it into a higher gear?'

Lockyer sighed, but she could tell he was going to relent, to give her the room to run the interview her way. 'So what do you want me to do in the meantime?' he asked.

'Stay with Olive and the aunt, see how they interact, get a feel for that part of the extended family – and then we can both head back to the office for the post-mortem,' Jane said. There was a slight pause. 'What do you think . . . sir?'

'I think I feel like a lackey,' Lockyer said, turning away. 'I'll be here when you're done – boss.'

Jane cringed. She was going to pay for ordering him around. He was SIO, yes, but this was *her* investigation, so she was the one who had to make the decisions – it was his job to monitor, and make sure things moved ahead at a decent pace. The funny thing was, it didn't even feel that odd. In the past, when he had been running a case, she might have been the junior officer but she was forever chasing and cajoling him to make sure the admin side of things stayed on track. He was in charge, no question; but she also felt like she was running things sometimes. She smiled. He was right. They didn't have a conventional working relationship at all, but it felt good. Things had been strained, on and off, for a while, but despite his new overprotective streak, Lockyer was back to being her boss and someone who was on her side.

She knocked on the door of the tech room, opened it and poked her head around the corner. 'You guys all set in here?'

'Yes, boss,' the tech officer said. 'Ready when you are.'

Jane nodded, smiled at Marie the social worker, and stepped back into the hallway. She straightened her skirt, pushed her shoulders down and walked into the video suite. 'Sorry to keep you waiting, Harvey,' she said, taking a seat next to Cathy. The CPO had already positioned herself opposite Harvey, with her hands folded in her lap. 'How are you feeling? Are you OK if we continue?'

'Sure,' he said. His tone was bordering on petulant, but Jane decided to ignore it for now. It would take him a while to come down from his run-in with Carl, so she would just have to be patient.

'Good. That's good,' she said, settling herself on the sofa a comfortable distance from the CPO. 'Can you talk us through what happened, Harvey – from the night before last, up until we met yesterday morning, please?'

Harvey looked at Jane like she was insane, but he didn't say anything. He just sat back and crossed his legs, his ankle resting on his knee. It was an open pose in terms of body language, but she thought it was more basic than that. He was being questioned by two women. He was asserting, however subconsciously, his masculinity.

'Dad and me watched a film,' he said. 'The new *Hobbit* movie. Olive didn't like it. She called Mum to say goodnight, then she went to bed with Dad's phone to play Candy Crush. She's always bugging him to use it 'cos she can't get the app on her phone . . . not enough memory or whatever. She's *obsessed* with it.' He rolled his eyes. 'She's on, like, level six hundred, or something. Anyway . . . me and Dad watched the film.'

'Any good?' Jane asked.

'It was all right. Not as good as the *Lord of the Rings* films.'

'Those were great,' Jane said, although in truth she had only watched half of the first one and fallen asleep. She had read the books when she was a teenager and loved them, but felt the magic had been lost in translation to the big screen. 'Can you remember what you and your dad talked about?'

Harvey shrugged. 'We didn't really talk. We just watched the film.'

'And how did your dad seem; OK?'

'Sure. He was fine. He was a bit pissed off because the whole flat stank of smoke, but that was it. He *wasn't* depressed,' Harvey said.

'Smoke?' Jane asked, sidestepping the reference to Richard Taylor's state of mind.

'Dad did a barbecue for me, Olive and a mate of mine, Ben. Dad went a bit overboard with the lighter fluid. Two of the neighbours complained about the smell – everyone had their windows open 'cos it was sunny.'

'That must have made him pretty unpopular.'

Harvey threw his hands up in the air. 'Now you think one of the neighbours did it?'

'No, no. I wasn't saying that at all, Harvey. Listen, I know you're angry, and I know you're frustrated, but I'm just asking questions here. I just want to get as much information as possible to help me build up a picture – that's all. The cause of your father's death has not been confirmed yet.' As she had said to Lockyer, Dave wouldn't give a conclusive answer until after the post-mortem, and even then, 'conclusive' might not get them very far.

'That's even more stupid,' Harvey said, crossing his arms and sinking back into the sofa. Now he *did* look like a fourteen-year-old boy. 'He didn't just die.'

Given everything she had learned so far, Jane couldn't help but agree with him: she didn't see Richard Taylor just up and dying in his sleep, and the suicide theory wasn't sitting well with her either. 'Please keep going, Harvey,' she said. 'Can you do that for me? Just keep telling me what happened, and let me worry about what it does or doesn't mean.'

The room was silent for a minute before he continued. 'We watched the film. Didn't talk about much . . . nothing I can remember. When it finished I went to my room. I don't know what Dad did. Went to bed too, I guess.'

'Any idea of the time?' Jane asked. She felt like she was treading on eggshells. One wrong step and Harvey could blow up again.

'About half-eleven, I guess. I texted my mate Ben at midnight, and then I went to sleep.' Jane was about to ask another question, but Harvey beat her to it. 'I checked my phone last night, just to see. I guessed you'd want to know,' he said, pulling a fake smile but then looking down at his hands. He wanted to help. It was obvious, but he was fighting his instincts.

'Did you hear your father moving around in the night . . . going to the bathroom, anything like that?'

'No.'

'What about you? Did you wake up? Hear anything?' She noticed Harvey flinch. 'Did you hear something?' she asked.

'I thought I heard . . .' He stopped speaking, his eyes fixed.

'What? What do you think you heard, Harvey?' She could see how uneasy he was. He was shifting in his seat.

He said, 'I probably dreamed it, but I thought I heard Dad shout.'

'What did he shout?'

He closed his eyes. 'I don't know. It was just a shout, or maybe it was a bang . . . it woke me up.'

'Did you hear it again?'

'No,' he said, his eyes still closed. He had balled his hands into fists. His knuckles were white.

'It's OK, Harvey. You're doing really well,' she said. 'What happened after that?'

'Nothing,' he said, opening his eyes and looking at her. 'I went back to sleep. When I woke up again it was morning . . . I got up, went for a pee. Got a drink of milk. Put the kettle on for Dad. Went to wake him up, and then . . .' He drifted into silence.

'It's all right, Harvey. Take your time,' Jane said. It was like talking to Peter – trying to encourage him without being 'annoying Mummy' and making him angry or upset. It was a hard balance to strike.

'I said something like "Morning, Dad" or "I've put the kettle on" – I can't remember exactly. Anyway, he didn't say anything. He didn't answer me, so I . . .' Jane held her breath. 'I went over to the bed and I knew. His face was a funny colour. He didn't look right. I touched his arm. It was cold – even through his pyjamas it was cold, freezing cold.'

'Keep going, Harvey,' Jane said. She felt Cathy stiffen next to her.

'I don't know what happened next. I think I shouted – I shouted for Olive to come – she came in and I told her Dad was dead. She cried, said we should call Mum. I got the phone, dialled 999 and then that was it . . . people were everywhere. They made me and Olive sit in her bedroom with the door shut until . . . I couldn't just sit there. I had to do something.'

'What did you do while you were waiting for the police?'

'Nothing,' he said, looking down at his hands again. 'The lady kept me on the phone, talking 'til the police rang the buzzer.'

'Who let them in?'

'I did.'

'OK.' Jane let her mind run over everything he had just said. 'Harvey, I need to ask you a question.' She waiting for him to look up at her before continuing. 'What made you think that someone had killed your father? People *can* die suddenly – it does happen, even in someone as young and fit as your dad. These things can happen.' Harvey was shaking his head. 'Tell me why you think someone killed him.'

'I guess I knew,' he said with a shrug. 'Mum said it would happen.'

'Your mother said your father was going to die? That someone was going to kill him?'

Harvey was shaking his head. 'It was a few weeks ago,' he said. 'Mum came to pick us up, and her and Dad started fighting . . . she started it, but I heard Mum say . . .' Jane could see his indecision, his fear, as if it was etched on his face. He put his head in his hands. 'She said . . . "you'll end up dead. Is that what you want? Do you want to die?"'

CHAPTER TWELVE

Richard – June

Richard looked at himself in the mirror. He didn't look good, and if he was honest, he didn't feel that good either. The past week had been a revelation. Both good and bad.

He had met Nicola when he was still a teenager. He had maybe had sex with four women before her: hardly Casanova. They had been serious by their second date, chosen the same profession, even the same university; so there was no time for the one-night stands and general promiscuity that seemed to go hand in hand with the usual uni experience. Most of his friends had spent the entire five years bed-hopping. Richard had never regretted that. He had been happy – but now, looking back, he couldn't help thinking that a bit of shagging about might have done him some good, prepared him for what was happening to him now.

He was discovering that not everything was about romance and commitment. His date, the date he had been so terrified about, had progressed to sex within ten minutes of them meeting. It was alien to him, but he couldn't deny that it had felt good. Scrap that: it had felt amazing. He had never been *so impulsive and spontaneous in his entire life. He was a planner. Always had been. He had always tried to plan ahead. His education, his marriage, Harvey and Olive's education – everything was mapped out ahead of time. Back then he hadn't liked surprises, bar the arrival of his children, of course, but now he was discovering a whole new side to himself. He splashed some water onto his face, towelled off and walked through to his bedroom. He started pulling off the sheets. As he took off the duvet cover, the smell of sex filled his nostrils. It was pungent and almost tangible. He reached into his jeans pocket for his mobile and tapped out a message.*

Got any time this afternoon?

He debated whether to add a kiss, but decided against it. This relationship, if it could be called that, was not about romance. It was about fun and freedom. His phone beeped with an incoming message. As he read it, a huge smile spread across his face.

Time? For you? Who wouldn't?? x

Richard messaged back a time, and then looked at his watch. He had three hours.

He walked through to the kitchen carrying the bundle of sheets in his arms. He shoved them in the machine and grabbed a liquitab from the box under the sink. He set the machine to a quick wash before grabbing his gym bag from the hallway and his keys from the hall table. A quick workout was just what he needed to clear his mind of all his doubts and get him ready for an afternoon of fun. He pulled the door to the flat closed behind him and swung his bag up over his shoulder. The smile that had taken up residence on his face was making his cheeks ache. How could anything that resulted in this amount of excitement be bad? He jogged down the stairs and out the main front door, the afternoon playing out in his head like a movie. His responsible side might be struggling with the 'new him', but his brain and body were both on board and raring to go. He jogged to his car and clicked the central locking. As he climbed in, he glanced at his reflection in the rear-view mirror. He looked better.

CHAPTER THIRTEEN

1 August – Friday

Lockyer sidestepped Dave as he made his way to the other side of the mortuary table. No one had spoken for the past thirty minutes other than Dave mumbling into his Dictaphone and muttering instructions to Patrick, who was assisting with the post-mortem. They were still doing the external examination. Richard Taylor's body had been photographed, and every item of clothing and errant fibre collected and logged. The mortuary suite was quiet. It felt respectful, which Lockyer knew was Dave's intention. He was genuine and earnest when it came to his responsibilities to the deceased. Lockyer moved back as Patrick started examining Taylor's scalp and hair.

Lockyer realized he was far more comfortable here than he had been at Caterham Road. Dave often said the dead were easier to deal with than the living, and given this morning, Lockyer was beginning to think he had a point. Olive had not fared well after her interview. By the time he joined her and the aunt in the family room, Olive was sucking her thumb and twisting her fingers around the same section of hair over and over again. The aunt, Kate, had tried to coax the girl out of her stupor, but to no avail. Lockyer had pulled Marie aside after Harvey's second interview to get her professional opinion. Regression, she had told him, was common and entirely natural in the weeks and months after a traumatic event, but she'd assured him that Olive would bounce back. 'These things just take time,' she'd said. Lockyer rubbed his face, remembering too late he was wearing surgical gloves. The rubber stretched and snapped back on his cheeks. When he swore under his breath he got a stern look from Dave. He mouthed an apology. As soon as there was a body on his table, Dave's sense of humour vanished.

'Would you do my post-mortem, Dave?' Lockyer asked, taking off the gloves, throwing them in the bin and grabbing a fresh pair. 'If I needed one.'

'Why? You planning on going somewhere?' Dave asked without looking up from the body.

'Not today, no,' Lockyer said, 'but you never know.'

'It can be arranged,' Dave said, his mouth tight. 'I keep telling Patrick here just how weird you are, but he never believes me . . . well, here's your proof, Pat. Who asks a question like that?' He looked at Lockyer over the top of his glasses.

'I just wondered if it might be a conflict of interest, or something,' Lockyer said, holding out his hands. 'Hey, buddy . . . if you don't want to do it, I respect your decision.'

'You would have no choice,' Dave said. 'You'd be dead.'

'Good point,' Lockyer said, smiling.

'I think,' Patrick said, as he examined Richard Taylor's hands and fingers with great dexterity and care, 'he's trying to pay you a compliment, boss.'

'Is he? Well, in that case, thank you, Michael.'

Lockyer stepped aside again as Dave made another pass

of the body. 'You are very welcome. Now, have you got anything I can report back on?'

'You're reporting back to Jane now?' Dave said, looking sideways but again over his glasses. It was becoming a trademark. 'The tide has certainly turned.'

'Ha ha, very funny. As SIO, of course, I'm still *in charge* . . . when am I not? However, Jane is the lead detective and is running the case, so *yes*, in a way I'm reporting back to her, but only as her superior.'

'Well, that makes perfect sense,' Dave said, shaking his head. 'I'm so glad I asked.'

'I get it,' Patrick said with a shrug.

'Thank you, Patrick,' Lockyer said, motioning a high five without making contact. He didn't want to change his gloves yet again.

'I don't know why you're sucking up to him,' Dave said. 'I'm the one who signs off on your bonus.'

There was an audible snort from Patrick's side of the mortuary table. 'Bonus? What bonus?' he said, laughing. Lockyer couldn't help joining in, if only because Dave's expression made him feel like a naughty kid in class.

'All right, all right. Enough levity, gentlemen.' Dave gave them both a stern look. 'Shall we?' He gestured to Richard Taylor's body.

Lockyer cleared his throat. 'Of course,' he said. He caught Patrick's eye, but managed to look away before cracking up again. 'So, as I said, DS Bennett wants, or rather, needs to know if this poor guy was murdered or not.'

'Possibly,' Dave said. 'As I said before, we've got the fibres on the nose and mouth and some broken blood vessels. There is a small amount of injury to the tongue, but other than that there doesn't appear to be any other sign of trauma. Not that I can see, anyway. Patrick, anything?'

Patrick had moved down to Richard Taylor's legs. 'No, nothing out of the ordinary . . . wait,' he said. 'Boss, can I borrow your penlight?'

Dave pulled the slim white penlight off his apron and handed it to Patrick. 'What have you got?' he asked. Lockyer couldn't help stepping forward to get a better look at whatever it was that had Patrick so interested.

'Give me a second.'

Lockyer watched as Patrick shone the light on one, then another section of Taylor's right thigh. He repeated the action several times before looking up at them and saying, 'Here, look.' He used the penlight and a pencil he had taken from his lab coat to show them both what he was looking at. 'There, there and there. Can you see them?'

Dave leaned closer. 'Well spotted, Patrick,' he said. 'Really well spotted. Mike, come and take a look. This could be interesting.'

Lockyer was already there, hovering behind them both, eager to get in between them. 'Show me,' he said, straining his eyes at the pale skin on Taylor's thigh.

'See them?' Dave asked.

Lockyer narrowed his eyes, moved his head back and then forwards to let his eyes focus . . . and then, yes, he saw it. 'Oh yes,' he said. 'Are those what I think they are?'

'Yes,' Dave said. 'They are.'

*

'Sorry I'm late,' Jane pushed through the double doors of the mortuary suite.

'That's quite all right,' Dave said. 'We're almost done here.'

'Problems?' Lockyer asked.

Jane recognized the subtext to his question. She had been insistent on getting the interviews with the children done so she could get back for the post-mortem, and here she was waltzing in well over an hour late. 'Nicola Brown,' she replied, pulling on a pair of gloves and glancing at the mortuary table. The internal exam was well under way, Taylor's chest opened, the skin and muscle held back. It always reminded her of a butterflied chicken: consequently, she didn't eat poultry.

'The ex-wife?' Dave said, looking at her over the top of his glasses. Jane wasn't keen on the new look. He reminded her of her biology teacher at school, Mr Hughes. He was always angry, frustrated by his class's pitiful knowledge and underwhelming enthusiasm for a subject he thought was the be-all and end-all of everything. She realized, now that she thought about it, that he had a point.

'I was stuck on the phone for half an hour,' she said, tipping her head back to ease the tension that was building in her shoulder muscles. 'She wasn't happy with the state her children returned home in . . . and that's putting it mildly.' Her ears were still ringing from Nicola Brown shouting at her down the phone. 'Apparently the girl has continued regressing, sucking her thumb, not really talking; and the boy, Harvey, is bouncing back and forth between aggressive and sullen.'

'They were video interviewed this morning?' Dave asked, moving around Patrick, who was removing samples of blood from the vena cava. From what Jane could see, Dave was preparing to remove the organs for weighing and examination.

She nodded. 'Yes. The girl did really well, didn't she, Mike?'

'She was fine. A few tears at the end, but overall I thought she handled the whole process well,' he said. 'It was only afterwards that she seemed to go downhill.'

'Pretty standard, I would guess,' Dave said, speaking to Jane but looking at Patrick. The two of them seemed to work by way of telepathy. Patrick used a scalpel to make an incision in the pulmonary artery. He looked at Dave and they both examined the artery, nodding, then Dave mumbled into his Dictaphone before Patrick began cutting the various arteries and veins in order to remove the heart.

'Yes,' Jane said, putting on a disposable apron. 'But that's not what her mother wanted to hear. Mike spoke to the social worker . . .'

'Marie,' said Lockyer.

Jane ignored the dig, but realized she had started calling Lockyer Mike, not 'boss' or 'sir'. How long had she been doing that for? He had asked her, more than once, to use his first name, but until now she had resisted the change. 'Marie, yes. And she said it would pass, that it was perfectly normal, and that Harvey's aggression was all part of the grieving process, especially given his ADHD. It was just unfortunate that both children decided to have their extreme changes in behaviour *after* we had interviewed them.'

'She'll get over it,' Lockyer said, waving her over. 'Besides,' he added, 'you've got bigger fish to fry.' He gestured over the table at Dave.

'Go on,' Jane said.

Dave removed his gloves, turned and pulled on a fresh pair that Patrick was already holding out to him. He moved to the far end of the table and beckoned Jane to follow him. As she did, she looked at Richard Taylor's face. Despite the colour changes in his skin and the fact that his entire torso had been cut open, he still looked as if he was sleeping. It was creepy. She watched as Dave took a penlight from his pocket and, with a flourish, directed it at Taylor's right thigh. 'Take a look. Tell me what you see.'

Jane stepped forward and leaned over the body in order to get a better view of where Dave was directing his light. She moved her head from left to right, searching. She was about to ask what she was meant to be looking for when she spotted it. 'Is that a needle mark?' she asked.

'Yes,' Dave said. 'Six needle marks, to be precise.'

Jane straightened up and looked from Dave to Lockyer to Patrick. 'Any evidence of drug use?'

'None,' Patrick said. 'Nothing on the external examination. We're about to check the liver, kidneys and heart now, but . . . '

'He's not a drug user,' Dave said.

'OK,' she said, turning her attention back to Dave. 'Suicide. An overdose of some kind?'

'Possibly,' he said. 'Patrick will send the bloods off for the basic tox screen, which I'd expect back fairly quickly, but he's taken a second lot of bloods which I'll send off to the toxicology lab if nothing's found in the first screen.'

'There's something else,' Dave said. 'The left side of the tongue has several lacerations.'

'Meaning?' she asked, moving up to the head as Patrick opened the mouth and showed her the damage to Taylor's tongue.

'I didn't think too much of it at first,' Dave said, as if embarrassed, 'but it could indicate a seizure.'

'Right,' Jane said, adding each piece of information to the flow chart she had created in her mind. 'Any history of epilepsy that we know of?'

'His medical records haven't turned up yet,' Dave said, 'but even then, it could have been his first seizure. A seizure happens due to changes in the brain's electrical activity. There are any number of reasons why this might happen.' He removed his glasses. 'Head injury, an aneurysm, hypoglycaemia, misuse of drugs or alcohol, brain hypoxia.'

'Hypoxia,' she repeated, 'reduced oxygen to the brain . . . caused by suffocation?' She looked down at Taylor's nose and mouth. The fibres were long gone, but she had seen them in situ yesterday morning.

'Put it this way,' Dave said. 'I've not finished my examination, but given what I've ascertained so far, I wouldn't be happy listing the death as natural causes. Suspicious death, suicide – I don't know yet. But I'm fairly confident he didn't die in his sleep.'

Jane nodded, pressing her middle fingers on her eyelids, trying to stop the headache that was forming. 'OK, so we've got the fibres on the nose and mouth . . . damage to the tongue which *might* indicate seizure and/or applied pressure from suffocation, *and* the puncture wounds. Is it just me, or does that sound like one thing too many?' she asked. 'If it was an injected overdose, then the puncture wounds and the

CLARE DONOGHUE

seizure could fit – but then the fibres don't. He was lying on his back.'

'Well, about that,' Dave said. 'Lividity backs that up, in the main – the majority of the blood has settled to indicate the victim died on his back. However, I noticed a small, *very* small amount of blood settling on the right bicep and right shin. It could – and I'd like to stress *could* – mean he died on his front.'

'What, and someone turned him over? Posed the body?' Jane's pulse quickened as she spoke.

Dave held up both hands. 'It's possible, yes.'

'They'll have to put that on your tombstone, Dave,' Lockyer said, stepping forward. 'Everything and anything seems to be *possible* when it comes to PMs.'

'That's because it often is,' Dave said. 'If it was an easy science, a definitive science, there'd be very little need for *your* lot at all.'

'Guys,' Jane said. They both turned to her. When neither spoke, she decided to press on as the puzzle in her mind shifted. 'Let's just think this through. If Taylor overdosed, then it would make sense that he injected himself; standing up, sitting down or lying down . . . on his back. Few people decide to kill themselves whilst face down in a bed, so the fibres, broken blood vessels, don't fit.'

'What if he passed out – fell face first onto the bed?' Lockyer asked.

'What, and then turned himself over after he'd died?'

Lockyer frowned. 'Good point,' he conceded.

'The suicide doesn't fit for me,' Jane said. Dave was nodding in agreement.

'I have to say I agree with you,' he said. 'In my experience, people who take their own lives don't go to the trouble of hiding the evidence . . . the needle, the drug used – all should, would, be present at the scene.'

'Of course,' Jane said, feeling as stupid as Lockyer had a few moments before.

'And why would the guy choose a night his kids were staying with him to top himself?' Lockyer added. 'Suicide is out for the time being.'

'Agreed,' she said. 'In which case, *someone else* administered an unknown substance . . .'

'While the victim was face down on the bed . . .' Dave said.

'And they held his face into the pillow, suffocating him . . .' Lockyer said.

'And then repositioned the body so it would look like he had died in his sleep . . .' Dave offered.

'Which,' Jane said, 'accounts for the injection sites, the fibres, tongue damage, signs of hypoxia, possible seizure and the anomalies with lividity.'

'My only problem with that,' Dave said, 'is that very few drugs are that fast-acting, meaning that suffocation would have to be the primary cause of death – and I'm sorry to tell you, but the evidence of suffocation is very minor. To suffocate a man of this size would take considerable force. I would expect significant bruising and blood-vessel damage around the eyes, nose and mouth. I would also expect to find defensive wounds on the victim's hands or arms. There's no way a man of his size could have been suffocated without A, being aware of it, and B, fighting his assailant – overdose or no overdose.'

The answer hit Jane like a physical blow. 'Unless he was injected *beforehand*, and therefore unconscious or semi-conscious when the suffocation took place.'

'That sounds more plausible,' Dave said.

'I'm afraid I have a tiny issue with that,' Lockyer said.

Jane felt the headache step up a gear and shift to her temples. She loved this part of an investigation, thrived on the solving of the riddle; but that only worked if the riddle *could* be solved. The lack of a clear solution was enough to keep her up at night, and she had the feeling that this case was going to do just that. 'Go on,' she said, bracing herself.

'All that works,' Lockyer said. 'It's a tad complicated, but it works . . .' She couldn't help but breathe a small sigh of relief. At least he wasn't going to blow the entire theory out of the water. 'But how would you inject someone without them knowing? Not once, but six times? Even if the guy was sleeping that's got to be impossible, surely?'

Jane looked at Dave. He shrugged. 'He has a point,' Dave said.

'Bugger,' she said, pushing her shoulder blades together, arching her back and blowing out a frustrated breath. 'I thought I had it then.'

'Give me time to finish the internal exam, and I'll chase up the medical records,' Dave said. 'That might give us more to work with, but if not, I'll put a rush on the bloods and see if that can resolve Lockyer's tiny issue.'

Jane smiled at the innuendo. 'Thanks, Dave,' she said with a sigh. 'Patience is a virtue, they say.'

'It seems we're agreed, then,' Lockyer said.

'On what?' she asked.

'It's not natural causes . . . no one's buying it's a suicide . . . sooo, that only leaves us with door number three – death under suspicious circumstances. Which means your team are up, DS Bennett.'

'Category A,' she said.

'Looks that way.'

Jane folded her arms. She had hoped, despite the children's statements and her gut feeling, that she might be passing a suicide case back to the coroner, or at a push a determination of death by natural causes; but that wasn't to be. She would await Dave's official report, but it looked like she would be opening a category A investigation: murder by unknown assailant, risk of anxiety and/or danger to the public.

'Time to talk to the ex-wife,' Lockyer said.

'Yes.' Jane nodded. 'I guess it is.'

CHAPTER FOURTEEN

June

Message from Dee_28:

Hey Rich,

You've gone quiet. Is everything OK? Did I say something to scare you off? I hope not. Don't worry about meeting up. If you don't want to or you're not ready, or whatever, that's fine. I know how busy you are. It was only an idea. I'm working tonight and tomorrow lunchtime anyway, so don't stress.

Anyway . . . I survived my first Friday night! I know, you're amazed. It was OK actually. The pub was absolutely packed but I managed to hold my own. Even Alfie (a.k.a. my shithead boss) was impressed. He said I could work tonight and he's given me two shifts next weekend too. At this rate I might just be able to make my rent this month and NOT have to resort to my last-resort BJ ☺

Sooo I'm rambling . . . sorry. Be good to hear from you. You can PM any time. I've got the messaging app on my phone now so I can talk to you any time, day OR NIGHT!! Ha ha, only kidding.

Speak soon.

Dee xx

CHAPTER FIFTEEN

2 August – Saturday

Jane pushed the straw into the carton of apple juice and handed it to Peter. 'Here you go, honey,' she said, taking the opportunity to ruffle his hair while he was within arms' reach. 'What do you say?'

'Thank you,' Peter said, his mouth making an exaggerated O shape as he tried to get the straw into his mouth. As soon as he made contact he began sucking as if he was trying to siphon a petrol tank from a hundred yards away.

'Slow down,' Jane said, reaching out to him, but he darted away. 'Slow down,' she said again, trying to stop herself from shouting. 'There's plenty in there . . . you don't have to drink it all in one go . . .' Her pleas fell on deaf ears, as usual. She opened her mouth to try again, but decided not to bother. He couldn't seriously injure himself with a carton of apple juice. She watched as he headed for the swings. To an observer he no doubt looked relaxed, skipping along; but Jane saw him through different eyes. He kept turning every few seconds to check she was still there. She massaged her temples. This separation anxiety was exhausting. He wouldn't let her leave without a fuss, but wouldn't let her near him either. She felt overwhelmed and bereft all at the same time.

Was she doing a good job? At work, she would say an unequivocal yes. She had recovered and retaken her place as senior DS on the squad with the minimum of fuss; but when it came to Peter, she wasn't so sure. He was struggling. He might not say so, but she could tell. He was anxious – more anxious than usual. Jane couldn't help thinking his stress levels were linked to her, to the stability that she was failing to provide. She also couldn't deny that this sudden onset of concern might have something to do with the email.

She logged into her Facebook account maybe once a month, tops. It was a good way to keep tabs on the friends she wasn't seeing – that would be all of them – and it made her feel connected to people, even though she never posted anything or revealed her presence in any way. She didn't know why she had decided to log in last night, but when she had, there had been a little red number one next to the messages icon.

None of her actual friends would bother messaging her on Facebook. They emailed her work address – that way they were guaranteed a response, eventually. When she clicked to open the message and saw his name she had dropped her Kindle, which had landed with a bang on her parents' kitchen floor. It had taken ten minutes and a reboot to get it to turn on again. By the time she got back to the message, Jane had been sweating, her mouth dry, her heart racing. No surprise there. Andy had always had that effect on her. *Andy Boyd.* Even the name gave her shivers, good and bad.

'Don't let him wind you up,' Celia Bennett said from the

bench next to her. Jane froze, not daring to look at her mother. How did she know? 'I don't know why you let him get to you,' she continued. Jane stayed mute. 'He knows he's doing it,' she said, patting the back of Jane's hand. 'You just have to learn not to rise to it.'

Jane was just about to ask what the hell her mother thought she was doing going through her emails, when the penny dropped. She wasn't talking about Andy. She was talking about Peter. Jane shook her head. 'He doesn't do it on purpose, Mum,' she said, her voice harsher than she intended.

Her mother huffed out a breath. 'That's what you think.' Jane was about to argue, but managed to hold her tongue, knowing her anger was misplaced.

Just thinking about Andy made her angry. Did he really think he could waltz back into their lives after eight years? If he did, then he was either disturbed or deranged. She looked over at Peter, at the sunlight bouncing off his pink cheeks. He was growing so fast. Every day she felt him growing further away from her. She clasped her hands together. She wanted to shake herself out of it, to tell herself how stupid she was being. With a deep breath she stood up and walked towards the fence that surrounded the children's play park. The grass was still damp from yesterday's downpour, but she didn't care. She bent forward and rested her arms on the blue-painted fence. Peter, her parents and her job. Those were her priorities, in that order – most of the time. Peter was doing OK, he was coping. Her father was on the mend, and her mother was – her mother. She closed her eyes and with ease, shifted her brain back to work mode: her preferred setting.

After the post-mortem she had spent several hours

reading over the transcripts from Harvey and Olive's interviews. The children's versions of events seemed to tally up until the discovery of Taylor's body. Olive had said she got up at six or six-thirty to go to the bathroom; saw Harvey's bedroom door open and heard him talking to their father. That concurred with her brother's account as he said he got up and went to ask his father if he wanted a cup of tea. After this point the accounts differed. Harvey said he found his father not breathing and shouted for Olive. He said she came into the room and he told her their father was dead. He said Olive wanted to call their mother, but Harvey dialled 999, and was then on the phone with despatch until the first responder arrived and he let them into the flat.

Olive, on the other hand, said her brother came and banged on her door, shouting that their father was dead and then dragging her by the wrist into their father's room. She said it was Harvey who wanted to call their mother, and that she was the one who said to call 999. Then their stories re-converged and Olive confirmed that Harvey called the police, and the two of them were in their father's room until the police arrived.

Jane took a deep breath and pursed her lips. Discrepancies in a traumatic incident were common, if not expected, but something was niggling at her. Peter waved at her, a goofy grin on his face. She smiled and waved back.

She wondered what Olive's and Harvey's home life was like. She had spoken to Nicola Brown, and so would hazard a guess that when they were with their mother life would be somewhat regimented. But what was their father like with them? From the little she had gleaned so far she had the feeling that Olive was the 'favoured' child, whereas Harvey was the 'problem'. Harvey had said his sister was delicate. Of course favouring one child over another didn't make Nicola or Richard bad parents. Jane knew how it worked in families. She looked at the other children playing in the park, glancing at the various benches to pick out their respective parents. It didn't take a genius to figure out the hierarchy when you watched families in the park as much as Jane did. The first child was worshipped right up until the point that number two arrived. After that, the parents' wonderment and affection shifted. The first child became a shadow called upon to perform fetch and carry duties for the second in line. No doubt she would be the same, if she had another child.

Her eyes settled back on her son, who was holding onto the swing, refusing to let anyone else come near him or it. She smiled. She would never have another child. One was perfect. Peter was perfect. The sun came out from behind a cloud and warmed her. She closed her eyes and lifted her face to it, but her mind wouldn't settle. If it was possible for a brain to fidget, that was how Jane's brain felt most of the time: fidgety. Part of her was here with her mother and son, enjoying some quality time, part of her was thinking about her father and, despite herself, Andy. But the majority was working on her action list, because that was her way of compartmentalizing her life. If she focused on work, on a case, she could blur the rest.

She opened her eyes and searched the play park for her son. He had left the swings. He was now sitting at the centre of the roundabout in a little Buddha pose while other children took turns spinning him as fast as they could. He appeared to be enjoying the experience, but she kept her eyes on him just in case that changed. Without thinking, she held out her fingers and started counting off tasks in her head. She needed to get an update from the territorial support group on the house-to-house enquiries. They had searched Richard Taylor's home the day before, but were still collating everything. The TSG's were the best officers for the job. They worked fast and would follow instructions to the letter.

'We need to start thinking about heading back,' her mother said, walking up behind her and jolting her out of her thoughts.

'Are you sure you're OK at home with the both of them?' Jane asked, regretting the question the second it left her lips.

'How many times?' her mother said, straightening her skirt with a sharp pull. 'I'm absolutely fine.'

'OK, fine, but you know where I am if you need me.'

Her mother laughed. 'Yes, dear, I know where you'll be,' she said, walking away. 'At the office.'

Jane took a deep breath in through her nose and held it for a couple of seconds. She let the breath out, closed her eyes and waited for her heartbeat to return to normal.

'Come on, darling,' she heard her mother call back to her. 'I don't like leaving your father for too long.'

Jane grumbled to herself, gathered up their things, Peter's coat, jumper and shoes. Peter was waving at her from the entrance to the park. She watched as he jumped up and down on the spot, squealing with delight. 'I won't let anyone hurt you,' she whispered. 'Ever.'

*

Jane lengthened her stride, but Lockyer was still ahead as they turned the corner on Belmont Grove. They had run along Lewisham High Street, taken a right at Kings Hall mews and then fought their way through the undergrowth to run alongside the railway line to the end of Cressingham Road. It wasn't a path per se, but it meant you could run next to trees rather than curry houses and run-down kebab shops. This was their second lap. She had managed to keep up with Lockyer until now. 'Are you trying to kill me?' she shouted as she stopped running and bent over, her hands resting on her knees. The sun felt hot on her back. Her heart was hammering in her chest. She felt as if her eyes were pulsating in rhythm. She saw Lockyer's trainers appear in front of her. 'When I asked if you fancied a run around the block, I meant a run, not a race.' She straightened up, wobbling on her feet.

Lockyer reached out and steadied her. 'You're unfit,' he said.

'Well,' she laughed. 'That is extremely helpful, thank you.'

He smacked her on the back and started jogging on the spot. 'Come on,' he said. 'Let's do one more lap. You can lead. I'll keep pace with you.' Jane rolled her eyes, took a deep breath, walked a few steps before breaking into a run. She took in as much air as she could to persuade her aching muscles that continuing to run was a good idea. She could hear Lockyer just behind her. 'That's it, pick up those knees,' he said, darting past her, his knees coming up to his chest like a footballer. There wasn't a bead of sweat on him. He looked so bloody healthy. Jane knew, without looking, that she had taken on the colouring of a ripe tomato and her hair would be stuck up at odd angles as it fought its way free from her hairband. She had never been able to exercise without looking terrible. It was embarrassing. Every instructor and trainee at Hendon had seen Jane puce at one time or another. They had nicknamed her PJ – Puce Jane, a name she had thankfully left behind. 'Deep breaths . . . get that blood oxygenated,' Lockyer shouted over his shoulder.

If she'd had the strength or the energy, she would have sprinted after him and tripped him up so he would come crashing down on that handsome face of his. However, given that her vision seemed to be wavering, she decided a sprint was a push too far. 'You go on,' she called. 'I'm gonna head back.'

He turned, stopped and started walking back towards her. 'Lame,' he said when he reached her side. 'No worries, I was about done anyway. It's good to cool down. Let's walk back via Caterham Road, save having to inhale all the fumes on the high street.'

'Fine,' Jane said, forcing herself to walk without limping, which right now was difficult. Her calves were killing her. She shaded her eyes from the sun.

He fell in step beside her and nudged her shoulder with his arm. 'No need to sulk just 'cos you run like a girl.'

She looked sideways up at him. 'That's because I *am* a girl,' she said. 'Besides, I've got a briefing in . . .' she looked at her watch, '. . . in thirty minutes, and I look like shit.' She saw him open his mouth. 'Don't say anything.'

He held up his hands, smiling. 'Wouldn't dream of it, ma'am.' He cleared his throat. 'So, what do we have to look forward to in today's briefing?' he asked. 'Fill me in. I'm all ears.' He tugged at his ears.

'Why are you in such a good mood?' she asked. Right now she would welcome a bit of his usual brooding demeanour. Ever since the email from Andy, her own mood had darkened by the hour. She wanted to delete it, but every time her finger hovered over the button she hesitated and found herself reading it again. He wanted to see her – to talk.

'It's the weekend. I'm *technically* not working tomorrow, so I'm looking forward to a day off. Is that so unusual?'

'Yes,' she said, feeling her pulse return to normal.

'What are you so wound up about?' he asked. 'Given the interviews with the kids yesterday and Dave's findings in the PM, I would have thought you'd be happy.'

'Why's that?' she asked, half wanting to tell him about the email. But what would be the point? She had to deal with Andy in her own way – when she was good and ready.

'Well,' he said. 'You've got a disgruntled ex-wife who may or may not have threatened Taylor two weeks ago. You've got the suggestion that drugs were used to sedate Taylor before he was suffocated. The ex-wife is a dentist – a partner in her own practice – so, easy access to drugs if she wanted them.'

Jane moved behind Lockyer to let a woman with a push-chair pass them. She rocked her head from side to side. 'That's true,' she said, 'but we don't have the tox screen back yet to confirm what drugs, if any, were used. And as for the motive – the angry ex-wife – Taylor and Brown divorced three years ago, separated well before that. Why would she all of a sudden decide she couldn't live without him, or rather, that *he* couldn't live without *her*?' She turned right onto Belmont Hill, thankful that the sun was now behind her.

'Who knows,' Lockyer said with a shrug, 'but it's the

simplest explanation, which as a rule is the one that turns out to be right. You said the indoor team found evidence on Taylor's laptop and iPad of Internet dating. Maybe Brown found out he was dating, and that pushed her over the edge? You said yourself there was something a bit off about her.'

As they crossed over to Caterham Road Jane noticed him looking left and right, his hand hovering behind her back. 'It makes sense,' she said.

'So, tell me where you're at,' he said, dropping his arm but putting himself on the road side of the pavement. The overprotective bit had been a hindrance in the office but she couldn't deny it felt good to have someone looking out for her. Maybe she should talk to him – show him Andy's email, even. Maybe he would offer to go and find Andy, to warn him off. She smiled at the thought. Now that would be perfect.

'Hellooo?' he said.

'Sorry. Update, right.' Jane ticked boxes in her head. 'The TSGs have started the house-to-house this morning, so they'll be updating me on that. The evidence they collected on Thursday and Friday is with the exhibits team, so we'll be looking to see if any fresh avenues of enquiry come from that.' She looked sideways at the house on Caterham Road where Harvey and Olive had been interviewed. She could do without being stuck in that tech room again. She shuddered. Her fear of enclosed spaces had gone from something and nothing, to something bordering on significant. However, she realized with some relief, this was the first time in a day or so that she had thought about what had happened to her back in May. Andy's forced re-entry into her life wasn't all bad, then.

She went back to her mental checklist. 'Anne Phillips is

coming in to talk to the team about the family. She's the FLO assigned to Brown and the kids. She's been observing them since Thursday, so she should have some insight into the family dynamic, and Brown's reaction after the kids came back from interview. I'll be prepping Penny, Franks, Aaron and Chris for interviews after tomorrow morning's briefing.'

'Who've you got so far?'

'Tomorrow I've got Nicola Brown,' she said, 'and Adam Oxenham, Richard Taylor's best friend. Cathy the CPO is going to speak to Ben Nicholls at Caterham on Monday. He's the kid who came over for the barbecue at Taylor's the day before.' She looked down at her fingers as if the names were written there. 'Also on Monday we've got . . . Tom Brown and Kate Franklin, Nicola Brown's brother and sister. I'm sending Aaron and Penny over to speak to Taylor's colleagues at his dental practice Monday morning . . . oh, and I've asked Franks to call Chantelle Bullion, the woman I met outside Taylor's flat, to follow up.'

'Sounds good,' he said.

'Mmm.' She nodded, still absorbed by her mental check-list. 'I'm video-interviewing Brown here, first thing. Oxenham is due in mid-morning; Penny will interview him. I'll get Franks and Chris to go to the brother and sister's home addresses on Monday. No sense having them in at this stage.'

'What about press coverage? How do you want to handle that?'

'If Roger will agree to it, I'd prefer to keep things quiet until end of play Monday, at least,' she said as they approached the back gates to the station. She reached up and touched her face. It felt warm but not volcanic, so with any luck she might just avoid looking like a freak in the briefing. 'If this turns out to be a spousal murder then I'll be downgrading it from a category A, in which case I would rather avoid alerting the locals. As soon as there's even a whiff of "killer on the loose", the phones will go nuts. The team will end up spending the majority of their time fielding calls from worried residents or more likely, nosey neighbours keen to dob in their local butcher, or the guy from number 30 that just "doesn't seem right in the head".'

Lockyer laughed. 'Well, I'm speaking to Roger after the briefing, so I'll put forward the case for keeping things quiet for now.'

'Does he want an update on the case?' she asked.

'Of course,' he said, smiling. 'That's one of my many jobs as SIO – keep the top brass informed, weekend or no weekend. Not that Roger's in the office, obviously.' He keyed in the security code before holding the door open for her. 'Now I'm off to get showered; and I suggest –' he said, looking her up and down – 'you do the same.'

She was thinking of a sarcastic response when her phone buzzed. She unzipped the pocket of her running trousers and took it out. It was a text and three missed calls. 'Funny,' she said, 'I never heard my phone ring. Did you?'

'Nope,' he said, following her down the hallway.

'I've got three missed calls and a text from Anne Phillips, asking me to call her.'

'Better call her, then.' Lockyer held open the door to the stairwell for her.

She was already dialling the number. She stood at the bottom of the stairs, Lockyer beside her. Anne answered on the third ring. 'Anne, it's Jane,' she said. 'You were trying to get hold of me?' She listened as Anne spoke. 'Where?' she asked.

Lockyer gestured next to her, mouthing, 'What's up?' She held up her hand for him to wait.

'Are you sure?' she asked. She didn't know what to make of what Anne was telling her. 'OK, call Marie and see if she can come in for the briefing. It's in –' Jane looked at her watch – 'ten minutes, but she'll make the end if she leaves now. OK?' She nodded. 'Good. Thanks, Anne.' She hung up the phone, put it back in her pocket and leaned against the wall.

'What was all that about?' Lockyer asked.

Jane pulled out her hairband and ran her hands through her hair. 'Anne's concerned about Olive. I've asked her to get Marie, the social worker from the interviews, to come down to the briefing.'

Lockyer wrinkled his brow. 'Err, yes. I heard that much. Why? What's wrong with Olive? Is it the regression?'

'No,' Jane said, shaking her head. 'Anne thinks Olive may have been abused . . . there are bruises and other injuries.'

'Well, there you have it,' he said.

'Sorry?'

'You didn't like the jealousy motive for Nicola Brown – so how does protecting her kids from an abusive father strike you?'

'It would make more sense,' Jane said. 'However, the fly in that ointment is when Anne asked Olive how she got the bruises, she said her brother did it. She said it was Harvey.'

CHAPTER SIXTEEN

Saturday

I should feel guilty but I don't. It might not have gone according to plan, but that doesn't mean I didn't succeed.

How does someone who does this for a living feel? A contract killer, working for the government. Do they feel guilt? They must be handed a dossier: this is the target, this is their life, this is the time to do it and this is how much you'll be paid. Do they take pride in a job well done, or do they sometimes look at the folder in front of them and think – this man doesn't deserve to die? If they had been handed a dossier on Richard Taylor, would they hesitate or, like me, would they do what was necessary? Or better still, what about a serial killer? One of those ghouls they're always showing on Channel 5: the Barn Butcher. Did the Barn Butcher start out with his morals intact? Did he feel guilt? I guess what I really want to know, what's making me curious, is: did he mean to kill, that very first time?

What comforts me is this: every action has a consequence.

He acted – there was a consequence.

What will my consequence be?

CHAPTER SEVENTEEN

2 August – Saturday

'I'm not making excuses,' Lockyer said, covering the microphone on his mobile and whispering, 'How much?' to the woman behind the stall and pointing at a T-shirt embossed with the words *Grumpy Old Man*. It was Dave's birthday next month.

'Yeah, right,' his daughter said, her tone flat at the other end of the phone.

'Look, honey, I've got a lot on,' he said. Dave was his mate, but fifteen quid for a T-shirt – *no thank you*, he mouthed, shaking his head. The woman's smile vanished.

'It's not 'til next month,' Megan whined. 'It'll be a couple of hours out of your life. I've got to be a bloody bridesmaid. Can't you do it for me, Dad?' Lockyer could hear the emotion in her voice. He scanned the next stall. He loved Lewisham Market. It was one of the few six-day markets still going. You could get everything from a bunch of bananas to a leather jacket. Lockyer took a deep breath in through his nose. There had been a quick shower this morning, soaking the tarpaulins that covered some of the stalls. Now the sun had burnt off the moisture it was heating the canvas, giving off a smell of hot plastic. It reminded him of going to a circus in France when he was a kid: the striped big top, baking in the heat.

'Megs, I can't. I . . .' he began, bracing himself for the impact of his daughter's displeasure.

'I really want you to be there,' she interrupted. 'I've spoken to Mum about it, and her and Brian would love you to come.'

He laughed and wandered through the market, letting the range of colours and smells stimulate his senses. 'Your mother said she would "love me to come"?'

There was a pause before his daughter replied. 'She said she was totally fine with you coming. I've got a plus one.'

'Can't you take a friend . . . a boy, perhaps?' he said. The delay in her retort made him pause. 'Oh, so there's a *boy*,' he said, stretching out the word. 'Who is he?'

'There's no . . . I don't want to . . . I don't know what you're on about,' she said.

Lockyer would never consider himself to be a 'reader of people', other than suspects, of course, but even he could tell his daughter was lying. 'OK, OK,' he said, turning on his heel and heading back towards the station. 'You don't have to tell me who he is . . . I'll find out eventually.' His comment was met with silence.

'Look, I just don't want to be like some Billy-No-Mates in a hideous dress, that's all,' she said finally.

He walked through the gates and raised his hand to a group of officers sunning themselves in the car park. There was no denying the glamorous life of a copper. He smiled. 'You're being silly, honey. Grandma and Grandpa will be coming down from Scotland, no doubt . . .' He shuddered at the thought of Clara's parents. To say they disliked him was an understatement. 'And Aunty Jill will be there . . . Uncle Kevan, your cousins . . . not to mention Brian's family.' Again, silence greeted him. He could picture Megan now – arms folded, head down, eyes on the floor. She might be nineteen and a 'woman now', as she so often told him, but she still sulked like a kid. From the age of two, her reaction to being told off or refused something had been the same. He could see her now, standing at the top of the stairs in her pink bunny pyjamas, refusing to go to bed, her chubby arms folded, her face puce with anger.

'They all come in twos,' she said. 'I'll be the only person on my own. I'll look like some kind of freak of nature.'

Lockyer blew out a breath, looked to the heavens and shook his head. 'So take the mystery fella,' he said, smiling at Dixie, who was behind the reception desk. He pressed the button for the lift. 'Surely it's better to go with a date than your dad?'

'It's not like that,' she said. 'I'm not ready for that . . . I mean, I don't have anyone else I can ask . . . that I want to ask.'

The doors of the lift opened and Lockyer stepped in, holding his phone closer to the doors as he was bound to lose signal – if he was lucky. The doors closed. He looked at his phone. He still had two bars. Typical, he thought. When you wanted your phone to work, it didn't. When you could do with a five-minute reprieve, it decided to defy the laws of phone-signal crapness and work like a dream. He took a deep breath and blew it out, his lips vibrating. He couldn't believe what he was about to say. 'Is there a reception?'

There was a squeal from the other end of the line. 'Yes . . . but you don't have to stay for all of that,' she said. 'You can just stay for the meal if you like and then go. It's a free bar. It's all in one venue so you don't even have to drive anywhere . . . well, other than driving home. Or you can stay in the hotel – I can book you a room so you can drink, but you can go and hide as soon as you want to.'

He stepped out of the lift, cursing his mobile's connectivity, and walked towards Roger's office. 'Fine, I'll come,' he said, accepting defeat with as much grace as he could muster. He should be used to it by now, given that he couldn't remember the last time he had actually *won* an argument when it involved his daughter.

'Perfect,' she said. 'I'll bring the invite over tomorrow. You still having the day off? Are we still going to see Uncle Bobby?'

'Yes and yes,' he said.

'Cool, I'll see you tomorrow. Thanks, Dad.'

'See you tomorrow.'

'OK, bye. It'll be a good day, I promise. Brian's loaded.'

Lockyer ended the call and looked down at his phone. 'Lucky old Brian,' he said under his breath.

'Don't suppose you're moving offices, are you?' Lockyer asked, as he pulled out a chair and sat down. Roger's office was one of the nicest on the floor. It overlooked a tree-lined street and St Stephen's Church. Lockyer wasn't one to get hung up on a view, but he would bet Roger wasn't greeted by the smell of chip fat and curry when he came into his office in the morning.

'Why? You think you're next in line for this one?' Roger asked, raising his eyebrows.

'Well . . . '

'You've got an office,' Roger said, holding up one finger. 'You've got an office with a window.' He held up a second finger. 'I'd say you're pretty lucky to have that. Besides, I'm not going anywhere.' He turned, picked up what looked like an oil can and started spraying a bonsai with a fine mist of water. 'My daughter gave it to me,' he said. 'I'm trying not to kill it.'

Lockyer noticed a large number of brown leaves. 'I'm not sure you're winning,' he said. 'How long have you had it?'

'A week,' Roger said.

Lockyer laughed. 'I'd give up.'

'Sod it,' Roger said, dropping the can on a filing cabinet with a bang and coming back to his desk. 'So –' he sat down – 'what do you have for me? How is DS Bennett getting along?'

Lockyer took out his notepad. He had taken notes throughout the briefing without really thinking. It was as if Jane had possessed him somehow and was forcing him to be super-efficient. It was annoying. He left it closed. If he couldn't remember details from twenty minutes ago then he didn't deserve to be a detective, let alone SIO. 'Interviews with victim's work colleagues, the ex-wife, victim's best mate, ex-wife's siblings and about half a dozen others have been scheduled for tomorrow and Monday. Some here, some at their home addresses or offices. TSGs are continuing their house-to-house. There are numerous sightings of Taylor from the day before the murder – jogging in the morning,

Sainsbury's a bit later and then on Gipsy Hill with the kids just before lunchtime. Neighbours confirm he was in the back garden for the majority of Wednesday afternoon, barbecuing with his kids. No sightings after that – which fits with the kids' version of events, that they stayed in and watched a movie.'

'What movie?' Roger asked.

Lockyer frowned and thought back to Olive's interview. He couldn't recall her mentioning the film, other than to say they watched one. Then he remembered the transcript from Harvey's interview. '*The Hobbit*,' he said. Roger shrugged. 'Anyway, no one saw or heard anything unusual during the night except one resident.' He had written down her name, but couldn't recall it now. Roger waved a hand for him to continue. 'She said she went to pick up her sister from the station at gone midnight, and the lights in Taylor's flat were out.'

'Right, so we're assuming he had a normal day, nothing untoward, and he and the children were tucked up by midnight?'

'That's right,' Lockyer said. 'The same resident thought she heard a shout in the middle of the night, which would correlate to the interviews with the kids. But she couldn't say what time it was, or what the shout sounded like.'

'Helpful,' Roger said.

Lockyer found himself nodding, although he wasn't sure whether Roger was being sarcastic or not. 'That's everything from the house-to-house, so far,' he said. 'There's no evidence to suggest that Taylor was in debt, or had a problem with drugs or alcohol, or was in any trouble with local gangs. No record of him on our database. He was single, as far as we're aware. No one ever saw him with a woman other than his ex-wife, either out and about or at his home address.'

'Right,' Roger said. 'What else?'

'The tech guys are working on his computer and iPad at the moment. He's a member of two dating sites, password-protected. They're in the process of getting access so they can see what women, if any, he's been talking to and whether he's met anyone in person.'

'Is Jane considering jealousy as a motive?' Roger asked. 'Either the ex-wife or a spurned lover, perhaps?'

'Possibly,' Lockyer said, 'but I'll come to that.'

'Fine. Keep going.'

Lockyer brushed his nose with his hand to give himself a second or two to remember what was next. His mind had gone blank. He looked at the notepad, sighed and opened it, reading over his notes. 'Oh, yes,' he said, kicking himself for forgetting the most significant part of the whole briefing. 'Anne Phillips, the FLO assigned to the family thinks the young girl, Olive, may have been abused by her brother.'

'The brother?' Roger asked, sitting forward. 'He's only thirteen, isn't he?'

'Fourteen,' Lockyer said. 'He's a big lad and he isn't averse to throwing his weight around.'

Roger smiled. 'Ah, yes. I did hear about that. Got the jump on you and Dave?'

'Not exactly,' he said.

'What does Jane think?' Roger asked, tipping back in his chair, turning his head and staring, it seemed, at his dying bonsai.

'Jane doesn't think the boy is capable of hurting the sister,' he said.

'And you think differently?'

'Yes,' he said. 'When I heard about the possible abuse I thought – and still think – the most likely scenario is that Taylor was hitting Olive, the ex-wife found out about it and killed him. The fact that he might have started dating could be an added incentive, in my opinion. Maybe the boy – Harvey – saw his dad knocking Olive about and thought he'd follow in his footsteps, but I still think the abuse would have started with Taylor.'

'What's the next step?' Roger asked, making a note on the pad in front of him.

'Jane's interviewing the ex-wife in the morning – the social worker and FLO are then going to bring Harvey down to Caterham Road for a follow-up video interview tomorrow afternoon.'

'Who's Jane using for the interview?' Roger asked, getting up, walking over to the bonsai and resuming misting it with the can.

'She's doing it herself,' Lockyer said, glad Roger wasn't looking at him.

'Really?'

'She sat in on the last one, so it makes sense for her to be there, to keep things consistent for Harvey. A CPO will be there.'

'OK. Good, that's good. Anything else?' Roger asked. Lockyer could tell his interest had waned and that he was, at this moment, far more focused on his tiny tree.

'No,' Lockyer said. 'I think that's it.' He stood up, keen to leave. 'Oh, Jane did say she wanted to keep the press out for now.'

'Good thinking on her part,' Roger said. 'No point agitating the locals if it turns out to be the ex-wife, as per your scenario.'

'For sure.' Lockyer edged towards the door.

'Great. And Jane?' Roger asked, turning to face him. 'She coping with this one?'

'Absolutely, sir,' Lockyer said without hesitation. 'She's doing an excellent job.'

Roger nodded. 'Good. She's made of strong stuff, that one. We're lucky to have her.'

'Yes, sir,' he said, his hand already on the door. 'Same time Monday?' Roger nodded but didn't speak, so Lockyer took the opportunity to make his exit.

CHAPTER EIGHTEEN

Richard – June

Richard sat staring into his coffee. His heart was thudding in his chest. He wasn't sure how to feel or how to process what had just happened. The conversation had been so easy, as if they had been made to talk to each other. He had laughed, without embarrassment. He had blushed, which, instead of making him feel pathetic, had made him feel amazing. The electricity that had sparked between them still seemed to be hovering over the table, charging the air around Richard's head.

He blinked several times, and stared out of the window at the evening traffic. Was this what people meant when they talked about the thunderbolt? He smiled, but then it hit him. Guilt. It extinguished the charge around him, and brought him crashing back into the reality of his surroundings. He was in a mediocre restaurant in Crystal Palace. There was nothing pure and ethereal about this moment. He was behaving like a stupid kid. His date couldn't have been any more sweet, sincere, beautiful or wholesome. Why the hell would anyone like that want him, after what he had done in the past couple of weeks? He wouldn't, that's for sure. If Olive ever came home with someone like him – someone who had been led around by his dick – Richard would tear him a new one and throw him out on the street. His daughter was worth better than that: better than a guy like him.

Richard drained his coffee and put a couple of twenties on the table. He nodded to the waitress and held up his hand as he went to leave. His phone beeped in his pocket. He took it out and read the message.

Fancy a fuck?

Richard deleted the message and walked out into the street. The sound of car horns and a group of lads shouting drowned out his thoughts. His phone beeped again. He stopped and opened the message.

No one has ever turned me on like you do – I want you to fuck me till I can't walk straight!!

The emoticon that came with the message had a tongue that was poking in and out of the round yellow face. He cringed, his finger hovering over the delete button. Should he reply? The last few hours flashed through his mind in a montage. He deleted the message, then went to his contacts and deleted the contact. He was done trying to be the kind of guy who could 'fuck' without feelings. His heart sank as his phone beeped again. He almost looked away as he opened the message, but then he started to read it and his heart started to thud harder in his chest again.

Hey, thanks for dinner. I had a great time, I really did . . . but I don't think I can see you again. I kinda got the feeling that maybe you're already seeing someone and I'm sorry but that's just not me. Maybe that sounds pathetic and maybe that's why I'm still single but I don't want to be mucked around. Sorry x

Richard stepped aside as a group of girls wearing pink Stetsons staggered past him. They were singing, although he couldn't decipher the tune. One of the women grabbed his arm.

'Hey,' she said. 'Hey, girls.' She dragged back two of her Stetson friends. 'Julie's gotta get a kiss from a stranger. I've found one!'

Richard tried to disengage, but found himself surrounded by pawing hands and alcohol-soaked breath. 'Thanks, but I don't think so,' he said, trying to back away.

'What's your problem?' one of the women shouted as she stumbled against the window to the restaurant. Richard could feel people turning to look at the spectacle that he had somehow ended up in the centre of. 'No one's asking you to tongue her . . . just give her a kiss, you big fag!' The girl in question, Julie, was shoved into his path. Her dress was too short. She was wearing too much make-up, and her eyes were bloodshot and not focusing on him or anything else. He reached out and took her arm to stop her from falling.

'Oooooh . . . here he goes,' another woman said.

He bent closer and gave Julie a kiss on the cheek. As he pulled away, he whispered, 'Might be time to head home.'

A roar of laughter greeted his comment. 'He's trying to take her home . . . dirty bastard . . . she's not that kinda girl.' With

that, the group dragged the almost-unconscious hen away, throwing insults back at Richard as they went.

He looked down at his phone, his decision made. He tapped out a message.

I was seeing someone. I'm not any more. I don't want to muck you around. I'm a good guy. I'll prove it to you, if you let me take you out again?

The reply came back straight away.

I was hoping you'd say that!! ☺ Call me xx

Richard pocketed his phone and started the short walk back to his flat. With each step, it was as if a weight was being lifted. This was who he was. This was the kind of man he wanted to be. He had taken a brief detour from the right path, but maybe he was about to be given the opportunity to redeem himself.

CHAPTER NINETEEN

3 August – Sunday

Jane was waiting for the lift with Penny, Sasha and Aaron. She had to resist the urge to press the call button again; she had pressed it twice already. 'You'd think this was a ten-storey building, the amount of time this lift takes to arrive,' she said, looking at her watch.

The interviews weren't for another ten minutes. There was plenty of time to get down there, but she still felt agitated. She couldn't stop thinking about what Anne Phillips had said at the end of the briefing yesterday. The look on Lockyer's face told Jane he agreed with the FLO. 'It'd be quicker to walk at this rate,' she said, pressing the button again.

'Let's take the stairs, then,' Penny said. 'I could do with the exercise.'

'You've got to be kidding,' Aaron said, pinching the back of Penny's arm. 'You're as fit as a whippet.'

'Fit as a butcher's dog,' Sasha said.

'What?'

'That's the expression,' she said. 'Fit as a butcher's dog.'

'Whatever.' Aaron waved Sasha's correction away. 'You

121

need to eat something,' he said, turning back to Penny. 'Something with the fat still in it.'

'You offering to buy me dinner?' Penny asked.

'Oh, he can't do that,' Sasha said. 'His *girlfriend* wouldn't like it.'

'Of course,' Penny said. 'Who else knows about your *new* girlfriend, Aaron?' she asked, widening her eyes. 'Jane, had you heard about Aaron's hot new bit of stuff?'

Jane shook her head.

'I – I . . .' Aaron stammered. He was blushing.

'Don't let the mean girls wind you up.' Jane sighed, unable to fully engage in the banter. No one spoke for a moment.

'You all right, ma'am?' Penny asked.

Jane turned to see all three of them looking at her with concerned expressions. 'I'm fine,' she said, folding and unfolding her arms.

'A lot of balls in the air,' Penny said.

'Something like that.' She still hadn't deleted the message from Andy. If she wasn't going to reply, then what was the point of keeping it? She had been asking herself the same question since she first read it on Friday night.

'Is the alleged abuse still bothering you?' Penny asked.

Jane looked at her and shrugged. 'I'm not happy with Anne's assessment, no,' she said, 'but I guess time will tell.' She fell silent again, relieved when Penny didn't push any further.

Jane had spoken to Harvey on a number of occasions now, comforted him even. There was nothing about his behaviour to indicate he was capable of hurting his sister. Of course he was angry, as he had demonstrated more than once; but who could blame him? He was a child. He had found his father dead. He had been thrown head first into a police investigation, a murder investigation. The anger he had displayed so far was, in Jane's opinion, a natural reaction under the circumstances. From what she could gather, he was very protective of his sister. Olive was the baby of the family. There might be some resentment as the older sibling. She had considered that, but to cause physical harm? It didn't feel right. He was as vulnerable as his sister, if not more so. He was the eldest. He was the one who looked out for his sister and mother. Now, without his father, that responsibility would weigh even heavier.

'After you,' Aaron stood back to let her and the others out once they arrived at the ground floor.

Jane lengthened her stride to get out in front, and walked alone down the corridor towards the interview suite. 'Brown and Oxenham?' she said to the sergeant on the desk.

'All settled in and ready to go,' he said, handing her two folders.

'Thanks.' She opened the first. It was Adam Oxenham's sign-in sheet. She passed the folder to Penny. 'OK,' she said, turning. 'Sasha, you're with me; Aaron, you're with Penny.' Each of them nodded. 'Pen, you'll probably be done before us, so we'll debrief in the office before lunch. OK?'

'Yes, boss,' Aaron and Sasha said in unison. Penny nodded as she and Aaron headed off to the second interview room.

'Let's go,' Jane said to Sasha, walking further down the corridor to the fifth room. The young DC had been on the team for a while, but other than briefings, Jane hadn't had much one-on-one time with her. 'As I said before, if you have a question, write it down and I'll add it to my list.'

'Yes, ma'am,' Sasha said, straightening her skirt once and then again.

'You OK?' Jane asked.

'Yes, ma'am; just . . . '

'Nervous?'

'I've done a ton of interviews,' Sasha said, running her fingers through her hair which, now that Jane looked, was a lot blonder than usual, 'but this is my first with a suspect.'

'Person of interest,' Jane corrected.

'Sorry, person of interest.'

'You'll do fine,' Jane said. 'I'll be leading the interview, so just listen, take notes and keep in mind the points that we talked about. You might pick up on something that I miss. Eyes and ears open, and don't be afraid to stop me if you have something to add or ask. OK?' Sasha nodded and smiled. Jane knew how she felt. She had felt it herself a long time ago. It was a combination of fear and excitement. Fear that the interviewee would fool you, sidestep your questions, or worse, say 'no comment' throughout. But the exciting part was the chance, however slim, that you might get a confession – the dream outcome.

Jane put her hand on the door. If either of Lockyer's theories was true, then Nicola Brown had murdered her husband out of revenge or jealousy. Nothing about Jane's dealings with the woman so far gave her the impression that Nicola was the type of woman to break down and confess – not in the first interview, anyway. Jane opened the door.

'Nicola,' she said, ushering Sasha in before following.

'Thanks so much for coming in.' Nicola Brown nodded. Her face appeared calm, her eyes clear. Jane smiled. 'Sorry, would you mind moving to the other chair?' she asked. 'The closer you are to the recorder, the better.' She took her own seat, but kept her eye on Nicola as she moved across to the seat right beside the digital recorder.

'Better?' Nicola asked.

'Perfect,' Jane said, still smiling. 'As your Family Liaison Officer, Anne will have explained that today's interview will be under caution. Your ex-husband's death has been listed as suspicious, so it's important we have everything documented from here on in.'

'I understand,' Nicola said.

'And you're sure you don't want a legal representative with you?'

Nicola was shaking her head. 'No, it's fine,' she said. 'I understand how this works.'

'Right,' Jane said. 'As long as you're sure.'

'I'm sure.'

'Great. Well, let's get started, then,' Jane said, pressing and holding the record button until the red light appeared. 'Interview with Ms Nicola Brown at –' she looked up at the clock on the wall – '10.14 a.m. on Sunday the 3rd of August, in connection with the death of a Mr Richard Taylor on Thursday 31st July. Present are myself, DS Jane Bennett, senior officer; DC Sasha Thomas; and Ms Nicola Brown. Ms Brown has been offered and declined legal representation.' She looked up at Nicola. 'Ms Brown, this will be an interview under caution. As such, you do not have to say anything. But it may harm your defence if you do not mention when questioned something which you later rely on in court. Anything you do say may be given in evidence. Are you happy to proceed?'

Nicola leaned towards the recorder and said, 'Yes.'

'Good.' Jane sat back and opened her pad on the table in front of her. 'Nicola, would you mind telling me your whereabouts between 8 p.m. on Wednesday 30th July and 7 a.m. on Thursday 31st July of this year?'

'I spent the evening at home,' Nicola said, enunciating each word. 'Twenty-eight Clevedon Road, Penge.'

'Can you remember what you were doing?' Jane asked.

Nicola was shaking her head. 'Nothing in particular,' she said. 'I did a couple of loads of washing; I'm using a different detergent that's meant to keep the clothes fresh for seven days. I don't think it works, but I live in hope. Anyway, after that I had dinner, a stir-fry with prawns; fresh, not frozen, I went to Waitrose that morning. After that I did some ironing in front of the television, the children's bed sheets. I'm working my way through the first series of *The Fall*. I spoke to the children before they went to bed. A friend popped over, Chantelle Bullion. Her daughter Kirsty is friends with Olive. She stayed for a drink or two, we chatted and then she left around half-eleven, twelve maybe. Then I had a shower and went to bed. I think that's everything.'

'You've got a good memory,' Jane said, noting down the mention of Chantelle Bullion's name. She was the woman who had approached her outside Taylor's flat the morning his body was found. Jane had asked Franks to follow up with a phone call, but he hadn't reported back with anything yet.

'I'm not stupid, detective,' Nicola said, breaking into Jane's thoughts. 'I knew you would need me to account for my whereabouts as soon as I got the call.'

'Of course,' Jane said. 'So what time, would you say, did you speak to the children?'

'Olive phoned at half-eight just to say good night,' Nicola said without pausing. 'She was going to bed. She wanted to tell me about her day – she's fallen out with one of her friends . . . you know how fraught friendships can be at that age. It's this girl from her class, Freya, I don't know her surname, anyway, she called Olive fat – which is ridiculous – but then they got into a spat about it, and . . . '

Jane found herself half-listening as Nicola relayed, in minute detail, the ins and outs of her daughter's row. The level of recall made Jane uneasy. It was too good – too precise. In her experience, 'truth-tellers' summarized: I was at home, I had dinner, watched TV, went to bed. Whereas someone who was either embellishing or inventing a story did just that: they told a story, going into elaborate detail about matters of little or no significance. 'Did you say you spoke to Harvey as well?' Jane asked when the story about Olive's fight had finally come to an end.

'Only briefly,' Nicola said. 'He was watching a movie with Rich. Once he's watching the TV nothing, short of an earth-quake, can break his focus. It was one of the *Hobbit* movies, I think. Harvey loves the first lot. He watched all three films and *then* read the book. Harvey isn't a big reader, so I was thrilled.'

'Do you remember what you and Harvey talked about?' Jane asked.

Nicola looked at the recorder, then down at her hands. 'Not really, no,' she said, shaking her head.

'Did you speak to your ex-husband?'

'No. He shouted out in the background . . . said he'd drop the kids home after five the next day.'

'Had that been previously agreed?' Jane asked.

'Yes. The only difference is I was going to pick them up, but Rich said he would drop them back.'

'Any reason for the change in plan, that you know of?'

Nicola shook her head. 'No clue,' she said. 'I didn't even think about it.'

'Is it unusual for your husband to change plans regarding the children?'

'Ex-husband,' Nicola corrected. 'Rich's never been very good at times, dates, that kind of thing. I'm a planner. He's not.'

Jane nodded, and looked down at her list of questions. 'How long have you and Richard been separated?' she asked, ringing the word 'alibi' in her notes and adding some question marks, careful not to let Nicola see.

Nicola sat back and crossed her legs. 'We divorced three years ago, but we separated over five years ago.'

'Can you tell me the reason the marriage ended?' she asked, watching for Nicola's reaction to the question.

'Yes,' she said, as if Jane had asked whether she wanted milk in her coffee. 'Rich had an affair with someone from his work. I found out about it, asked him to move out. He suggested we stay together for the kids. I refused, but agreed he could stay in the marital home until he found somewhere else suitable to live. But we weren't "man and wife" –' she used her fingers to create inverted commas – 'after that.'

'Did you sleep in separate bedrooms?'

'Yes.'

'That must have been difficult, especially with young children. How old would Harvey and Olive have been then?'

'They were six and eight when we separated but Olive was almost nine, and Harvey eleven before Rich actually moved out. They never knew. They were in bed before us, and Rich was up before them. It wasn't an issue,' she said. 'I made sure it wasn't an issue.'

Jane was struck by how detached Nicola Brown seemed. Her ex-husband had been found dead only four days ago, most likely murdered, and yet she didn't seem fazed at all by his death, by the interview, by anything. Was it shock? She had shown some emotion a few days ago that appeared genuine – but the phrase 'she's a cold fish' kept circling Jane's thoughts. 'It must have been difficult for you,' she said.

Nicola shrugged. 'At first, perhaps. To be honest, the marriage had been going downhill for a while. We had grown apart. We were different people. When I met Rich he was dynamic, ambitious and exciting. As he got older, he just seemed to get slower . . . weaker. The kids were my priority then . . . as they are now. Maintaining their routine was my main concern.'

'That's impressive,' Jane said, thinking it was anything but. She couldn't imagine deceiving Peter like that, whether he was aware of it or not. Andy's email flashed into her mind. She needed to reply, to see him and hear him out. A lump pushed its way up her throat, but she managed to catch it in time and force it back down. Now was not the time. 'Did you ever discuss reconciling?' she asked.

'All the time,' Nicola said, rolling her eyes. 'Rich was desperate to make things work, to get things back on track, but I just couldn't do it,' she said. Jane chanced a sideways glance at Sasha. Was it just her, or did Nicola Brown have tears in her eyes? 'The thought of him with someone else was just too painful. I couldn't get past it. Once the trust is gone, it's gone, you know?'

Jane was staring, still trying to figure out if the woman was about to cry, when she realized Nicola was expecting a reply from her. 'Of course,' she stuttered. 'Trust can be a difficult thing to rebuild.' Again she thought about Andy.

'I loved Rich,' Nicola said, dabbing at her eyes with her fingertips. There were no tears, and the sheen that had been there seconds before had disappeared. 'He was a good man, a wonderful father, but I just couldn't see him the same way after that. I wished nothing but good things for him. I can't imagine why anyone would want to hurt him,' she said, bowing her head. Jane looked at Sasha and raised an eyebrow. The woman should get an Oscar for that performance.

'How are the children coping with their father's death?' she asked.

Nicola shrugged. She looked bored. 'As you'd expect, I guess.'

'What do you mean by that?' Jane asked, sitting back.

'Harvey's up and down, but he's doing OK. He'll be fine. It's Olive I'm concerned about,' she said. 'She's very sensitive. She always has been. She *had* been doing OK, until Friday.'

Jane knew what was coming; Nicola's voice was rising. 'She was practically catatonic once *you* lot had spoken to her.'

'The death of a parent is very traumatic for a child, especially at Olive's age,' Jane said.

'Don't you think I know that?' Nicola was shouting now. 'She's my daughter. Her father is dead. You're telling me her father has been killed. Someone has come into that house while my children were sleeping, and killed him. What if my children had been hurt?'

'I think we should take a break,' Jane said. Nicola was panting, her hands shaking. 'Nicola, would you like to get some air?'

'No,' she said, not looking up.

'A drink?' Jane asked. 'Coffee?'

There was a pause. 'OK,' Nicola said, still looking down at her hands.

Jane leaned forward. 'Interview suspended at 10.40.' She stopped the recorder and stood up. 'Sasha, can you get Nicola a coffee? I'll be back in a sec.' She left the room, closing the door behind her.

'Jane.'

She turned at the sound of Lockyer's voice. 'Hey,' she said. 'I thought you had the day off?'

'I did . . . I do. I just swung by to grab some paperwork and took a call from comms.'

'What have they found?' she asked, lowering her voice and moving away from the door to the interview room.

'They've managed to access Taylor's messages on one of the sites, although it's more of a forum,' he said.

'And?'

'He was talking to a woman called Dee for about three months, April to June. It's not clear whether they've met up or not, despite her asking several times, but according to comms some of the messages are a bit steamy,' he said.

Jane couldn't help laughing, the tension from the interview leaving her shoulders as she did so. 'Steamy' – it was a word her father would use. Hearing Lockyer say it was somehow funny. 'Are you blushing?' she asked.

Lockyer screwed up his face. 'Err, no. I'm not a teenager, you know,' he said, crossing his arms and puffing out his chest.

'What did the messages say, then?'

'I don't know. I haven't seen the transcript, but I just thought you might want to know that he was definitely active on the dating scene; which, given what we know so far, might be significant while you're interviewing the ex.'

'Mmm; maybe. I'm not sure she's the jealous type. I'm not sure she really cares he's dead.'

'Well, she wouldn't if she killed him, would she?' Lockyer said.

'True,' Jane said with a tired smile. 'She's got an alibi . . . of sorts.'

Lockyer's lips turned down at the edges. 'Lying?'

Jane shrugged. 'I'm not sure, but either way, it doesn't cover her for the whole night. Just up until midnight.'

Lockyer nodded. 'Still time, then,' he said.

'Yep.' Jane's shoulders were aching, as if she had been lifting weights. 'Anyway,' she said, trying to shake off her lethargy, 'what's the gist of these messages?'

He cleared his throat. 'Comms said there's a lot of general

conversation about work, home life; and then there was some
– well, a lot of references to hand jobs, blow jobs, that kind
of thing.'

'OK.' Jane tried not to let his discomfort amuse her too
much. 'So he's been talking to a woman about jobs of all
varieties,' she said, smiling.

'Ha ha, very funny. Yes.'

'Last contact?'

'Dee's last email is 20th June, several unanswered before
that,' he said. 'Taylor's last reply was 4th June.'

'Interesting,' Jane said. 'I wonder why he stopped replying.'

'Why don't you ask the wife?' Lockyer suggested.

'I'm just giving her five minutes to compose herself.'

'Things getting a bit heated?'

'You could say that. I'm going to run back up to the office
and give my mother a quick call. Could you do me a favour?'

'Possibly.'

'Would you mind looking in on Penny, and seeing how
she's getting on with her interview?' She pressed her hands
together in a mock plea. 'She's in two.' He looked at his watch.
'Please?'

'Oh, all right,' he said.

'Thanks,' she said, already backing away down the
corridor. 'I'll see you in the morning at the briefing?'

'You will,' he confirmed.

She turned and jogged towards the lift. She would give
Nicola Brown ten minutes to drink her coffee and calm down.
She need her focused and clear for the next part of the interview. She didn't believe for a second that Harvey had hurt
his sister, which left her with two possibilities. Either Richard

Taylor had hurt their daughter, and Nicola had found out about it and killed him; or Nicola wasn't quite as happy for her husband to 'move on' with his life as she claimed. One or both could be deemed a possible motive for murder. Jane just had to figure out which.

CHAPTER TWENTY

3 August – Sunday

Lockyer knocked on the door to interview room two, and waited. When there was no answer he knocked again. Aaron, one of Lockyer's PCs who had been transferred over to Jane's team, opened the door a crack, saw it was Lockyer and opened it wider. 'Sorry, sir,' he said. 'I couldn't pause the tape.'

'No problem,' Lockyer said. 'I just wanted to have a quick word with DC Groves.'

He heard Penny give her apologies, and then she appeared at the door next to Aaron. She turned back into the room. 'Adam, PC Jones will get you a drink. I'll be back shortly.' Lockyer heard a muffled 'OK' before Penny left the room, shutting the door behind them.

'Do you want anything?' Aaron asked.

'No, thanks, I'm good,' Penny said. 'You'll have to go up to the first floor. The vending machine down here is out of order.'

'Has it ever been *in* order?' Aaron said with an awkward laugh. 'Sir,' he added, nodding at Lockyer. Was he blushing?

'What can I do for you, sir? Penny asked.

Lockyer turned back to Penny. 'Jane asked me to see how you were doing.'

'Has DS Bennett finished her interview?' Penny asked, frowning.

'No. She's had to run back up to the office. I was just leaving but she wanted to check how you were getting on with . . . '

'Oxenham,' Penny offered.

'That's right. He's a friend of the deceased?'

'Yes. He was best man at Taylor's wedding. They've known each other since primary school.'

Lockyer nodded. 'He must know him pretty well, then.'

'Well, you'd think so. He's not been very forthcoming. He could just be nervous . . . being interviewed, et cetera, but I feel like he's holding back.'

'What have you covered so far?' Lockyer asked, his interest piqued. 'One sec,' he added, taking his mobile out of his jacket pocket. He should be in the car now, driving home. He should be getting ready to see his daughter and his brother, but one hint of intrigue and he was taken in – hook, line and sinker. It was a trait that made him a good cop. The downside was that it also made him a crap father. He tapped out a message to Megan –

Running late. I'll call when I'm leaving the office x

– and debated adding a smiley face, but that would just scream guilt, so he settled for another kiss. 'Hit me with it,' he said. His pulse had kicked up a notch.

'I've asked how he knew Taylor, how long they'd known

each other for. How often they saw each other, what they did together. Does he have contact with the kids, the ex-wife; does he think Taylor was a good father – any problems? That kind of thing,' Penny said, shrugging.

'And?'

'His answers have been monosyllabic. I feel like I'm pulling teeth,' she said. He could see how frustrated she was. Penny took after Jane: she was a perfectionist. Jane would have asked her to get as much background information as possible, and with that, gain insight into the family. Penny appeared to be taking Oxenham's reluctance to talk as a personal failure.

'As you say,' he said, 'he might just be nervous about being called into the station. His best mate has been killed. There's a million and one reasons why people adopt the yes-and-no repertoire.' That was true, but Lockyer was already wondering if he would have better luck. There was a reply from Megan. He clicked into it.

Who's surprised?

No kiss. That was bad. 'Tell you what,' he said. 'I've got a few minutes. Why don't I come and sit in? See if a change of personnel helps loosen the guy up.' Penny stood aside and gestured for him to go ahead, just as Aaron arrived with two cups of coffee. 'Thank you,' Lockyer said, taking the drinks. 'I'm going to sit in with DC Groves for a few minutes. You can head back up to the office.' If Aaron was disappointed at being kicked out of the interview, he didn't show it, which impressed Lockyer.

Penny opened the door, letting Lockyer enter the room before her. 'Adam,' she said, 'this is DI Lockyer. He's the Senior Investigating Officer on this case. He's going to sit in with us for the rest of the interview, if that's all right with you?'

'Sure,' Adam said.

Adam Oxenham was a big guy. He was built like a rugby player, or a boxer maybe: thick-set, his arms and chest rippling with muscles under a super-tight T-shirt. Lockyer set down the drinks and held out his hand. Adam seemed to shrink before his eyes. 'How's it going, Adam? Those must take some upkeep,' Lockyer said pointing to the guy's arms. They were huge. 'How often are you in the gym?'

'Every day.' Adam shifted in his seat.

'Not surprised,' Lockyer said, taking a seat next to Penny. 'At least you get your money's worth. I've been a member of my local gym for years. I hardly ever go. I can't stand being cooped up inside, you know?'

'Yes.'

'But I guess you need the weights,' Lockyer said. 'Me . . . I just run.' Adam nodded. Penny was right about one thing: the guy was uncomfortable. 'DC Groves,' he said, gesturing towards the recorder, 'please go ahead.'

Penny pressed and held the record button until the red light showed. 'Interview with Adam Oxenham, Sunday the 3rd of August, 11.10 a.m. Present are myself, DC Penelope Groves, and DI Mike Lockyer, Senior Investigating Officer. Adam, are you happy to continue?'

He nodded.

'Could you answer, please?' Penny asked. 'For the sake of the tape.'

'Sorry,' Adam said. 'Yes.'

'Great.' Penny took out her notepad. 'So, Adam, we were talking about Richard and Nicola. You were best man at their wedding, I believe?'

'That's right.' Adam was looking at Penny, but his eyes kept darting back to Lockyer. He was used to making suspects uncomfortable, but he hadn't even said anything yet.

'Did you know Ms Brown before?'

'Before what?'

'Before she and Richard got married,' Penny said.

'As Rich's girlfriend, yes,' he said.

'Were you friends?'

'No.'

Lockyer felt Penny throw him a look. No wonder she was frustrated, if the entire interview had been like this. 'Doesn't sound like there's a lot of love lost between the two of you,' he said.

'No,' Adam said.

'Could you expand on that, do you think?' Lockyer asked, moving his head until Oxenham was forced to look at him. 'Did something happen to sour the relationship?'

'With Nicola?'

'Yes, with Nicola,' Lockyer said. He waited. Adam was fidgeting in his seat, his face flushed.

It was obvious he wanted to talk. Whatever he had been holding back for the past hour was exhausting the poor guy. 'We're here for Richard,' Lockyer said. 'The whole team is working to find out what happened – to find out why someone would want to harm Richard. It's important . . . No. It's *imperative* that if you know something, anything that you think could help, you tell us, Adam, you need to tell us now.'

Adam was shaking his head. 'I can just imagine the crap she's been telling you . . . the injured party – the poor-little-wife routine,' he said, looking up at Lockyer. His eyes were red-rimmed. It was clear he was trying not to cry. 'She should have been an actress.' He was spitting the words out. 'I would never want to break Rich's trust – never – but I can't just sit here, knowing the lies she's telling you about him.'

Lockyer sat back in his chair, Penny following his lead. 'Go on,' was all he said. Adam's expression made it obvious he didn't need any further encouragement. The floodgates were open.

'Sorry, Nicola.' Jane took her seat opposite Richard Taylor's ex-wife. 'That took longer than expected. You got your drink, then?' She gestured to a half-drunk coffee.

'Yes.'

'It's not very good, I know,' Jane said, grimacing. 'I always think it tastes like soil. It's way too earthy, you know?' Nicola didn't answer, but grunted her agreement. 'So, are you happy to continue?'

'How much longer is this going to take?' Nicola asked, looking at Sasha rather than Jane.

'Not long.' Jane turned to Sasha. 'Anything you need to add at this stage, DC Thomas?'

'No, ma'am,' Sasha said.

Jane nodded, sat forward and pressed record. She stated who was present in the room, the time and the date before sitting back. 'So, Nicola. We were talking about the children and how they were coping,' she began. 'You said before that neither Harvey nor Olive was aware that you and your husband had separated.'

'Ex,' Nicola said.

'Sorry, ex-husband.'

'That's right.' Nicola folded her arms.

'Did your ex-husband have a good relationship with the children after the separation?'

'Of course he did,' Nicola said, screwing up her face as if Jane's question was the height of idiocy.

'I only ask because children can act up after a break-up . . . play their parents off against each other, push boundaries, break the rules, that kind of thing,' she said.

'Harvey had some trouble, especially after his ADHD diagnosis . . . that, and his dyslexia,' Nicola said, as if things could not possibly get any worse. 'But it was nothing really. He was back to normal within a couple of weeks.'

'What kind of trouble?' Jane asked.

'Fighting.'

'Who was he fighting with?'

'It was nothing, as I said.' Nicola glared at Jane. 'A couple of older boys were picking on Olive. Harvey stuck up for her, told them to stop. They didn't, so he ended up getting into a fight.'

'Has he always been protective of his sister?' Jane asked.

'Yes, very. Ever since she was a baby. Olive had whooping cough when she was only three months old. She would cough until she went blue.' Her face paled at the memory. 'Harvey was only two at the time, but he never left her side. Rich and I took it in shifts to sleep in with Olive, so we were on hand in the night if she had an episode.' She put her hand over her mouth. 'I would put Harvey to bed, but he wouldn't stay there. I would wake up and there he'd be, curled up asleep on the floor next to his sister's cot.' A tear rolled down Nicola's cheek. Jane handed her a tissue, taking the opportunity to gauge Sasha's reaction at the same time. It felt like they had been talking to a different woman before. 'They're so precious,' Nicola added in a whisper.

'That must have been terrifying,' Jane said, and she meant it. As soon as Peter was born she had found herself in a constant state of paranoia. Every hiccup, every time his cry had a different cadence, she worried that something was wrong. If he had turned blue she would have had a coronary on the spot.

'It was what it was.' Nicola scratched her cheek with the tip of her nail. 'Next question?'

Jane cleared her throat and looked down at her notepad to disguise her surprise at Nicola's rapid change in attitude. 'Did Harvey and Richard ever argue?'

'No more than any father and son; less, probably. Rich was a pushover when it came to the kids,' Nicola said, rolling her eyes. 'As I said . . . weak.'

'How about Olive? Did your ex-husband and Olive ever have disagreements? Or Olive and Harvey, perhaps?'

Nicola shook her head. 'God knows what you're trying to get at,' she said. 'If you want to know something, you should just ask. I really don't have time for this.'

'Olive has several bruises on her right arm and there is a burn on her left arm, at the wrist.' Jane indicated the position of the burn on her own wrist. 'Can you tell me how she got the bruises, and when and how the burn happened?'

Nicola shrugged, her face expressionless. 'Do you have children, detective?' she asked, raising an eyebrow. She didn't wait for Jane's answer. 'Mine are permanently covered in cuts and bruises, Harvey especially. How he manages to rip so many pairs of school trousers is beyond me. Don't ask me how they hurt themselves. I'm just the one who cleans them up and forks out for their new clothes.'

'And the burn?' Jane asked.

'God knows,' she said, without even a flicker of interest – no longer the overprotective mother, it seemed.

'Olive said the burn had happened at the barbecue – that Harvey was responsible.'

'You have got to be kidding me,' Nicola said, laughing. 'You may as well tell me Santa Claus was responsible. Let me be clear, detective . . . *it never happened*.'

'Why would your daughter lie?' Jane asked. 'Could she be protecting someone else? Your ex-husband, perhaps?'

Nicola held up a finger. 'First off, my daughter is not a liar, detective,' she said through gritted teeth. 'Second off, my ex-husband may have been a lot of things . . . a negligent father, he was *not*. You . . . or one of your lot, have put words in her mouth, and she's just repeating them back to you. I will speak to her about the burn, but I can assure you, it will have been an accident.'

Before Jane could press any further, there was a knock at the door. 'Excuse me, Nicola,' she said, pushing back her chair. 'Sasha, can you pause the interview for a moment? I'll be right back.'

When she stepped out of the room, Lockyer was standing a few paces away. He was transferring his weight from one foot to the other. To a casual observer it might look like he needed the toilet, but Jane knew him better than that. He was excited. 'What are you still doing here?' she asked, walking towards him.

'You having any luck with Taylor's ex?' he asked, raising an eyebrow.

'She's up and down like a yo-yo, to be honest,' Jane admitted. 'Angry, sullen, aggressive, sad – she's an emotional Olympian. I'm knackered just listening to her.' She closed her eyes and then opened them again.

'Want some help?'

'So that's why you're still here,' she said with a sigh.

'I've been sitting in with Penny on the Oxenham interview. He had a lot to say.'

'Tell me.'

'Has she told you about her affair?'

'No,' Jane said, shaking her head.

'Has she told you about Richard's affair?'

'Yes. She said he slept with someone from his dental practice.'

'Did she happen to mention that the someone was a *guy*?'

CHAPTER TWENTY-ONE

3 August – Sunday

'I need to ask you again, Nicola,' Jane said. 'Are you sure you don't want to have legal representation?'

'I've been here for over two hours,' Nicola said. 'Just get on with it, will you?'

Jane took her seat, and indicated for Lockyer to take the chair next to her. 'This is my colleague, Detective Inspector Lockyer. He is the Senior Investigating Officer in relation to your ex-husband's case. I have asked him to join us, as new information has come to light that I would like to discuss with you. Are you happy to continue?' For the first time since Jane had met her, Nicola Brown looked uncomfortable. 'Nicola?'

'You can bring in the Mayor of London, for all I care,' Nicola said, her arms folded, her face sullen.

'I'll take that as a yes.' Jane began the tape for, she hoped, the final time today, stating who was present and the time. 'Nicola, do you know Adam Oxenham?'

'Yes.'

'Can you tell me about your relationship with Mr Oxenham, please?'

'Relationship?' She screwed up her face. 'That's a joke. We have no *relationship*, but if you mean how do I know him – he was a friend of my ex-husband's.'

'A close friend?'

'Yes.'

'He was best man at your wedding, I understand?' Lockyer said.

'Rich's choice, not mine.'

'So, would it be fair to say the two of you don't get on?' Jane asked.

'That would be fair to say, yes.'

'Can you tell me why that is?' Lockyer asked. Jane watched Nicola look from Lockyer to her, and then back again. Before she'd been able to storm back into the room demanding answers, Lockyer had managed to stop her so they could discuss how to handle the interview. His suggestion that they take alternate questions appeared to be working. Nicola Brown did not look happy.

'He was a bad influence.'

'A bad influence?' Jane repeated. It made Adam Oxenham sound like a teenager. 'How so?'

'I'm sure he won't have told you himself,' Nicola said. 'He's never been very good with words like *reality* and *truth*. He's a drinker. He's always been a drinker. After a night out with Adam, Rich would come home barely in control of his bodily functions . . . in fact, sometimes even that failed him. It was embarrassing.'

'You and your ex-husband were separated over five years ago, divorced for three – correct?' Lockyer said.

'That's right.'

'That's a long time,' Jane said, 'and yet your dislike for Mr Oxenham doesn't appear to have dissipated.'

'That's because he's a liar,' she said. 'He's always filling Harvey's head with rubbish . . . with lies.'

'Such as?' Lockyer asked.

'Look,' Nicola said, sitting forward, locking eyes with Jane. 'I just don't like the guy. I never have, and I don't like him around my kids . . . not that I need to worry about that any more,' she added, smiling.

'What makes you say that?' Jane asked.

Nicola sighed, rolled her eyes and looked at Jane. The dual questioning technique seemed to be aggravating her – exactly what Lockyer had intended, and exactly what Jane wanted. She was tired of listening to this woman lie. 'With Rich gone, my children will have no need to see Mr Oxenham again, ever.'

'Isn't he a legal guardian?' Lockyer asked. It was a piece of information that Jane had received by email seconds before walking back into the interview room; and it wasn't the only piece of news she had received.

'I have an appointment with my solicitor next week,' Nicola said.

'Not wasting any time,' Lockyer observed.

'I have a busy practice to run, and two children to care for, Detective Lockyer,' Nicola said. 'I don't have time to waste. Though it's obvious you lot do.'

Jane gave Lockyer a sideways glance, and sat back in her chair. He followed suit. She let the silence stretch, but kept her eyes on Nicola. She knew Lockyer was doing the same.

It was time. 'Nicola,' she said. 'DI Lockyer spoke to Mr Oxenham earlier this morning—'

'And?' Nicola interrupted.

'He gave us a different version of events, in relation to your separation from your ex-husband,' Lockyer said.

'What a surprise,' she sneered. 'Let me guess: I went crazy after Rich had the affair, trying to get him back, acting like a woman possessed, throwing myself at him . . . something like that?'

'Not exactly,' Jane said.

'No,' Lockyer reiterated. 'Not exactly.'

Silence fell on the interview room again. Neither Jane nor Lockyer spoke. Nicola's expression began to change. Her cheeks were flushed, her eyes darting in all directions. 'I . . . I don't know what he's said,' she stammered, 'but whatever it was, it'll be lies. It's always lies with him.' Another beat passed before Lockyer took a breath and began to speak.

'Mr Oxenham does allege that you have been attempting to reconcile with your husband for the past five years; that you have gone to some lengths to try and persuade him.'

Each word seemed to hit Nicola Brown like a blow to her torso. 'What lengths?' Her voice was almost a whisper.

'Letting yourself into his flat in the middle of the night, and getting into bed with him naked . . . offering sex. Things of that nature,' Lockyer said. Nicola's entire face went a deep shade of scarlet. 'Does that sound familiar?'

'That only happened once,' she said.

'I see.' Lockyer noted something down on his pad. Jane leaned towards him, but couldn't see what he had written. 'Adam agrees with your version of events, inasmuch as your ex-husband did have an affair with someone from his dental practice. However, where your accounts differ . . . Adam claims Richard's affair was with a male colleague, a fact you omitted.' Nicola sat motionless. 'Adam went further to say that your ex-husband had been struggling with his sexuality for a number of years. The affair was a result of that struggle,' Lockyer continued. 'According to Adam, Richard confessed to the affair and told you that he was, in fact, gay.'

'That's not true.'

'Adam claims your reaction to your husband's infidelity and the disclosure about his sexuality was not good, to say the least. Understandable, perhaps,' Lockyer said, 'given the circumstances.'

'Do you have anything to say, Nicola?' Jane tapped her notepad to break the woman out of her stupor. Nicola shook her head.

'Adam claims you threw Richard out of the house and refused him access to the children for a period of six months,' Lockyer said. 'Is this true?'

'I – I . . .' She opened and closed her mouth like a stranded fish.

'Is it also true that you only allowed your husband back into the marital home on the strict understanding that the breakup was to be kept from the children, and that his sexuality would not be revealed until the children were sixteen and eighteen respectively? Is that correct?' Lockyer asked. Nicola said nothing. 'And further, that he would take responsibility for the marriage breakup when the divorce was finalized, and maintain the story that he had had an affair with a woman from his dental practice?'

'I was angry,' she said in a whisper.

'Mr Oxenham also alleges that you and he had a brief affair early on in your marriage,' Jane said.

Nicola's face went a deep shade of burgundy. 'I can't believe he would stoop this low.'

Jane wasn't done yet. 'Adam also told DI Lockyer that your ex-husband was about to come out as openly gay, and that he wanted to tell the children,' she said.

The silence seemed to fill the room, with only the sound of the air conditioning breaking it. Jane felt as if each revelation was building a framework for a motive. She tried to put herself in Nicola's position: an ambitious woman, a known and respected figure in the community, a mother, a member of the Parents' Association. Being left by a partner was humiliating. It eroded your self-esteem. Jane knew that well enough; but to be left for a guy – would that be worse? She didn't know, but from the expression on Nicola's face, it seemed so.

'Richard wasn't *gay*.' The way Nicola said the word 'gay' made Jane shift in her seat. 'It was Adam who wanted him to be gay,' she said. 'That's what this is all about. He's a fantasist, always has been. Did Adam tell you he was gay?' she said, looking at Lockyer.

'He told me he was bisexual, yes,' Lockyer replied.

Nicola's face contorted into a grimace. 'Bisexual . . . that's a cop-out. He was always coming on to Richard, making excuses to touch him. It was disgusting and desperate. Rich told him no, but you know how *gay* men are.'

'No,' Jane said, trying to keep her voice level. 'I don't.'

'Neither do I,' Lockyer said.

Nicola shrugged, her lip curled upwards. 'Anyway, Rich

wasn't gay. He was a shitty husband and a pretty ineffectual father, but he wasn't gay.'

'Your word against Adam's, I suppose,' Lockyer said.

'I suppose it is.' Nicola pulled a fake smile.

Jane took out the transcript that Chris had run down to her before the interview had restarted. 'Actually,' she said, 'it isn't. After gaining access to Richard's computer, we have found evidence that he was, in fact, openly homosexual, and that he was dating – had been dating for several months, at least. We also have testimony that you threatened him as recently as a couple of weeks ago; that you said –' Jane opened her notepad and flicked back to her interview with Harvey – 'that you said, "You'll end up dead. Do you want to die?" Do you have anything to say, Nicola?'

'I want to talk to my lawyer,' was all she said.

CHAPTER TWENTY-TWO

Richard – July

Richard pushed his feet into his trainers and tightened the laces before leaving the flat and jogging down the stairs. He slipped his door key into his right sock and pulled the front door closed behind him. He turned right and started to run up Gipsy Hill. The roads were quiet, but that wouldn't last. Rush hour would kick off in about an hour. He needed to get his run done, get home, shower and get back to his dental practice for the two final patients of the day. He tapped his chest pocket, and then remembered. Today was the first time he had come out without his mobile. It was pathetic, really, but he hadn't wanted to miss a text or call from Eric. Things had moved quicker than he could have imagined. It was as if it had always been this way: he had always been gay, he had always been open, he had always been with Eric. He had always been happy. It was weird and a bit unsettling, but Richard couldn't repress a smile as he ran. He pushed his legs to go faster, enjoying the sun on his face.

As was the way with ying and yang, not everything in his life was going quite so well. He turned right at the church onto

Highland Road, and slowed his pace a little. Ben's mother had called last night. Her opening gambit had been that she needed to talk to him about Harvey. No parent ever wants to hear those words, because you know the 'talk' is not going to be good. Sandra had said, 'He's usually so good, so helpful, but I'm sorry to say, Rich, but I really struggled with him at the weekend.'

As soon as Richard asked for more detail, he regretted it. According to Sandra, Harvey had been rude, but worse than that, he had been aggressive. He and Ben had somehow managed to get into a fight over nothing. 'I could see he was sorry, but he wouldn't apologize,' Sandra had said.

What could Richard say to that? There was nothing he could say. He had apologized, and said he would speak to Harvey. Ever since Harvey had turned thirteen, it had been like raising Jekyll and Hyde; but then, maybe all teenagers were the same. Richard had tried to talk to Nicola about it – not this incident, he wasn't stupid – but he had tried to tackle the issue, with no success. 'He's a teenager, Rich. He's acting like a teenager. Man up.'

But something in Richard's gut told him it was more than just a phase. Something else was going on in his son's life, and for the first time ever, Richard wasn't privy to it. Moreover, his involvement wasn't wanted. He was going to take Harvey out for a curry tonight, to talk to him. Olive had been peeved to be left out, but Richard knew he needed to give Harvey his full attention. Of course, the downside of being a good father was that he couldn't see Eric tonight, which was pissing him off more than it should.

More than anything, he wanted to talk to his children, to

explain how things were and to introduce them to Eric. But he needed to talk to Nicola first, and that was a conversation he would cross a continent to avoid. He wasn't worried about the kids. Olive would love Eric, of that he was in no doubt – but, given his current demeanour, he wasn't so sure about Harvey. Boys were different. He doubted Olive differentiated between gay and straight. She was part of the equality gener-ation, exposed to every minority and demographic from such a young age that it was just accepted. No questions asked. He still remembered walking into the lounge and noticing that one of the children's television presenters only had one arm. He had asked his daughter why, and to his surprise she had looked at him, oblivious.

He smiled as he continued onto Lunham Road. Kids today just accepted differences. They didn't question them, let alone reject or fear them. Not like Richard's generation. He knew already that he was going to lose friends over his 'choice'. He knew, because he had heard some of his friends talk. They didn't like 'gays' because they found the sexual mechanics repul-sive. The word Geoff had used was abhorrent. Richard shook his head and increased his pace. He didn't want to think about that now. He needed to focus on his kids, on Harvey, and try to figure out what was wrong before he dropped another bomb-shell into the poor kid's world.

CHAPTER TWENTY-THREE

4 August – Monday

Jane pulled into the station car park off Lewisham High Street, found a space and turned off the engine. She rested her head back and stared up at the blue, cloudless sky. Her brain was aching under the strain of too much information coupled with not enough time to process it. She lifted her sunglasses and rubbed her eyes, glancing at herself in the rear-view mirror. She looked pale. No wonder, given her day yesterday.

The interviews with Brown and Oxenham had gone well, but they had been exhausting. By the time she pulled into the driveway at her parents' house, she was about ready to drop. She had cooked supper for the whole family. Her father had eaten well, and so had Peter; but her mother had picked at her food. It was obvious something was bothering Celia Bennett, but in an act of self-preservation, Jane had decided to turn a blind eye. She had enough on her plate.

After dinner she had retreated to her room to compose a reply to Andy:

Hi, thanks for your email. I am fine. Busy. Be good to meet up. Where are you staying? Give me your number and I'll call you to arrange. Jane

This had been changed dozens of times, until she ended up with:

Yes, we can meet. What's your number?

He hadn't replied yet. Maybe he wouldn't. She hoped he wouldn't. She looked out the passenger window at the sunshine, and wondered how long it would take to retrain to be a garden designer or some other profession that meant a lot of time outdoors. As the idea grew, she remembered the rain of recent days and decided maybe gardening wasn't for her after all. She closed her eyes.

The knock at her bedroom door the previous night had been quiet. Her mother had poked her head around the door and said, 'Have you got a second, darling?' Even now, it sounded so innocent; but when was something her mother said ever really 'innocent'? The bomb was still falling through the air when Celia Bennett left the room for Jane to 'have a think'.

The sound of her mobile ringing made her jump. She reached into her handbag and ferreted around until her fingers closed around the vibrating phone. It was Dave. She tapped the speaker button.

'Hello, Doctor,' she said with a smile. 'I was just trying to find a reason to hide in my car and avoid the office.'

'Happy to oblige, always,' he said.

Just hearing Dave's voice made her shoulders relax. He

was such a tonic. The only other person who had this effect on her was her father, and maybe Anthony Hopkins – well, his voice, anyway. 'Did you get my email?'

'I did,' he said. 'I emailed over the preliminary post-mortem report earlier. You'll have it when you get into the office. I'll get the full one to you end of business today or early tomorrow, does that suit?'

'Sure, sooner the better,' she said, letting her eyes wander around the car park, watching other officers climbing out of theirs cars, ready for the day – or not, if their tired expressions were anything to go by. Most of her team had been in all weekend. Rest didn't really come into it when you had an active murder investigation.

'I've got Taylor's medical records,' Dave continued.

'Yeah – anything interesting?' she asked, not holding her breath.

'Actually, yes.'

Jane sat forward and started searching in her handbag for her notepad and pen. 'That's a first,' she said. 'Hang on, let me just find a pen.' Her fingers closed around her purse, a nail file, a rolled-up magazine, some loose tampons and finally the cold barrel of a biro. 'Got it,' she said. 'Go ahead.'

'Taylor had type two diabetes,' he said. 'Diagnosed a year ago.'

'Medicated?' Jane made a note to speak to the territorial support team who had searched Taylor's address.

'Yes and no,' Dave said. 'Yes, he was prescribed metformin and insulin; but from what I can gather, he hasn't been taking up his prescriptions.'

'That's odd, isn't it?'

'Not really,' Dave said. 'A fit guy like that . . . I don't mean to stereotype my gender, but men who are diagnosed at his age can often have a hard time coming to terms with the diagnosis. In actual fact, I spoke to Taylor's GP this morning. He said Taylor was determined to control the diabetes with diet and exercise, figured he could reverse the condition.'

'Is that even possible?' Jane asked, surprised that a man of Taylor's background would be so cavalier with his health.

'In the short term it can have a positive effect, yes, but long-term, Taylor would have needed medication to help balance his levels,' Dave said. 'There was no real physical evidence in the post-mortem to suggest damage from the diabetes, so he was doing well with it.'

'The TSGs never flagged up finding any drugs in the flat,' Jane said, drawing a ring around her note to follow up with the search team.

'Well . . .' Dave said, 'I took the liberty of calling and checking with them this morning, too.'

'Wow, you *are* keen,' she said, smiling. Jane wasn't precious about her cases, and she wasn't one for worrying about anyone stepping on her toes, so if anything she was pleased by Dave's proactive morning.

'No drugs were found,' he said.

'Yeah, I didn't think there had been.'

'During the internal examination, Patrick found small fragments of white tablets in Taylor's stomach. I've sent them off for analysis, and sent some more bloods off to a lab in Reading that can test for insulin.'

'Why do I feel like you're drip-feeding me this

information, Dave?' Jane asked, feeling the first needle of frustration. She was too tired to play games.

'OK, OK,' he said. 'Sorry; Patrick and I have spent the past two hours sleuthing. I feel like Columbo.'

Jane smiled at that. 'You're beginning to look a bit like him, too,' she teased.

'Charming.'

'Go on. What have you and Watson come up with?' She sensed Dave was about to embark on a monologue involving a lot of medical jargon.

'In the post-mortem we discussed the possibility that a sedative of some kind might have been used to put Taylor out, to facilitate injection and/or suffocation – yes?'

'Yes,' Jane confirmed.

'Well, it occurred to us, Patrick and I, that an overdose of metformin can result in lactic acidosis,' he said.

'Lactic acidosis.' She scribbled it down, hazarding a guess at the spelling.

'The symptoms include weakness, drowsiness, a depressed heart rate, feeling light-headed and fainting.'

'Hold up, Dave,' she said. 'I don't mean to rain on your detective parade, but you're suggesting someone force-fed Taylor his own diabetes pills and then waited for them to take effect so they could inject him with another drug *without* him noticing?'

'Sarcasm is the lowest form of wit, Jane,' he said. 'I am not quite that stupid.'

'Sorry, Dave, go on,' she said, aware that lack of sleep, PMT, a murder investigation, her mother dropping the bomb that they might be moving and Peter's father crawling out from the rock he had been hiding under – all combined – were making her a little fractious.

'Taylor's GP said he was taking metformin sporadically: when he had eaten a particularly fatty meal, for example. He had cooked a barbecue that day, hadn't he? Sausages, burgers . . .'

'So you think Taylor overdosed on the metformin himself?' Jane tried to disguise the scepticism in her voice.

'Actually, it's perfectly plausible,' Dave said. 'People who self-medicate are very susceptible to overdose.'

'Okaaay.' Jane stretched out the word. 'I'll buy that; keep going.'

'If Taylor had inadvertently taken too much of his metformin he would have been extremely drowsy, if not semi-conscious – and therefore not able to fight off an attacker.'

'But the attacker wouldn't know that, Dave,' she said. She hated to say it, but Dave should really stick to pathology – sleuthing, it seemed, was not his strong point.

'Hence the fibres,' Dave said, sounding very pleased with himself.

Jane was about to protest, when the penny dropped. 'You think the attacker held Taylor face down while they injected him?'

'Bingo,' he said.

'OK, let's work with that,' she said, taking a deep breath and scribbling more notes on her pad. 'So you've dealt with the tablet fragments, pending the test results, but what makes you think the injected substance was insulin – I'm assuming that *is* what you think, given you've sent the bloods to a lab in *Reading* – I hate to think what that will cost.'

'It was actually Patrick who came up with it,' Dave said, without apology.

'Go on, then, spill.' Jane scratched her nose where her sunglasses were beginning to pinch.

'It's possible Taylor died of a hypoglycaemic attack.'

She started to write the word down, but stopped halfway. 'How are you spelling that, Dave?'

'Hypo,' he said, 'and then g, l, y, c, a, e, mic.'

'And that is?'

'A severe drop in blood sugar. Not enough glucose gets to the brain. The initial effects can be relatively minor, such as loss of attention, confusion – but in more severe cases it can lead to seizures resulting in brain damage, coma or death.'

'Aha,' she said, 'now I see where you're going.'

'It fits with everything we know,' Dave said. 'Taylor's system would be very sensitive to insulin, given his condition and the fact that he hadn't been taking his medication properly. Six shots of insulin would have been ample to kill him.'

'God,' Jane said. 'That is cold.'

'Murder often is,' he replied.

Jane tapped the biro against her teeth and scanned her notes. 'So you can prove this?'

'Ah,' Dave said.

Jane blew out a breath. 'Of course, nothing is ever simple in this game. Tell me.'

'To prove Taylor died of a hypoglycaemic attack, I would need to demonstrate three things – high levels of insulin, low C-peptides, and the blood itself would need to be a hypoglycaemic sample.'

'And Taylor's wasn't . . . isn't?' she asked, balancing her

CLARE DONOGHUE

mobile on the dashboard. It was getting sweaty in her hand. Her car was turning into an oven. She opened her door a crack, relieved to feel a cool breeze.

'No, because the blood samples were taken post-mortem. Glucose levels in the blood decrease after death, as do C-peptides, so there's no way to diagnose hypoglycaemia post-mortem.'

'But we still have the tests to come back on the tablets and the bloods?'

'Yes,' Dave said. 'If what Patrick and I have come up with is correct, then we should be able to confirm the presence of metformin for definite – or whatever the fragments contain.'

'And the insulin?'

'That's the tricky one,' he said. 'Insulin can be metabolized within hours, leaving the bloods clear.'

'A great way to kill someone, then,' Jane said. 'To hold Taylor down, semi-suffocate him, inject him six times, wait for him to die and then reposition the body so it would look like death by natural causes.' She couldn't help picturing Nicola Brown. It took a cold fish to perform a cold-hearted act.

'That's what we thought,' he said, 'but we'll have to wait and see when the results come back. Patrick has taken a sample of fluid from around Taylor's eye. It's a backup in case the bloods come back clear of insulin. Of course,' he said, 'if you can find me the discarded EpiPens, then . . . '

'Oh, sure,' she said. 'As if I'm that lucky.'

CHAPTER TWENTY-FOUR

4 August – Monday

Lockyer watched as Roger and Jane paced the room in sync. He didn't know if it was the promotion, or something else, but Roger seemed more agitated than usual – and Jane wasn't faring much better. 'Look,' he said, addressing them both. 'We're further along than we were.'

'I'm not sure I agree with you there, Mike,' Roger said. 'I was hoping you would be coming here to tell me you were charging, or at least on the road to charging, someone. Are you?' he said to Jane. She shook her head. 'Exactly. I agreed to keeping the media out on the basis that this case would be downgraded from a category A by this morning. Are we there yet?'

'No,' Jane said, shaking her head again.

'Not yet,' Lockyer qualified, 'but we have a hell of a lot more information than we did. We have a motive, possibly two for the ex-wife. And, thanks to Dave –' he glanced at Jane – 'and pending some toxicology report, we have a possible method too.'

'Which is?'

'I'd rather wait for the test results—' Jane began.

Lockyer interrupted. 'Taylor was a diabetic. Dave found fragments of pills in his stomach, and from the PM he thinks it's possible Taylor died of hypoglycaemia – a severe drop in blood sugar brought on by six injections of insulin.'

'Shit,' Roger said. 'So Nicola Brown is the prime suspect?'

'Yes,' Lockyer said, at the same time as Jane said, 'Maybe.'

Roger threw up his hands. 'Well, at least you two are on the same page. That's some comfort.' Lockyer looked up at Jane, who was pacing in front of him. She looked tired. He could see that a lack of sleep and the lack of progress were taking their toll on her, which was the last thing she needed or he wanted. With everything that had happened and that was happening with her father, this amount of stress couldn't be good for her.

The sun was bouncing off Roger's window right into Lockyer's face. He pushed his fingers into the back of his neck, and closed his eyes. An image of Jane lying on muddy ground flashed into his mind. He opened his eyes, and the vision vanished. It was hard to believe the Hungerford case had ended almost three months ago. Lockyer was still having nightmares about it, so he could only imagine how Jane must be feeling.

'There's circumstantial evidence on the ex-wife, but nothing chargeable, sir,' she said.

'Nicola Brown has possible motive, keys to Taylor's flat – she's a dentist, knows about drugs, injections – I think that's more than circumstantial, Jane,' he said, knowing it wasn't, but feeling frustrated by her lack of faith.

'We don't have the tox screens back yet,' Jane countered. 'And her alibi has been confirmed.'

'You said yourself that the alibi only covered her until midnight,' Lockyer pointed out. 'Dave said the attack would have happened in the early hours. Plenty of time for her to drive over there, let herself in, and get home again afterwards.'

'We're checking CCTV on all possible routes,' Jane said, looking at him. Her expression seemed to say, *aren't you meant to be on my side?*

'Good,' Roger said.

'What we know so far suggests premeditation, planning,' Lockyer said before he could stop himself. 'We're not looking at a spurned lover or a bungled robbery; there was no sign of forced entry.' He heard Jane take a deep breath. 'All I'm saying is, the investigation is moving forward. So we don't have a chargeable suspect yet – but we do *have* a suspect. We just have to prove it now.' Roger covered his face. 'Yes, Roger, we need to keep it as a category A for now. But that's not the end of the world.' He could feel Jane looking at him. 'I'm just saying, for day five, we're in pretty good shape.'

'Jane,' Roger said, as if Lockyer hadn't spoken. 'What's next?'

Jane stood up and resumed pacing. 'The majority of the interviews with peripheral folk are happening today. Comms are briefing me after this meeting about what they've turned up on Taylor's computer. We'll need to interview and rule out any men he's spoken to or met through the dating sites.'

'Mike just said we're not looking at a spurned lover here . . . notwithstanding his ex-wife being a spurned lover, that is,' Roger said.

'No,' Jane agreed, 'that's right, but it's too soon to rule it out. Who knows what kind of guys Taylor talked to or met from these sites? A friend of mine was talking to a bloke for over a month – she was really excited – she was about to meet him. She showed me his profile pictures to see what I thought. He was using fake photos.'

'Surely that's not unusual?' Roger asked, sitting down behind his desk, folding his arms and putting his feet up on the edge of his bin. Lockyer noticed the top of a dead-looking bonsai tree poking out.

'No, it isn't,' she said, 'but the photos the guy was using for his profile were of Ted Bundy.'

'Jesus.' Roger shook his head. 'What is wrong with these people?'

'I'm guessing, a lot.'

'OK, so you need to rule out the sites,' Roger said. 'Got it. What else?'

Jane sat down too, folding her arms, mirroring Roger's body language. 'Both children need to be re-interviewed. I'll go over to the house and sort that today. We can't disclose Taylor's sexuality, but we need to see if they knew – and, of course, discuss the bruises on Olive.'

'Sounds sensible,' Roger said.

'And Brown needs to be re-interviewed too,' she said, 'with her solicitor . . . but I'm going to hold off on that until after the test results come back and the CCTV footage has been examined. If she is our prime suspect, I don't want to waste holding hours until I feel we have something more concrete.'

'Absolutely.' Roger was nodding.

Lockyer nodded too. He couldn't disagree. He might be frustrated, but Jane knew how to get a case through to trial.

She was just being cautious, something he was not known for.

He shifted in his seat. It was lazy police work just to focus on the ex-wife, and here he was pushing for it. Why was he trying to shut this case down? He looked at Jane. Her face was pale. The longer a case dragged on, the more it took out of you. Lockyer looked down at the floor as the reality of what he was doing settled on his shoulders. Dave was right. He needed to back off and trust Jane to tell him if she needed help.

'I agree,' he said. 'There are two clear lines of enquiry at this time – the ex-wife, and Taylor's possible contact with guys from the dating site.' He looked over at Jane. She smiled.

'OK,' Roger said. 'In that case, we need to release a statement to the press regarding Taylor's death . . . '

'I'll liaise with the press office and put something together,' Jane said. 'I want to keep the details to a minimum: death under suspicious circumstances . . . several lines of enquiry . . . nothing to suggest a threat to public safety.'

'Unless we're dealing with a nutjob from the Internet,' Roger said, raising his eyebrows.

'Let's see who he talked to first,' she said. 'I'm already running a historical check for similar cases. If we get a hit, then I'll adjust the statement. If not, then we're hopefully looking at an isolated incident, personal to Taylor.'

'That would be good,' Roger said. Lockyer was still looking at Jane. Her eyebrows had disappeared beneath her fringe. 'What I mean by that,' Roger clarified, 'is that we've had a rough year so far. The crazies have been coming out of the woodwork. We – the department, not to mention the borough

– could do with a break from the high-profile cases, don't you think? Barely a month has gone by without one or both of you ending up in the tabloids because of stalkers, serial killers or people being buried alive. Enough's enough, already.'

'The worries of a superintendent,' Lockyer said, getting up. 'If only the *crazies* of south-east London would do us all a favour and chillax.'

'You'll update me later?' Roger looked at Jane.

'We both will,' Lockyer answered, ushering her out and closing the door behind them.

'We both will?' Jane said, walking away from him. He paused, and then broke into a jog to catch up with her as she headed for the lifts. He almost barrelled right into her when she turned and stopped in the doorway. 'Look, sir,' she said, looking at her hands. She was back to calling him 'sir'. That wasn't a good thing. 'You're SIO. I report to you. You report to Roger. I get that.' He opened his mouth to speak, but she held up her hand. 'I am OK,' she said. 'I can handle this case.'

'I know you can,' he said, feeling every inch the idiot. Judging by her expression, and by his conversation with Dave, Jane knew what he had been doing for weeks – and yet it had taken him until just now to figure it out.

'I feel like—'

'I'll stop you there,' he said. If he had to have any more conversations about feelings, he was going to go insane. 'I know,' he said looking at her. 'Consider this an official backing-off, OK?'

She nodded. 'OK. As long as you understand—'

'Enough said,' he cut in. 'I've got a few things to do. Brief me once you've spoken to comms, and we'll go from there. OK?'

'Yes, sir.' Jane pressed the button for the lift, and turned away.

Lockyer crossed the open-plan floor towards his office. He shut the door, walked around his desk and sat down. He took out his phone from his jacket pocket and tapped out a text to Dave.

You owe me a pint!

Thirty seconds passed before his phone beeped. He opened Dave's message.

Why's that then?

Lockyer tapped out a reply:

Because you were right and that irritates the hell out of me!!

Another few seconds passed. Lockyer's phone beeped.

When will you learn, Michael? I am ALWAYS right!

CHAPTER TWENTY-FIVE

4 August – Monday

Jane repositioned the earpiece from her hands-free kit and knocked her windscreen wipers up to full speed. It was throwing it down. This was more the type of weather she could handle. Like her son, she loved sunshine, but only when she wasn't working. Rain and dark clouds went with her profession – and, today, her mood.

Andy's phone number was burning a hole in her pocket, or rather her handbag. 'I agree with you, Mother,' she said, putting the car into third gear and then changing it back to second as the traffic ground to a halt in front of her. She had been on the phone to her mother for the entire journey from the station to Penge. The conversation, like the traffic, was very much stop–start. People in summer clothing and flip-flops were scattering in every direction, trying to escape the downpour. She watched a mother trying to drag two very wet children under a shop awning.

'Your father agrees with me,' Celia Bennett said. She was mid-rant, and not really listening or indeed asking for Jane's response.

'I do, too,' she said, more to herself than anyone else.

'I won't allow him to spend his entire school holiday either glued to the television or on that PMT,' Celia said.

'It's a PSP, Mum, not PMT,' she said. 'PMT is pre-menstrual . . . '

'I don't care what it's called,' her mother said. 'I care about Peter's mental development, as should you. How is he ever meant to get better when he's locked away in his room? He may as well be surgically attached to the damn thing and *I* won't always be here to watch him . . . to look out for his wellbeing.' Jane tried to ignore the dig, but it stung. It was as if her mother was saying that without her, Jane would fail. How did she think she could raise Peter alone? Without her mother, who would watch him, take him to school, pick him up? 'I don't think you are taking this seriously, Jane.'

'I am,' Jane said, her voice flat. 'I'll talk to Peter when I get home, and we'll set up a time chart for the PSP, OK? I'll be home by four, five at the latest.'

'You said that yesterday. And might I remind you that yesterday was a Sunday – a Sunday, Jane. You might not be godly, but Sunday is supposed to be a day of rest.'

'Mother, you're not religious.'

'So?' her mother snapped. 'What difference does that make?'

'How's Dad doing today?' she asked, changing the subject.

'Your father is as stubborn as you are,' Celia said. 'He won't stay in bed. He won't rest. He insists on eating bread with the butter spread so thick you could take a dental impression, but what do I know? Nothing, apparently. I'm not a doctor. I'm not his mother. Well, I'm your mother and I'm telling you this is not on, Jane. It's just not on.'

Jane took a deep breath, and waited. She wasn't sure which part of the current discussion 'wasn't on', but she knew that interrupting her mother would be pointless. It was best to let her finish. 'I am running myself ragged trying to look after those two, and what thanks do I get? None, that's what,' Celia said. 'Your son – my eight-year-old grandson – tells me to go away and get out of his room, and my husband – your father – tells me I'm a pain in his arse, and that I can shove my low-fat recipes where the sun doesn't shine.' Jane bit her lip. 'What a bloody cheek. A bloody cheek.' Celia was breathing hard at the other end of the line.

'What can I do to help, Mum?' she asked in the most non-confrontational tone she could muster.

'You can start by letting me off this phone,' her mother said. 'I've got a million and one things to do. I don't have time to update you on the state of the world every five minutes. Be home by five, or I shall feed your dinner to the fish.'

Two things jumped out at Jane. One – that the fish would no doubt die if Celia Bennett threw in a whole bowl of no-fat beef bourguignon; and two – that her mother had called her, not the other way around. She swallowed both incendiary pieces of information and just said, 'OK, Mum. I'll see you at five.'

'You're acting like this move is an easy decision for your father and me,' Celia went on, as if that had been the topic of conversation the entire time. 'We can't all be selfish. *Someone* has got to think about your father's health, about

172

what's best for him. He needs fresh air, peace and quiet. He needs a break, Jane. He's worked hard all his life. He deserves to enjoy his twilight years.'

Jane had to hold her breath to keep from shouting. She covered the speaker and blew out the breath. 'I told you, Mum. I understand. I'm just trying to get my head around it, that's all.'

'Then why are you being so dismissive?' her mother barked. 'It's as if you don't care . . . well, why should you? You're always at the office – you don't have time for your son or your father, let alone me.'

'Look, Mother,' Jane said, unable to keep the anger out of her voice now. When her mother wanted to pick a fight, she knew just how to push Jane's buttons. 'You only dropped this *move* on me last night. Peter and I will miss you terribly if you move away from London, but as I told you last night, I will support your decision, whatever it is. I love you both and don't want to see you go, but right now, at this minute, I can't do anything or say anything that will make you feel OK about moving away. Give me some time to get used to the idea. Can you do that?'

'You obviously have far more important things to be doing than talking to me. If and when we decide, I'll be sure to let you know . . . give you plenty of notice.' The line went dead.

Jane took out the earpiece and shoved it into the ashtray as she slowed to a stop outside Nicola Brown's house. She blinked back tears. She didn't have the strength to withstand her mother's guilt transferral. She inched forwards, looking ahead for a space, and accelerated when she spotted brake lights at the end of the street. Once the other car was clear, she parked and turned off the ignition, put her head in her hands and closed her eyes.

She should be overjoyed at the thought of some distance between her and her mother. If it weren't for Peter and her father, she might be. She sat back and took another deep breath. That wasn't true. She loved her mother. A smile played at the corner of her mouth. But that didn't mean she couldn't fantasize, for just a moment, about what it would be like to be free. Her mobile started to ring. With some trepidation, she unplugged it from its charger and looked at the screen. She let out a sigh of relief. It was Dave.

'Lucky me,' she said, her voice thick. 'Twice in one day.'

'You OK?' he asked.

Damn his sensitivity, she thought. 'I'm good,' she said, clearing her throat. 'You have more news for me?' She didn't want to *talk* any more, she just wanted to work.

'Some,' Dave said. 'Have you got a pen?'

'Yes,' Jane said, finding one in her bag. 'Go ahead.'

'Taylor tested positive for chlamydia and HSV,' Dave said.

'HSV?'

'The herpes virus.'

'That's quite common, isn't it?' she asked, making a note that Taylor had been sexually active on her pad.

'Yes, both are very common STIs. More so in people in their early twenties, but that's not to say other demographics aren't susceptible.'

She hesitated. 'Would you be able to tell if Taylor had had anal sex . . . recently, I mean?'

'I didn't see any damage on the external examination, but let me take another look,' Dave said without hesitation. 'The lining of the anus is very thin, so there may be evidence internally. Any particular reason?'

'It's been suggested that Taylor was homosexual, bisexual or at the very least curious,' she said, thinking about the Internet sites Taylor had frequented. 'I've left Mike back at the office checking into possible contacts or partners, but if there's evidence of sexual intercourse, then at least it gives me a better idea of where Taylor was in terms of relationships.'

'You don't have to be in a relationship to have sex, Jane,' Dave said.

'No, of course not,' she said.

'If you're trying to save his blushes, Jane,' Dave said, 'I think it's a bit late for that.'

She shook her head. 'I know. You're right. It's just that he . . . Taylor wasn't *out*, out. According to a friend of his he was struggling to come to terms with his sexuality. He wanted to come out, but he never got the chance.' She fell silent. 'I'm being stupid,' she admitted. 'I'm trying to save him from a prejudice that isn't even there.'

'It's all right,' Dave said. 'It's your job. Taylor is your responsibility. The fact that he's dead is irrelevant. You feel protective. It's quite understandable, Jane.'

She couldn't help chuckling. 'Dave,' she said, 'you are a wonderful man.'

'Why, thank you, Jane,' he said in a grandiose voice. 'I do try.'

She smiled. 'Anything else?'

'Yes. I meant to tell you earlier that Taylor's blood alcohol levels were high, considering the time lapse – 0.14 – not high enough to account for his death, but high enough to assume he would have been under the influence, and high enough for me to recheck his liver and kidneys.'

'And?' Jane asked. She could feel the weight of her argument with her mother lifting. Thank God for her job, she thought.

'There was some damage,' Dave said. 'Not enough to suggest a significant problem, but enough to tell me that he overindulged.'

'Binge drinking?' she asked as she noted it down.

'Possibly,' Dave said. She put a tick next to her note.

'Great,' she said. 'Thanks, Dave. As ever, your help and insight are invaluable.'

'You are very welcome, as always,' he said.

Jane said goodbye and ended the call. She closed her eyes and pushed her shoulders down. Dave always made her feel better. He was so calm, so measured – which was amazing, when you considered the atrocities he bore witness to every day. She felt as if she had received a virtual hug. She climbed out of the car, locked it, put her handbag over her head to fend off the rain and jogged towards Nicola Brown's house. Her good feelings seemed to evaporate as she approached the 1930s half-brick, half-render house. She didn't imagine Nicola was going to be in an agreeable mood after yesterday's revelations. Anne Phillips' car was parked on the other side of the street – so Jane would have an ally. At least, she would when it came to the mother. Jane and Anne were yet to agree when it came to Harvey.

CHAPTER TWENTY-SIX

4 August – Monday

Lockyer was sitting in the briefing room with Chris and Aaron, listening to the rain as it hammered against the windows.

'It's forecast to rain all week,' Aaron said, not looking up from what he was doing.

'Priya's stuck at home with Layla,' Chris said. 'I think it's driving her a bit nuts.'

Lockyer couldn't help tuning into their conversation. 'I think it's probably the six-month-old baby that's driving Priya nuts, Chris, not the rain,' he said.

'Either way,' Chris said, 'she's not happy with me.'

'Why?' Aaron asked. 'Because it's raining?'

'No,' Chris said, with a look of guilt and confusion. Lockyer recognized the expression as that of a new father. If in doubt, you were in the wrong. That first year could be very challenging if you didn't grasp that idea right out of the gate. 'I was meant to get a rain cover for the pram. I thought I'd ordered it.' He looked doubtful. 'To be honest, I thought she'd ordered it, but apparently not.'

'Women,' Aaron said, with a knowing nod. He met Lockyer's eyes but dropped them to the ground, a look of panic on his face. Lockyer might have been imagining things, but he felt like Aaron had been acting differently around him in the past week or so. Or, he thought, pushing his eyes open with the tips of his fingers, it could just be that the three of them had been stuck in this room together for the past three hours.

Every fibre of Lockyer's being wanted to break free. He wasn't used to feeling this cooped up on a case. True, his role as senior DI had meant spending a significant amount of time in the office, but now he was SIO as well, he felt like he was back to doing grunt work. Wherever he turned, someone from Jane's team or his own was handing him a stack of paperwork or a memory stick. His team was working on two stabbings over at Wendover House on the Aylesbury Estate. With a jumbled mass of 1950s high-rises, it was one of the largest estates in Europe. The city planners were just asking for trouble cramming three thousand homes into a square mile, but with a crime reported every four hours, two stabbings was almost a slow day. He should be knocking on doors and tramping around the estate but instead he was stuck checking, signing off and rechecking action lists for both teams. It was boring as hell.

At least with the Taylor case – or Jane's case, as he kept having to remind himself – he had been sitting in on interviews, picking out suspects, doing something. Or rather, he had been until Jane had asked him to look into Taylor's dating history; ever since then, he'd been buried beneath a pile of paperwork. Comms had provided thousands of transcripts taken from Richard Taylor's computer, tablet and phone. It was taking an age to wade through them all, and it wasn't easy reading. Lockyer couldn't remember the last time he had felt uncomfortable prying into a victim's life. In fact, even the word 'prying' had not entered his vocabulary in years – but for some reason, Richard Taylor's messages were getting to him. It wasn't the sexual content. Lockyer had seen and read worse, a lot worse. It was the emotion. It was evident that Taylor had suffered. His emails were an electronic record of his struggle to come to terms with his sexuality. Looked at as a whole, even Lockyer could identify the five stages of grief – grief for the life that Taylor was turning his back on.

With a heavy sigh Lockyer flicked back to the first section of emails, taken from a chat room Taylor had used back in February. Each message was like a fishing expedition – asking for contact, but not knowing or wanting to admit to himself why.

Does anyone know how to stop mice getting in? I'm on the second floor.
I'm looking for a local handyman to help with a kitchen installation – recommendations welcome
Looking to make friends locally – divorced
Does anyone else struggle to get a reply on here? Or is it just me!

In isolation the notes would have meant very little, but in context they weren't as benign as they seemed. It was a male-only chat room. The site itself was littered with references, the rainbow flag was the backdrop for the webpage – the image at the top of the screen was of two male symbols interlinked. No one in their right mind could possibly see

179

this chat room as anything other than what is was: a way for men to connect, talk and if they were so inclined, meet up. There were posts about group meet-ups at the weekend that 'everyone was welcome' to attend. Lockyer sighed again. This was Richard's denial stage – his innocent questions and enquiries put out into the ether, not quite being able to accept the responses he would no doubt have received.

The batch Chris was on represented Taylor's anger. Chris had started to read out a line of messages until Lockyer had asked him to stop. For some reason, hearing Taylor's fury out loud made him feel even worse. Some guy had emailed Richard with what could only be described as a sexually explicit request. Richard, shifting between denial and anger, had lost the plot. In his reply there was an abundance of 'How dare you?', 'What are you? Sick or something?' and the ever-reliable, 'If I ever find you I will kick the shit out of you.' It was sad, almost pathetic, to see a man's life laid bare. His private thoughts were being pored over by three male police officers. To their credit, Aaron and Chris had been nothing but professional. If either had shown even the slightest mirth at their assignment Lockyer was pretty sure he would have fired them on the spot. This was no joke. This was Taylor's life.

He clasped his hands around the back of his neck and pulled at his aching muscles. He couldn't help thinking about his own marriage, about how hard his separation from Clara had been. Like Taylor, Lockyer's divorce had come about as a result of his own actions. Clara wasn't to blame. Neither was Nicola, though Lockyer had trouble finding any sympathy when it came to that woman. She was cold. Clara was never cold. He had hurt her. She had ended it. It was as simple as that. He could still remember what it had felt like, sitting in his new flat trying to reason his way out of the situation. *It would have happened anyway. We were never right for each other. She would have left me in the end. If I hadn't done it, she would have.* How did he know Taylor had felt the same? Because he was looking at a raft of emails from Richard to his ex-wife when she had kicked him out and was refusing to let him see the children. The pain, anger, regret and self-righteousness made Lockyer cringe. 'You never understood me,' Taylor had written. 'I tried to talk to you a million times, but you just wouldn't listen.' Lockyer shook his head. He had done the same. He had tried to blame Clara for his mistakes. It was a classic manoeuvre: when you feel bad, shift the blame to whomever you can.

Next came self-pity. How could she do this to him? What had he done to deserve this? Without her and the children, Taylor claimed, he had nothing to live for. The phrase had jumped out at Lockyer when he had first read it but now it just sounded like a plea. Taylor was begging Nicola to let him back into his own life. His last messages would have made a grown man cry, the utter desolation in Taylor's voice moving.

Lockyer glanced at the rain still running in torrents down the glass, turned over several pages and started to reread a whole stream of messages between Richard and a guy called Frank. It had been Richard who had initiated contact. It was clear from the tone of his messages that he had moved past denial, anger, bargaining and depression into the acceptance portion of his journey. He was now a paid member of a gay dating site. The messages dated from early May up until mid-June. What started out as a couple of messages quickly turned into dozens of emails back and forth. Richard talked at length about his job and his two children, though Frank, who claimed to be in his early twenties, was far more interested in Richard on his own. It was Frank who started the flirting, the suggestive messages, but Richard wasn't slow to react. Lockyer wasn't a prude, not by a long shot, but he was somewhat taken aback at the speed with which Taylor had become comfortable talking about sex, explicit sex. The guy had been living as a hetero-sexual for forty years, but he was all over the innuendos like a pro.

Lockyer rubbed his eyebrows. He knew what Megan would say – that he was 'behind the times', not even aware of how dating worked these days. And she was right. He didn't have a clue, and this glimpse into another man's dating life showed just how true that was. He had never sent Clara a dirty message, not that he could recall. Then he remembered. He had received and sent maybe half a dozen sex texts. He still had them on his phone. He still looked at them at night, but they belonged to another time, a time that had only lasted for a heartbeat before it was gone.

'God,' he said, pushing his chair back, startling Chris and Aaron, 'this is depressing the shit out of me.' He headed for the door. 'I'm going over to Bella's to get a coffee. Feel free to take five if you want.' Neither of them moved. They just looked up at him like obedient children. 'I'm coming back,' he said, although he was already thinking he probably wouldn't. Chris and Aaron looked at each other then back at Lockyer.

'I'm fine, sir,' Aaron said, his face reddening.

Lockyer blew out a breath. What was wrong with this kid?

'We'll keep at it,' Chris said with a determined nod.

'Whatever.' Lockyer pulled the glass door closed behind him. He didn't need to suck up or impress the boss. He *was* the boss. He had done his time in that respect. Just thinking about a hot cup of coffee, and maybe a maple-syrup danish, was enough to make him salivate. Peering into Richard Taylor's life had been exhausting. Lockyer felt drained. There were actions to be raised, guys from the emails to speak to, to interview; but right now he needed a change of scene.

As he headed down in the lift he could see Bella's cafe in his mind, the fading gingham decor and the overwhelming yet comforting smell of coffee and air freshener. He could hear the bell that rang over the door when someone walked in off the street. He had always loved that place. For the briefest of seconds he saw *her*, standing in the doorway, the bell chiming above her head. She was smiling. He jabbed his finger again and again on the button for the ground floor. He shook his head. It was almost six months since it had happened, but to him it still felt fresh, raw. She still came to him in his dreams – or nightmares, as they so often were. He rubbed at his temples. Now wasn't the time to go back, to relive it all again. Never look back: that should be his new motto. Looking back only brought him pain.

CHAPTER TWENTY-SEVEN

5 August – Tuesday

Jane pulled at her running shirt. It was clinging to her, sweat dripping down her back. She had jogged down to Ladywell Fields to make some phone calls in peace and quiet, but it seemed a good portion of Lewisham's three hundred thousand residents had decided to invade her sanctuary. When the sun shone, a Londoner could sniff out a blade of grass from a thousand yards.

She walked to the bridge and stopped to stretch her calves. There were half-clad bodies everywhere. The tennis courts were packed and every inch of grass seemed to be taken up with prostrate figures soaking up the sunshine, each with their own booming music. The competing tunes made Jane's head hurt, but then, it didn't take much after the amount of red wine she had put away last night. She wedged the phone between her shoulder and ear so she could still hear Lockyer but could also rub her eyes. The line was terrible, but that didn't appear to be bothering him. A reflux of acid fought its way up her throat. She uncapped her water bottle and took a big swig, hoping to dilute the alcohol still slithering around her system.

After re-interviewing both Harvey and Olive she had needed something to ease the tension. Although she hadn't realized until she was eating her breakfast this morning that she had managed to polish off a bottle and a half of Merlot. The wine had given her enough courage to call Andy. She was meeting him tonight after work. She held her fingers on her eyelids and applied gentle pressure. No wonder her head hurt.

'Look,' she said, feeling exasperated, 'I don't know, but the bruises are there. Anne saw them. She agrees with me.' The phone crackled and died as the signal dropped out. She waited. He would call back. This was Lockyer. He always called back.

She was still trying to process yesterday's events after she and the children had arrived at Caterham Road for the re-interviews. Anne had pointed out the bruising on Olive's wrists and lower arm from the safety of the tech room, and shown her a photograph of a burn that was further up the girl's arm, hidden by her T-shirt and jumper. Jane had reacted as she would have expected: she mentally processed the injuries with interest, but without emotion. She had worked with the Child Abuse Investigation unit for two years before Lockyer recruited her, so was accustomed to dealing with the emotive imagery that, sad to say, went with the job. But her calm demeanour hadn't lasted. She and Cathy the CPO had been mid-interview with Harvey when he had sat forward, obviously tired, and pulled at his neck. The action had revealed purplish bruising at the top of his right shoulder.

Her phone rang. She answered it. 'You were saying?' she said.

'What did . . . say?' Lockyer asked. The signal was still terrible. She was missing every other word.

'Say that again,' she said, resisting the urge to shout. It drove her bonkers when her mother did that. She would be chatting to Aunty Alice, who in fact was not a family member at all but some woman who had looked after Jane when she was a baby. Alice had moved up to Scotland to live on a farm in the middle of nowhere. It was obvious when her mother was talking to Alice, because the volume of her voice was enough to deafen the entire neighbourhood. 'Scotland is too far for you to shout, Mother,' Jane had said a million times. However, listening to the crackle of the phone line and Lockyer's broken sentences, she was tempted to try the Celia Bennett method of communicating. He was only two miles away, sat in the office. If she shouted loud enough, he might just hear her. 'Why don't we just talk when I get back?' she suggested. 'The briefing's in an hour.'

'What . . . Harvey say?' he said again.

Jane blew out a breath and pushed her fringe back from her forehead. She hadn't run that hard, but the combination of heat and booze was making her sweat like a pig. 'Harvey said he couldn't remember where the bruises on his neck had come from,' she said, assuming that was what Lockyer had asked. 'He said he probably got them while he was playing football or play-fighting with his mate Ben. Ben Nicholls, the one who was at the barbecue.'

'And Oli . . . '

Jane continued her conversational guesswork. 'He didn't

know how Olive got the bruises either. He said she bruises easily.'

'Do you . . . it could . . . been Taylor,' Lockyer said in between crackles, '. . . or . . . mother?'

She shifted the phone to her other shoulder and resumed rubbing her eyes. 'Could be,' she said, 'could be a family member, could be accidental. Social services are going to visit the house and make an assessment. I get the feeling something is going on, but neither Harvey nor Olive are talking.'

'Doesn't make sense to protect . . . father, not now . . . dead,' Lockyer said.

'He's still their father,' she said. 'Anyway, that's where I am with the kids.'

'. . . nowhere,' he said.

She wondered what the missing word at the beginning of that sentence was. An expletive, perhaps. 'I'll fill you in on the rest when I get in,' she said. 'When I can actually *hear* what you are saying.'

Lockyer was laughing at the other end of the line. 'That's a first,' he said. 'You're not . . . this keen . . . hear what I . . . to say.'

'Can't argue with you there, sir,' she said. 'I'll see you in a bit.' She started making her own crackling noises before ending the call.

She looked over at a group of teenagers who were passing round an iPhone, each howling with laughter before passing it on. Her curiosity to know what video clip or picture they were looking at was piqued, but then she remembered that they were teenagers, and their sense of humour and hers were no doubt poles apart. She nodded a greeting to an old man making his way across the bridge before retracing her steps to the one bench that was unoccupied. It was under a canopy of trees, and covered in graffiti and dried bird shit. No one wanted shade, it seemed. Lucky for Jane, as she had some calls to make that didn't require an audience.

Comms had managed to get contact information for the majority of guys Richard Taylor had corresponded with. There were three profiles from one of the dating sites that led nowhere: false names and email addresses. No surprise, really. Jane had set up her own profile on Match.com last year and other than her email address, most of it was fiction. Not flat-out lies, but the truth adjusted enough to ensure that no one would be able to recognize her from her description. All the sites said you needed to display a picture, which Jane understood. She would never respond to anyone without a photo; but for her it was different. In her job, it just wasn't safe. It came as no surprise that she went six months without receiving a single message.

She picked up her landline and dialled the number for Eric Tang. He was forty-five years old and lived in Penge, just a couple of streets away from Taylor's ex-wife. The irony wasn't lost on her. The phone rang half a dozen times before a voicemail message kicked in. Jane left her name, number and the time of the call before asking Tang to call her back. From what Lockyer had told her yesterday, Tang had met Richard Taylor in June. There had been a tranche of emails before phone numbers were exchanged. Once that happened, their correspondence was by telephone or text. The texts and calls went right up to and past the date of Taylor's death so Jane had to assume that Tang was still in contact with Taylor right up until the murder, and, it seemed, unaware that Taylor was no longer able to answer – or at least, wanting it to look that way. Jane would ask him to come down to the station for a chat on the record, get things on an official footing straight away.

A gaggle of girls bundled past her in what could only be described as swimwear, flesh very much on show. The Ravensbourne River, which ran through Ladywell Fields, was not the best swimming spot, but given the amount of oil the girls had on Jane guessed their aim was sun-worshipping, not swimming. She took a breath and closed her eyes, listening to the thwack of a dozen tennis rackets hitting a dozen yellow fluffy balls. If it weren't for the cacophony of warring music it would be a relaxing scene, almost idyllic. A large group of thirty-something women were gathered on the other side of the river with rugs, chairs, a picnic and speakers. Who brought speakers to a public place, for goodness' sake? They were adults. Did they have no consideration? Jane had to stop herself as she began the familiar climb onto her high horse. She mentally stepped down, and smiled. She was being an old git. It was sunny. It was the school holidays. People were having fun. It wasn't their fault she had to work.

She unfolded the piece of paper in her hand, and dialled the next number on the sheet. Derek James, a.k.a. Dee. He was thirty-four, lived in Peckham and worked at a local bar – a bar Jane had never heard of. According to the transcripts, Richard had been talking to Dee for a few months, April to early June. Their contact had stopped, but it wasn't clear from the correspondence whether they had ever met in person.

Derek had offered his phone number a few times but it hadn't shown up on Taylor's phone records. The phone rang twice before someone answered.

'Hello,' a male voice said.

'Good morning,' Jane said. 'Can I speak to Derek James, please?' It was a private mobile number, but still, she didn't want to assume the man who had answered was Dee until he confirmed it himself.

'Speaking.'

'Derek, my name is Detective Sergeant Jane Bennett. I'm with Lewisham Police. Are you free to speak for a moment?'

There was a slight pause before Derek said, 'Yes. Sure. What can I do for you, officer?'

His formality didn't surprise Jane. Despite a widespread lack of respect for the police force amongst the less salubrious groups of south-east London, the average Joe was, in her experience, respectful and co-operative on the whole. It harked back to a bygone era, but it was always nice to hear. 'Can I ask, Derek, does the name Richard Taylor mean anything to you?'

There was a longer pause. 'Yes,' he said, 'and you can call me Dee. Everyone does.'

'OK, Dee. Can I ask how you know Mr Taylor?' Jane could hear that the phone was being muffled. It sounded like Dee was on the move. 'Dee, are you still there?' She heard a door bang shut.

'Sorry, yes, I'm here,' he said. 'I just came out back for a break,' he said. 'Is it OK if I smoke?'

'Sure,' Jane said. That was a first. No one had ever asked her permission to smoke on the telephone before. She heard the telltale spark of a lighter, followed by a deep inhalation. 'I was asking about Richard Taylor,' she said as a prompt.

'I met Rich online,' he said.

'When would that have been?'

'Um, April, I'd guess.'

'When you say you met online, what do you mean by that?' Jane asked, opening out the sheet and turning it over so she could make notes on the back with the tiny pencil she had brought with her.

'In a chat room,' Dee said. 'Justformen.com,' he said with a snort, 'like the hair dye?'

'I know the one,' Jane said.

'He was nice . . . Rich, I mean. He was funny.'

'Did you and Mr Taylor ever meet up in person?'

'No,' Dee said without hesitation. 'I think he was a bit shy, you know. I'm not sure he was totally comfortable with . . .' He seemed to be searching for the words. 'I don't know. He just didn't seem one hundred per cent on the whole thing, if I'm honest. Is he OK?'

'Why do you ask?' Jane said, shifting the phone to her other ear. It was cooler in the shade, but she was still sweating. She decided to cut out alcohol for a week, to do a proper detox.

Dee laughed, but there was no humour in his voice. 'Well, forgive me, but I don't get a lot of calls from the cops, and Rich stopped talking to me a while ago . . .' He was silent for a moment. 'And I saw that news report last night about the suspicious death in Gipsy Hill, so now I'm thinking . . .'

'Was a name given in the report?' Jane asked, knowing full well one wasn't. She had prepared the statement with the press office herself. She had signed it off.

'No,' he said. 'I didn't think anything about it at the time . . . well, that's not true. When the cop off the telly said Gipsy Hill, I immediately thought of Rich, not because I thought it involved him but because I hadn't heard from him, you know? I was really hoping he liked me . . . as much as I liked him.' Jane noted that Dee was talking about Richard Taylor in the past tense. 'But then, with you calling me . . . a detective, asking about Richard . . . somehow it makes sense.'

Jane debated asking again why he thought the report and Richard might be connected, but decided against it. It was clear from Dee's voice that he had put two and two together and she didn't have time to play games. 'I am sorry to inform you that Richard Taylor was found dead on Thursday the 31st of July.'

There was a sharp intake of breath from the other end of the line. 'Oh God,' Dee said. His voice sounded muffled, like he had put his hand over his mouth. 'What . . . what happened?'

'I am not at liberty to discuss the details with you at this stage, I'm afraid, but I can say that his death has been listed as suspicious,' she said. 'We are speaking to anyone who may have had contact with Richard in and around the time of his death.'

'You never really know someone, do you?' he said, his voice flat. 'I mean. He sounded like a nice guy, a decent guy. He talked about his kids, his job. He just sounded like a normal guy, but I guess . . . he wasn't.'

'Why do you say that?' Jane asked.

'Because normal guys don't die under . . . suspicious

circumstances,' he said. 'People don't kill nice, normal guys for no reason, do they?'

Jane wanted to say that he would be surprised how many 'normal guys' had been murdered since she had joined the squad, but instead she said, 'There's nothing to suggest that Mr Taylor was involved with anyone, or anything, untoward. But I do need to ask you, Dee: in your correspondence with Richard, did he ever say anything to intimate that he was worried or anxious in any way? Did he talk about anyone else – any name you might recall?'

'No,' Dee said. 'I got the feeling he was seeing or at least talking to other guys, but he never said anything, and I guess I didn't ask because I didn't want to know. You can't really expect exclusivity with this kind of thing, can you?'

'I suppose not,' Jane said, thinking Internet dating did no good for someone's self-esteem if they were there for honest soulmate-seeking purposes. How were you meant to decipher the players from the real deals?

'He didn't really talk about himself much,' Dee continued. 'I mean, he told me about his kids, what he did, that kind of thing; but he mainly asked me about me. He was good at that, at listening. He was always really upbeat . . . super supportive. I've not long been in south-east London and I've just got this new job – which I hate.' His voice had dropped to a whisper. 'Rich was really nice about it. He made me feel better.' There was a pause. 'I can't believe he's dead. It doesn't feel real, you know? I know what he looked like – well, what he looked like in his photos – I guess I felt close to him after all this time talking. Closer than I've felt with any guy for a while. It's so weird. I can't get my head around it.'

'I can imagine it is a shock, Dee, and I'm sorry for that,' Jane said. 'Would you mind coming in to the station at some point this week, just to make sure we've covered everything?' She didn't get the feeling she was talking to a cold-blooded killer, but if her time on the force had taught her anything, it was that you couldn't trust a first impression. The Hungerford case flashed into her mind. Her skills at reading people had failed her that time. Her throat pinched at the memory. She shook her head, dislodging the feeling of unease that was trying to settle on her shoulders. Not everyone lied, she thought. But then her nightmares from May were replaced with the thought of Andy: yet another case of bad judgement on her part.

'Why?' Dee asked.

She pushed the thoughts of Andy and the Hungerford case away and said, 'It would be good to get an account of your relationship with Richard on record, and if you were willing, I would like to take a DNA sample and some finger-prints,' she said.

'Of course,' Dee said without hesitation. 'When do you want me to come in?'

'Any day this week is fine,' Jane said. 'If you come in to Lewisham Station on the high street and ask for me, DS Jane Bennett, one of my officers will come down and sort out the interview and sample. OK?'

'Yes. And, Detective Bennett . . .'

'Yes, Dee?'

'Thank you,' he said. 'If you hadn't called, I would never have known. Rich would have never replied to my emails and I would have just thought . . . well, I'd have assumed that he'd gone off me. I have been thinking that. So thank you. It probably sounds bad, but not knowing would be worse, you know?'

'I know what you mean,' Jane said. She said her goodbyes and hung up the phone. She felt like she had just been given an insight into Richard Taylor's life. A real insight – not some analysis of data or message he had sent or received. It was obvious that Richard had had a profound effect on Dee, despite their never having met in person. Jane would bet that was rare in the world of Internet dating – it was such an anonymous medium that to make a real connection must be nigh-on impossible. She had not achieved anything close to the kind of feelings Dee was talking about.

She pictured Richard Taylor lying on his bed. She looked across the river at people enjoying the sunshine, enjoying their lives.

It was tragic. Taylor's life had ended before it could really begin.

Lockyer picked at some lint on the knee of his trousers, and continued to nod. It was baking outside and he was sitting on a very uncomfortable yellow bucket-style armchair, listening to Frank MacIntyre. There were two windows in the lounge and both were open, but they had been fitted with restriction bars, so neither opened more than a few inches. It was only the fourth floor, but the longer he sat here the more tempted Lockyer felt to throw himself out of a window, so perhaps the bars were there for good reason.

He had been listening with depleting patience for over forty minutes, and so far none of the information gleaned appeared useful. Lockyer would have cut the interview short and escaped back to his air-conditioned car, but Frank was one of only two men Richard Taylor had talked to online that he had gone on to meet in person. Lockyer had been regretting his decision to visit MacIntyre at home from the moment he arrived. The guy had verbal diarrhoea and was in the habit of saying 'like' at the beginning, end and sometimes the middle of every sentence. Lockyer felt as if his eye was beginning to twitch every time the word was repeated. It was an affliction of the young, it seemed. He remembered Megan going through a 'like' phase. It had driven him nuts then, and it was having the same effect now.

'Like, we met up quite a few times,' MacIntyre said, taking a slug from the can of Red Bull he was holding. 'It's hard to know exactly how many, like.' He appeared to be running solely on nervous energy, so Lockyer doubted the energy drink would help. 'I reckon we saw each other every night for a while, like, a lot. You know what I mean?'

Lockyer managed to still his aching brain long enough to answer. 'Yes,' he said. 'You saw a lot of each other.'

'Yeah,' MacIntyre said.

'Over what kind of period?' Lockyer asked. His question was received with a frown. 'How long were you seeing Taylor for?' he said again.

MacIntyre blinked several times before he said, 'What, like, how long each time?'

'No,' Lockyer said, repressing a smile. 'I mean, how long were you seeing each other for? A few weeks? A month?'

'Oh, a few weeks, like, two weeks maybe,' MacIntyre said. 'Yeah, two.'

'But you talked online before that?'

'Sure,' MacIntyre said, as if the answer should have been obvious.

'Are you financially stable, would you say?' Lockyer asked, not sure if the change of tack would help or hinder the interview. MacIntyre seemed to be having trouble staying focused on one topic for more than a minute. He had told Lockyer, at length, that he was in his second year at Goldsmiths Uni studying economics, though how often he went to lectures was anyone's guess. Economics just didn't seem this kid's speed.

'Like, I'm not loaded but I'm not poor, like,' he said, gesturing around the room.

Lockyer looked around him. It was wall-to-wall IKEA. Did MacIntyre think his decor presented an impression of affluence? 'Are you currently receiving any benefits?'

'Err, no,' he said as if Lockyer had insulted him. 'I'm no scrounger, like. My folks help me out with the rent for here, and I work over at the Prince of Wales some nights, like.'

'Right,' Lockyer said, doing some mental maths. 'The reason I ask, Frank, is that when I was checking Richard Taylor's bank records, I noticed that there was a transfer to an F. T. MacIntyre. I was wondering if that might be you?'

MacIntyre blushed. 'I don't know. I guess it could be me.' He looked up at the ceiling. 'Oh yeah,' he added, his eyes widening, 'Rich lent me a few quid for my phone and that.' He seemed pleased with his answer and sat back on the long grey sofa, which looked as uncomfortable as Lockyer's bucket chair.

He sniffed, aware not for the first time of the smell of

marijuana. University, a.k.a. 'the stoner years', he thought. 'For your phone', he repeated. 'Hmm, the transfer was for seven hundred and fifty quid. That's some phone bill, Frank.'

'I wanted . . . a couple of things, like', MacIntyre said, sitting forward again, rocking back and forth a little. Lockyer felt almost cruel. 'I was . . . Rich wanted to . . . '

'Have a think', Lockyer said. 'Take your time. What was Richard Taylor giving you money for?'

Two beads of sweat popped out on MacIntyre's forehead at the edge of his buzz cut. His left leg had started to shake in his skinny jeans. Sweat patches had started to form under the arms of his Calvin Klein T-shirt. His face was going from red to white like a set of flashing Christmas tree lights and he was mumbling to himself whilst biting the skin at the edge of his thumb. 'Seven hundred . . .' he said with a mouthful of skin, 'I don't remember, like, it being that much. I guess, like, it could have been for my leccy bill, or something.'

'You had an electric bill for over seven hundred pounds?' Lockyer said, his tone incredulous.

'Err . . .' MacIntyre was using his hand to try and steady his leg. The result was that the entire left-hand side of his body was now shaking. He was so skinny Lockyer was sure he would shake himself apart at this rate.

'Have you got a copy of that bill, Frank?' Lockyer asked, keeping his expression blank. It was hard not to smile. The poor guy looked like he was about to soil himself. 'I'll need to take a copy for the file.'

'I don't . . . he didn't . . . I don't.'

'OK', Lockyer said. 'No worries. If you don't have the bill

then a bank statement showing the payment to the utility company will be fine.'

'I . . . he . . . I . . .'

'Take a breath, Frank.' Despite himself, Lockyer felt a bit sorry for MacIntyre. He was only a young guy, and if today's reaction was anything to go by, he was unaccustomed to being questioned by the police. Lockyer had the feeling that despite the affected speech and the grunge-chic look, MacIntyre came from money. University wasn't cheap. Neither was renting alone in your second year of uni. Someone was footing the bill for his education, his digs and his IKEA obsession. Pub work didn't pay that well, and Lockyer would swear he kept hearing a posh accent slip through on the occasional word or phrase. 'Would you say you and Richard were dating . . . that you were an item for those weeks?'

MacIntyre was shaking his head. 'No, like, we were more like . . . more like . .' He seemed to be searching for the right words. 'Fuck buddies,' he said at last.

Lockyer put his hand to his face to hide his expression and to stop his eyebrows disappearing into his mop of hair. 'Charming,' he said. 'So, your relationship was mainly sexual, then?'

'That's it, just sex.' MacIntyre cleared his throat. He was pulling at his T-shirt.

Lockyer paused before asking the next question. 'Were you charging Taylor for sex?' He felt bad asking, but it had been his first thought after he had read Taylor and Frank's emails and seen the money transfer.

'No, man. I'm not, like, some rent boy.' MacIntyre sounded affronted.

Lockyer held up his hands by way of an apology. 'Sorry, had to ask,' he said. 'Did you and Taylor ever meet up at his place?'

'Like, once – twice, maybe.'

'OK. Did you ever meet his kids?'

'Didn't know he had kids,' MacIntyre said, getting up and pacing back and forth.

'He's got two, a boy and a girl,' Lockyer said. 'He never mentioned them?'

'Nope,' MacIntyre said. 'Like, we didn't talk about that kinda thing, you know? We didn't really *talk*.'

'I can imagine.' Lockyer looked down at his notepad, which contained very few notes. He wasn't sure what to make of MacIntyre. He couldn't figure out what MacIntyre might need seven hundred and fifty quid for, and he knew the guy was lying about not knowing about Taylor's children. Lockyer had read the transcript of their conversations. Taylor had been up-front about his family, his kids, his life to date as a heterosexual: the lot. He hadn't held anything back. The lying MacIntyre didn't fit with the nervous trustafarian sitting in front of him.

'So the kids weren't at Taylor's flat in Gipsy Hill?' he asked. 'Not on the times you visited?'

'Nah, nah. I only went in a couple of times for—'

'Thanks, you can skip the details,' Lockyer said. 'Did you ever stay the night?'

'No, never,' MacIntyre said. 'He was funny about his flat, private, like.'

Lockyer could tell he wasn't going to get any further. The edge of the bucket chair was cutting off the circulation to his legs. 'And the physical side of your relationship lasted for how long?'

'Like I said . . . a couple of weeks, tops.'

'And you stopped seeing him because . . . ?'

'Rich wanted to date.'

'He wanted a relationship with you?' Lockyer asked, hoping his tone didn't sound as surprised as he feared it did.

'No.' MacIntyre shook his head and came back to the sofa, perching on the edge. 'He wanted to have a proper boyfriend, someone like him.'

'Like him?'

'His age, interested in antiques and whatnot . . . smart, basically.' The resignation on MacIntyre's face was difficult to look at. He didn't seem to consider himself very worthy which, despite his annoying 'like' affectation, was a shame. As far as Lockyer could tell, the kid was OK. Not Mensa material, but surely he had a lot more to offer than his body?

'Did Taylor ever talk to you about another guy, about anyone else?' he asked.

'No, no one I can remember, like.'

'Did he ever seem worried, unhappy, anxious at all?'

'Nah,' MacIntyre said, shaking his head and screwing up his face. 'What's he got to be worried about?' Realizing what he had said, he added, 'Well, like, he's dead, so yeah, that's not good, but before that . . . he's got money, got a nice place, got a family.'

'Frank,' Lockyer said, 'would you mind coming over to Lewisham, to the station so we can get this chat on tape . . . take some DNA and fingerprints?'

MacIntyre seemed to think about it for a minute before saying, 'Sure, whatever, like.'

'Great. How are you fixed for tomorrow?' he asked.

'In the day?' MacIntyre asked.

'Preferably,' Lockyer said.

'I'm seeing a uni mate, like, in the morning. I can be with you for eleven?'

'Great,' Lockyer said. 'Come to the main reception and ask for me and we'll get this all wrapped up, OK?'

'Sure,' MacIntyre said, getting up and walking Lockyer to the door.

As they passed in the doorway MacIntyre reached out and touched Lockyer's arm. 'I'm sorry he's dead, like,' he said. 'He was all right. He was nice to me, you know?'

'Yeah, I know.' Lockyer patted him on the shoulder. 'I'll see you tomorrow, Frank.'

When the door closed, Lockyer could hear MacIntyre moving back to the sofa. Within ten seconds he heard the click of a lighter. He didn't begrudge the guy a spliff to ease the tension. After that interview, Lockyer was tempted to knock on the door and join him.

CHAPTER TWENTY-EIGHT

Richard – July

He couldn't wait for this week to end. Eric was taking him away for the weekend. They were booked into a fancy hotel right on the seafront in Brighton. Just the thought of the sea air and the smell of fish and chips made Richard want to cancel his patients and go now. He didn't want to have to wait another two days.

He repositioned the light and tuned out the mumbled conversation his patient was trying to have with him. 'Open a bit wider, please,' he said as he picked up the needle. 'You'll feel a sharp scratch and then a little pressure . . . there, OK?' His patient nodded, although tears had collected in the corners of her eyes. 'Mandy,' he said to his assistant. She leaned forward and dabbed the tears away with a tissue. 'Won't be long before that takes effect,' he said, sitting back and staring out of the window. He usually liked the small talk, the short-lived banter and exchange of gossip he had with each patient, but today he just couldn't be arsed. He wanted to be in Brighton. He wanted to be with Eric.

His meal out with Harvey had been a success of sorts.

Harvey had apologized. Said he would call Sandra and apologize, but refused to say what the fight was about. When Richard tried to push him he had folded his arms and taken on the sullen, stony face that was becoming all too familiar.

If that was all he had to worry about, then life would be good. No, life would be great – but now Nicola was on his case. She had somehow got wind that he was dating, and she'd hit the roof. The kids must have told her that Adam had looked after them for a couple of evenings. Rookie error, he thought. That was his mistake. Not that he was surprised by his ex-wife's reaction. Given their past history, a bit of histrionics was nothing compared to what he knew she was capable of.

Mind you, if her partners ever saw the content of some of her emails, she would be in a lot of trouble. She wanted him to stop, but how could he? He had a life. He was a good father. It wasn't as if he was doing anything in front of the kids. They were being completely sheltered from the whole thing, much to Eric's chagrin. He so wanted to meet the kids, to become part of the family. Richard wanted that too, more than anything – but the timing had to be right. It was too soon. Things with Harvey were a bit better, but Richard wanted to see real improvement before he risked telling him the truth. Part of him wondered if the kids knew – not consciously, but somewhere deep down.

'Ready?' Mandy asked.

'Sorry, yes.' He smiled down at his patient. 'You'll feel some pressure, but you shouldn't feel any pain, OK?' He picked up the drill and pulled down his glasses. 'OK, here we go.'

The hum of the drill helped to clear his mind, to clear out the unnecessary worries. It was Wednesday. He only had to get through two more days, and then he and Eric would be free. He imagined them walking hand in hand, looking around the antique shops, having afternoon tea at the Grand. If only Nicola could see how happy he was. Maybe then she would lighten up – or rather, maybe then she would let him go. He knew she didn't really want him any more. Those feelings had disappeared years ago, but she couldn't stand the idea of anyone else having him, let alone a guy. It was the ultimate insult, according to her. 'Suction,' he said, sitting up to give Mandy room to work.

He knew Nicola would be a nightmare – but what the hell was wrong with Adam? They had been best friends for as long as Richard could remember. They were more like brothers. When Adam had come out as bisexual, he hadn't cared. Why would he? In hindsight, maybe part of him had recognized himself in Adam, but his head hadn't been ready to face that truth. He applied some pressure. 'Almost done,' he said.

He had told Adam about Eric the previous night. But instead of the gushing support and excitement he had expected, Adam had been cold and disinterested – and, if Richard wasn't mistaken, jealous. 'Give it a few more weeks, Rich mate, and then I'll believe it's something serious,' he had said. 'You thought the last one was something special too, remember?'

Bringing up Frank was cruel. Not Adam's style at all. He knew how bad Richard felt about his time with Frank – he had been beating himself up ever since. To put Eric in the same category was an insult to Richard, but worse, an insult to Eric. What was wrong with people?

Did no one want him to be happy?

CHAPTER TWENTY-NINE

6 August – Wednesday

'What happened to you yesterday?'

Lockyer looked up from his coffee, a bite of danish filling his mouth. He had snuck over to Bella's for breakfast before going into the office. It was one of the few independent coffee shops left in the area – authentic south-east London. He liked not knowing what cakes and pastries they would have in, rather than the identical selection always on display in the bigger chains. He swallowed and smiled. Jane was standing in the doorway, the bell jangling above her head. His hiding place had been rumbled, it seemed. She looked pissed off. She also looked wet. 'Is it raining?' he asked.

'No wonder you're a detective,' she said, her voice thick with sarcasm. She put her hands on her hips.

He clenched his teeth and sucked in a breath. 'Can I get you a coffee?' He motioned to the waitress, who hurried over to his table. It wasn't table service, but Natasha (she had told him to call her Tash) had said she was happy to serve him. 'Tash, can you get my colleague a coffee . . . Americano, Jane?'

'Thanks,' she said to Natasha, not to him.

'So what's got you so riled?' he asked, motioning to the chair opposite. It was moulded red plastic, to complement the red-and-white gingham table cloths – they were plastic too.

Jane blew out a breath. 'I've just got off the phone with Nicola Brown.'

'Social workers paid her and the kids a visit, did they?' he said.

'Yep, and to say she's not happy would be beyond an understatement.' Jane fiddled with the menu, her hair dripping into the sugar. She looked beaten. 'She's making an official complaint against me, and the department, and social services –' she held up her fingers, counting off the items – 'and she's telling anyone who'll listen that Adam Oxenham murdered her ex-husband in a fit of jealousy.'

He nodded his head, but didn't speak.

'Oh, sod off,' she said.

'What did I do?' he asked. Jane shrugged and sat back as Natasha brought over her coffee and gave Lockyer a winning smile. Sweet girl, he thought.

He looked over at Jane. She was seething. He couldn't recall ever seeing her this unhinged. 'Dare I ask what child services said?'

She picked up her cup, her eyebrows rising with it. 'They have, and I quote, "checked both of the minors and confirmed that there is evidence of recent and historical bruising consistent with abuse".'

'What have Harvey and Olive said?' he asked. He had first-hand experience of Harvey's strength. Despite his age, he seemed like a lad who could handle himself – but then, that meant nothing when it came to domestic abuse. Lockyer shook his head, annoyed to be caught out by his own gender stereotyping.

'Still nothing,' she said.

'Any updates on the television appeal?' he asked, deciding a change of subject was a good idea.

'Good response so far.' Jane rocked back and forth in the red plastic chair, cradling her coffee. 'A few calls have come in from people suggesting they heard a shout in the night.'

'The kids heard a shout, didn't they?'

'And the neighbour,' Jane said. 'Olive said she heard a bang, but she could have mistaken a shout for a bang.'

'Taylor calling out when he was attacked?'

'Before the attacker got his face in the pillow . . . I'm guessing,' she said, reaching over to his plate and taking a corner of his danish. 'It's being repeated tonight after the evening news on ITV and the BBC, so we'll see what comes in overnight.'

'And you still don't think Harvey could have hurt his sister?' he asked.

'I honestly don't know any more. The more time passes, the muddier this case becomes.'

Lockyer looked at his watch. 'Look, I've gotta go. I've got a few things to do before a second interview with Frank MacIntyre, one of Taylor's exes. He's coming in at eleven. I wanted you to sit in – have you got time?'

Jane sighed, but nodded. 'Sure,' she said. 'I've got an interview with Eric Tang, Taylor's other ex, in ten minutes. I spoke to him on the phone yesterday. He's been abroad on business, flew back yesterday morning. He'd been calling and calling, but hadn't heard back from Taylor since Wednesday last week . . . the day before the murder. He seemed pretty cut up.'

'I'm guessing he's the one Taylor texted on the Wednesday suggesting a late-night meet-up?'

'That's him,' Jane said. 'He claims they didn't meet up because he had to work, video calls with the US . . . he figured Taylor wasn't replying because he was pissed off with him. His account fits what we know. There's no suggestion Taylor left the flat. He was watching the film with Harvey until midnight at least.'

'Fair enough,' he said. 'Alibi?'

'Not really,' she said. 'He flew out to Stockholm on the morning of the murder at ten-thirty. Sasha's checking his flights and his phone records for the Skype calls.'

'So he's not in the clear,' he said.

'Nope,' Jane said with a shrug of her shoulders, 'but then who is?' He returned her shrug. 'Let me finish my cuppa,' she went on, 'speak to Tang, and then I'll meet you down at the interview rooms just before eleven. OK?'

'Nice one.' Lockyer stood and put a tenner on the table. 'That should cover it.' He raised his hand and said his good-byes to Natasha. She smiled. 'See you back there,' he said, the bell jingling as he left.

Jane wanted to cry. She hadn't come over to Bella's to talk to Lockyer about work. She hung her head and closed her eyes. Her evening with Andy had not gone well. She could feel the tears wanting to come. She sipped her coffee, and tried to push them back.

As soon as she walked into the bar at the Novotel hotel over in Greenwich she had regretted ever replying to Andy's email. He wasn't there, of course. When was he ever on time, or where he said he would be? Never. She should have known.

She had sat up at the trendy teak-stained bar and downed one vodka and tonic, and then another. The alcohol had hit her tired system like a bullet. She had moved to a table so that she could have the reassurance of a chair with arms.

She stirred a heaped spoon of sugar into her coffee. She didn't take sugar, but she needed something to take the bitter taste out of her mouth. The waitress was clearing away Lockyer's cup and plate, looking at Jane – in an attempt to engage her in conversation, it seemed. Jane looked down at the table. She wasn't in the mood for small talk.

Andy had walked into the bar like a film star attending a premier. He was wearing a pair of black jeans and a crisp white shirt, the top two buttons opened at the neck. His dark hair was longer than she remembered, shiny, with not a single hint of grey. His face was tanned, his chin covered in a day or two's stubble. 'Janey,' he had said, approaching the table like a panther on the hunt. She cringed at the memory, clutching her coffee cup a little tighter. Just seeing him had made her flustered. She had pushed back her chair too hard, and banged her hip against the edge of the table. There was an angry bruise there when she checked this morning. He had just smiled and planted a warm kiss against her cheek as if he hadn't noticed her gaffe, while at the same time waving the barman over.

She had forgotten how slick he was. Life, it seemed, was effortless for people like him. He just glided through, untouched by the shit Jane felt buried in. Not that she was bitter, of course. She rubbed her tired eyes and pushed her empty coffee away from her.

'Are you sure I can't get you anything else?'

She looked up as the waitress made another pass of the table. Jane was, after all, the only customer, so it made sense the girl was being attentive. 'I'm fine, thank you,' she said. 'I've got to be getting back.' She slid out of the chair, handing the girl the cash, and headed for the door.

'See you again, detective,' the waitress said.

'You too,' Jane said, stepping out into the rain.

She didn't even bother to run or cover her head. She needed to wash away the memories of last night. More than that. She needed to wash away the scent of him. Two bottles of wine, a hotel room, discarded clothes. It was too clichéd for words. She felt sick to her stomach. 'You're pathetic,' she muttered to herself.

CHAPTER THIRTY

6 August – Wednesday

Eric Tang was tall, his physique toned. He was wearing blue slouch jeans and a plain white T-shirt. His skin was smooth, his forearms the colour of fudge ice cream. His eyelashes were long, his eyes dark. Jane couldn't believe he was in his forties. She would have believed him if he had said he was in his mid to late twenties. He sat back in his chair, feet squarely planted on the floor, hands resting in his lap. The Eric she had spoken to on the phone had been close to hysteria, whereas today's Eric seemed calm and measured. He answered her questions in a clear voice. Most people would be flustered under these circumstances, but not this guy.

'Eric,' she said, 'you were saying that you met Richard in June. Is that correct?'

He nodded, running his thumb along his jawline. 'Yes. We started talking on the first of June and met on the tenth,' he said. 'I only joined the dating site the week before. Rich was one of the first guys I spoke to . . . the only guy I spoke to.'

'Would that be considered quick?' she asked. From what Lockyer had said, Richard had still been seeing MacIntyre at the beginning of June. She wondered if Eric knew, and if he did, how he felt about it.

'I don't know,' Eric said with a shrug. 'It was my first . . . and last time on a dating site. Do you think it's quick?'

'That's not for me to say,' she said, knowing she sounded judgemental. 'What were the arrangements for your first date? Where did you meet? What time?'

He sighed at her question. 'As I said yesterday, we met at my house in Penge late afternoon so we could swing by Borough Market for a wander, and then we headed over to Crystal Palace for a meal at the Tamnag Thai on Westow Hill. Richard must have picked me up at about four. I think – or rather, I know – Rich was surprised we *went* anywhere. He had been thinking our date was more of a . . . hook-up,' he said, reddening, 'but as soon as we met, he knew . . . we both knew there was something there, something more. I'm not a one-night-stand kind of guy . . . never have been.'

'Was Richard?'

Eric reddened further, clenching his fists in his lap. 'He's been murdered, detective,' he said, his voice low. 'I'm not here to listen to a character assassination.'

'Not at all,' she said, holding up her hands. 'I am simply building up a balanced view of Richard's life from everyone who knew him. I'm afraid his sex life comes into that.'

Eric sniffed. 'No,' he said. 'Rich wasn't like that either.'

'So when you started seeing each other, you were . . . exclusive?' she asked. Part of her wanted to back off the subject, but the detective part wanted to push just a little bit further to see how Eric would react. She wasn't disappointed.

He banged the table with his fist. 'I told you. Rich was *not* like that.'

Well, at least that confirmed her suspicions. Richard hadn't told Eric about Frank MacIntyre, or if he had, Eric was not going to admit it. Given what Lockyer had said about the brief relationship, she wasn't surprised. Eric was clean-cut, moral. She somehow doubted that Richard's dalliance with promiscuity would have met with his approval. 'Fine,' she said. 'Let's move on.' He nodded and unclenched his fists, but she could see that he was struggling to control his emotions. 'Do you think it was hard for Richard . . . to come out as homosexual, I mean?'

'Hard?' Eric said, shaking his head. 'That, detective, is an understatement.' He took a deep breath and closed his eyes for a second before refocusing on her. 'I knew who I was when I was still a kid. I came out when I was sixteen. My family and friends were supportive, nurturing. *I* was lucky.'

'And Richard wasn't?'

He scoffed. 'No . . . he wasn't. Can you imagine living a lie for forty years?' he asked.

It sounded like a genuine question, so she decided to answer. 'I understood Richard only came to realize . . . or accept his sexuality fairly recently.'

'What, you don't think he always knew?' He sounded incredulous.

'I don't know, Eric. That's why I'm asking,' she said, keeping her voice level.

He shook his head. 'He was never allowed to be who he was. He met his ex-wife when he was still a kid. They had children because she wanted to . . . because she trapped him.'

214

She was taken aback by the anger in his voice. 'He was a good man, a decent man. He stood by her, stood by his family. He did everything for them – and when he finally slipped, finally let his true self come out in that silly affair, what did she do? She rejected him, threw him out . . . and she's been punishing him ever since.'

'You're referring to—'

'Nicola, of course,' he said, interrupting her. 'She's a real piece of work.'

'Did Richard talk much about his ex-wife?'

'Ha,' he said, 'that's all we talked about.' He hung his head for a moment. 'That's not fair. We talked about Nicola a lot, but only because Rich was at a loss. There was no way she was going to let him come out . . . she would never have allowed him to tell the kids . . .' He stuttered to a stop.

The intimation in his statement was clear. 'Did you ever meet the children, Eric?' Jane asked.

He shook his head, but didn't look at her. 'No. Rich wouldn't allow it.' She could hear pain in his voice. It seemed to sit side by side with his anger. She wondered how much it would take to tip the balance either way. 'He said right from the start that he wanted to keep it quiet, keep them separate until we knew . . . knew how we felt about each other.'

'He sounds like a good father,' she said, and at that second she meant it, but as soon as the words left her lips she thought about the bruising on Harvey and Olive. Could Taylor have been an abusive father? It didn't seem to fit the man Eric was describing, but then, abusers were clever. Her days in child protection had taught her that.

215

She remembered a mother who on the surface seemed sweeter than sweet, desperate to protect her offspring from some external abuser. She smothered her children in kisses and affection whenever Jane was there – and yet the bruises, the welts, the burns kept appearing. If it hadn't been for a neighbour reporting a disturbance in the middle of the night, they might never have known it all came from that same doting mother. They had arrived at the flat to find all three children cowering under the kitchen table while their inebriated mother yelled and screamed at them, a meat tenderizer in her hand. It explained the pattern of some of the bruising, which had so far confounded the entire team. Jane cleared her throat to empty her mind and get back to the interview.

'He always put the kids first, but we both knew he had to sort things out with Nicola . . . before we could move forward, be a real couple,' Eric said. 'She threatened him all the time.'

'Threatened him how?' Jane asked.

'Oh, she was inventive.' His tone was bitter. 'She told him he would get AIDS or hepatitis and die . . . she told him he deserved to die . . . that he was disgusting.' He stopped, panting for breath.

'Go on, Eric; what else?' The threat Harvey had overheard made more sense now.

'She told him that if he kept seeing me – or anyone, for that matter – she would stop him seeing the kids. She would move away, so he could never find them. She would say anything to get him to do what she wanted. It was hard for Rich. He'd been compliant his whole life. To break away was . . . difficult.'

'How did Richard react to his wife's threats?'

'He didn't,' Eric said. 'He just listened. He just let her rant at him. He didn't know what to do, but things were coming to a head.'

'How so?'

'Rich had decided to tell the kids without Nicola's permission. He was going to sit them down and talk to them and explain. He needed to . . . we needed to. What life would we have otherwise?'

Jane wondered if Eric was deluding himself. It sounded so familiar. *I will tell her. Things will change. It's you I want to be with. I'm just waiting for the time to be right.* How many other clandestine relationships followed this pattern? All promises, but no action. Andy had been just the same. She felt sick even at the thought of his name. She cleared her throat again. Richard Taylor had managed to conceal his sexuality for, if Eric was to be believed, most of his life. Surely lying would become second nature to someone like that?

'Did Richard tell you anything else about his relationship with his ex-wife, other than his struggles with the children and his sexuality?'

'Only that he thought she was a hypocrite . . . that she had shagged about with a friend of his.'

'Did he ever tell you the name of the friend?' she asked, writing down the word *affair* followed by Oxenham's name and a question mark. After Sunday's interviews it had been Adam's word against Nicola's, but it sounded like Adam might have been telling the truth about his affair with Nicola.

'No, no, he didn't,' Eric said. 'It winds me up just thinking about it. She got all high and mighty about him having an affair, keeping those kids from him – but then she's doing the same thing all the time.'

'Did Richard seem upset about his ex-wife's infidelity?'

'No,' Eric said without hesitation. 'He didn't want her.'

She looked down at her notes. 'Listen, Eric, I think we're about done for now,' she said. 'Would it be OK if I called you if anything else comes up?' He nodded, but didn't speak. She took the opportunity to make another few notes. Next to Eric's name she put: *angry, frustrated*. Then she wrote: *on the edge – come to a head*? Then she underlined the words *threats*, *Nicola*, *affair* and *friend*. She was about to stop the tape when she remembered something. 'Sorry, Eric. Just one more question. Did Richard have any illnesses . . . take any medications that you know of?'

Eric raised his eyebrows. 'Rich was a fitness freak. He wouldn't take any medication *voluntarily*,' he said, his face flushing. 'I mean, no, not that he told me.'

'Thank you, Eric.' Jane stopped the tape. 'That'll do for today.'

CHAPTER THIRTY-ONE

6 August – Wednesday

Jane took shelter from the rain in the doorway of St Stephen's. She had ten minutes until the interview with Lockyer and MacIntyre was due to start; she didn't have time for this. 'Look, Andy,' she said, trying to keep her voice from shaking. 'Like I said, it was a mistake . . .'

'A mistake?' he said. 'A mistake you made twice.' He was laughing. 'And seemed to enjoy.'

'I wasn't thinking. I was drunk, Andy,' she spat back at him.

'Oh, please, Janey,' he said, his voice silky. 'You were the one who suggested we go up to my room . . . and you were the one who came on to me.' She couldn't disagree with him. She wished the booze had resulted in memory loss, but in truth, she could remember the whole sordid thing. It had been her fault. 'I just wanted to see you,' he said, 'to talk about Peter, but you looked so good, and you seemed so lonely, so sad . . . I just couldn't help myself. You felt so good.'

'Stop,' she said. 'Just stop.'

'Hey, look, I'm sorry you're feeling bad about it, but I'm

not sorry it happened. I didn't expect it, Janey, but I don't regret it.'

She leaned her face against the cool stone of the church, hoping for some kind of divine intervention, or at least a reprieve from the sickness that was overwhelming her. He had a power over her that she would never understand – had never understood. His voice, his face – she felt powerless and weak. She was like an addict, desperate for a fix of his poison. She had asked for this. She may as well have begged him to hurt her. 'I can't . . . I can't see you again,' she stuttered. Silence. 'I just can't, Andy.' She could feel the tears coming. She had let him in again. She had opened herself up to him, and now she was paying the price. She heard him take a deep breath.

'OK,' he said. 'Maybe you need a couple of days to process things – I get that, but I need to see you again. I want to see Peter. I want to be part of his life . . . your life.' Bile filled her cheeks. She was shaking her head. 'He's my son, Jane. I have rights.'

'Rights?' she said, her voice a low rumble. 'You have to be fucking kidding me. You only know his name because I told you. You only know he exists because I told you. You don't have a *right* to anything. Peter is my son, and I won't let you hurt him.' She wanted to add that she wouldn't let him hurt her, either; but of course she had done that herself. 'You are nothing to him. You are nothing to me. Last night was . . . was a mistake. I don't know how I was taken in again by your whiter-than-white smile and your smarmy, perfect-guy shit. You are and have always been the most selfish, cruel man I have ever had the misfortune to meet.' She realized she was shouting. People entering the church were looking at her, putting down their umbrellas whilst exchanging worried glances, but she couldn't stop now. 'You left. I told you I was pregnant and you fucking left . . . went back to your *wife* . . . the wife you told me you were separated from. How many others are there, Andy? How many other wives and girlfriends have you screwed and then screwed over? How many kids are out there who you've fathered and then abandoned?' She took a deep breath.

'You're angry,' he said, as if it had nothing to do with him. 'I wanted to be with you, Janey, you know I did. But the timing wasn't right. What could I do? My wife wanted to reconcile . . . to work on things. I made a vow. Surely you can understand that I had to try?' He made it sound like the most reasonable point in the world.

'And how long did you try for?' she asked, not really needing to know the answer.

He coughed at the other end of the line. 'It was difficult. This whole thing has been difficult.'

'My son is not a *thing*,' she said, fighting to stay in control.

'I couldn't call,' he said in a soft voice. 'I was ashamed.'

Jane was shaking her head. 'For eight years,' she said, 'for *eight* years you couldn't call? You dropped off the face of the earth. I couldn't find you, even with my connections, so the CPS sure as hell couldn't find you. What did you do – change your name, move to another country? Is that how you escape all of your responsibilities? Just run away and hide?'

'It wasn't like that . . .'

'Oh, please, Andy. I've heard it all before.'

'I was no good for you then,' he said in a pleading voice, 'but now . . . now I'm ready.'

'*Now* you're ready?' she yelled. '*Now* you're ready?'

'OK, I'm sorry,' he said. 'I'm sorry. What can I say? I was in the wrong. I am in the wrong, but I'm trying to make up for that now.'

She could feel him wheedling his way in like a parasite burrowing into the flesh of its host. For the briefest second, she allowed herself to believe he was telling the truth, that his words were sincere, but then she shook the mirage away. This was how he operated. He smothered her in apologies and charm, made everything seem so perfect with his oily words, but he had never changed – never kept his word. Peter deserved to have a father; she knew that. But he deserved to have a father who loved him, who would cherish him – not a guy who would break his heart over and over. She pictured Peter's sweet little face. 'No, Andy. No.'

A few beats of silence passed before he answered. 'I'll speak to you again when you've had time to think, Janey. Peter needs his father, and legally, that's me.' He disconnected the call.

She was left staring at her mobile, a cold sweat covering her face. Her hands were shaking. She wandered into the street, the rain soaking her hair. What had she done?

Jane placed both her hands flat on the interview desk to steady her jangling nerves. Lockyer had asked her if anything was the matter before they came in, but she had just shrugged and told him everything was 'fine'. How could she talk to him now? She would have to admit what she had done.

'Ready, Frank?' Lockyer asked.

'Sure thing,' MacIntyre said.

He was nothing like Jane had expected: nothing like Eric. MacIntyre was pale and wafer-thin, but aside from his malnourished appearance Jane noticed that his jeans were branded – ripped, but the kind of rip you paid for – and his T-shirt didn't look like it came from Primark, either. He was a visual conundrum. As she looked at him she thought two things. One: what had attracted Richard to this waif? And two: MacIntyre didn't look strong enough to blow the froth off a cappuccino, let alone sedate and suffocate a grown man. She blew out a breath, ignoring the look that Lockyer gave her. This interview was going to be a waste of time.

'Thanks for coming in, Frank,' Lockyer was saying. 'This is my colleague, Detective Sergeant Jane Bennett. She's running the investigation into Richard Taylor's death.'

'Right, cool,' Frank said, his lips turning down at the edges. 'That's different, like.' He looked from Lockyer to Jane and back again. 'Must be weird having a lady for a boss,' he said to Lockyer. 'Mind you, that *Prime Suspect* copper was a lady, wasn't she? Not the same these days, I guess.'

Jane took a deep breath. 'How true,' she said. She felt Lockyer's shoulders tense next to her. If he started laughing, she might hit him. 'Anyway, Frank, thanks so much for coming in this morning.'

'Not a problem,' Frank said.

'As DI Lockyer explained, this will be a recorded interview, but you are under no obligation to be here and are free to leave at any time. OK?'

'Nice,' he said.

Jane leaned forward and started the recording. She took the opportunity to push her heel into Lockyer's foot. To his credit, he hid his reaction well by shifting in his seat and clearing his throat. 'So, let's get started,' she said. 'I know you spoke with DI Lockyer yesterday about your relationship with Richard Taylor, but there were a couple of points I wanted to follow up on, if that's OK?'

'Sure,' Frank said, folding his arms and sitting back in his chair.

'You told DI Lockyer that you met Richard in person towards the end of May, is that right?'

'Yeah.'

'And where did you meet?' she asked.

Frank looked up at the ceiling, squinting his eyes. 'Curry house in Forest Hill.'

'You live there?' Jane asked.

'Not in the curry house, like,' he said looking confused. 'That's where I met Rich.'

'Sorry, yes,' Jane said, 'I realized that. You live in Forest Hill, though, don't you?'

'Oh yeah, got a place up the hill,' he said. 'It's nice, like.' He was nodding at Lockyer as if waiting for confirmation.

'So you met for a meal, then?' Jane said.

Frank shook his head. 'No, we met outside and then went back to mine.'

'Right, I see,' Jane said. She could hear the judgement in her voice. As if she was any better. 'Did you ever go to Richard's place in Gipsy Hill?'

Frank was nodding. 'Yeah, a couple of times. Nice place.'

'But you didn't stay over,' Lockyer interjected.

'That's right,' he said, smiling at Lockyer.

Jane glanced at Lockyer's pad as she formulated her next question. 'Did Richard tell you much about himself, about his life?'

'A bit,' Frank said.

'Did he tell you he had kids?' she asked, knowing from the transcripts that he had, but also knowing that MacIntyre had denied all knowledge to Lockyer. He opened his mouth, but shut it again. He looked at Lockyer, then turned back to Jane. Whatever he wanted to say, he was having trouble spitting it out.

'Frank, when we spoke yesterday, you said—' Lockyer began.

'I know,' MacIntyre said, cutting Lockyer off mid-sentence. 'Like . . . you have to understand that I was a bit . . . I'm not used to having police in my gaff.' He was folding and unfolding his arms, and rocking in his seat.

'It's all right, Frank,' she said, trying to catch his eye. 'You find out an ex of yours has been murdered. That kind of news would throw anyone, make them nervous . . . maybe make them forget things?' She waited for a few seconds. 'Is there something perhaps you meant to tell DI Lockyer yesterday, and forgot?' she asked. 'Or . . .' She stretched out the word, as if thinking, when in fact she knew just what to ask. It was written on Lockyer's pad. 'Or perhaps since you spoke to DI Lockyer yesterday you've remembered something, realized you'd made a mistake?' She could see by Frank's agitation that he was right on the edge. One more nudge, and he would cave. 'Frank, people lie to us every day. We're the police. We're used to it, aren't we, DI Lockyer?'

Lockyer did an exaggerated nod. 'Happens all the time,' he said.

'We don't hold that against people,' Jane continued. 'It's an automatic reaction. Copper turns up at your door, makes you nervous, you forget your own name, right?' MacIntyre was nodding, his eyes downcast. She tapped the desk to get his attention. When he looked up, she said, 'A fib here and there doesn't matter, Frank. The important thing is to tell the truth when you're in here – when it counts.' She sat back in silence. Lockyer mirrored her body language.

Frank bit his thumb. 'OK, like,' he said. 'I didn't tell you before, I mean I didn't tell you everything yesterday –' he gestured to Lockyer – 'because I didn't want to get into any trouble, like. You know?'

'Of course,' Jane said.

'Right, well,' he said, his words coming out in a rush. 'I borrowed the money.'

'The seven hundred and fifty quid?' Lockyer offered.

'Yeah, yeah. Rich lent it to me so I could get a tattoo . . . '

'That must have been some tattoo,' she said, knowing her own had only cost forty quid.

'I wanted this lion, eagle-type thing here,' MacIntyre said, pointing to his arm, 'but . . . '

'You never got the tattoo,' Jane said.

MacIntyre rubbed his eyebrows. 'No . . . I chickened out,' he said.

'And you never returned the money?' Lockyer asked.

MacIntyre shook his head. 'I know I shoulda done, but, like, it was when we were pretty much finished, so I thought . . . '

'You thought you'd keep it.' Jane finished his thought process for him. He nodded. 'OK,' she said. 'That's not a hanging offence, Frank. What else?'

Frank looked at her, then over at Lockyer. 'I kinda told your man here that I never knew Rich had kids . . . never met them.'

'And that wasn't the case?' she said.

'Not totally, like,' he said, holding up his hands. 'I met the boy.'

'Harvey, Richard's son?' Jane offered.

'He never said his name, but yeah, that's him, yeah,' Frank said. 'Him and his mate didn't, like, *approve* of Rich's lifestyle, I guess. Told me to feck off, said they'd kick my head in, that kinda thing.'

'When and where was this, Frank?' Jane asked, leaning forward.

'I dunno exactly,' he said, 'June maybe. I was just leaving Rich's flat after . . . after, you know . . . '

'Yes, we know,' Jane said.

'. . . Well, the kid and his mate were waiting for me outside. Roughed me up a bit and said if I came back, they'd make me regret it . . . or whatever.'

Jane wrote the name *Ben* on her notepad, and circled it. From the interviews so far it was clear that Harvey and his best mate Ben Nicholls were close, but that they also fought. Ben had been there the day of the barbecue. Harvey had texted Ben to confirm the time he had gone to sleep on that Wednesday night; he had even suggested some of his bruises had come from run-ins with Ben. She circled his name again. 'Can you describe both boys?'

'Err, I can try, like,' MacIntyre said, scratching his head. Jane watched, fascinated by his facial expressions as he dragged his brain on an unwelcome workout. 'But I don't think his mate was a kid – he looked older.'

'Did you get his name?' Lockyer asked. Frank was shaking his head.

'Can you tell me his height, weight, build, what he was wearing?' Jane asked, feeling frustrated.

MacIntyre looked at Lockyer. 'Tall. Blonde, I guess. Big guy. That's all I can remember, honest.' He looked about ready to crawl out of his skin.

Jane sat back and let Frank's words wash over her. Ben Nicholls was blonde, but he wasn't that big – not from the photograph she had seen. She would check again when she got back up to the office. She sighed. If MacIntyre's story was true, then Harvey had lied – or at least withheld the truth – about his father, and his little run-in with MacIntyre. But the thing that was really bugging her was the 'friend'.

'So what do you think?' Lockyer asked, pushing his feet into his trainers without bothering to undo them. They had about an hour before the rain returned with a vengeance, and he had no intention of wasting that time cooped up in the office.

'I think I'm getting a bit pissed off with people lying to me,' she said.

He looked at her. Her cheeks were red, and they hadn't even started running yet. 'Oh, come off it,' he said, in the hope that he might be able to lighten her mood. 'You said yourself people lie to us all the time. And you're right – they do.'

She shook her head and started jogging on the spot.

'I know, but I wish that just once . . . that for one day, I could ask a question and someone would tell me the truth. The whole truth.'

'Ahh,' Lockyer said, pushing her into a run. 'You should know better than that. People only tell the truth, the whole truth and nothing but the truth when they're under oath . . . and even then, they still struggle with the concept. Why are you taking this so personally?' He could see she was about to respond, but then she stopped herself and kept going. He shrugged and kept pace next to her.

She was so up and down at the moment. It was beginning to drive him nuts. He was meant to be the one with the personality problems – barking at everyone in the team for no discernible reason and flying off the handle as and when he pleased. It was one of the perks of being him, of being the boss. Jane was meant to back him up, calm him down, do all the things she used to do; but despite being a lot closer to her now than ever before, he couldn't seem to get her to talk to him or to snap out of it. It wasn't clear whether their runs, which seemed to be becoming a regular thing, were a boss-and-colleague type of thing or 'friend time'. He lengthened his stride and decided to just run. If she wanted to talk, she would. It was exhausting trying to figure out what the 'right' thing to say was. He and Dave had met in the Crown for a drink on Monday night, and between the two of them they had tried to piece together their limited knowledge of women in order to come up with a solution. Six pints each, and they came up with squat.

'You still happy to re-interview Oxenham tomorrow at his place?' she asked as they turned onto Gilmore Road.

'Sure,' he said, taking a deep breath to push away the stitch that was taking hold in his left side as he jumped to avoid a strip of grass and a pile of dog shit. The pavements themselves were dry, but the rest of the ground was sodden from the deluge. He noticed that Jane had increased her speed, pumping her arms, so he adjusted his stride to stay level with her. A car sped past them, doing well over the speed limit. Lockyer started to memorize the number plate, but then stopped. The road was quiet.

'I'm going to need to bring Harvey in again,' Jane said, turning her head away from him. 'Get his side of the story on MacIntyre and find out who this mysterious friend is.'

'I guess,' he said. 'You think it's Nicholls?'

'That would make sense, yes,' she said, puffing out a breath.

'Who interviewed him?' he asked.

'Cathy the CPO . . . and Aaron.'

'Aaron's in. I spoke to him earlier,' he said, remembering again how jumpy the kid was – but then, that was nothing new these days. 'You can check with him when we get back.'

'Thanks,' she said speeding up again. 'I'm aware of that.'

'Jeez, what's got you all psycho?' he asked, unable to stop himself.

'I'm not being psycho,' she said, looking at him over her shoulder.

'Really? You could have fooled me.' Lockyer stopped, and waited for her to do the same and walk back to where he was standing. 'What is going on, Jane?' She was shaking her head, staring at the pavement between them. 'Is it the case?' She shook her head. 'Your dad?' he tried. Again she shook her head. 'Your mother . . . Peter . . . what?'

'I . . . I've done something stupid,' she said. He was alarmed to see a tear drop onto her cheek.

'What?' he said.

'It's Peter's dad,' she said. Another tear rolled down her face.

Lockyer racked his brains for his limited knowledge of Jane's personal life. Peter's father had left when Jane was three months pregnant. He had not been heard from since. Lockyer mined his memory for more information, but nothing surfaced. 'Go on,' he said.

'He got back in touch, said he wanted to see Peter . . . see me,' she said, kicking at a weed with the toe of her trainer.

'Right,' he said, stretching out the word.

'I *saw* him,' she said, looking up at him.

Lockyer recognized the expression of guilt and shame on her face. 'Ahh,' he said. 'And I'm guessing that wasn't a good idea?'

She was shaking her head again. 'He's bad news for me, for Peter . . . he's a nightmare . . . I don't know why I ever agreed to meet him, why I ever thought . . .' She drifted into silence.

He clasped his hands together, searching for the right words. It was quite amazing how shit at this he was. 'Look,' he said, reaching forward and taking her hand, feeling embarrassed by the gesture but now unable to withdraw. 'Everyone makes mistakes. Just don't make it again . . . if it's not what you want.'

'It's not what I want,' she said.

'Then put it out of your mind,' he said, brightening his voice. 'You did it. You feel bad. Let it go. No point punishing yourself. You've done nothing wrong.' He stopped speaking when he had run out of platitudes. He wished Megan was here, so he could ask her for help. His daughter would know just what to say.

'He's texted me,' she said. 'He's talking about lawyers – saying he'll fight for joint custody.'

It was Lockyer's turn to shake his head. 'Bollocks. That is not going to happen,' he said. 'This guy's been absent for, what, seven years?'

'Eight.'

'Has he ever paid child support? Or seen Pete since he was born?'

'No.'

'Then he's pissing in the wind,' Lockyer said, triumphant. 'Leave it with me.'

'Mike, no, I didn't mean to get you involved—'

'Tough shit,' he said, giving her what he hoped was a reassuring shove. 'I will do some digging . . . on the quiet,' he added, when he saw her eyebrows disappear beneath her fringe. 'I will find out this scum's situation, and if he comes for you, we will be ready. OK?' She opened and closed her mouth. 'Good,' he said. 'That's settled, then.' He cracked his neck and pulled her next to him so they were standing side by side. 'Now, we're going to finish our run, and then you are going to sod off for a couple of hours and get some rest. Got it?'

He didn't think she was going to respond, but then she said, 'Yes, sir,' as she broke into a run. He fell into step next to her, chancing quick glances at her face, but her expression was unreadable. He felt a familiar well of anger stir in his gut. This guy had nothing but bad things coming if he messed with Jane again. Lockyer would make sure of that.

CHAPTER THIRTY-TWO

7 August – Thursday

Jane turned the jar upside down and let the last of the honey dribble into the steaming mug of hot water. She swallowed, wincing at the sensation. It was like trying to swallow a Ferrero Rocher whole. She stirred her drink and took a sip, grateful for the heat that numbed her throat for a second. She had stopped taking her painkillers. They were affecting her judgement – or at least that was how she was justifying it. She needed to blame something; the booze wasn't enough.

'Jane?'

She heard her father moving around in the lounge. 'I'm coming, Dad,' she called back, flicking on the kettle to make her father the cup of tea she had forgotten about. She had been checking her phone every couple of seconds to see if Lockyer had replied. He had told her to take time for herself yesterday. She would have done as he asked, but there hadn't been any time. She took the teabags down from the cupboard and went to the fridge for the milk.

The team had needed briefing, and she had to get up to

speed with where everyone was in relation to the investigation and all the interviews. There was nothing groundbreaking, other than a thirty-minute time lag between the children finding Taylor's body and the logged call with 999. That needed to be clarified. The calls about a shout in the night were still coming in to the action line, so she had dropped an email to Dave to ask his opinion and find out where he was with the results on the fragments of tablets and the bloods he'd sent up to Reading.

The kettle clicked off and she poured the boiling water into her father's mug, topping up her own at the same time. She had arranged everyone's schedules for today. Everyone knew what they were doing, but she still felt bad about taking the morning off. She looked at her phone again. A message flashed in her inbox. She snatched up the phone and clicked into the email. There was no hello or greeting, just two lines of text.

Jane, it would have been helpful and perhaps more prudent to have sorted out the timesheet yesterday but hey, not to worry, I'll hold down the fort. I will supervise the morning briefing as per your notes. See you later.

It had been poor form on her part to turn her nose up at time off only to take it the next day, on her terms, but she hoped he understood. She reached up and held her throat for a few seconds before tapping a message back.

Much appreciated. Thank you. I'll be in by midday, latest. I'll keep my phone with me.

She pressed send, picked up the two drinks and walked down the hallway to the lounge. She stood in the doorway for a moment and watched her father as he shuffled from the television to his chair, clutching the remote control in his hand. He had a habit of forgetting he had it with him. She sighed, tried to shake off the pain taking hold of her heart, and went into the room. 'Here you go,' she said, putting his tea on the little table next to his easy chair. He had never been allowed an easy chair before; Celia Bennett had forbidden anything of the sort in her house. They were for old people's homes and daytime television adverts. But things had changed. Jane stroked the back of her father's hand as he sat down. He looked up at her and smiled. He was still in there, the father she knew and had always adored, but there was no doubt that John Bennett was a shadow of his former self. Jane had heard the expression throughout her life, but until now she had never really understood what it meant. Her father had lost a significant amount of weight, it seemed, overnight. It was as if some phantom had snuck into his room, shrouded by darkness, and sucked out the very essence of the man Jane knew. He moved with a laboured pace, careful or perhaps nervous about where he placed his feet. It was as if the fear of another stoke was crippling him. It didn't help that the weight loss made his eyes look sunken, the lids drawn back from his eyeballs so he looked frightened or shocked all the time.

Jane felt the tears wanting to come. She swallowed them back, this time relishing the pain in her throat, needing it to keep her grounded, to stop her thinking.

'Nice to have you here, honey,' her father said. His speech

was fine; Jane kept telling herself that, but she couldn't help listening out for a slur.

Jane smiled. 'Glad to be here, Dad. It's been a tough couple of weeks.'

'Work or home?' he asked.

'Both,' she said, but then shook her head. She wasn't going to tell her father about her run-in with Andy; that might kill him. And she couldn't handle another discussion about the move. Her mother had been trying to encourage, or perhaps torture, her with property details of places they were 'considering' near Bristol. 'No, no,' she said, 'it's work really. I'm just not myself at the moment.'

'Did you really expect to be?' he asked.

The simplicity of his question silenced her for a moment. She stared out the window at the sunshine. Who would have thought that sunshine in August would feel like a novelty? At least it was shining on her morning off. She didn't care if it rained later. 'They'll be having a good time,' she said, deciding to change the subject. 'I bet the beach will be quiet. We were forecast more rain.'

'Mmm, I expect so,' he said, before picking up his mug. Jane looked away, unable to bear the tremor in his hand. 'Peter will be getting your mother to do just what he wants, and your mother will be protesting but loving every minute of it.' He smiled at her.

She laughed. 'How true. I wonder how many ice creams he'll manage to wangle out of her.'

'Well, as it happens, your mother had a plan to deal with such requests,' he said in a conspiratorial voice.

'You've got to be kidding me,' Jane said, amazed, as she

so often was, by her mother's unpredictable and yet predict-able behaviour.

'Not a bit,' he said blowing on his tea and then taking a long drink. He made an appreciative sound and nodded at her. 'Good cuppa.'

She smiled. She wanted to cry at the normality of it all, but managed to hold herself together. 'So? How is she plan-ning to divert Peter from multiple ice creams?'

Her father looked confused for a moment, but before she could prompt him his face cleared and he said, 'She's going to tell him that the man in the ice-cream van picks his nose.'

Jane burst out laughing, surprising herself as much as her father, who jumped at her reaction but then threw his head back and joined her. She belly-laughed for what felt like ages before she managed to calm herself down. 'Oh,' she said, coughing and laughing. 'She is something else . . . she's really something else.'

'Well,' her father said, chuckling, 'you know how Peter is about food hygiene. He's obsessed with our dishwasher. If your mother or I touch his dinner plate or, God forbid, accidentally put a finger in his water glass, he goes nuts, won't touch it. Your mother figured, why not use some of his . . . idiosyncrasies to her advantage.'

'Well, good luck to her,' Jane said, giving her dad a warm smile. He picked up the remote and turned on the television. '*This Morning*?' he asked. 'They've got a piece on the South Bank that I wanted to see.'

'If we must,' she said, flopping back on the sofa. According to her father, the South Bank was the jewel in south-east London's crown.

'Come on, Jane,' he said. 'It's got everything. The London Eye, the Tate, the OXO tower, the Imperial War Museum . . . the National Theatre, and now we've got the Shard looking over everything. It's something for this borough to be very proud of.' He returned his eyes to the screen. 'I should record it, really. Your mother will be sorry to miss it.' Jane doubted that would be the case, as Celia Bennett didn't share her husband's obsession with all things south-east London, but she didn't argue. She also decided not to point out that the South Bank might indeed represent the best of south-east London, but it didn't do a great deal to represent the fifty-four thousand low income homes or the two thousand reported crimes a month. The division of wealth was extreme, but she guessed her father didn't need or want to hear about that right now.

Instead she thought about her mother, negotiating ice-cream terms with Peter. She couldn't help laughing. She didn't know who to feel more sorry for: her mother or Peter. If her mother thought she could outsmart Peter, she would be very disappointed. Jane had been trying to get the upper hand for eight years and had failed. If Peter wanted something, even as a baby, he had a way of getting it. She settled herself into the sofa and tucked her legs up under her.

One of Jane's favourite memories, exemplifying both Peter's intelligence and his determination, was a trip they had taken to a friend's house in Margate. On the way there Jane had explained to Peter that it wasn't polite to ask people to give him biscuits, which he did, wherever they went. He seemed to associate all strangers with biscuits. So, in the car, when

Jane had told him it was rude to ask for biscuits, he had been confused but agreed to 'be a good boy' and do as she asked.

All went well. They arrived and managed to get in to Becca's house, coats off, no dramas. There were a few dicey moments when Becca was making them a coffee but Peter, to his credit, hadn't said a word. Then, about ten minutes into the visit, he asked Becca if she had any nice tins. Of course she said she did. When she produced them, Peter had admired the tins for some time before saying, 'Do you keep anything in your tins?' When Becca removed the lids to reveal biscuits, Peter had not flinched. He had just looked at the contents without interest. But when Becca said, 'Would you like a biscuit?' he had beamed. Jane could still see his face now. He had looked at her, said 'thank you' to Becca, and then taken a fistful of biscuits. Jane smiled. Now *that* was clever. Celia Bennett didn't stand a chance.

Her phone buzzed in her pocket. She had turned it to vibrate so as not to disturb her father. She pushed herself up from the sofa and went into the hallway, closing the door to the lounge. She pressed the answer button on the phone. 'Bennett,' she said.

'Hi, boss, it's me,' Penny said. 'Sorry to bother you. I just wanted to check a few things with you . . . if that's OK?'

'Of course, don't be daft.' Jane sat down on the stairs.

'I've booked Harvey in for re-interview at Caterham at three o'clock. Is that OK?'

'Perfect,' she said, nodding. 'Either DI Lockyer or myself will sit in for that one. Is Cathy good to attend?'

'Yes, she'll be there, and I've confirmed with Marie, too,'

Penny said. There was a brief pause before she went on, 'I thought DI Lockyer was with Oxenham this afternoon?'

'He's heading there mid-morning,' she said, ignoring the tone in Penny's question. Lockyer had held his tongue with her about her impromptu morning off, but she would guess he had been a bit more vocal in the office.

'OK, great,' Penny said.

'Anything else?' she asked, running her hands over her mother's perfect stair carpet. It was deep and soft, and not a thread was out of place. Celia Bennett hoovered it in definite lines every other day. It showed.

'Umm, yes; Aaron said he'll speak to comms re the thirty-minute delay on the 999 call, see if it's a system error or the kids' memories giving us the time lag.'

'I'd lay bets on it being the kids,' Jane said. 'Remembering the exact time you found your father dead in his room would tax anyone's memory.'

'I can only imagine,' Penny said. 'I saw the little girl yesterday when I was over there sorting the follow-up video interview for Harvey. She was in a bad way.'

'Really?' Jane asked. 'Anne didn't mention anything in yesterday's briefing.'

'I know. I was a bit surprised by that,' Penny said.

'Is it the regression?'

'Maybe,' Penny said. 'I think it's that, and . . . '

'And?' Jane prompted.

'All the questions from the social workers about the bruises, about the burn. I think that's thrown her.'

'I would imagine,' she said, 'but until the kids tell us what's going on, I'm afraid the questions are going to have to continue.' Penny didn't respond. In fact, the pause was so long that Jane found herself looking at the screen to check they were still connected. 'You there?'

'Sorry, yes,' Penny said. 'She's had a few accidents.'

'Who has?'

'Olive, she's . . . wet the bed once or twice, according to her mother.'

Jane was always impressed by Penny's sensitivity and discretion. Not many coppers would bother about saving the blushes of a twelve-year-old; but then, she reminded herself, Penny wasn't your average DC. She sighed. 'It's happened before,' she said, 'when her parents first split up. It's a reaction to the stress. It happens with some kids, Pen.'

'I guess,' she said. 'Anyway, that's everything for now.'

'Good,' Jane said, 'and thanks, Pen. I'm glad you told me. I'll be in later, OK?'

'Sure, see you then.'

Jane ended the call and leaned back against the banister. She thought about the long-term damage abuse and trauma could cause a child. She thought about Olive, about her bed-wetting, and then she thought about Peter. Andy wasn't a hitter but he was an emotional abuser, of that she was in no doubt. Olive and Harvey had not been protected from their abuser, whoever that was, but there was no way Jane was going to let an abuser into Peter's life. Not today. Not ever.

Lockyer was sitting in Adam Oxenham's lounge, which appeared, like the man, to be all about size. The coffee table was made out of railway sleepers. The sofa was a black leather corner thing that took up more than half the room, with an accompanying easy chair that Lockyer was sitting in, and the television, also massive, was mounted on one wall. He looked out the window as a bunch of teenagers walked past. They were shouting and laughing, pushing each other into the road.

'Sugar?' Adam called from the kitchen.

'No, thanks,' he called back, 'just milk.' He heard the sound of the fridge door closing before the door to the lounge opened and Adam walked in carrying two mugs of steaming coffee.

'Here you are,' Adam said, handing one of the mugs to Lockyer and walking over to the sofa. 'Sorry for the wait . . . my kettle's buggered.' He shook his head. 'Paid an arm and a leg for it . . . so much for the price tag, eh?'

'Sure,' Lockyer said, unable to get excited or involved in a conversation about kettles.

'So what can I do for you?' Adam asked. 'I appreciate you coming here. I've got a session with my trainer in an hour. There's no way I'd have made it over to Lewisham and back.'

'Not a problem.' Lockyer took a sip of his coffee. It didn't taste like the freeze-dried stuff he had at home.

'I know,' Adam said, as if reading his thoughts. 'It's the new barista-style stuff you can get. It costs a fair bit, but it tastes like a coffee you'd get in Starbucks or whatever, doesn't it?'

He nodded, taking another sip. 'It's good.'

Adam smiled, but then his face fell. 'I figured I'd be seeing you again,' he said.

'Really?' Lockyer said. 'What made you think that?'

242

'I knew Nicola would give you the run-around. I hate to think what she's told you about Rich . . . or me, for that matter.' He waited, looking at Lockyer as if he expected him to fill him in on what Richard's ex-wife had had to say. He would be waiting a long time.

'Right,' Lockyer said, shifting to one side to avoid the ray of sunlight that was blinding him.

'I still can't believe he's gone.' Adam was shaking his head. 'It just feels surreal, you know?'

'Yes,' Lockyer said, 'I know what you mean.' It wasn't until the platitude was out of his mouth that he realized it was true. He knew, all too well, that feeling of being in an altered universe where things just didn't make sense. It wasn't that he couldn't come to terms with the loss of her. It was more that this life, the one he was living now, was new, separate somehow. It was as if time had stopped when it happened, and then a new tangent of existence had begun. She would never exist in this time, in the world he now inhabited. He blinked, and realized Adam was staring at him. 'So, if I could ask you a few follow-up questions . . . that would be great.'

'Of course,' Adam said, 'whatever I can do.'

Lockyer resisted the urge to look at his watch. He was meeting Megan for lunch, and after he had let her down the other day, he didn't want to be late. 'Were you aware of any illnesses or medications that Richard might have been taking?'

'Sure,' he said. 'Rich was a diabetic, not that he'd admit it. He didn't take his meds – he could be stubborn sometimes.'

'But he had prescribed medication?'

'Yes.'

'Do you know where he kept his meds?'

Adam paused, his eyes flitting to the floor and then the ceiling. 'God knows,' he said. 'Somewhere in the flat, I'd imagine . . . the bathroom? I don't know. Is that what you wanted to ask me? Why are you asking me that?'

'Just asking,' Lockyer said. 'Nothing to worry about. Let me see,' he said, taking out his notepad and tapping his teeth with his pen. 'What else was there, what else . . . ? Ahh, yes. I wanted to ask you a few questions about Richard's relationships, if I could?'

'OK,' Adam said, his tone wary.

'During the course of the investigation, we have spoken to a number of individuals who knew Richard, a couple of whom I guess you could describe as . . . boyfriends,' he said.

'Right.' Adam's face was blank.

'You were reluctant, when we talked before, to tell us about Richard's sexuality,' Lockyer said. 'Any reason?'

'Not my secret to blab,' Adam retorted.

'Fair enough. Did Richard ever talk to you about his relationships once his marriage ended?'

'Not really, no,' Adam said, taking a sip of his coffee. 'I mean, we talked about it a lot when Rich finally told me he was gay, but I tried to leave him to it, and once he started doing stuff for himself . . . online, I mean, I pretty much backed off.'

'Why's that?'

'Just because,' Adam said. 'He needed to find his feet, figure out what he wanted.'

'Richard knew you were bisexual?'

'Of course,' he said. 'He was always great about it . . . well, obviously I guess it makes sense that he was, but back then, when I first came out, we were just kids. He didn't judge me. He wasn't that type of guy, you know?'

'I see,' Lockyer said. 'Did you ever want to be more than friends?' Adam frowned, but didn't speak.

'You knew each other a long time,' Lockyer said. 'You were best friends.'

'She told you I fancied him, didn't she?' Adam's face was pulled into a scowl.

'Who?'

'You know who,' Adam said, with a wave of his hand. 'I told you: she lies.'

'So you were never attracted to Richard?'

Adam hesitated. 'No.'

'OK,' Lockyer said, holding up his hands, 'just asking.'

'Yeah, right.' Adam's tone was sarcastic. He shifted his position and stared out of the window.

'Did Richard ever express an interest in you?'

Adam looked down at his coffee cup. 'Nah. I wasn't his type, you know?'

Lockyer nodded, though in truth he had no idea what Adam meant. 'OK, let's move on,' he said, watching as Adam clenched and unclenched his jaw. It occurred to him that pissing this guy off might not be such a good idea. Under normal circumstances Lockyer would consider himself more than capable of handling an aggressive or violent witness, but in Adam's case, he needed to rethink things. The guy could knock him on his arse if he felt so inclined. 'So did Richard ever tell you about the guys he was talking to online?' he asked, leaning forward and putting his mug down on the oversized coffee table.

Adam seemed to think about the question, taking a long, deliberate sip of his drink before turning back to Lockyer. 'Sometimes,' he said. He had started to shift in his seat. 'Some of the guys talked about sex, but Rich didn't like that. He had some fun with it, don't get me wrong, but it wasn't him, you know?' Lockyer nodded but didn't speak, in an attempt to force Adam to fill the silence. 'There was a guy over in Penge, and one Peckham way, I think, but he didn't tell me much more than that.' He sighed. 'Anyway, there were a few he talked to about feelings and whatnot, but they ended up coming to nothing. Rich was a bit naive. He would get really excited thinking he had found someone special, but then the messages would just stop. That's just how it is. You can't take it personally, but Rich did. He took it as a rejection.' Adam shrugged. 'I tried to warn him, to steer him in the right direction, but like I said, he could be stubborn when he wanted to be – wouldn't be told what to do – ever since we were kids. It was his way, or no way.'

The comment struck Lockyer. It was the second time Adam had mentioned Taylor's stubbornness. Nicola Brown had said her husband was weak. From what Jane had said, Eric Tang had said pretty much the same, though in much kinder terms. Even Frank's account made Taylor sound like someone who put others first. Lockyer began to wonder if the impression they had of Taylor was entirely accurate. He thought about the bruising and the alleged abuse. His jaw hardened. A bully wasn't strong – a bully was weak, but people were still drawn to them. Something occurred to Lockyer. 'Did you ever meet any of Richard's . . . dates?' he asked.

'No,' Adam said, folding his arms, his muscles bulging beneath his T-shirt.

'Never?'

'No.'

Lockyer turned his mouth down at the edges and cocked his head on one side. 'You've been to Richard's flat on Gipsy Hill?'

'Sure, loads of times.'

'Spend a lot of time with the kids?'

'A fair bit, why?' Adam asked, his knuckles white around his mug. 'I'm Harvey's godfather.'

'Nice,' Lockyer said. 'Ever spend time with them alone?'

There was a noticeable pause before Adam replied. 'Once or twice. Sometimes Richard's regular babysitter would get sick or whatever, and I'd watch the kids.'

Lockyer was nodding. 'Sure, sure. Ever spend time with them outside the flat?'

Adam looked confused. Whether it was genuine or not remained to be seen. 'Me and Harvey watched the footy sometimes . . . I'd take him to local games, you know?'

'Who do you support?'

'Crystal Palace. Tickets cost a fortune, but the friendlies aren't too bad.'

'So you and Harvey . . . you get on?'

'Course,' Adam said. 'He's a good kid.'

'Does he ever confide in you?' Lockyer asked.

'What do you mean?'

'Well, being a teenager isn't easy,' he said. 'Talking to a *friend*, rather than your dad, would be easier . . . you know.' Adam opened his mouth, but didn't speak. 'Did Harvey know his dad was gay?'

Adam's face froze. 'How would he?'

Lockyer looked at his watch. He didn't have time to dick around. He was meeting Megan in twenty minutes. 'It has been alleged that an individual, possibly Harvey, threatened one of Richard's *dates*.' Adam reverted to opening and closing his mouth. 'According to the witness, Harvey wasn't alone.' As soon as he finished speaking, he knew he was on the right track. Adam had paled.

'All right,' he said, holding up his hands, his coffee mug swinging on his thumb. 'All right, yes, Harvey knew about his dad. He was shocked, upset or whatever. He knew his dad was seeing someone. He wasn't happy about it, so he asked for my help. He figured if he warned the guy off then that would be the end of it. He just wanted to make it stop. I didn't see the harm. We didn't hurt the guy.'

'Right,' Lockyer said. 'And this was when?'

Adam shook his head. 'I don't know.' He looked down at the floor. 'July, maybe.'

Lockyer sat back, schooling his expression. Frank claimed the threat had happened in June. He wouldn't be surprised if Frank had his dates wrong, but the fact remained that Richard was no longer seeing Frank in July – hadn't been seeing him for over a month. However, he *was* seeing Eric. Lockyer had the feeling he had just unearthed someone else's lie. There appeared to be an epidemic when it came to this case. He rubbed his eyes. Jane was not going to be happy.

CHAPTER THIRTY-THREE

Richard – July

Richard picked up two bags of barbecue briquettes and threw them into the trolley. He debated paper plates, but a quick glance at his daughter made him change his mind. Even the sight of non-recyclable material could send her into an hour-long lecture on greenhouse gases and global warming. When he was twelve, he had been stealing cigarettes from his father to smoke with his friends.

'Can we have prawns, Dad?' Olive asked, one hand resting on the trolley.

'Sure,' he said, picking up a tray of ready-made kebabs. 'Harvey, can you grab some chicken?'

'A whole one?'

Richard smiled. 'If you're very hungry, sure. If not, then just a few chicken breasts will be fine.'

'Whatever,' Harvey said.

'Sarcasm is the lowest form of wit,' Olive said, leaning into the trolley and lifting her feet off the floor. 'That's what Mum says.'

'And she's right.' Richard poked his daughter in the ribs. 'Right, what else do we need?'

'Salad?' Olive offered.

'Burgers,' Harvey said, 'sausages and steak.'

'That should just about cover every member of the meat family, plus deal with our five a day. Go for it.' He watched his children wander off to get their preferred items. Olive smiled back at him. Harvey, by contrast, was sullen and agitated. He was at a loss.

He thought about Eric and felt his mood soften. He was flying to Stockholm in the morning on business. Richard was desperate to see him before he left, but with the kids staying over, he couldn't. He took his mobile out of his pocket and tapped out a message.

If I can get the kids into bed early do you fancy a late-night rendezvous? I can sneak out!! x

He went to put his phone back in his shorts pocket when it started ringing. He grinned and pushed answer. 'Yeees,' he said.

'Just got your message,' Eric said.

'I'll see how it goes, but . . . '

'I can't, Rich,' Eric said. 'As much as I'd love to see you, I'm not done packing, I've got a ton of work to do and I've got two Skype calls with the US at God knows what time.' There was a pause. 'Can you wait six days?'

Richard resisted the urge to sulk. 'I suppose,' he said.

'Look, I've gotta go, I'm just heading into a meeting about networking issues in New York. Love you.'

'Love you too,' he said, but Eric had already hung up.

He thought about Harvey. Maybe another male role model would do him some good. Eric was an IT director and a self-confessed geek. That should appeal to Harvey's technical side; and Eric was also football mad. Harvey loved it when Adam took him to a game, but that happened rarely. With Eric it could become a regular thing, a way for them to bond.

He found himself imagining today's shopping trip, but with Eric by his side. He smiled at the image, but then remembered his argument with Adam the night before. Adam's feelings had been clear. He thought the whole relationship was 'clichéd' and 'a fantasy of Richard's own making'. 'You think Nicola is gonna let you stroll around town hand in hand with your new boyfriend with the kids in tow?' Adam had said. 'You need to get real.'

Richard sighed. If he didn't know any better, he would say Adam was jealous; but jealous of what? He had been openly bisexual since his teens. He dated whoever he wanted. He was never short of offers. His family accepted him for who he was. He had everything. So why was he so mad at Richard? Why did he begrudge him happiness?

'Got the meat,' Harvey said, throwing the packets into the trolley with a thud.

'Great,' Richard said, his voice a monotone. Olive appeared with two bags of salad and a cucumber. She placed everything in the trolley, where it wouldn't get crushed.

'Now what?' Olive was hopping from one foot to the other like a jogger maintaining her heart rate. At least she was enjoying herself.

'We need buns, lighter fluid and ketchup,' he said. 'Harv,

you get the ketchup. Olive, you get some buns and I'll go and get the lighter fluid . . . last one to the till pays.' Olive dashed off, still young enough to enjoy the competition. Harvey just rolled his eyes and walked off, dragging his feet. 'Would a smile kill you?' Richard called after him.

He made his way to the household goods aisle. He was becoming more depressed by the minute. Was Adam right? Would he ever get to live his life the way he wanted? He gave the trolley a hard shove before yanking it back to him. Not if Nicola or Adam had their way. He shook his head. Eric made him happy, and vice versa. He had been a good friend; a good husband, up to a point; and he had been a devoted father. It was his time now. The kids weren't babies any more. If they couldn't handle his choices, then he was prepared to suffer the consequences. They would come around. It would just take time.

He wouldn't change his mind. The decision had been made.

Even the thought sent a shiver down his spine. He picked up the lighter fluid and chucked it in the trolley, defiant. He no longer cared what anyone thought. For the first time in his life, he knew what he wanted. He knew who he wanted, and it was Eric. He had fallen into marriage, nervous and unsure. He had stumbled into fatherhood. Eric had been a breath of fresh air, blowing through his life, clearing away all his cobwebs of self-doubt.

He wasn't scared. He wasn't unsure.

He was going to ask Eric to marry him.

And no one was going to ruin this for him.

CHAPTER THIRTY-FOUR

7 August – Thursday

Lockyer shifted in his chair in the tech room before re-focusing on the three television screens. The wide shot showed Harvey sitting on one sofa, a glass of water in his hand, with Cathy the CPO and Marie the social worker sitting opposite. Harvey looked a lot younger than the last time Lockyer had seen him. 'Jeez,' he said in a hushed voice. 'He looks like shit.'

'Doesn't look like the same kid, does it?' Bill, the tech guy, said.

'You're telling me,' Lockyer said. The ten-minute break from the video interview had done nothing to revive the kid. He looked pale and listless.

A light flashed on the wall in the other room, behind Harvey's head. 'They're ready to continue,' Bill said. Lockyer sat back, ignoring the cramp in his calf. He hated this room.

'Harvey,' Cathy said, crossing her legs, sitting back and resting a clipboard on her knee. 'I only have a few more questions I need to ask, to clear up a few things. OK?' The first part of the interview had only lasted ten minutes, but Harvey had seemed to shrink with each question. His bravado, his anger, his whole being had been replaced with the demeanour of a small boy who looked frightened to breathe. He nodded now, and muttered under his breath. The sky had clouded over, throwing gloom over the video suite. 'Harvey?' Cathy said again.

Harvey looked up. 'I'm fine.'

'OK,' Cathy said. 'We were talking about your dad . . . '

'You were trying to find out if I knew he liked *guys*,' Harvey snapped.

'What makes you say that?' she asked. Lockyer could see she was genuinely surprised by Harvey's statement.

Harvey shrugged. 'Because that's what you do, isn't it? You never ask a question straight out. You go round the houses . . . over and over, trying to trip me up.'

'No one is trying to trip you up, Harvey,' Marie said, her voice soft.

'Well, then, why don't you just ask me?' he said, shaking his head. 'All that crap before about *did I know if he ever dated anyone after my mum?* Did I ever see him with *someone* else . . . not did I see him with a woman . . . but *someone*. I'm not stupid, you know?'

'We know that, Harvey,' Cathy said.

'So just ask,' he said, folding his arms.

'OK. Harvey, do you think your father was homosexual?'

He took a deep breath. Lockyer did the same. Harvey hung his head. 'Yeah,' he said, 'I knew.'

'Did your dad tell you?' Cathy asked, repositioning her clipboard.

He was shaking his head. 'No.'

'So what made you think your father was homosexual?'

'You can say *gay*,' he said.

'All right. What made you think your father was gay?'

'It wasn't one thing,' Harvey said with a shrug. 'I heard him talking to someone on the phone, a guy . . . his voice sounded different. I – I . . .'

'It's OK, Harvey, go on,' Cathy said.

'I saw some emails and texts, some websites . . . that kinda thing.'

'Did you talk to your father about what you had seen?' she asked.

He was shaking his head again. 'He would have been mad . . . he hated snooping. My mum used to do it when they were married. She used to go through his phone, stuff like that. Dad would have flipped out if he knew I'd been reading his emails.'

Lockyer knew where Cathy would go next with her question. Harvey was right. They had been trying to find out if he knew his father was gay, but that wasn't where the line of questioning ended. 'Did you ever see your dad with a guy?' Cathy asked.

'No,' Harvey said, his face reddening.

'No one ever came to your dad's flat?'

'No,' Harvey said again.

'So you never met any of your dad's male friends?' she asked, her tone firm. A twitch started in Harvey's left cheek. 'The thing is, Harvey, we've spoken to a number of people who claim to have had a run-in with someone claiming to be Richard Taylor's son. If that wasn't you, then . . .'

'It was me,' he said in a whisper.

'Right,' Cathy said. 'Thank you, Harvey.'

'You have nothing to worry about, Harvey,' Marie said. 'You are not going to get into any trouble. We just need to know the truth, that's all. OK?'

He nodded. 'I figured he'd stop if I . . . warned the guys off, you know?'

'So what happened?' Cathy asked. 'Tell us what happened, Harvey.'

Within ten minutes Cathy had managed to extract the entire story. Mind you, the kid was about ready to burst, he was that keen to get it all off his chest. Lockyer had been right. Adam Oxenham had been telling the truth. He had backed Harvey up and threatened Frank, but it had been Ben Nicholls, Harvey's best mate, who had been there the week before Taylor died. He was staying over when Harvey spotted his father sneaking out of the flat. Olive had been in bed, so Harvey and Ben had followed and seen Taylor with another guy. The description matched that of Eric Tang. Lockyer had already texted the information to Jane. She would be speaking to Tang later on this afternoon. He didn't envy the guy that phone call. Lockyer shifted in his seat. His arse was all but numb. He had a follow-up call of his own to make.

Adam Oxenham had been up-front, once he was pushed, about the threats against Frank. However, he had neglected to say he had always been, and still was, in regular contact with Harvey by text and email. Harvey had told Cathy that neither he nor his sister had been allowed to contact Adam since their father's death, but that Harvey had disobeyed his mother. He was still talking to Adam by phone and they had even met up a couple of times. The fact that Adam had withheld the information was irritating, but that wasn't the only part of it that made Lockyer uncomfortable.

'Thank you, Harvey,' Cathy said. 'You've done really well. Do you feel OK?'

He nodded and sighed. 'Yeah, I feel . . . better.'

'Good.'

'Are we done now?' he asked, sitting forward on the sofa.

'Just a few more questions,' she said. 'Ten minutes, tops.'

Harvey didn't look pleased. He slumped back into the sofa, his mouth straightening into a tight line. Lockyer wondered how much more Cathy was really going to get out of the kid. He looked knackered, and to be fair, he had just spilt his guts. Truth-telling was an exhausting business; Lockyer knew only too well. He had been less than truthful with Clara when they were married, but the energy required to maintain a lie was nothing compared to the all-consuming drain of admitting his wrongdoings.

'Harvey, did your dad have any illnesses that you know of? Did he take pills for anything?'

'He had stuff for his diabetes,' Harvey said, 'but he never took it.'

'Right,' Cathy said nodding. 'Do you know what he was meant to take?'

He shook his head. 'No. Mum was always going on at him about it . . . saying it was irresponsible not to do what the doctor had told him, you know?'

'Sure,' she said. 'Do you know where he kept his medication?'

Harvey shrugged. 'Nope.'

'Good. Almost done,' she said.

'Good,' he said.

Cathy paused for a few moments. It was enough to make Lockyer sit forward in his seat. Marie had done the same. 'Harvey, we talked earlier about the burn on your sister's left arm . . .'

'She burnt herself on the barbecue tongs,' he interrupted. 'I told you that . . . it was an accident.'

'That's right,' Cathy said. 'We also talked about the bruising on your neck and shoulder.'

'Yeah.'

'And you don't know how you came to get these bruises?'

'No.'

'Your sister has bruises, too,' Cathy said. 'You don't know anything about these either?'

Harvey seemed to flinch at the mention of his sister's bruises. Lockyer wondered if Cathy had picked up on his reaction. 'Do you and your sister ever fight? Did you guys ever fight with your dad?'

'You're doing it again,' Harvey said, looking down at his feet.

'What do you mean, Harvey?'

'You're asking questions, but you're not asking the question you *want* to ask.'

'What's the question I *want* to ask?' Cathy said, shifting further forward on the sofa. Marie mirrored her body language. Lockyer realized he was doing the same.

'You want to ask if my father did it,' he said.

'Did he?' Cathy asked. 'Did your father cause the bruises on your neck and on Olive's arms?'

A single tear rolled down Harvey's cheek. 'He . . . he didn't mean to . . . He just got angry sometimes.'

CHAPTER THIRTY-FIVE

7 August – Thursday

'So?' Jane asked, pulling out a chair and sitting down on the other side of Lockyer's desk.

'Taylor was physically abusing the kids,' he said without preamble.

'Shit,' she said.

'According to Harvey's statement, it all started about six months ago . . . about the time Taylor was coming to terms with his sexuality. He says his father started drinking more than usual and would sometimes . . . lash out.'

Jane blew out a breath. 'Dave said there was evidence that Taylor had been binge-drinking,' she said with a sigh. 'His blood alcohol was high the night he died.'

Lockyer shrugged. 'You know how it is . . . people portray one persona, but in private they're someone . . . something else.' He seemed to be waiting for her to speak, but for once she was lost for words. All she could think about were the kids – the ordeal they had been, and were still, going through was hideous.

'We need to bring Brown back in, push a little harder and

see if we can get her to admit that she knew about the abuse,' Lockyer said.

'And if she does?' she asked. 'Her admitting knowledge of the abuse is not proof that she killed him, Mike.'

'No, but it sure as hell cements her motive, Jane,' he said, his tone indulgent. He held up his hands balled into fists. 'Here's what we know. One –' he extended his thumb – 'Brown had keys to Taylor's flat. Two, according to Harvey, she knew about Taylor's diabetes.' He held up his first finger. 'Three, Brown's profession means she has experience of administering drugs. Either she knew where Taylor kept his drugs . . . or it would have been easy for her to get access to prescription medication, needles. She would have it all, and let's be honest, she's no weakling. I reckon she could hold me down if she really wanted to.'

Jane pushed her fingers into the nape of her neck and tipped her head back. 'We still don't know what drug, or drugs, were used . . .' she said as her mobile started to ring. She took it out of her trouser pocket and looked at the screen. 'Speak of the devil,' she said, putting it to her ear. 'Dave.' She listened. 'Yes . . . right . . . OK. Great, send it over.' She said her goodbyes and hung up.

'So?' Lockyer said, his head cocked on one side.

'He's still waiting on the tablets, but the bloods are back. Taylor's insulin levels were significantly high, suggesting an overdose. I'll have to order another search of Taylor's address.'

'There,' Lockyer said, 'you see?'

'It's not enough to bring Brown in, Mike,' she said, giving him a stern look.

He looked at her and rested his hands on his desk, palms down. 'It's enough to arrest her on suspicion,' he said.

Jane leaned back in her chair and tried to pull together her muddled thoughts. She had had another Facebook message from Andy, but she'd been too chicken to read it as yet. The morning off had been meant to give her some breathing space, let her get back up to speed – but if anything she felt more weighed down, more sluggish. 'Let me just think this through,' she said. Lockyer waved his hand for her to continue. She took a deep breath in through her nose and closed her eyes. 'If we can't find Taylor's drugs, then I'd have to get access to Nicola's prescription records – check for anomalies,' she said. 'Olive will have to be re-interviewed. She'll have to back up Harvey's testimony about the abuse.'

'Good point.'

'I'd need to speak to child services about what we do about custody of the kids, if we do bring Nicola in,' she said.

She heard Lockyer push his chair back, stand up and begin pacing. She knew the routine. He was waiting for her to come around to his way of thinking. 'You've got an FLO in place and the aunt's staying there . . . she's registered as a guardian, so that's sorted.'

She opened her eyes and sat forward, frowning. 'The thing that bothers me is, if Nicola knew Taylor was abusing the kids, why on earth didn't she stop him seeing them?'

'Maybe she did,' he said. 'Maybe she decided to stop him seeing them permanently.'

Jane sighed as his point hit home. 'I can't argue with that,' she said.

'Good, because I've already spoken to Roger and the CPS

and everyone agrees we can arrest but, as you say, we'll need more to charge . . . which, if I'm right, we'll get when we question her and from the stuff you want to put in place.' Jane could feel her jaw tightening as he spoke. He had spoken to Roger? He had spoken to the CPS? 'Now, hang on,' he said as if reading her thoughts. 'I know this is your investigation. I spoke to Roger right after I'd finished up with Harvey. He called me. I am, after all, SIO for this case.' He pulled his lips back, showing his teeth. 'Now I'll admit that I got a bit carried away and called the CPS on my way back to the office . . . while I was stuck in traffic . . . just to run things by them and set up a dedicated person over there for us . . . for *you* to talk to.' He looked at her. He looked more defiant than apologetic.

'Got it all sewn up, have you?' she asked, crossing her legs. 'And what about the others?'

'What others?' he asked, looking at her as if she was barking mad.

'Brown is not our only suspect,' she said, 'as much as you're pushing for that.'

'Go on,' he said, as if daring her to challenge him.

'OK. Working on your motive, means and opportunity theory, we've got . . . Oxenham, for one. He had spare keys for the flat, knew about Taylor's diabetes, he's physically strong, and he displayed jealousy over Taylor's relationship by threatening Frank MacIntyre. And he doesn't have an alibi.' She held up a hand to stop Lockyer interrupting. 'Eric Tang,' she went on. 'He was frustrated by the continued secrecy of their relationship, held back by Nicola and the kids. He doesn't have an alibi. He said he didn't know about the diabetes, but

I got the feeling he wasn't being entirely truthful . . . which wouldn't be a first.' She sniffed. 'He could have had keys and withheld that info . . . '

'I think you're going to have to add one more to that list.'

Jane turned to see Penny standing in the doorway to Lockyer's office.

'Who?' she asked.

'Child protection just called,' Penny said. 'They've talked to Ben Nicholls, to get his account of the threats made against . . . we're assuming, Eric Tang.'

'Don't tell me,' Lockyer said, laughing, 'we're bringing Ben in for questioning. He did it.'

Jane rolled her eyes at him and looked back at Penny. Penny wasn't laughing. 'He's not right, is he?' she asked with trepidation.

'No, no,' Penny said. 'It's not Nicholls.'

'Well, come on, then,' Lockyer said. 'The suspense is killing us.'

'Nicholls claims Harvey was very agitated and extremely aggressive when they fronted up to Tang,' Penny said. 'He claims he had to stop Harvey physically attacking the guy . . . that Harvey had a knife.'

'You're kidding.' Jane and Lockyer spoke in unison.

Penny was shaking her head. 'And that's not all,' she said. 'Nicholls says he didn't admit to the confrontation when he was first questioned because he was scared . . . scared his involvement might implicate him in Taylor's murder.'

'Why would it?' Lockyer asked. 'We're not connecting the threat to Tang to Taylor's murder.'

'No,' Penny said, walking into the room and handing them

both a piece of paper. 'This is the transcript of the interview. Nicholls said he was scared because Harvey had made threats that night . . . the night they confronted Tang. Nicholls claims Harvey was amped up after the confrontation and said he'd kill his father if he didn't stop seeing the guy.'

'Christ,' Jane said.

'So Nicholls figured he'd better not say anything, in case we thought he was involved?' Lockyer offered.

'That's about the size of it,' Penny said. 'Sorry.'

Jane put her head in her hands. 'This is crazy,' she muttered. 'He's just a kid.'

'A kid with a history of aggression and poor impulse control,' Lockyer added.

CHAPTER THIRTY-SIX

Thursday

*I'm getting the distinct feeling that this will all be over soon.
I had a dream last night that I was wearing handcuffs and
lying on a bench in a prison cell over in Lewisham. The cuffs
were cold and heavy against my wrists. There was a hatch
in the door. People kept opening it and looking in at me –
judging me. Who cares? Let them judge. They don't know.
They can't know what I've been through, what he put me
through. The phone keeps ringing. They want to talk about
this. They want to talk about that. 'It's all routine.' That is
all they keep saying. Over and over. 'It's all routine.' They
must think I'm stupid.*

*I'm not. I'm not stupid. I know what they're thinking, what
their veiled questions really mean. They make everything sound
so seedy. That's because they don't understand. I suppose I'll
get my chance to explain at some point, to make them see why
I did what I did. Why it was the only way. But I will do it on
my terms, not theirs. I won't be forced. I won't be trapped. I
will do what is necessary to remain outside their net until
I am good and ready.*

CHAPTER THIRTY-SEVEN

8 August – Friday

'Come on . . . you have to bring her in now,' Lockyer said, putting his hand out to usher Jane across the road.

He had dragged her out of the office for 'a walk', but in truth he wanted to be away from flapping ears for five minutes. She was fighting him all the way on the Brown arrest, throwing suspects at him left and right. The only thing that piqued his interest was Harvey and the allegations his best mate, Ben Nicholls, had made; but Jane wasn't even entertaining that. She was still set on Eric or Adam. It was idiotic.

As they crossed the street he glanced back, up to Roger's window. If anyone understood the hierarchy battles, it was him. As SIO it was Lockyer's job to move the case forward, push for results – in his humble opinion, Nicola Brown was that result. Jane's job as lead detective was, by contrast, to make sure things were done according to procedure, that nothing was missed. The dynamic created a natural combative element, but her attitude was driving him nuts. He understood she had a lot on her mind, what with her recent sex mistake with her ex; but she shouldn't be bringing that crap into the case.

He let her step up onto the curb first, the church tall and imposing on their right. Sure, he wasn't perfect and had been known, on occasion, to get things wrong, to let his personal life interfere with his judgement, but he was positive he had never been this annoying. He would ask Roger. He stopped. Best not to ask questions he didn't want the answer to.

'You said yourself that the CPS advised us to get our ducks in a row *before* we made any arrest,' she said as they passed the arches of St Stephen's.

'For crying out loud, Jane,' he said. Several heads turned in their direction. 'For crying out loud,' he repeated, lowering his voice. 'She lied about her alibi and there are direct threats in the emails.' Comms had restored reams of deleted messages from Nicola to Taylor on Taylor's personal computer. They made for difficult reading. 'What more do you bloody want?' How could she not see that this was the logical next step?

'How do we know Chantelle Bullion is telling the truth?' she asked, as they overtook two old ladies with Zimmer frames.

'Because she's got no reason to lie,' he said, exasperated. 'You said yourself that she was jumpy the morning you saw her outside Taylor's – the morning the body was found. No bloody wonder. Nicola had spent the night before ranting and raving about Taylor – threatening to stop him . . . *whatever it took.*'

'But . . . '

'But nothing,' he interrupted, sidestepping a mother with a double stroller. God, twins, what a nightmare that must be.

The woman had the rain cover secured over the two squabbling toddlers. It was baking hot; they would be cooking under there. He turned away. 'Chantelle gets a call from Nicola telling her to say they were at Nicola's house in Penge, not Chantelle's on that Wednesday night . . . being that Chantelle's is walking distance from Taylor's . . . and that she needs her to keep the content of their conversation to herself . . . for the sake of the kids. She gives her some cock and bull story about the kids being taken into care if the police brought Nicola in for questioning, and as the ex-wife, that was standard procedure. The poor woman was intimidated – she didn't know what to do. Nicola manipulated her . . . made her think she had to lie to protect the kids, or whatever. Brown is a piece of work, I'm telling you.' Jane stopped at the barrier and turned, the noise of the roundabout traffic drowning out her words. 'What?' he shouted.

She motioned for him to follow her along the path, past the roundabout and to the right towards Greenwich. Once they were clear of the noise she turned. 'I'm not disagreeing with you,' she said, her voice firm.

'It sure sounds like you are,' he said.

'I just don't want to jump too soon,' she said. 'The TSGs are searching Taylor's property as we speak.' She reached into her trouser pocket. Her phone was ringing.

'What now?' Lockyer asked. He wasn't finished. He didn't want to go back to the office until they were in complete agreement – until she agreed with him. He tried to gauge the content of the conversation, but her expression was unreadable. She turned on her heel and started walking back towards Lewisham High Street. Great, he thought. Now they would never finish this conversation. He followed behind, shaking his head.

By the time they had reached St Stephen's she was saying goodbye and hanging up. 'So?' he asked, unable to control the irritation in his voice.

'We've got a problem,' she said, taking off her sunglasses and striding towards the entrance to the station.

'What?' he asked. She glanced over her shoulder. He jogged to catch up with her. 'What?' he said again.

'That was Anne,' she said.

'The FLO?'

'Yep.' Jane was shaking her head. 'Olive has fresh bruises.'

'What?'

She stopped and turned. 'Olive has fresh bruising on her left thigh and right arm.'

'Is Anne sure?'

'Yes . . . she's got child services to confirm. They're at the house now.'

'And Brown?'

'She's going nuts,' Jane said. 'Penny's bringing her in . . . she assaulted one of the social workers.'

'I guess that's forced your hand,' he said, trying not to sound smug.

'I guess so,' she said, not looking at him.

CHAPTER THIRTY-EIGHT

8 August – Friday

Lockyer held the door of the interview room open for Jane, Nicola Brown and her solicitor, Sadie Willmott, who had arrived within an hour of Nicola's arrest. Willmott's offices were in Fleet Street, a half-hour journey, minimum, with no traffic; and yet within forty-five minutes of the custody sergeant's call Willmott walked, unflustered, into Lewisham police station. Some might say the woman's prompt arrival was a little too convenient. Jane was one of those people. She would lay bets that Ms Willmott had been prepped before-hand for just such an eventuality. She gestured for the two women to take their seats as she sat down herself.

She was still irritated that she had been forced into this situation, but Lockyer was right. The assault charges, which had now been dropped, gave Jane the perfect opportunity to arrest Nicola on suspicion of Richard Taylor's murder. Surprise was a useful tool to unbalance a suspect – and to say Nicola Brown was surprised when Jane read her her rights was an understatement. 'Shall we get started?' she asked.

Nicola didn't blink. She had regained her composure since

the pre-interview disclosure. When Jane had produced copies of the emails from Nicola to her ex-husband she had blanched and shouted about privacy and data protection, but Willmott had put a hand on her arm and spoken to her out of earshot. After that, Nicola was more tight-lipped. She nodded when she was shown the current evidence, but made no further comment.

Her reaction so far was not unusual. Innocent or guilty, people being pushed to explain uncomfortable or embarrassing aspects of their personal lives would go through a myriad of emotions, anger and frustration being the front-runners. Interviewees would shout, bang their fists and protest in the strongest of terms that they were not enjoying the experience. Who could blame them? This was not a fun place. However, if Nicola Brown thought portraying a calm exterior now would preclude her from body-language analysis, she was wrong. Jane was watching her every move and gesture.

'Right,' she said, starting the tape and listing who was present in the room.

'My client has a statement,' Willmott said.

'Go ahead,' Lockyer said, sitting back and looking over at Jane. Nicola's brief had said the plan was for Nicola to read a prepared statement, and then continue to a no-comment interview. It was Jane's intention to change the second part of that plan.

Nicola took the piece of A4 paper she was holding and began to read. It was very much a woe-is-me epistle. She was the injured party: the ex-wife raising two children after her husband's affair. Her response to her own emails was laughable. She may as well have pleaded insanity. She claimed that she had not been in her right mind when she wrote the emails – that it was possible she had been drinking, but that she was now teetotal. What she neglected to cover was why she had lied when giving her alibi. As soon as she was finished, she sat back and folded her hands in her lap. She looked disdainful, as if she was untouchable. Jane was determined to change that.

She leaned forward. 'Nicola, during disclosure we showed you a number of emails sent by you to your ex-husband. Can you confirm that you sent these emails?'

'No comment.'

'There are over one hundred and seventy, spanning a period of just over three years. Can you recall the content of these emails?'

'No comment,' Nicola repeated.

'The emails were sent from your personal computer, which is password-protected. Have you given details of your password to anyone else?'

'No,' Nicola said, a self-satisfied look on her face. Her brief flinched. Jane didn't.

'So it stands to reason, then, that you would be the only person with access and therefore, the only person able to send the emails in question. Wouldn't you agree?' Jane asked.

Nicola blinked several times, surprised, it seemed, to be caught out. A no-comment interview was never wasted. They were annoying, but they could still provide crucial evidence. An unfavourable inference could still be gained if there were inconsistencies between an interview response and that of the prepared statement, coupled with the evidence given at trial. In her statement, Nicola had confirmed she had sent the emails. To say 'no comment' in the interview, but then confirm her password was secure, was a slip on her part. A few more of those and Jane would really be getting somewhere. And she for one would feel a lot more comfortable to be on firmer ground – to be within spitting distance of a charge. 'Did you ever threaten your husband verbally, Nicola?' she asked.

'No comment,' Nicola said, glancing at Willmott for reassurance.

'What did you hope to achieve by sending these messages to your ex-husband?' Jane asked.

'No comment.'

'Were you hoping for a reconciliation?'

'No comment,' Nicola said, but without meaning to, she also shook her head.

'Then why send them?' Jane asked, ignoring the warning look from Willmott. 'In the emails you openly insult and belittle your ex-husband,' she went on, looking down at the transcript in front of her. 'You tell him, on numerous occasions, that he was . . . a bad lover, a bad father . . . that you found him physically abhorrent . . .' Jane tapped her pen on the pages. 'It just seems very one-sided.' She looked up at Nicola; there was confusion on her face. 'Breaking up under any circumstances can be very difficult, but with children I'd imagine it's even harder. But then, wouldn't the messages be more varied?' Again she looked at Nicola, whose brows were bunched together in a deep frown. 'It would seem to make more sense to me to see a balance of dialogue . . . *I love you, I hate you, come back to me . . . I never want to see you again.*

Do you see what I mean?' She could see that Nicola knew exactly what she meant. There was not one positive word in any of the emails. Not one. On the flip side, there were no less than six direct threats to Taylor's life. 'And yet,' Jane said, pushing forward, 'we have received testimony, which you yourself confirmed, that you have, on at least one occasion, let yourself into your ex-husband's flat and propositioned him with sex.' Nicola blushed and stared down at her hands. 'The two behaviours just don't seem to fit . . . not to me, anyway.'

'I would agree,' Lockyer said, from his seat next to her.

'Would you like to comment on that, Nicola?' Jane asked.

She wanted to. Jane could see that Nicola was dying to talk, to argue. The silence lengthened until Willmott leaned forward and touched Nicola's arm. 'Would you like DS Bennett to repeat the question, Nicola?' she asked.

Nicola shook her head. 'No,' she said. 'No comment.'

'In your statement, you talk about your husband's affair,' Jane said. She was about to lower the boom. 'We have recorded testimony, as yet unconfirmed, that you also had an affair . . . an affair with one of your ex-husband's closest friends.' A muscle in Nicola's cheek began to twitch. Her eyes widened and she uncrossed and recrossed her legs before crossing and uncrossing her arms. It was obvious that it was taking every ounce of her willpower not to speak. Another little push, and Jane would have her. 'The affair was brief, but from what I understand, it was at the beginning of your marriage, many years before your husband's indiscretion.'

'There was *no* affair,' Nicola growled. Her brief reached out, but Nicola snatched her arm away. 'There was never an affair,' she said. The look she gave Jane was nothing short of murderous. '*He* forced me. It happened on two separate occasions. I had been drinking. It was not consensual.' The only emotion in her voice was anger – a pure rage.

'Are you saying you were raped, Nicola?' Jane asked, softening her tone.

Nicola waved away her brief's protestations again. 'Yes.'

'Did you go to the police?' Lockyer asked.

'No,' she said. 'I was newly married. He was my husband's best friend.'

'Can you tell me the name of your attacker?' Jane asked.

'You *know* his name, detective,' she spat back. 'Adam . . . Adam Oxenham.'

Jane took a breath. 'These are very serious allegations,' she said. 'Do you wish to take this further?'

Nicola dropped her head for the first time in the interview. 'No,' she said. 'I didn't then, and I don't now. The *only* reason I am even telling you is that I need you to understand the type of man he is.'

'And what type of man is that?' Lockyer asked.

Nicola turned her icy gaze to Lockyer. Willmott sat back in her seat and shrugged. Her job, it seemed, was done. 'He is a liar. He manipulates people to his advantage . . . he's a sociopath.' If her account was true, then her grudge against Oxenham might well be justified; but there was no way Jane was going to let Nicola divert the interview to her own agenda.

'Can I ask, Nicola: have you ever smacked your children?'

Nicola blinked, the change in topic taking her by surprise. She turned to Willmott, but the woman seemed to have lost interest. Her expression seemed to say, *hey, I've been trying to advise you and you've ignored me so far. Sort this mess out yourself.* 'I . . . not since they were little, no,' Nicola said.

'You are aware, of course, that child services have confirmed the presence of both historical and recent bruising on both of your children?'

'I know,' Nicola said, her face dropping a shade.

'You are also aware that one of the children has alleged that their father, Richard Taylor, caused these injuries?'

Nicola was shaking her head. 'I know that,' she said, 'but I don't believe it. As I told you before, my ex-husband was many, many things, but violent was not one of them.'

'Is it possible he may have changed in the years since your separation? One of the children also claims that your ex-husband had started drinking, drinking heavily. Were you aware of that?'

She nodded. 'So I've heard,' she said, 'but I still don't believe he would have hurt the children.' Her support for her ex-husband, a man she seemed to, at times, detest, was odd. 'And if he did,' she added, 'it's not something that is going to be repeated, is it?'

'Because your ex-husband is dead?' Jane asked.

She shrugged. 'Yes. He can't hurt them any more.'

Jane exchanged a glance with Lockyer. Nicola's statement could be taken in a number of ways, but did she realize that by saying it she was cementing her own motive? She had never, and still didn't, strike Jane as someone who would say things without thinking. Mind you, despite wanting to break Nicola's 'no comment' plan, Jane had never expected to get this response. Maybe there was more to this woman than she realized.

'There is a problem with that, though, isn't there?' Lockyer said.

'Yes,' Jane agreed. Nicola looked from one to the other, and then down at her hands. 'As you know, child protection confirmed new bruising on Olive this morning.'

'It wasn't me,' Nicola said in a quiet voice.

'If it wasn't you, then . . .' Jane didn't get to finish her sentence. Nicola Brown put her head in her hands and began to sob. Willmott looked as bemused as Jane felt. In her previous interview with Nicola, Jane had found the woman's emotional yo-yoing exhausting. Today, it seemed, was no different.

Nicola said something, but it was muffled by her hands.

'Can you repeat that, Nicola?'

'I don't *know* who hurt Olive, but I . . . I have an idea,' she said in a whisper.

'Who do you think hurt your daughter?' Jane asked, her voice firm.

'Harvey,' Nicola said without hesitation. 'I think Harvey may have hurt his sister.' Her body was further wracked by sobs.

'I think we need to take a break,' Willmott said. 'I need to speak with my client.'

Jane nodded. 'Of course,' she said. 'Let's take a five-minute break.' She stopped the tape. She could feel Lockyer staring at her.

'What do you think?' she asked, the moment the door to Lockyer's office was closed. Willmott had taken Nicola Brown to the exercise yard for some fresh air. Lockyer's face was tight.

'If you're asking if I still think Brown is the prime suspect, then yes, I still think that,' he said. 'Sure, Harvey has a history of aggression, what with his ADHD. He's a soft target . . . the fact that it's his mother pulling the trigger is what's bothering me.'

'OK,' she said, not wanting or indeed having the energy for a debate.

'Jane,' he went on, 'she *claims* she didn't know about the abuse . . . and then in the same breath says it couldn't have been Taylor. There's no way she didn't know, and she said it herself: Taylor couldn't hurt them any more. Not now he's dead.' He sat down in his chair with a thump.

'I agree,' she said. 'Her behaviour . . . her moods are erratic. What do you think about the rape allegation?'

'It might explain why Oxenham told us about the "affair" up front, to make sure his side of the story was the first heard,' Lockyer said. 'The last time I spoke to him, he was certainly very interested to know how Nicola had reacted to his claims.' He steepled his fingers under his chin. 'It would also explain Brown's open hostility towards the guy . . .'

'And why she wouldn't want him around her kids,' Jane added.

'Mmm,' Lockyer said. 'I've been thinking about that.' He pushed his chair back and went to stand by his window, looking back at Jane, his eyes blank. 'Oxenham's relationship with Harvey was bothering me. Why was he so close to Harvey and not Olive? Why is he Harvey's godfather but not Olive's? He takes Harvey to football matches, but not Olive . . . '

'You're not thinking . . .' she began.

'No, no,' he said, shaking his head, 'nothing like that. Although I'll admit that it did cross my mind when I found out Oxenham had been contacting Harvey and meeting up with him on the quiet since Taylor's death; but no. What I'm wondering now is, *why* is Oxenham so interested in Harvey?'

Jane chewed at the edge of her thumbnail as she moved the idea around in her mind like a puzzle piece. 'It could give Oxenham more of a motive,' she said. 'The jealousy was one angle, but this provides a different slant.'

'Exactly,' he said. 'Let's see what Nicola has to say.' He looked down at his watch. 'We should head back down.'

'What about Harvey?' she asked.

He looked at her. 'Let's just see what else Nicola has to say before we go any further down that road,' he said. 'If Harvey *has* lashed out – and that's a big *if* – it may be due to a number of factors . . . a learned behaviour from Taylor's abuse, or simply a physical reaction to the stress he's under. As you've said on more than one occasion, Harvey's been through a very traumatic experience.'

'Has he?' she asked, raising her eyebrows.

Five minutes later, Lockyer and Jane were back in the interview room. Nicola had, again, managed to regain her composure, but her eyes were still wet. Lockyer doubted it would be long before the waterworks began again.

'Are you happy to continue?' Jane asked, looking from Nicola to Willmott.

When both nodded, Lockyer leaned forward and started the tape, detailing for the record who was present, that this was the second part of the interview and that Nicola was still under caution. The forty-eight hour holding clock was counting down, but Lockyer had the feeling they wouldn't need the full amount of time. Despite Nicola's renewed poise, there was a fizz of tension in the room. Whatever she had to say, she was going to say it now, whether her brief liked it or not. From Willmott's expression, it appeared she had all but given up on her client.

'Nicola,' Jane said. 'You were telling us about Harvey . . . that you think he might be responsible for the recent bruising on your daughter, Olive.'

Nicola glanced at Jane and then turned to Lockyer and began to speak. 'Harvey hasn't been the same since his ADHD diagnosis,' she said. 'He coped well with the dyslexia, but the ADHD seemed to be too much for him . . . too much to process.' It was obvious from Nicola's demeanour that she knew what she had to say. It felt as if she had rehearsed the speech – as if she had wanted to say the words for some time. 'Richard wouldn't accept that Harvey was different – that he needed extra attention. I suggested we move schools to give him a better chance . . . but Richard wouldn't have it. He said it would make Harvey feel *different*. That it would make people treat him differently.' She sighed and clasped her hands together. This was yet another version of Nicola Brown. Her personality had more sides than a set of dice.

'How did his behaviour change?' Jane asked.

'He struggles in school,' Nicola said, ignoring Jane's question. 'His teachers say his concentration has gone downhill, as have his grades. At first I thought it would just take time for him to adjust, to adapt to this new diagnosis, but now I realize he never did . . . never has. He's been in trouble at school for fighting – I've been battling a suspension for months, but his teachers are beginning to lose patience. He fights in school. He fights with his friends.'

'Ben Nicholls,' Lockyer offered.

'Yes, Ben,' she said. 'They seem to fight every time they see each other. It's almost always over something silly, but I know it's Harvey who makes it physical.'

'Has he ever been physical with you?' Jane asked.

Nicola was shaking her head. 'No, no,' she said. 'He wouldn't dare.'

Lockyer shot a quick glance at Jane. He hoped she was listening to what Nicola was saying. He hoped she wasn't being distracted by this new information. It was still clear to him that Brown was a piece of work who might or might not be trying to push the blame onto her own son. 'Did you ever witness him being aggressive with Olive?' he asked.

Again, she shook her head. 'No, never. Harvey is usually so protective of his sister. I think this is how it all started,' she said, looking from Lockyer to Jane and back again.

'How what started?' he asked. Nicola squared her shoulders. Lockyer felt like he was watching a play. Everything she said felt too rehearsed – she was too prepared.

'Harvey knew about Richard's *sexual preferences*,' she said. In his mind she may as well have said 'ta-daah' at the end, like a magician's flourish at the end of a trick.

'How?' Jane asked.

'He only admitted it to me . . . very recently,' Nicola said, looking at Jane and tipping her head to one side, as if to say, 'Who'd be a mother, eh?'

'What did Harvey tell you, Nicola?' Lockyer said, forcing her to look at him.

Nicola took a deep breath and placed both her hands flat on the table. 'He had been reading his father's emails . . . texts, that kind of thing,' she said. 'He knows it was wrong, but he said his father was acting differently, what with the drinking . . . so he wanted to find out if something was wrong.'

'And how did he react to the knowledge of your ex-husband's sexuality?' Jane asked.

'I don't know,' Nicola said. 'I only *just* found out that he knew at all, but from what I can get out of him, he was upset . . . understandably so. It transpires that Rich . . . my ex-husband was sneaking out at night . . . when the children were staying there.' She sounded aghast. 'Apparently, Harvey witnessed one of these clandestine meetings and was, again, very upset.'

'And?' Lockyer asked. He felt Jane turn to look at him. His tone sounded harsher than he had intended. It felt as if Nicola was leading them all on a merry dance, and he for one didn't feel like taking part.

'I don't know,' she said, her eyes wide. 'I just thought you needed to know.'

Lockyer decided to cut to the chase. 'Do you think your son is responsible for your ex-husband's death?' he asked without pausing. If she wanted to displace blame, he was going to force her to do it head-on.

'God, no,' she said, her hands flying up to her mouth. 'No, no. That's not what I mean at all.' Her reaction seemed genuine, but then, all of her personalities *appeared* genuine. 'I told you,' she said. 'I believe . . . I know who killed Rich.'

'Who?' Jane asked. Willmott had sat forward and opened her mouth to speak. Lockyer looked at her and waited, but she just closed her mouth and sat back. She really was done.

'Adam,' Nicola said. 'I told you that, but . . . '

'But what, Nicola?' Lockyer asked. How many other people was she going to point the finger at? Harvey, Adam – who was next? A tear rolled down Nicola's cheek. He had to resist the urge to roll his eyes. He turned to look at Jane. She appeared rapt – hanging on Nicola's every word. Was he the only one to see this woman for who she really was?

'I can't be sure,' she said, 'and the last thing I want is for Harvey to be in trouble, but I think . . . I'm worried he knows something . . . that he might even have been . . . *involved*.'

'Involved in your husband's murder?' Jane asked, her voice sympathetic.

'Ex-husband,' Nicola corrected. 'But, yes,' she said, a slight tremor in her voice. 'I knew something was wrong . . . I just *knew*. That's why I couldn't, I couldn't leave him alone in this.' Her eyes pleaded with Jane. 'I watch television, detective. I know how these things work. I know, as the ex-wife, I'm the prime suspect. I knew the second I heard about Rich's death that I would be implicated and I couldn't allow it,' she said, hurrying on before Lockyer could interject. 'I couldn't risk you people . . . the police making a mistake. You hear about it all the time. People being charged and held by mistake. I couldn't risk that happening to me. I couldn't risk leaving my son alone. Whatever he's done, he's still my son.' She panted, out of breath.

'Is that why you provided a false alibi?' Jane asked.

'Yes.' Nicola pushed away tears with the back of her hand. 'I didn't know what had happened, but I was . . . I was worried. He'd been so different . . . so angry about everything. I didn't want him to be alone.'

'I see,' Lockyer said, trying very hard to control his temper. He couldn't believe Jane was lapping up this bullshit.

'But you don't.' Nicola barked. 'It's Adam. He's dangerous. He wanted Richard but he could never have him. He . . . he *raped* me, but not because he wanted me.' Fresh tears were filling her eyes. 'He wanted to *be* where Rich had *been*,' she spat. 'He's sick . . . sick in the head. He wanted Richard, and when he couldn't have him, he killed him. Now . . . now he wants my son.' She covered her face and resumed her sobbing.

'Nicola,' Jane said. 'Does Adam believe Harvey is his son?'

Before Nicola could answer, there was a knock at the door. Lockyer made his apologies and stood up, opening the door a crack. When he saw Aaron's expression he opened it wider, stepped out and shut it behind him. 'Yes,' he said, not even bothering to wait for Jane to join them. It was obvious where her head was.

'I've just had a report from the TSGs, boss,' Aaron said.

'And?' Lockyer was unable to disguise his impatience.

'They've found a dozen EpiPens, six empty, and two packets of metformin. One of the blister packs is missing a total of twelve pills,' Aaron said. 'They've been bagged and sent straight to the lab for fingerprinting and analysis.'

The door opened, and Jane pushed her way out. 'What is it?' she asked in a hushed voice.

'TSGs have found the drugs at Taylor's address,' Lockyer told her. 'They've gone off to the lab. Little Miss Perfect in there won't be able to talk her way out of fingerprints, now, will she?'

Jane either didn't hear his jibe, or chose to ignore it. 'Where were the drugs found, Aaron?' she asked.

'Behind an airbrick,' he said.

'Ha.' Lockyer hoped he looked as smug as he felt.

'Where in the flat was the airbrick?' Jane asked, again ignoring Lockyer.

'In the boy's room,' Aaron said. 'The airbrick was on the back wall, underneath Harvey's bed.'

Lockyer opened his mouth and closed it. Jane turned to look at him. 'Still feeling smug?' she asked.

He wanted to say no, but Aaron's words had rendered him speechless.

CHAPTER THIRTY-NINE

8 August – Friday

Jane looked both ways before pulling out of the station car park, reaching into her handbag for her sunglasses as she did so. A black cab swerved in front of her, forcing her to switch lanes, which resulted in horns blaring and offensive gestures coming at her from behind. She held up her hand by way of an apology.

'What a dick,' Aaron said from the passenger seat.

Jane was about to agree when her phone started ringing. It was sitting in the cup holder in the centre console. She couldn't see the screen. She reached down, but another car pulled out in front of her. 'Shit,' she said, slamming on her brakes.

Aaron picked up her phone without being asked and said, 'No name.' He held up the phone to show her. 'Number ends in 353.'

That was Andy's number. 'Ignore it,' she said.

Aaron touched the screen. 'Oops, sorry,' he said. 'I was trying to mute it but I think I hung up on them instead.'

Jane shook her head. A dropped call would be just the

kind of ammo Andy craved for his poisonous messages. She was keeping a careful log of all of his phone, text and email communication. He thought he was being clever, spreading his harassment across every medium, but he was messing with the wrong person. This was Jane's territory. She knew how to log and detail every single contact, even down to Andy's three rings and hang-up that he had taken to doing for the past two nights.

He was trying to wear her down. He had used a similar method when she refused to date him. She had believed – correctly, it transpired – that he was still married. He had tried to break her resolve, and succeeded, by bombarding her with messages, cards and flowers. In the end it had been easier to give in than continue to ignore his advances. Not this time, though. She was wise, or wiser, to his tactics. If he thought she was going to be that easy to manipulate again, he was stupider than he looked.

'Don't worry about it,' she said, taking the phone from Aaron and throwing it into the handbag at her side.

'They'll call back if it's important,' he said.

'That they will,' she said, with a resignation that went through to her bones. Andy had only been back in her life for a week, and already he had managed to weaken her to the point of tears and hysterics – not once, but several times. She flicked on her indicator and switched back into the left lane. It would take a while to get to Penge if the traffic didn't ease up. She checked the clock on her dashboard. She had promised her mother she would be home in time for dinner. *Fat chance of that*, she thought.

She had never arrested a minor on suspicion of murder

before. She couldn't believe she was going to do it at all, but given the location of the insulin and metformin, what other choice did she have? Lockyer, despite his desire to see Nicola Brown charged, was in complete agreement, but he had fought back when she suggested turning Nicola loose. 'Not until the fingerprints are in,' he had said. The lab was good and they had received a request to process the prints as a matter of urgency, but it would still take a day or so. The normal waiting time on a request was usually weeks, not days. Jane had made the point to Lockyer that whatever happened, the fingerprints wouldn't be back before Nicola's forty-eight hours' hold time ran out. This had not pleased him, so instead of fighting, she had acquiesced and agreed to keep Nicola in custody for the time being.

She stopped at the lights and pushed her sunglasses further up her nose, pulling down her visor. It was a beautiful day. It didn't match her mood or what she was about to do.

'Boss,' Aaron said. 'Can I ask you something?'

She looked at him, then back at the road. 'Sure, Aaron. What is it?' She supposed it would be Aaron's first arrest of a minor under these circumstances too. Maybe he was as unnerved as she was.

'You've got kids, right?' he asked.

Now that she hadn't expected. 'Yes,' she said. 'I've got a little boy.' It was the first time today she had thought about Peter. It seemed to warm her from the inside out. He had been up when she got home last night because he was too excited from his day at the beach and couldn't possibly go to sleep until he had given Jane a blow-by-blow description of his day. She smiled.

'How do you think you'll handle him dating?' Aaron asked.

Jane glanced at him. 'He's eight, Aaron,' she said. 'I don't think I need to worry about that for a while.' She looked over her shoulder and changed lanes, following the signs to Sydenham and Crystal Palace.

'Sure, yeah,' he said, falling silent.

'Why do you ask?' When he didn't answer, she turned to look at him again and remembered the conversation in the lift the other day. The girls had been teasing Aaron. 'Is this about your new girlfriend?' she asked. He blushed scarlet. 'I'll take that as a big fat yes,' she said, grinning. It had been a while since she had allowed the office banter to dull her senses. It was like a drug that deadened the solemn nature of the job. She sank into the feeling, as if getting into a warm bath. 'Come on, then,' she said, 'spill.' Aaron looked like he would prefer to get out and run alongside the car than stay where he was and be questioned, but as she was doing about forty, he had little choice. 'Come on . . . I'll ask Penny and Sasha if you don't tell me.'

He grunted next to her. 'It's nothing,' he said, his face still puce. 'I just wondered what . . . what parents thought about their kids dating. I mean, my folks don't care but like, I'm twenty-five, so why would they . . . '

'Right,' she said, trying to decipher his point and the subtext of his ramblings all at the same time. 'You're not mucking around with someone underage, are you, Aaron?' she asked, frowning.

'No, boss,' he said. 'Course not.'

'But she's younger?' Jane asked, picking up on his obvious anxiety.

'Yeah,' he said. 'She's nineteen.'

'That's plenty old enough,' she said. 'Just about right for a guy your age.' As she spoke, she realized she hadn't given a man dating advice in her entire life. She had spoken to Lockyer about one woman in particular, but that didn't count. She teased Dave about being single – although the word on the street was that he had been seen around town with Dr Jeanie Crown, a decomposition expert who had helped out on the Hungerford case. The memory of their first meeting almost dented Jane's reverie, but she pushed the bad memories away and held on to the good. Jeanie was sweet, petite and from what she could remember, very funny. Good on Dave, she thought.

'I don't think her dad would approve,' Aaron said, pulling at the knees of his trousers.

'What does *she* say?' Jane asked, making the right by the Pawleyne Arms.

'She says he'll be fine . . . she's pretty relaxed about the whole thing.'

'Well, then, trust her instincts,' Jane said, turning onto Clevedon Road. 'She knows her father best, after all.'

'True,' Aaron said. 'Look,' he said, pointing up ahead, 'there's a space.'

Jane accelerated. 'Well spotted.' She pulled the car in behind Anne's Nissan Micra. They both fell silent as she turned off the engine. 'Right, you ready for this?'

'As I'll ever be.'

She smiled and patted his leg. 'You'll do fine. Come on.'

She climbed out of the car. Seeing Aaron's nerves had helped. He was the rookie here, not her. She needed to remember that.

Jane stepped up to the front door and pressed the bell, Aaron close behind her. She heard the chime ring out. It was one of those modern doorbells that you could programme to any tune you wanted, a bit like a mobile phone. Nicola, or perhaps the children, had chosen the chimes of Big Ben.

Jane took a step back and waited. Years ago, she had changed the settings on her own phone so when the answer-phone kicked in the voice of a celebrity would answer, asking the caller to leave a message. Jane had thought it was funny: voices of the Queen, Prince Charles, Alan Sugar. She remembered once, when it was set to the voice of Graham Norton, Peter's teacher had left a message to say that Peter was ill and someone needed to collect him from school. The delay before Miss Hinks spoke, together with her tone, made it clear she did not share Jane's sense of humour.

She rolled her head around her shoulders and pushed the bell again. The sun was out. Maybe they were in the garden. She had called Anne before she left the office to prepare her for their arrival. The aunt, Kate, had been staying with the family ever since Taylor's death, so she would be there to help Anne with Olive once Harvey was taken into custody.

'Maybe they're outside,' Aaron offered.

'That's what I was thinking.' Jane tried the door handle. It wasn't locked. 'Hello?' she said as she opened the door, walking in and down the hallway. 'Anne? It's me.' She glanced back at Aaron and shrugged.

She pushed open the door to the kitchen and stopped. Anne was lying on the floor, a chair askew next to her. 'Christ, Anne,' Jane said, rushing over and dropping to her knees. Aaron stayed in the doorway. 'Anne, are you all right?' Jane gave her a small shake, but there was no response. 'Anne,' she said again, rubbing her knuckles back and forth on Anne's chest to bring her round. She looked around the kitchen, and then back at Aaron. 'Is anyone home?' she shouted. There was no answer. The back door was wide open, thrown back on its hinges.

'What's going on, boss?' Aaron asked with a grimace.

'I have no idea,' she said.

CHAPTER FORTY

8 August – Friday

Jane's handbag was on the floor next to her. She reached in for her mobile, took it out and dialled through to despatch. Her call was answered on the second ring. 'This is DS Jane Bennett speaking,' she said, taking a calming breath when she heard the panic in her voice. 'I need an ambulance to . . .' She thought for a second, '. . . to SE20, 28 Clevedon Road. Officer down. Anne Phillips – Family Liaison. She's unconscious.' She listened and answered the questions that were being fired at her, all the time cradling Anne's head in her lap. She felt her stir. 'I don't know,' she said, looking around her. 'Yes . . . yes . . . hold on, I think she's coming round.' Anne's eyelids were moving. 'Myself and PC Aaron Jones arrived on scene five minutes ago . . . so she's been out for at least that, but that's all I can tell you right now.' She nodded. 'Great . . . how long?' There was a pause while the woman on the other end of the line checked her system. 'Ten minutes . . . great. And can you please put a call through to DI Lockyer at Lewisham HSCC, telling him the situation, and tell him I'll call to update him ASAP.' She stroked Anne's forehead. 'Thanks.' She hung up the phone. 'Anne?' She gave her another gentle shake. Anne's eyelids fluttered for a moment before she opened her eyes and looked at Jane.

'Jane?'

'Hey,' she said, smiling. 'How are you doing?'

'I . . . I don't know . . . what happened,' Anne croaked, trying to sit up.

'No, no,' Jane said. 'You stay where you are for now, OK? It looks like you've taken a tumble. Do you know where you are?'

Anne was shaking her head. 'God, my head,' she said, trying to raise her arms to her head.

'Just stay still,' Jane told her. 'An ambulance is on the way.'

'I . . . I don't need an ambulance,' Anne said again, trying to push herself up into a sitting position, holding on to Jane's arm for support. 'I . . . how long was I out for?'

Jane shook her head. 'I don't know,' she said. 'We've only just got here.' She looked over her shoulder at Aaron, who seemed frozen to the spot. 'Aaron, check the house, will you?' He nodded, the movement mechanical, but did as she asked and left the kitchen without a word.

'Where is everyone, Anne?' Jane asked. 'Where are the kids?'

Anne bent her knees, leaned forward and hung her head. 'I – I . .'

'Don't worry,' Jane said. 'It'll come.'

Anne cleared her throat. 'Kate,' she said. 'Is she here?'

'Not that I know of,' Jane said. 'I called out when we arrived, but we only found you.'

A frown wrinkled Anne's forehead. Jane could see she was straining to remember. 'She went out . . . she went out to the supermarket,' she said.

'Right,' Jane said, her voice soft, 'and the kids? Did they go with her?' She knew that couldn't be the case. She had called Anne from the station, explained that she and Aaron were on their way over to arrest Harvey. There was no way Anne would have allowed Harvey to leave the house – not with anyone – not under any circumstances.

Anne was shaking her head. 'No, they were here. I was looking after them.' Her brow furrowed again. 'I was here,' she said, looking up at the kitchen table. 'I was sitting at the table . . . with Olive. She was telling me about . . . about Henry VIII, his wives.' She closed her eyes. 'We were looking up pictures of Anne Boleyn on the iPad.' Jane sat back on her heels and stretched up to look on the table. Sure enough, the iPad sat open, its screen black.

'And Harvey?' she asked.

'I don't know,' she said, looking at Jane. 'I remember talking to Olive and then . . . nothing. I must have passed out.'

'Has this ever happened before?' Jane kept her tone gentle and reassuring.

Anne shook her head. 'No, no . . .' She fell silent. A minute passed where neither spoke. Jane could hear Aaron's footsteps climbing the stairs. 'Wait,' Anne said. 'I was . . . Olive and I were laughing . . . we were trying to remember the rhyme, the one about the wives.'

'OK,' Jane said. 'And then what happened?'

'Harvey came in . . .'

'Yes,' Jane said, her eyes settling on a heavy frying pan lying under the table.

'He was upset.'

'Upset . . . about what?'

Anne shook her head. 'I don't know,' she said. 'He was crying . . . I asked him what was wrong.'

'And . . .' Jane said, her heart thudding in her chest as the implication of the discarded frying pan began to dawn on her.

Anne shook her head. 'I don't know . . . I don't know,' she said, reaching up to the back of her head and wincing. 'I can't remember.' Her hands had started to shake.

Jane rubbed Anne's back. 'It's all right,' she said, looking over at the back door. It was hanging off its hinges. She looked again at the frying pan and cocked her head on one side, trying to pull together her jumbled thoughts. Had the damage to the door been caused by someone fighting to get in – or to get *out*? Could Harvey have attacked Anne? Given Jane was here to arrest him for the suspected murder of his own father, it wasn't much of a stretch to believe him capable of assaulting a stranger – a stranger trying to prevent him leaving the house, perhaps? She stopped mid-thought. She needed to check on Aaron.

'Where's Olive?' Anne asked, her expression pained.

Jane shook her head. 'I don't know,' she said, pushing herself up, using the kitchen table for support. 'Aaron's checking the house now. Will you be OK for a second?'

Anne waved her away. 'Go, go,' she said. 'I'm not going anywhere.'

Jane turned and left the kitchen, her pulse racing. She listened for Aaron's footsteps. 'Aaron,' she called. 'Anything?'

'No,' he called back. She climbed the stairs, listening all the time. 'I'm just checking . . . the mother's room now,' he said. 'All the other rooms are clear.'

Jane stopped on the last stair. She could hear Aaron moving around at the other end of the hall. She could hear Anne downstairs, muttering to herself. She could hear something else. She could hear someone breathing – breathing hard. Without moving from the spot, she turned and looked around her for the origin of the sound. The doors to the bathroom and the children's bedrooms stood open. She followed the sound along the landing, towards Nicola Brown's bedroom. There was a door halfway along the landing, a cupboard of some sort. She took a step towards it as Aaron appeared in the doorway. She put her finger to her lips and pointed to the cupboard. He nodded and took two steps towards her, so they were flanking the door. 'This is DS Jane Bennett,' she said in a loud voice. 'I am going to open the door now . . . please stay where you are.'

There was no answer, but Jane heard a strangled sob. Aaron had heard it, too. She widened her stance and readied herself for whoever was behind the door. She reached for the handle, turned it and pulled the door open in one swift motion.

It took a moment for her eyes to adjust. Curled up on the floor of an airing cupboard was Olive. The girl turned her face up to Jane's, tears streaming down her cheeks. 'I couldn't stop him,' she said, burying her face in her hands. Her entire body was shaking.

'Harvey?' Jane said, her voice quiet.

Olive lifted her head again, her words choked by tears. 'He's gone,' she said, her words hitching. 'We were . . . sitting . . . at the table. He bust down the door – he came in – he . . . he grabbed my brother – he grabbed Harvey and tried to . . . to take him . . . but . . . Anne wouldn't . . . wouldn't let him.' Tears were coursing down her pale cheeks. 'He hit her,' she said. 'He hit her so hard.'

'Who did?' Jane asked, kneeling down to get closer, to hear the girl's muffled words.

'*Adam*,' Olive screamed. 'He hurt Anne and took my brother.'

Jane's breath stopped in her throat.

Nicola Brown had been telling the truth.

CHAPTER FORTY-ONE

Friday

I can't keep hiding – running. I'm tired of this whole mess.

The police will be here soon. They'll ask their questions, as they do, but they never ask the right ones. If they did, I think I would confess everything just to have it over with. It was fun to begin with – to get away with it – to stay one step ahead of them all the time, but that's over now. They forced me to act. Did they really think I would just give up? They still don't seem to have grasped the kind of man Richard Taylor was.

CHAPTER FORTY-TWO

9 August – Saturday

'Traffic's still looking for Oxenham's car,' Jane said, slumping down at the incident room table. The glass was cool against her bare forearms. It had been a very long night. The rain was hammering against the windows, for which she was grateful. She wasn't sure her tired eyes could cope with sunshine this morning.

She glanced at her mobile. She had two missed calls from Andy, and four from her mother. She couldn't cope with those either. She had texted her father to make sure all was OK at home, on the off chance her mother was calling with an emergency, rather than a bollocking for Jane not only missing dinner but failing to come home at all last night. She rubbed her eyes, trying to focus.

'We've been through every name on the list. We've covered everyone – everyone who knew Harvey or Oxenham, who might be hiding them or have at least helped them. I've had every spare officer out searching addresses, questioning people. There's no sign of them anywhere,' she said. 'Air support has scrambled a helicopter to assist, although in this weather I'm not expecting much. I've put out an All-Ports Warning to try and stop Oxenham taking Harvey out of the country, but other than that . . . it's a waiting game now.'

'They've been gone for well over twelve hours,' he said.

'I know,' she said, shaking her head. 'I know.'

'What about Anne?' he asked.

'They took her over to Kings A & E yesterday. They kept her overnight for observation, but she'll be OK. She was severely concussed. Her husband John's with her.'

'She remember any more?'

'No,' Jane said. 'She doesn't remember anything after Harvey walked into the kitchen.'

Lockyer shrugged and began pacing back and forth, folding and unfolding his arms. 'Where the hell would Oxenham take him?'

She ran her hands through her hair once, then twice. 'I have no idea.'

'What did Brown say?' he asked, a harder tone to his voice.

'Not much,' Jane said, feeling exasperated. She was getting a bit tired of Lockyer's attitude towards Nicola Brown. 'She's terrified Adam has abducted her son . . . or that her son might be somehow involved in his own father's murder. She wasn't in the best of states to answer questions, but to be fair to her, she gave us a pretty comprehensive list of everyone Harvey knew, plus contacts for Adam's work. Without her, we wouldn't have known where to even *start* looking.' Lockyer was shaking his head. 'Look, Mike, Nicola was in custody yesterday,' she said, catching his eye. 'The drugs were found in Harvey's room. It was Oxenham who broke into Brown's house, assaulted Anne and took off with Harvey. Nicola was here the whole time.'

'That doesn't mean she's off the hook . . . '

'You think she murdered her ex-husband and planted the discarded needles . . . the pills in her own son's room?' she asked, raising an eyebrow. He seemed to think for a second, and then shrugged. 'Exactly,' she said. 'Right now we need to focus on finding Oxenham and getting Harvey back.'

'And Harvey's involvement in all this?' he asked.

'I don't know,' Jane admitted, 'but it doesn't sound to me like he's a willing participant, does it?' Again, Lockyer shrugged. 'Look, let's just concentrate on finding them both,' she said. 'We can worry about who did what when we've got them in custody.'

'I can't believe you let her go,' he said.

She rolled her eyes. 'What did you want me to do? We've got an outstanding warrant on Harvey on suspicion of Taylor's murder. We now have the same on Oxenham. Holding Nicola on the same charge was making a mockery of the whole thing. They didn't all do it.'

'We don't know that,' he said, pulling out a chair and sitting down opposite her. He looked tired.

Who wasn't? She shook her head. She couldn't be arsed to argue with him any more. 'Whatever,' she said. 'It's done now. Besides which, Olive needed her mother. The poor kid was hanging on by a thread after yesterday.' Lockyer seemed to soften at the mention of Olive. He had arrived at the house in Penge within twenty minutes of Jane's call to despatch. He had carried a shivering Olive to her bedroom and sat with her while child protection checked her over. Jane knew how she felt when she was dealing with a kid who reminded her of Peter. It was, she guessed, the same for Lockyer. He was bullish and stubborn at times, but he was a father at the end of the day, and his daughter meant the world to him. Megan's involvement in a case they had both been on earlier in the year had showed that.

'So what now?'

'I've put in calls to Dave and to the lab, to chase up on the fingerprints. I've also advised them that they could be looking for two or three sets of prints,' she said, looking down at the smooth surface of the briefing table. She was tempted to rest her cheek against the cool glass.

'Three?'

'Yes,' she said. 'Taylor's, Harvey's and Oxenham's.'

He nodded. 'Sure,' he said, rolling his head around his shoulders and closing his eyes. 'I'm not sure I'm cut out for this SIO crap,' he said. 'I can't *stand* all this waiting. It pisses me off. I'm used to being . . . '

'. . . the one pissing *other* people off?' Jane smiled in spite of herself.

He opened one eye and looked at her. 'That,' he said sitting forward, 'is exactly right, and I, for one, prefer it that way.'

Jane looked at him. 'Right now, sir, I think I would too.'

'I bet you would,' he said, making a stupid face, 'but unfortunately this shitbox is your case, sooo . . . as SIO, I have to ask, where are we? I need a progress report, stat.'

Jane laughed and let her head drop onto the desk with a thump.

*

Lockyer dragged his hands down his face. His mobile was on his desk. He had put it on speaker when he could no longer endure his daughter's tirade banging against his ear. He had been *listening* for five minutes now. She hadn't drawn breath.

'. . . You promised,' she whined.

'Megs, I'm . . .'

'. . . working, I know,' Megan finished for him, her words snapping out of the phone. He had attached a picture to her contact card last week, so he was looking at her smiling face. It didn't match the voice. 'That's always your excuse,' she said. 'I just thought . . . I wanted you to be there when I asked Uncle Bobby to come to the wedding,' she said.

He ran a hand through his hair, his fingers catching on two knotted curls. He needed a shower, but a shower – like his daughter, like his brother – would all have to wait. Until Oxenham and Harvey were found, Lockyer, Jane and the team weren't going anywhere. 'I spoke to your mother,' he said, preparing himself for his daughter's response.

'When?'

'Last night,' he said.

'Why?' she asked.

'Because since you've decided to dump me and take your mystery man to the wedding, I figured I'd back out gracefully, so I emailed your mother to say I wouldn't be attending.'

'I never meant you not to come, Dad,' she said, sounding apologetic. 'I told her to add you and a guest to the list. I still want you there.'

'Well, lucky for you, your plan worked,' he said, puffing out a frustrated breath. His email to his ex-wife to make his apologies had not gone as he hoped. 'Your mother called me and insisted I come because she'd already confirmed numbers with the caterer . . . and she thinks it's only right for me to be there and show my support for her new marriage.'

'Ahh, that's brilliant,' Megan said. 'Besides, Uncle Bobby wouldn't be happy without you there.'

'Well, that's the other thing,' he said.

'What?' she asked, her voice wary.

'Your mother's not sure bringing Uncle Bobby to the wedding is a good idea,' he said, through gritted teeth.

'She what . . . ? Why?' Her voice had gone up an octave.

'Well,' he said, trying to keep his voice firm. 'She thinks perhaps it's not the best environment for him.'

'But you'll be there,' she countered.

'True,' he said, knowing he should have had the balls to stand up to his daughter in the first place and say no to attending his ex-wife's second marriage. 'But I have to agree with your mother, Megs. All those people . . . it'll just freak Bobby out. You know how stressed out he can get.' He sighed. It was over five years since Lockyer had found his older brother wasting away in a care home up North. Their maiden aunt, who had taken Bobby off their parents' hands when Lockyer was only four, had shoved Bobby in the home when she too found him too *difficult* to cope with. It made Lockyer mad every time he thought about it.

'He loves the outings Cliffview organize,' Megan said, her voice sounding sulky.

'That's totally different, and you know it,' he said.

'All the carers and the nurses say how much better he is,' she said. 'How much he loves our visits . . . *my* visits.'

'And he does,' Lockyer said, his tone soft. 'He has changed since you came into his life, honey, there's no doubt about that. He loves you very much, but he still gets anxious and upset if his routine changes or something out of the norm happens.' He took a breath. 'Do you really want to put him through that?'

'I . . .'

'I think your mother's right,' he said, thinking this must be the first time he had been on Clara's side in years. 'She's thinking of you and Bobby. If you drag your poor uncle to a wedding with hundreds of people, noise, music, strange food, he's going to throw a fit . . . literally. And that isn't fair on him, or you.' Lockyer had been there for a few of Bobby's fits now. They were gut-wrenching. He couldn't stand seeing his brother like that, but the thought of Megan witnessing it was even worse.

'But I would . . .'

'He's happy, Megan,' Lockyer said. 'He's content and happy where he is, doing what he's doing. He has me and he has you. He loves it at Cliffview. He enjoys the outings there because they are organized and run by professionals who know how to keep him relaxed. I know you think I've locked him away in there . . .' He didn't know how to finish his sentence.

'I don't think that, Dad,' she said. He could tell by her voice that she was calming down. 'I just want him to see more, be with people more, to be . . .'

'Normal?' He couldn't blame his daughter for wishing. He knew how many times he had wished his brother to be better, to somehow outgrow the autism – throw off its shackles. He wanted it for Bobby, but he also knew he wanted it for himself – to have the brother he had dreamed about as a kid. The guilt of wanting Bobby to change, for things to be different, had weighed on Lockyer for years – but since the truth had come out, since Megan had been visiting, things had changed. He had let go. Now he loved his brother for who he was. He didn't waste time worrying about who he wasn't.

'I've been there,' he said. 'You love your uncle, I know, but loving him means letting him be who he is. Not trying to change him, to make him fit your idea of what an uncle should be.'

'So you agree with Mum,' she said. 'You think I'm being selfish.'

'Your mum was probably angry when she said that . . . and she's planning a wedding, so she'll be doubly stressed. She didn't mean it, honey. Why don't you give her a call, straighten things out? I'm sure she doesn't want to . . .' He didn't get to finish his sentence, because Jane was at his door. She waved for him to join her before turning and running back across the office. 'Listen, I've got to go, honey,' he said. 'I'll give you a call as soon as there's a break in this case and you and me will take Uncle Bobby out for some ice cream or whatever, OK?'

He heard his daughter's heavy sigh. 'OK,' she said, resigned, it seemed, to the inevitable wait. He hated himself for always keeping her waiting. He said goodbye, told her he loved her and ended the call. He stood up and slid his phone into his pocket and sidestepped around his desk, pulling open the office door and jogging across the office.

'What is it?' he asked when he caught up with Jane at the lifts.

'Adam Oxenham is downstairs,' she said.

'Fantastic,' he said. 'That was quick. Did air support get him?'

She was shaking her head. 'No. He just walked into reception, handed himself in and asked to speak to you.'

Lockyer frowned. 'And Harvey?'

She was shaking her head again. 'Harvey isn't with him.'

CHAPTER FORTY-THREE

9 August – Saturday

Adam Oxenham was sitting in the interview room across from Jane and Lockyer. They had been questioning him for ten minutes, but so far gained very little. 'Adam,' Jane said. 'Did you have feelings for Richard Taylor?' It was like pushing a boulder uphill, getting this guy to talk.

He shifted in his seat and looked from her to Lockyer and back again. He clasped his hands together, his enormous biceps rippling as he did so. She couldn't help but imagine a heavy frying pan in his hand, see him hitting Anne. She balled her hands into fists in her lap. 'He was my best mate,' he said.

'Yes,' Jane said, 'we know that, but I'm asking if you ever had any romantic feelings towards Richard? From what DI Lockyer has told me, you didn't look upon Richard's recent dating too favourably, and I'm asking why that was?'

His mouth straightened into a tight line. 'Like I told *DI Lockyer*, I never had feelings for Richard. He was my buddy, that was it.'

'Were you jealous of the new life he was embarking on . . . his new relationships?' she asked.

He was shaking his head. 'No,' he said, but then shrugged. 'Maybe a bit . . . but not for the reasons you think. I've been single for a while.'

'So you were jealous,' Lockyer reiterated.

'All right,' he said, 'yes. I was jealous.'

'Angry?' Jane asked.

Oxenham shook his head again. He looked at Lockyer, but nodded his head towards Jane. 'Is she for real?'

'Yes,' was all Lockyer said.

Oxenham opened up his hands. 'Right,' he said, 'I guess I'll say it again. I did not kill, nor have anything to do with the death of my friend, Richard Taylor. Me being jealous he was getting laid is not enough for me to want to off the poor guy.'

'Other motivations have been suggested,' Jane said.

'What?' he said without pause. 'What possible reason would I have to kill my friend?'

'Tell us about Harvey,' Lockyer said, picking up on Jane's line of questioning. 'Tell us what happened yesterday.' They hadn't had much time to prepare before the interview, but one of the benefits of a long-standing working relationship was that, for the most part, she knew what he was thinking and vice versa. Jane realized the same rules did not often apply to their personal lives.

'Harvey called me,' Oxenham said. 'He said he was in trouble . . . that you guys were on your way over. He was frightened . . . agitated.'

'What did he have to be frightened about?' Lockyer asked.

'I . . . I don't know,' Oxenham said, although it was clear from his body language that he was lying through his whitened teeth. Jane usually found it easy to detach, to remove her emotions during an interview, but for some reason Oxenham had crawled under her skin the moment she entered the room. 'I asked Harv what was wrong, but . . . he wouldn't tell me. He just said he needed help, that he needed to get out . . . that the woman, the officer watching him and his sister, wouldn't let him leave.'

'So you rushed over there to help without knowing what the situation was?' Jane asked, incredulous.

'Yes,' he said. 'What else could I do? He asked for my help . . . I had to go.'

'Do you believe Harvey is your son?' Lockyer asked. Oxenham seemed thrown by the directness of Lockyer's question, but Jane couldn't decipher if his surprise was genuine or not.

'He *is* my son,' he said. He lowered his head. 'I can't believe she told you.'

'Who?'

'Nicola,' he said. 'She's never admitted it to me . . . never.'

'Nicola told us you *thought* Harvey was your son . . . that you *wanted* him to be your son,' she said, 'but she never said he was.'

'She's a liar,' he said, looking up at her.

'Funny,' Lockyer said. 'She says the same about you.'

'In fact,' Jane continued. 'Nicola's account of what happened between the two of you is somewhat different to yours.'

'Oh, sure. Told you I raped her, did she?' he said with a cruel laugh.

'Are you saying you didn't?' Lockyer asked, leaning

312

forward in his chair. Jane knew how he felt about violence towards women, sexual violence in particular. If he didn't take a breath he might end up smacking Oxenham, and Jane, for one, was in no mood to stop him.

'Course I didn't,' he said. 'She tried to pull that shit years ago . . . said she was drunk, that I forced her.' He shook his head. 'Not how I remember it, I can tell you.'

'Did Richard know?' she asked, putting a hand on Lockyer's arm. She hoped the gesture would tell him to calm down. He didn't flinch, but he did sit back in his seat, so maybe it had worked. Time would tell.

'No,' Oxenham said. 'I wanted to tell Rich, to come clean, especially when I found out about the baby, but *she* wouldn't have it. She said she'd tell Rich I raped her if I ever said anything – that I'd never see Rich again, or the baby.'

'That must have been hard,' she said, 'to be threatened like that . . . to stand by and see another man raising a child you believed to be yours.'

'It was,' he said, his voice quiet, 'but Rich was my friend. He was a good guy . . . a good father.' He rubbed his eyes. 'After a while I just accepted things,' he said. 'At least I got to see Harv – to see he had a good life.'

'But why?' Jane asked, looking at him. 'Why, Adam, would Nicola go to such lengths to keep your affair a secret? It can't have been just to protect her marriage. Perhaps she was trying to protect Harvey . . . from you?'

'That's bollocks,' he said. 'She denied it all, forced me to keep quiet because . . . because she . . . she *regretted* what we did,' he said in a lascivious tone. 'She's wound pretty tight, as I'm sure you've seen.' He looked at Lockyer and smirked, as if they were sharing a joke. Jane cleared her throat until Oxenham turned back to her. He shrugged and pulled his mouth down at the edges. 'She let loose,' he said, his tongue sounding wet in his mouth, 'more than she ever did with Rich . . . I know, we talked about that kind of stuff.' He sat back and pushed out his chest. 'She had a good time, I can assure you, but afterwards . . . well, she couldn't handle what we had done . . . guess it was a bit more . . . filth than she was used to.' He laughed again. 'I figured it was just the guilt of cheating, but there was more to it than that. She was disgusted with herself.' He shook his head. 'God knows why,' he said. 'She had nothing to be embarrassed about . . . but I guess some people can't handle letting go . . . really letting go.'

His words needled Jane's skin as if she had brushed against a load of stinging nettles, each sting swelling and itching against her crawling flesh. She could taste bile in her mouth. He sounded just like Andy. The same smutty justifications: the same grubby, wet words. It was clear that like Andy, Oxenham relished Nicola's distress, her disgust with herself and what the two of them had done together. For the first time since she had met her, Jane felt a sudden pang of sympathy for Nicola. Her denial, her repulsion at the entire affair, twisting their encounters into rape: because rape was more palatable than the torture of facing the truth.

Jane realized she was lucky. Andy had been gone, out of her life and out of her mind, for eight years. Nicola had been forced to endure the memory not only through her husband's friendship with Oxenham, but through her own son's attachment to the man she despised. 'I've got emails from Nic telling me to keep my mouth shut,' he said with another smirk at

Lockyer. 'I kept them . . . just knew she'd bring up this rape nonsense again. Happy to show them to you. The woman's got a dark side . . . trust me.' Jane couldn't speak; she was too disgusted with Oxenham and, moreover, with herself. She wanted to go home, to shower off the memory of Andy, of what she had done.

'We're not here to discuss the rape claims,' Lockyer said. 'We're here to discuss your involvement in Richard Taylor's death and to what extent you involved Harvey in his father's murder.'

Oxenham looked at Lockyer like he was mad. 'What have you been smoking?' he said, laughing. 'As I've said . . . several times . . . I *didn't* have anything to do with Rich's death. Neither did Harv,' he added, though the second part of his statement lacked the certainty of the first.

'In that case,' Jane said, finding her voice, 'why would you go to Nicola Brown's house, break down the door, attack a police officer and abscond with Harvey in tow?'

Again, Oxenham looked confused. 'Hang on, hang on,' he said. 'I never attacked nobody.'

'Really?' Jane said.

'No,' he said. 'Harv told me the copper was holding him, that she wouldn't let him leave. He said I'd need to come in the back door because the woman wouldn't let him leave – she'd locked him in.'

'So you kicked it in?' Lockyer offered.

'Sure,' he said, opening his hands. 'I kicked in the door, and there was Harvey and the copper.'

'And, according to you, what happened then?' Jane asked, shifting in her seat, an uneasy feeling settling into her bones.

'We tried to leave, but the woman . . . the copper, she was having none of it,' he said.

'What about Olive?' Jane asked. 'Where was she?'

'She was scared . . . she was screaming,' he said, looking contrite for the first time in the interview. 'She ran out of the kitchen.'

'And then what?' Lockyer asked.

'The copper grabbed Harvey, held on to him good and tight. She wouldn't let him go.'

'So you assaulted her to force her to release Harvey?'

'No, no.' Oxenham waved his hands back and forth. 'You've got this all backwards. She grabbed Harv and then he whacked her with something. I never saw what it was, but he whacked her hard. She went down, and that was it,' he said with a shrug, 'we left.'

'You left?' Jane and Lockyer said in unison.

'Yeah,' Oxenham said. 'I took Harvey back to mine, but he was so wired he couldn't sit still, so we went for a drive . . . you know, just to give him time, like, to figure out what he wanted to do. He reckoned you thought he killed his dad, you see. He was . . . I mean, I *did* say we should just call you lot . . . explain or whatever; but Harvey wasn't having any of it.' He shook his head. 'I didn't want to push him. Not with him acting like he was.'

Jane pushed her middle fingers into the corners of her eyes to stop her head thumping. 'So you're saying Harvey called you, said he was in trouble, that we were on our way,' she said, getting the facts according to Oxenham straight in her mind. 'Then he told you to come and get him, but that you'd have to kick in the back door because the Family Liaison

Officer had locked him in the property. So you came over, kicked in the door, tried to leave, the FLO grabbed Harvey to stop you taking him and Harvey knocked her unconscious – and then you just both walked out, calm as you like, went back to yours, before going for a drive to figure out what Harvey was going to do next? Is that what you're telling me?'

'He wasn't calm . . . neither of us were,' he said, 'but that's what happened . . . and I didn't *take* Harvey. He was the one who called me. He was the one who wanted to get out of the house . . . I just helped. I don't think he *meant* to hurt the woman – he wanted to get out – he was all over the place.'

Jane felt Lockyer shift next to her. 'So why are you here?' he asked.

'What do you mean?' Oxenham asked.

'I mean, Adam,' Lockyer said in an indulgent tone, 'if what you have just told us is the truth, then you went out of your way to help and protect Harvey from the bad guys, namely, us. And yet here you are, dobbing him in for assaulting a police officer. What's all that about?'

Oxenham appeared to think for a few seconds before he replied. 'I was worried,' he said.

'About what?' Lockyer asked.

'About Harvey,' he said. 'I woke up this morning and he was gone. He was so agitated . . . so angry.'

'Angry about what?' Jane asked.

Oxenham seemed to hesitate. 'About me . . . about me being his dad,' he said.

'Who told him you were his father?' she asked, knowing the answer from Oxenham's face.

He turned down his lip and shrugged. 'I did.'

'When?' Lockyer asked. 'And why?'

'The kid had a right to know,' Oxenham said, crossing his arms again, defensive.

'When did you tell Harvey you were his father?' Jane asked, again feeling like she already knew the answer to her question.

'I don't know . . . a couple of weeks ago, maybe a month,' he said. 'We went to a footy match and . . . and I just came clean.' He sounded so self-righteous, Jane wanted to lean across the table and slap him. 'He was so angry . . . with me, with his dad. He hated his mother for lying to him and for . . . for cheating on Rich. He's even started to resent his sister because she was Rich and Nicola's, whereas he wasn't. He told me he felt like an outsider in his own family.'

'Because of you,' Jane snapped. 'He felt like an outsider in his own family because of you . . . because you decided to *come clean*.'

'Did you even consider the consequences?' Lockyer asked. 'Did you stop to think how your *confession* would affect Harvey? How hurt he'd be?'

Oxenham shrugged again. 'I guess not,' he said. 'I guess I shoulda done.'

'And how was Harvey last night?' Jane asked.

'Angry,' he said, biting his lip. 'He was going on and on about his folks . . . saying they were liars, that the whole family was a lie. He kept saying he wanted to get things straight with his mother – to finish things. I've never seen him like that. He was crying and yelling. It was . . . scary,' he said, raising his eyebrows.

'How was he going to finish things?' Jane asked, the uneasy

feeling stepping up a gear, making the muscles in her legs twitch. 'What did he say he was going to do, Adam?'

'Nothing. I don't know,' he said. 'He just kept saying he didn't know what to do, that he didn't know what he was meant to do now . . . that he needed to see his mum, that he needed to ask . . . to get things straight. That's what he kept saying, that he needed to get things straight – to finish it.'

Jane turned to find Lockyer already looking at her. Nicola and Olive were alone at the house on Clevedon Road. The replacement FLO hadn't been assigned yet and the aunt, Kate, had left the night before because her mother-in-law had had a heart attack. She was due back today, but not yet – it was too early. 'We'll finish this interview later, Adam,' Jane said, not even bothering to look at him. She stopped the tape and pushed back her chair, Lockyer close behind her.

As soon as the door to the interview room was shut, he turned to her. 'We're in deep shit if he hurts his mother or sister,' Lockyer said.

She started to run down the hallway towards the exit. 'Then we'd better get over there,' she shouted back. 'Come on.'

CHAPTER FORTY-FOUR

9 August – Saturday

Lockyer accelerated away from the lights amid a screech of tyres. The roads were wet, making their progress slower than he would like. He had the squad car lights on and the sirens screamed a path clear in front of them.

'Watch out for that . . .' Jane began. He swerved around a woman pushing a pram, and pulled the car left onto Brownhill Road. '. . . And the . . .' Again, she didn't get to finish her sentence. Lockyer braked, waiting for the bus to spot him and pull out of the way. He put his foot down and yanked the wheel to the right, shooting down Plassy Road and then Sangley Road, leaving them in a blur behind him. His windscreen wipers swept back and forth at a manic pace as they tried to keep up with the pelting rain.

'We'll be there in three minutes,' he said.

'I hope we're alive when we get there,' was all Jane said.

He didn't have time to turn and give her a withering look, so he just refocused his energy on getting to Clevedon Road as fast as was humanly possible. The gearbox was protesting at him driving at almost fifty miles an hour in third gear, but he needed the control. The roads were slippery as hell, and everyone and his wife seemed determined to get in his way. He was swinging in and out of the Saturday morning traffic as if it was standing still. 'Where's backup?'

'They're en route,' she said, pointing at a cyclist who appeared and disappeared in an instant. 'There's no answer from the address – comms said the phone is most likely off the hook.'

'Christ,' he said, spotting the signs for Sydenham and Crystal Palace too late. 'Hold on.' He slowed enough at the traffic lights to ensure the crawling traffic was aware of his presence, and then he was gone, accelerating away in a spray of water.

'I've been holding on since we left the station,' she said, her legs braced against the dashboard.

'If we crash, the airbag will break both your legs,' he said, yanking the wheel left and turning onto the A213. She didn't answer but she didn't change her position either.

'How do you want to go in?'

'Hard,' he said. 'The kid doesn't have any weapons that we know of . . . frying pans and kitchen equipment aside.'

'Shouldn't we try talking to Harvey?'

'He's been backed into a corner, Jane,' he said, pushing the squad car up to sixty on the straight. 'People who are backed into a corner are unpredictable. I want him contained as soon as possible. I for one don't want to get into some drawn-out negotiation if he's got a knife to his mother's throat . . . do you?'

'No,' she said. 'Right,' she shouted. 'Right . . . now.'

'I know that,' he said, pulling the wheel to the right and

hovering his hand over the handbrake, just in case. She turned off the sirens and the lights. 'I think he'll have heard us coming,' Lockyer said, slowing as they approached the house.

'Maybe,' she said, 'but there's no sense freaking him out any further.'

Lockyer stopped four houses away and swung the car to the right, blocking the road. 'Let's go,' he said, turning off the engine and opening his door in one swift motion.

'We're not waiting for backup?' she asked, lowering her voice as she climbed out of the car.

'Nope,' he said, striding towards the house. Jane caught up with him at the door. He closed his eyes and a mental layout of the property appeared in his mind. The kitchen was straight ahead, the lounge to the left, stairs on the right, kids' bedrooms top right and left of the stairs, bathroom top of the stairs, straight ahead; and Nicola's room was at the front of the house, down a long landing. He could feel Jane tensing at his side.

'I think we should wait for backup,' Jane whispered. He turned to look at her, to tell her to get a grip, but stopped when he saw her face. She was frightened. She had been in this situation more recently than him, and the consequences for her had not been good.

He reached out and put his hand on her shoulder. 'I'm right here, Jane,' he said. 'We're going to take this kid down and no one is going to get hurt . . . not him, and not you, OK?'

She looked at him. Her face cleared. She nodded. 'OK. Go.'

He tried the door handle. It was unlocked. He pulled it

down and opened the door without a sound, then stepped into the hallway, Jane close behind him. 'Déjà vu,' she whispered.

'It's going to be all right,' he said, holding up his hand as he stopped at the bottom of the stairs. 'Listen.' He could hear someone crying. The sound was coming from the kitchen. He walked forward, motioning for Jane to follow. When he reached the kitchen door he pushed it open with his foot.

Sitting on the floor beneath the kitchen sink was Nicola Brown. She was clutching her shoulder, blood covering her hand and running down her arm. 'He's taken her . . . he's taken her upstairs,' she said, her voice a whisper. Her face was pale. She was losing a lot of blood.

'Back up will be here in two minutes,' Lockyer said backing out of the kitchen. 'Jane, stay with Nicola.'

'No chance,' she said as he turned. 'I'm coming with you.'

He looked at her but could see she wasn't about to change her mind. 'OK.' He turned to Nicola. 'Keep pressure on it.' Nicola nodded, but didn't speak.

Lockyer pulled the kitchen door to behind them. He wanted to at least try to secure the scene – to limit Harvey's options of escape. He crept towards the stairs, glancing back every couple of seconds to check Jane was still with him. She was pale, but he could tell she was focused, her fear in check. 'OK,' he whispered. 'We'll go up together, me on the right, you on the left. Got it?' She nodded. He put his foot on the bottom stair. The loud creak of a floorboard echoed through the hallway. 'Shit.'

'It's OK,' a voice said.

Lockyer looked up to the top of the stairs. Harvey was

sitting on the floor, slumped against the door to the bathroom. 'It's OK,' he said again. 'It's over.'

He climbed the stairs, never taking his eyes off Harvey. He looked from one of the boy's hands to the other. Both were covered in blood, but he wasn't holding a knife. He didn't appear to have a weapon of any kind, not that Lockyer could see.

'It's all right, Harvey,' Jane said from behind him. 'We're here to help.'

Tears coursed down the young boy's face.

'Where's your sister?' Lockyer asked, feeling a lump rise in his throat. 'Where's Olive?'

Harvey nodded his head at the bathroom door behind him. 'She's in there,' he said.

Lockyer took a deep breath. He was fighting the urge to hurl the boy out of the way so he could get to Olive. He couldn't help remembering the last time he had held a dying little girl in his arms. He reached out and steadied himself against the wall as the memory weakened his legs. He had saved that little girl, but was he in time to save this one? 'Harvey,' he said. 'I'm gonna need you to move away from the door . . . back away to the wall over there,' he said, pointing. 'OK?'

Harvey sniffed, pushed himself up until he was standing and stumbled, crying, over to the other side of the landing. Lockyer took the remaining stairs two at a time, his hand on the bathroom door, his heart in his mouth. 'It's locked,' Harvey said. Lockyer looked down at the handle and saw the stubby silver key in the lock. He turned it and the handle at the same time. 'Be careful,' Harvey said.

Lockyer pushed open the door, Harvey's words still echoing in his ears. *Be careful.*

Olive was sitting on the side of the bath as if leaning in to test the temperature of the water. Her legs were crossed, her left leg swinging back and forth, the heel of her shoe hitting the bath surround with a repetitive thud. Her white T-shirt was stained pink with blood. A bread knife lay on a white bathmat, it too stained with blood. She hopped off the edge of the bath and stepped over the knife towards Lockyer. He didn't move. He couldn't. He was frozen in place as his brain tried to process what he was seeing. 'I guess you're here for me,' she said, her face the picture of innocence. He backed out onto the landing. Jane was standing with Harvey, her arm around his shoulder. Harvey's face was wet with tears.

'What the . . . ?' Lockyer began.

Olive walked out of the bathroom and turned to look at Harvey.

'Only *babies* cry,' she said.

Her voice was sweet.

Her words were cold.

CHAPTER FORTY-FIVE

10 August – Sunday

Jane repositioned her legs to try and restore the blood flow. She and Lockyer had been stuck in the tech room at Caterham Road, together with Bill the tech officer, for the past forty minutes. She shifted in her chair, lifting her feet onto a pile of boxes. Lockyer gave her a sideways glance. If his expression was anything to go by, he was just as uncomfortable as she was – if not more so, given the length of his legs. 'I feel like a sardine,' she whispered.

'I *live* like a sardine,' Bill hissed from his place over by the television monitors and wireless equipment.

'How much longer, do you reckon?' Lockyer asked.

Jane shrugged. 'Cathy's broken Olive's initial silence, so I'm guessing it won't be too much longer, but who knows?' Olive had proven a tough nut to crack, but Cathy's wealth of experience with the child protection unit had won out, and the young girl was almost verbose.

'In your own words, Olive,' Cathy said, 'can you tell us what happened?'

'Sure,' Olive said, as if she had been asked to talk about her favourite school subject. 'After Ben went home . . .'

'Ben Nicholls?' Cathy asked.

'Yes. So, after Ben went home we had a bit of dinner . . . just leftovers from the barbecue – I made myself a salad. Dad and Harvey wanted to watch a film . . . so they did.' She shrugged. 'I hate all those *Lord of the Rings* movies, they're crap, so I asked Dad if I could play Candy Crush on his phone . . . can't get the app on my mobile,' she said with a sigh. 'Anyway, he said yes, so I went to bed.'

'What time was this?' Cathy asked.

'If you keep interrupting me, this is gonna take a really long time,' Olive said, her voice thick with sarcasm.

'You carry on,' Cathy said, 'but if I feel the need to stop you to ask questions . . . clarify any information, I will do that.'

'Whatever,' Olive said, tossing her head to one side. She was behaving as if she had been caught smoking or some other trivial infraction.

'She's like a different kid,' Lockyer whispered.

'I know,' Jane said. 'Who would believe that just last week she was a traumatized little girl . . . regression, bed-wetting . . .'

'She put it all on,' Lockyer said, sounding both shocked and impressed.

'She's an amazing actress,' Bill said. 'I've seen her previous interviews.'

'Please,' Cathy said in the other room. 'Go on, Olive.'

'I went to my room about *half nine*,' she said. 'Is that

better?' Cathy didn't respond to the jibe, so she went on. 'I had a quick look at my dad's messages . . . '

'Why?' Cathy asked.

'Because I always do,' she said, as if that was explanation enough. 'Anyway, I saw my dad had sent a text to *Eric*.' She scrunched up her face in apparent disgust at the mention of his name. 'Dad was planning to wait until me and Harvey were asleep and then sneak out and see *him* . . . leave us on our own in the flat, while he went out to see his fancy man,' she said with a sneer.

'Had you known about your father's sexuality for long?' Cathy asked.

'Long enough,' Olive said. 'He wasn't exactly subtle . . . none of his computers or stuff have passwords. It was all there in the history.'

'Did you talk to your dad about what you had seen?' Cathy asked, picking up her clipboard and resting it on her lap.

'No,' Olive said.

'What about your mother . . . or your brother?'

'Nope. I knew Harvey knew. He knew I knew. We just didn't talk about it. I mean . . . would you want to talk about your dad fucking other guys?'

Cathy didn't flinch at Olive's language, but Jane did. 'She's a piece of work,' Bill whispered. Jane couldn't help thinking she and Lockyer had said the same thing about Nicola. That they had both called her interviews 'performances', thought she was a consummate actress. Olive, it seemed, had inherited the same talents.

'Go on, Olive,' Cathy said, without answering Olive's question.

'Where was I?' she asked, frowning.

'You had read your father's message to Eric, arranging to meet him later that night,' Cathy said. How she managed to maintain her composure Jane would never know; but then, the child services team had seen everything. She doubted much surprised Cathy, or caught her off guard.

'Oh yeah,' Olive said, rolling her eyes as if to say, *me and my memory, eh?* 'I didn't want Dad to go out,' she said. 'I didn't want him to go and meet Eric. He'd done it before . . . snuck out at night. I'd seen him . . . so had Harv, more than once.' Her nose flared. 'I didn't want him to go, so I figured I'd stop him going.'

'How?' Cathy asked. 'How did you intend to stop your dad going out?'

'Well, I couldn't very well tell him I'd read his text, could I? I wasn't about to get into trouble for snooping when *he* was the one sneaking around.'

'So what did you do?'

'I went to the bathroom to see what stuff we had . . . '

'What do you mean, stuff?' Cathy asked, crossing her legs.

'Drugs and stuff,' Olive said, again as if the answer was obvious. 'But we didn't have much,' she went on, 'just paracetamol, cough medicine – the non-drowsy stuff. That kinda thing. So I sneaked into my dad's room and checked his bathroom.'

'And did you find anything in your dad's bathroom?'

'Sure,' she said. 'He had all his diabetic stuff . . . pills, injection pens, the lot. I took it all back to my room and read the instructions.'

'What did you intend to do with the medication you had found, Olive?'

'I just wanted to make him sleepy,' she said. 'Too sleepy to go out. That's all.' She was shaking her head as if the whole thing had been one big misunderstanding.

'What did the instructions say?' Cathy asked.

'I checked the Internet too,' Olive said. She seemed proud of her ingenuity. 'The pills . . . if you take too many, they can make you tired . . . same with the insulin. So . . . I went back into the lounge . . . I told Dad and Harv I needed to get something, but I just wanted an excuse. I asked Dad if he wanted a beer. As if he wouldn't. He had been drinking all day, practically.'

'And then what?'

'I got him a beer, opened it in the kitchen and chucked in the crushed-up pills.'

'How many pills did you put into your father's drink?'

'I don't know, a dozen . . . not too many,' she said. 'Anyway, I gave him his beer and went back to my room.' Jane shifted in her seat again. She didn't know which was worse: listening to Olive's emotionless account, or sitting in this room, which was feeling more and more like a coffin by the second. She felt a bead of sweat roll down her back. She shook the memory of the Hungerford case loose before it could even try to take hold.

'Anyway, I knew Dad had gone to bed 'cos he came in and got his phone,' Olive continued. 'I pretended to be asleep, but a bit later I went to check on him and . . .' She seemed to drift off mid-sentence.

'And?' Cathy prompted.

'He was sleeping,' she said with a shrug, 'but not like he usually does. He wasn't flat-out; you know, he wasn't snoring or anything.' She opened her palms to Cathy. 'I wasn't about to stay up *all* night watching him, so I figured I'd use a few of the EpiPens just to be sure . . . to knock him out properly.'

'Right, and did you?' Cathy asked.

'Kind of,' she said, using her hands like weighing scales moving them up and down as she bit her bottom lip. 'I managed to get two, maybe three in him, but then he . . .' Her eyes drifted away from Cathy's and down to her hands.

'Then what happened, Olive?'

'He woke up,' she said. 'I mean, he wasn't awake, awake, but he grabbed me . . . his breath stank of beer. He shouted something, but I couldn't understand him – he was slurring his words – still pissed.' She shook her head in disgust.

'You didn't think it might be an effect of the drugs you'd given your father?' Cathy asked.

Olive shrugged. 'Could have been,' she said. 'Didn't really think about it, but anyway, I must have shouted too, because next thing I know Harvey comes running into the room. He thought Dad was hurting me . . . which he *was* –' she lifted her chin – 'so Harv being Harv, he sort of barrelled between us, shoved me out of the way and got Dad pinned on the bed, his face in the pillow.'

'So your father and Harvey fought?'

Olive was shaking her head. 'Dad wasn't really fighting much . . . just flinging his arms about a bit,' she said, demonstrating by waving her hands in a feeble gesture. 'I still had the pens in my dressing-gown pocket, so I figured . . .' She gave another shrug. 'I just shoved in the rest . . . to be sure.'

'So you injected your father with a further two or three shots of insulin. Is that right, Olive?'

She nodded, disinterested. 'Sounds about right, yes.'

'What did your father do?'

'Not much,' she said, pursing her lips. 'He just lay there, so I told Harvey to get off and let him sleep it off, and we both went back to bed.'

'So your brother believed your father was attacking you under the influence of alcohol?' Cathy asked.

'Guess so,' Olive said, picking at some skin at the edge of her thumbnail.

'Right. So you gave your father an overdose of metformin, followed by an overdose of insulin, and then when you thought he was unconscious, you went back to bed?' Cathy asked. Her voice had changed. It seemed she could be caught off guard after all.

'Yeah,' she said. 'It wasn't 'til the morning when Harv went in that we realized he was dead.'

'And what did you do once you realized your father was dead?' Cathy asked, two bright red spots appearing on her cheeks. Jane hoped she could hold out a bit longer. If Cathy decided to break, then they would all be taking a break – but they would all have to come back, and Jane didn't think she would ever be able to come into this room again. Not voluntarily, at least.

'Well, I had to calm Harvey down, obviously,' she said. 'He thought he'd suffocated Dad in the pillow or something, so he figured it was his fault.'

'Did you tell your brother about the drugs . . . about the injections?'

'God, no,' she said. 'What if he didn't keep his mouth shut?' She grimaced. 'I'd hidden the stuff the night before. As soon as Harv was asleep, I took all the needles and stuff and hid them in his room.'

'Behind the airbrick?' Cathy offered.

'That's right,' she said. 'Harvey used to hide his marijuana stash there sometimes . . . he thought I didn't know about it, but I did.' She grinned, smug.

'So, after you calmed your brother down . . . ?' Cathy prompted.

'We rolled Dad over on his back, you know, so it'd look like he died in his sleep . . . which technically he did,' Olive's expression was still smug. 'Then I promised not to tell anyone what had happened . . . about Harvey suffocating Dad . . . then we agreed what we were gonna say, and Harvey called the police. That's it. It was an accident. The whole thing was an accident.'

'She thinks she's going to get away with this by saying it was an accident?' Lockyer said in a hushed voice, his surprise evident.

Jane shook her head. 'I don't believe for a second that she just *happened upon* the insulin and metformin idea the night of Taylor's death like she claims. My guess is she's been researching ways of incapacitating her father for some time, and *adjusted* the truth to make the alleged accident more plausible.' She took a deep breath. 'Having said that, she genuinely appears to believe Taylor's death was an accident, however it came about, so who knows what she's thinking.'

'That's one scary kid,' Bill said.

'You can say that again,' Lockyer said.

Lockyer walked into his office, around his desk, and slumped into his chair. Jane wasn't far behind him. She came in, pushed the glass door closed and dropped into the chair opposite him. 'That was,' he said, 'hands down, the most surreal interview I have ever been witness to.' Jane nodded. She looked tired. Not that Lockyer was surprised.

'You and me both,' she said, running her hands through her hair.

The drive back from Caterham Road had been surreal, too. They had called the CPS representative from the car to discuss the changes in the charges, the result of which was that Olive Taylor-Brown was going to be arrested and charged with the murder of her father and ABH against her mother, Nicola Brown. As yet Anne's assault charges had not been dealt with. Harvey would need to be held accountable; but neither Lockyer nor, it seemed, Jane was in any mood to cause the kid more distress.

Lockyer stared up at the ceiling. He tried to think back to what he had been like at twelve, what he was capable of at that age, but it was too long ago. He thought about Megan, about how she had been at a similar age. He was pretty sure it had all been about school, boys and make-up. She had been a normal, soon-to-be-teenager. Olive was anything but.

'Where's Harvey now?' Jane asked.

'He's staying with Ben Nicholls and his family until his mother has fully recovered,' Lockyer said, sitting forward.

'The hospital said they'll be releasing her tomorrow, in all likelihood. What about Olive?'

'They'll take her over to the closed unit at Orchard Lodge,' Jane said. 'They'll most likely hold her there for the time being.'

'I still can't believe it,' he said, and he couldn't. Not once during the interview had Olive shown even the slightest shred of remorse. After her assertion that it was all an accident, Cathy – who was amazing, in Lockyer's opinion – had pushed Olive. She had gone through the past ten days in exhausting detail, but neither the revelation about the abuse or Olive's obvious cruelty and manipulation of her brother had made a dent in the girl's casual demeanour. 'There's two things I don't get. Why did she attack Nicola, when she was doing pretty well at passing all the blame to her brother for Taylor's death? And why did Harvey never fight back?'

'Olive said herself that she hated her mother,' Jane said. 'Finding out about Harvey, about the affair with Oxenham – I think all the lies compounded until she couldn't help herself. She wanted out of that family, whatever it took. She'd said as much to Harvey according to his testimony. I think that's why Harvey came back to the house. I think he realized his mother was in danger – that Olive would stop at nothing to be free of the "dead weight" as she saw it.'

'He could have come to us, talked to his mother,' Lockyer said. 'He should have stood up to Olive years ago.'

'Well, he did in the end,' Jane pointed out, 'didn't he?'

'Bit late,' Lockyer said, thinking back to the day before, and Harvey locking his sister in the bathroom to stop her hurting their mother.

'It's built up over years, Mike,' Jane said. 'Nicola told us Harvey had been protective of his sister ever since she was sick as a baby. Instead of being grateful to have a big brother looking out for her, Olive just turned it to her advantage, forcing Harvey to do whatever she wanted, whenever she wanted. I've read the transcript from Harvey's interview yesterday. The poor kid worshipped his sister, but equally she frightened him – controlled him.'

'But he's twice, three times her size. Why didn't he fight back?'

Jane shrugged. 'He loved his sister,' she said. 'From what he said during his interview, Olive started testing the boundaries by hurting herself and blaming him back when she was only six. Their parents always believed her over Harvey, which just confirmed to him that it was Olive who was in control. After a while, I guess he just gave in.'

Lockyer shook his head. 'But what about his bruises? What about when she hurt him? Why didn't he show his parents . . . surely they would have believed him?'

'You'd think so, but he was too scared to cross his sister,' she said. 'She'd shown how far she was prepared to go.' She had only read Harvey's interview, but it was clear that his words were still impacting her. 'When she was six Olive ran to her mother crying, saying Harvey had shut her out of his room, and jammed her hand in the door. Nicola believed Olive. Why wouldn't she? Why would a six-year-old kid slam their own hand in a door? Kids are manipulative. They lie. We all know that, but no one . . . not even you would believe that a six-year-old would break a bone in their finger *just* to get their big brother into trouble.'

He blew out a breath. 'I get your point,' he said. 'I've just never heard of the *kid* being the abuser.'

'It happens,' she said. 'According to Cathy, it happens more than you'd think.'

'Harvey could have told us when child services discovered the abuse,' he said.

'He could have,' Jane said, 'but Olive had already covered that angle. She knew Anne had seen the bruises, so she knew it was only a matter of time before we found out. She told Harvey to say it was their father – that he had lashed out when he was drinking – which, given what we know about the night Taylor died, would have made sense to Harvey. In Olive's mind, Taylor was dead, so what did it matter if he took the blame? Her plan was only scuppered when we found the fresh bruising.'

'The fly in her manipulative ointment,' he said with a sigh.

'Exactly,' she said. 'She found out that Adam told Harvey about being his father and, being the charming child she is, she taunted him with it . . . said he wasn't really a member of the family . . . that he shouldn't worry about having killed his dad, because it wasn't his *real* dad.'

'So Harvey snapped and hit her?'

'Yep,' Jane said. 'Unfortunately for him, that meant she needed to bring him back into line, so she threatened him. She told him she would tell us that he had hit her, and then break down and tell us the whole story . . . that Harvey had killed his father . . . Taylor.'

'And he believed her.'

'Of course,' she said. 'Why wouldn't he? He thought that *was* what had happened. Besides, he knew what his sister was capable of. He was terrified, so when he heard we were coming over to *speak with him* he figured Olive had carried out her threat, and we were coming to arrest him. So he freaked. He called Adam to get him out, and when Anne tried to stop him, he panicked. He didn't mean to hurt her.'

'But he did,' Lockyer said.

'I know,' she said. 'I know, but when he was off with Adam, he realized he couldn't leave his mother with Olive. He realized he had to finish things – to come clean and stop his sister.'

They both fell silent for a moment. Lockyer stood up, pushing his fingers into the small of his back, and walked over to his window. He stared down at Lewisham High Street. The rain was gone, the sun was out. The traffic was busy, the smells were pungent – everything was normal. But this wasn't normal. What they were talking about was nowhere near normal.

'She showed no remorse,' he said.

'As far as Olive sees it, her actions are entirely justifiable,' Jane said. 'She didn't *intend* to kill her father, but his death, as it happens, met with her approval, because she wanted out of the family anyway. The whole thing was a lie as far as she was concerned. She didn't want a gay father. She was fed up with having a controlling mother, and Harvey was, she had just discovered, not even her brother. She believes she's better than all of them . . . that she's special somehow.'

'She's a very disturbed kid,' he said.

He turned to look at her. Neither of them spoke. There was nothing left to say.

EPILOGUE

27 September – Saturday

'I feel like a bloody idiot,' Lockyer said, pulling at the tie around his neck.

'You look very handsome,' Jane said, knocking his hand away. 'Well, the suit's nice, anyway.'

He ran a hand through his hair. 'I didn't have time to get to the barber's,' he said.

She frowned. 'Are there still such things as barbers?'

'Yes,' he said in the tone of a petulant child.

'And the last time you visited one was when?' She started to laugh. She wasn't lying. Lockyer looked good. He looked better than good, but the suit was an amusing fiction. The scuffed shoes and the crazy-Yeti hair were the real him, the man she knew.

'Oh, sod off,' he said, buttoning and then unbuttoning his jacket.

Jane smoothed down her dress and adjusted her pashmina. The sun on her back felt good. What had made her agree to this, after the week she'd had, she had no idea. She needed a gin and tonic or four. She was still reeling from her meeting

339

with the solicitors. Despite Andy abandoning her and Peter, never paying child support and never, not once, getting in touch with his own son – he was still entitled to visitation. She felt her anger surfacing, her face flushing. Whatever it took, she would not let Andy hurt Peter. She could feel the fury taking hold, but with a shake of her head and a hard swallow, she managed to force the pain away. Andy would not ruin today for her. Today was not about him.

'So,' she said, 'are you planning on being a miserable git for the entire evening as well, or can we expect a smile at some point?'

'What is there to smile about?' he said, gesturing to the head of the line-up.

Jane bit her lip. All the guests were kissing the bride and congratulating the groom before filing into the marquee. Standing next to her mother was Megan in a beautiful pale yellow dress. She looked so grown up. Jane knew that that, in itself, would bother Lockyer, but she was pretty sure it was the man standing next to his daughter who was causing him to clench his jaw every few seconds. 'Do tell me . . . what exactly is there to smile about?'

Jane opened her clutch purse and took out a lipstick to buy herself some time. Ever since she had seen Megan being escorted down the aisle by Aaron, she had known there would be trouble. Her and Aaron's conversation in the car all made sense now, as did Aaron's behaviour around Lockyer over the past few weeks.

She let out a breath. It was going to be a long night. She was still unsure how Lockyer had managed to rope her into attending his ex-wife's wedding and reception party in the first place, and now she was going to spend the whole time trying to stop him beating Aaron to a pulp. She applied a quick swipe of the lipstick, clicked the top back on and replaced it in her bag. 'Well, I can think of one thing to smile about,' she said.

'Surprise, surprise,' he said, still sulking.

'Well,' Jane said, hesitating, 'your daughter looks very beautiful.'

'She does,' he conceded.

'And . . . she looks very happy.' Lockyer huffed next to her, but didn't speak. Jane took a deep breath. 'Aaron's a good kid . . . man, Mike,' she said, correcting her error. 'Come on, he must have been terrified at the prospect of facing you.'

'Explains why he's been so jumpy around me lately,' he said.

'Exactly,' she said. 'Don't you think he deserves some credit for being man enough to come today, knowing you'd be here?'

'I suppose,' he said, narrowing his eyes.

'So do you think you could be happy for her . . . for them?' she asked. 'Just for today?' He didn't answer. 'Of course you are going to torture Aaron when we get back to the office,' she said, 'that's a given – but for today, do you think you could drop the angry-dad face and let them enjoy themselves?'

'I can be happy for *her*,' he conceded, 'but I fail to see how that's a positive for me.'

Jane nodded. 'Good point. OK. How about that your ex-wife seems very nice, and thrilled that you decided to come, because it means so much to Megan?' she offered.

'That's good for her. Not me.'

Jane thought for a second. She was running out of positives. Why had she agreed to come, again?

At least her family had been happy about her 'getting out'. As soon as she had asked her mother to look after Peter, and explained the reason, Celia Bennett had gone bonkers. Jane's father had even dragged his weary bones out of the house, insisting on helping her pick out an outfit and paying for it – hence the new purse, clutch or whatever it was. Her mother kept saying, 'Let him do this, darling. Who knows when we'll be able to do this again?'

She sighed. They had put in an offer on a house in Clevedon, near Bristol, and it had been accepted. Jane still couldn't believe it was really happening. She had thought, hoped even, that the whole 'we're moving' debacle was an elaborate torture her mother had cooked up to keep her and Peter close by; but no. They were set on moving, and even her father was excited.

She looked around for the bar. She could still see their faces when Lockyer had picked her up earlier. She smiled. It was fair to say that all the Bennetts were beside themselves. Lockyer was only picking her up because it was on the way to the wedding, but as Jane had climbed into his Audi and turned back she had seen her mother and father standing in the driveway, Peter between them, waving her off as if she was on her way to the prom. Lockyer might not be able to find the positives for today, but she was damn well going to try. Her family had found some joy in something different, in a change to their usual routine, and Jane was grateful for that. She would deal with the move when she was good and ready, but for now, she would remain in denial and enjoy herself. She pursed her lips and looked up at Lockyer as they approached the congratulations-and-kisses line-up.

He shook Brian's hand and kissed first Clara on the cheek, then his daughter. There was a pause, during which Jane and the group held their breath. Time seemed to stretch until Lockyer finally reached out and shook Aaron's hand. Aaron looked about ready to piss himself, but he managed to hold it together before nodding and stepping back behind Megan – for protection, Jane would guess. She said her own congratulations and thank-you-for-having-mes before taking Lockyer's arm. 'I've thought of a positive for you,' she said, as they walked away.

'It better be good.' His face was flushed.

'How about the fact that I am in a dress . . . an actual dress?' she said. 'I'm telling you, the likelihood that you will ever see me in a get-up like this again is slim to none, and I did it for *you*.'

Lockyer sighed, but reached over and took her hand, giving it a squeeze. 'That, DS Bennett, is a big positive for me. And I, for one, can't wait to see you manage those heels on the dance floor.' He laughed and walked into the reception, dragging her with him.

'Oh, I don't dance,' she said.

'Oh, you will,' he said. 'Because it's an order, and because it is the only thing about this debacle that really will be . . . *good* for me.'

OLIVE

I feel like a zoo animal, imprisoned behind glass – a hundred eyes on me day and night.

Every day they bring in someone new to talk to me. Each fresh face leaves with the same expression. They look at me, their faces relaxed, but their eyes give them away. They are horrified. They seem scared, as if at any moment I will transform into a demon and eat them alive. It's ridiculous. I'm not a demon or a devil. I'm not evil either, although that's what they think. I heard some of them talking. 'What made her like this, do you think?' they ask each other in hushed voices. 'Is it nature or nurture?' and my personal favourite, 'Have you seen her eyes? It's like staring into the abyss.'

It's silly really. I've tried to tell them what happened, that it was an accident and the rest, what happened afterwards, was just self-protection, but they aren't really listening to me. They ask me the same questions over and over. Why did I want to kill my father? Why did I use insulin? Why didn't I tell Harvey about the injection? Why did I let him think he was responsible? Why did I want to hurt my mother? Why did I hurt myself? Why did I hurt my brother? Over and over they ask, and over and over I tell them the same thing. I didn't kill my father. My father died in his sleep. The fact that I had given him some harmless drugs was happenstance. Am I sorry he died? I know I should be but I can't find the emotion. I've tried but it's simply not there.

The question they should be asking is, how did someone like me manage to survive in a family like that for so long? No wonder I fought back. Wouldn't you? Every one of them was a liar. Every one of them was weak. Every one of them sickens me to my stomach. Mum and Harvey have tried to visit me, to see how I'm doing, but I don't want to see them. Why would I? I didn't want to be part of that family when I was in it. Now I have a chance to divorce myself from the whole mess, I'm seizing it with both hands. I don't need them. I only need me.

Dad always used to say our actions have consequences. I believed that. I still do. So where was their consequence for lying, for cheating, for being sickening, pathetic human beings? What punishment did they get for fighting all the time when I was in my room trying not to listen? What punishment did they get for ripping apart our home so I had to sleep in two beds and be two people, one for her and one for him? What punishment did they get for favouring Harvey because he was thick – no, because he was special. Isn't subjecting me to neglect and disinterest, while they carried on with their selfish little lives, abuse? I think it is. I know it is. If I didn't fight for me, for my right to live a proper life, who would? Where was their consequence?

Action equals consequence.

What would you have done?

Do you think I'm evil?

ACKNOWLEDGEMENTS

They say the second novel is the hardest, but I must confess that this book takes the crown for me. I was keen, when I plotted *Trust No One*, to move away from multiple murders, featured in my previous books *Never Look Back* and *No Place to Die*. However, it turns out, the less murder and mayhem there is, the harder the author is required to work to maintain pace and tension. I hope I have managed to achieve both, but I guess my readers will let me know in due course!

The list of people to thank grows with each novel, but I wouldn't be anywhere without my fabulous editor, Trisha Jackson, whom I respect and adore in equal measure, and my agent, Hellie Ogden, and the team at Janklow & Nesbit. Hellie's enthusiasm and knowledge is second to none, and I am very lucky to have her by my side.

Pan Macmillan is often described as a family, and I'm thrilled to say that I feel very much a part of the clan. Kate Green is a new member, and, I'm delighted to say, my PR guru. I thought I was organized, but I am very happy to say that Kate puts my efforts to shame. There isn't much she doesn't know, and to say she's on top of things would be an understatement. Thank you to her for all of her support and I'm very excited to see where we go next with the Lockyer-and-Bennett team. I would also like to thank Natasha Harding, Eloise Wood, Stuart Dwyer, Neil Lang and Kate Bullows for all their hard work and support. I am enormously grateful and forever in your debt.

My continued thanks go to my US publishers St Martin's, Elizabeth Lacks and my editor, Kelley Ragland. Not forgetting my publishers Fanucci Editore in Italy, LYX in Germany (the books are beautiful) and De Fontein in the Netherlands.

Audible have done another fantastic job with the audio version of book two, *No Place to Die*, which is narrated by the very talented Imogen Church. Thank you.

Thank you to CLIC Sargent, a charity that cares for children with cancer, for including me in their 'Get in Character' campaign. Fans could bid to have a character named after them, and a big thank you goes to James Bullion, the winning bidder, for his generous donation. I hope you enjoy seeing your chosen name in print in *Trust No One*.

When it comes to researching a crime novel, you can never have enough contacts, and I am pleased to say that my list of people I can go to with obscure questions is growing. Mark and Sue, we don't talk shop as much as we used to, but your friendship and continued support means a lot to me. Leanne, we haven't even met yet but I have thoroughly enjoyed chatting with you, and the insight you gave me into policing practices involving minors was invaluable. I very much look forward to bending your ear a lot more in the future – lucky you! And finally, Basil – a big thank you to you for all your help on the pathology side of things.

As a writer, I spend a lot of time alone, which is OK, but without my family and friends I am sure I would go completely bonkers. So, a very big thank you to you all – you know who you are and what you do ☺.

Q&A WITH CLARE DONOGHUE

1. **Have you always wanted to be a writer?**

   In a word: no. It never even occurred to me to consider it as a profession. I was mediocre at English in school, and my tutor at Bath Spa would certainly tell you my grammar and general understanding of the English language was lacking and then some. But I loved reading. I couldn't get enough, and once I stumbled onto the crime/thriller genre, that was it – I was hooked. The more I read, the more I envied the authors not only for their talent but for their ability to enthrall a complete stranger with a work of fiction. So when, in the early hours of the morning, I finished a Mo Hayder novel and turned back to read her biography and discovered she had done an MA in creative writing at Bath Spa, I had my 'eureka' moment and decided to follow in her footsteps. The fact that I am now a published author is more of a surprise to me than anyone else.

2. **Can you tell us about your book deal moment?**

   Yes. It was a crazy and surreal day. I was standing in my parents' kitchen when my agent called with the good news. I was floored to hear that Pan Macmillan wanted me – I was even more floored that they were going to pay for something *I* had written! It took several days for the news to sink in . . . and to be honest, it's still sinking in. I feel like a fraud most of the time but I also feel very lucky to be working with such a prestigious publishing house.

3. **Can you tell us how the characters of Jane and Mike came into being?**
   Well, Mike came first. In the initial plot of *Never Look Back* there were no cops, but, as the bodies piled up, I realized that without a police narrative the story was going to be near impossible to tell, and so DI Mike Lockyer came into being. He had several name changes in the beginning but who he was never changed. In my mind he was a British version of Jeff Goldblum. I don't know why, and even now when I'm writing him he bears little resemblance, but that's who I see in my head – strange but true! Jane came a little later, and out of necessity, rather than anything else. My tutor at Bath Spa pointed out to me that Lockyer as a character was more empathetic than Claire Rayner. She said it was fine for a man to *have* feelings, of course, but for him to be expressing them in every piece of prose wasn't, shall we say, realistic when it came to gender traits. And so, Jane came in as the emotional counter-balance to Lockyer's strength. Like all characters, they have taken time to develop, but they are no longer cyphers telling a story, they are real people – well, as real as a fictional person

can be! Now when I'm writing from either's perspective, I don't have to think about how they would react to any given situation – I just know.

4. How long did it take you to write *Trust No One*?
I would say it took about three months of solid work to get the first draft finished.

5. Is there a particular place you like to write?
I just write in my lounge, sitting on the sofa. If I'm writing new material I like to listen to music, something chilled but with a beat so I can work away nodding my head like a loon, which I often do. If, on the other hand, I'm editing, then I like to have the TV on – I hasten to add that I don't watch it! I just put on a good Disney/ Pixar film and I'm away. I can get through two to three viewings of *Madagascar 2* without ever needing to take a break – again, I know that probably sounds weird but it's true!

6. What was the hardest part of writing *Trust No One*?
The lack of bodies. In books one and two there were a number of victims and potential people in peril, but in *Trust No One* there was a definite shift to a more psycho-logical angle. Murder and mayhem naturally assist with pace and tension, so the fewer bodies you have, the harder it is for the writer, it transpires (I didn't know that before I plotted it out!). I still really enjoyed writing the book, but it took me longer to get it right – I just hope readers like it.

7. Do you have a routine as a writer?

It depends what I'm doing. If I'm editing, then I tend to be very regimented – get up, have brekkie, start writing for about ten and then work through until five or six, depending on my energy levels. It's much easier to maintain concentration for prolonged periods because the hard part (the creating part) is already done and essentially I'm rejigging and making sure the plot runs smoothly. However, if I'm writing from scratch then I'm a bit more haphazard and have amazing procrastination skills. It can be mentally exhausting, but once I'm in the zone I usually turn out about two thousand words in a day. That implies I could write a book in about fifty days – I haven't achieved that yet but who knows, maybe one day I will!

8. How are you going to celebrate publication day?

I'm not sure what I'll be doing on the actual day, but in the past I've had a launch in my home town the week of publication. It's fast becoming a legendary event. It's a bit like *Four Weddings and a Funeral* – a good excuse to get all my family and friends together in one place – the difference being, it's a lot cheaper than a wedding and no one has to die, so it's a win-win!

9. Which books have inspired you?

Sooooo many books have influenced me over the years – both fiction and non-fiction. *Matilda* and *The BFG* got me started, but it was Stephen King who really got me hooked as a reader. As soon as I read *The Shining*,

I had to go out and buy and read his back catalogue. His characterization never fails to impress me. I also love Karin Slaughter, Tess Gerritsen, Mo Hayder, David Baldacci and numerous other crime and thriller authors. I'm adding to the list all the time.

10. **What advice would you give to aspiring authors?**
Be brave, be determined and, above all, listen. There's no point writing your masterpiece if you are never going to show it to anyone. Find a handful of people who you trust (and who like reading) and get some feedback. If they see a problem, don't justify yourself and explain why they aren't getting it – listen to them and take their comments on board. Edit, polish, do a course, whatever it takes to give you the confidence to get your manuscript out to some agents. This time listen harder – whatever they say, listen. They know what they are talking about. If you get this far and you're prepared to listen and adapt then you are in with a real chance of getting somewhere. In all seriousness – if *I* can do it then, trust me, anyone can.

Never Look Back

By Clare Donoghue

He's watching. He's waiting. He knows.

A chilling and compelling debut crime thriller set in south-east London. For all those who enjoy Peter James, Mark Billingham and Peter Robinson.

Three women have been found brutally murdered in south London, the victims only feet away from help during each sadistic attack. And the killer is getting braver . . .

Sarah Grainger is rapidly becoming too afraid to leave her house. Once an outgoing photographer, she knows that someone is watching her. A cryptic note brings everything into terrifying focus, but it's the chilling phone calls that take the case to another level.

DI Mike Lockyer heads up the regional murder squad. With three bodies on his watch and a killer growing in confidence, he frantically tries to find the link between these seemingly isolated incidents. What he discovers will not only test him professionally but will throw his personal life into turmoil too.

No Place to Die

By Clare Donoghue

Guilt for the past. Fear for the future.

The body of a female university student is found buried in Elmstead Woods, south London. The circumstances of her death are as unprecedented as they are frightening.

Two men admit to having had relationships with the girl just before she died.

Both deny murder.

Lewisham's murder squad detectives Jane Bennett and Mike Lockyer must untangle a web of deceit if they are to stop this monster before more innocent lives are lost.

extracts reading groups
competitions books new
discounts extracts extracts
competitions reading groups
books new extracts discounts
events books reading groups
extracts new titles reading groups
interviews events new
books events extracts extracts events books
discounts interviews new extracts
new books events events
events new events

www.panmacmillan.com

discounts extracts discounts books
extracts events reading groups
competitions books extracts new